DEFIANT

DAVE BARA'S
THE LIGHTSHIP CHRONICLES

IMPULSE
STARBOUND
DEFIANT

DAVE BARA
DEFIANT

Volume Three of the
Lightship Chronicles

DAW BOOKS, INC.
DONALD A. WOLLHEIM, FOUNDER
375 Hudson Street, New York, NY 10014

ELIZABETH R. WOLLHEIM
SHEILA E. GILBERT
PUBLISHERS
www.dawbooks.com

First Printing, January 2017
1 2 3 4 5 6 7 8 9

DAW TRADEMARK REGISTERED
U.S. PAT. AND TM. OFF. AND FOREIGN COUNTRIES
—MARCA REGISTRADA
HECHO EN U.S.A.

PRINTED IN THE U.S.A.

AUTHOR'S NOTE

This book represents the end of a trilogy. Four years ago when I signed the contract for The Lightship Chronicles series with DAW Books, I had no idea what a fun ride I was in for.

Working with my (Hugo Award winning!) editor Sheila Gilbert and DAW's co-publisher Betsy Wollheim has been the best experience of my life. Whatever comes next, more books in this series or something else, this has been the experience of a lifetime for me. I hope every aspiring author out there gets the chance to work with people as great as I have been blessed to work with. Being with DAW has been like being part of a family, and I will be forever grateful for that.

There are simply too many people to thank for getting *Impulse*, *Starbound*, and *Defiant* into print, but I'd like to mention a few in particular. Joshua Bilmes and everyone at JABberwocky Literary; Michael Rowley, who was my editor at Random House UK; Joshua Starr, who turned my books into something printable at DAW, and all the people who have helped with promotion and publicity. I hope we all have great success in the future.

To the struggling writer out there still trying to break through, I wish you good luck, great timing, and finding people who believe in your work. It's the best feeling in the world to have a family like I have had behind me.

Here's to future adventures.

Dave Bara

September 2016

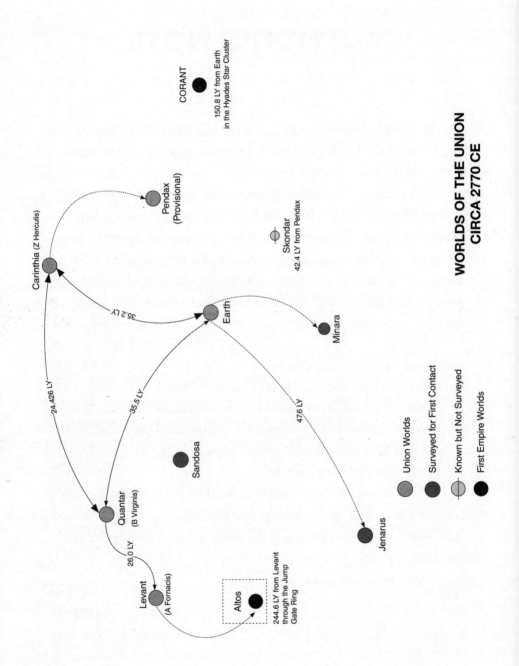

WORLDS OF THE UNION
CIRCA 2770 CE

CORANT

150.8 LY from Earth
in the Hyades Star Cluster

Pendax
(Provisional)

Carinthia (Z Herculis)

Skondar

42.4 LY from Pendax

35.2 LY

Earth

Minara

24.426 LY

35.5 LY

47.6 LY

Sandosa

Quantar
(B Virginis)

26.0 LY

Jenarus

Levant
(A Formacis)

Altos

244.6 LY from Levant
through the Jump
Gate Ring

Union Worlds

Surveyed for First Contact

Known but Not Surveyed

First Empire Worlds

Prologue—On Carinthia

Six Weeks After the Attack

held my wife's hand tightly. It was small inside my own, and I was glad of that. I wanted her to feel protected, cared for, and even loved in these difficult moments, and any gesture toward that end was to the good as far as I was concerned. Lady Karina Feilberg, Princess of Carinthia, was holding vigil, as we all were, waiting for her father to die.

Grand Duke Henrik had faded fast after the attack on his home world. Within weeks he had taken ill, then was confined to his bed, in and out of consciousness. As I watched him now from across the bedroom he had shared with his wife for so many years, he seemed peaceful but not altogether content. There were still signs of the struggle of life, of unfinished business. He was a stubborn man, and he would go when he damned well pleased; that much was clear. But go he would.

The Earthmen had offered some of their miracle technology to keep him going for months more—perhaps even a year—but he had refused in one of his clearer moments of lucidity. I couldn't blame him. His wife was gone. His first son had betrayed him and their world, bringing down a devastating atomic attack on Carinthia. He would likely never see that event avenged, but I had vowed in my own heart to bring about justice for him, the man who had become my father-in-law, if I was given the opportunity by the universe.

But for now it was enough just to hold my wife's hand and let her know I was here for her if she needed me.

The bedroom curtains were open, and the late winter sun of Carinthia's star, Zeta Herculis, shined yellow-gold light into the room. That light nearly reached the elaborate medical bed that tended to the grand duke, mostly with automated protocols. A web of tubes and wires moved about his body as if alive, monitoring and taking readings, then applying treatments as necessary. Two doctors were always present, and at least six other technicians monitored his condition minute by minute from medical display stations spread throughout the spacious room, often consulting quietly amongst themselves.

Karina and I sat together on a large sofa in the middle of the room. It felt odd, us being there, just stuck in the room while everything happened around us. But it had been this way for two full days now. Karina had only rested when I insisted upon it or when her brother Benn was there to keep watch over her father for her. She knew Benn would inform her of any sudden change in the grand duke's condition.

In some ways I envied Benn. He was busy running the government, trying to coordinate the massive effort of all the Union worlds to aid Carinthia in her recovery. It was going much faster and better than expected, but there was still a long, hard slog to go, no doubt of that. But at least he had the distraction. Karina had none of that and wouldn't leave her father's side in any case.

As for me, I could only say that the vigil was a way to avoid my own problems. I'd had many since the Battle of Pendax. Nightmares, sudden anxiety, even depression, not wanting to face the day. Karina had helped me through much of that in the weeks after the attack, as had the Green Court's doctors, but there was no panacea. I had wiped out over thirty thousand human lives defending the Union. That would take a toll on anyone.

But now I had to think of Karina and her fear of losing her father and facing the grief of his inevitable passing. I focused all of my energy on supporting her, and through all of this, support her I would. "For better or for worse" is what the Vicar of KendalFalk had said on the night we were married. This time on Carinthia was undoubtedly the worse, and I wondered if the better times would ever come.

The double doors to the duke's bedroom opened suddenly, and Prince Benn came through, trailed by a small entourage of uniformed advisors. He came directly to Karina. She and I rose from the sofa to greet him.

"Has he said anything more?" asked Benn.

"No," replied Karina, shaking her head. "Just the one request for you to come."

Benn nodded and then went to his father's bedside, the doctors parting to let him pass. Karina let go of my hand and followed, standing on the opposite side of the bed from her brother. I held back, waiting for confirmation regarding what I should do. Respect for the family in these times was critical, and I was extended family only, not blood.

I looked at Benn and realized I didn't really like him much. I felt he had made mistakes, or at least different choices than I would have made, leading up to the attack on Carinthia. He had always held me at a distance, even after my marriage to Karina. I didn't mind. I still respected him and his position in the family as the prince regent. My loyalty was to my wife and went further only minimally. These were difficult times for us all.

Karina touched her father's arm to rouse him. He rolled around a bit, then opened his eyes.

"I'm here, Father," said Benn in German. My ear com translator worked so fast that it was almost seamless. I "heard" the words in German, but my mind comprehended them in Standard English.

The grand duke opened his eyes and looked first at his son, then at his daughter.

"Out with them," he said, waving his arm. "All of them . . . out." I assumed he meant the doctors. They all put their equipment in automated mode and shuffled out slowly. The automated medical monitor tried to adjust things according to the readings it was receiving, but the duke demanded that it be shut down as well. Benn nodded to the primary doctor, who put the device in standby mode, then exited the room. I turned to follow him out, assuming the duke wanted a few last moments with his children.

"Not you, Peter," he said weakly, and in Standard. "You are family now. . . ." He coughed harshly. "You stay."

I made my way to Karina's side. Benn didn't look happy at this turn of events, but there wasn't anything I could do about that. It was the grand duke's choice. He looked to his second son.

"Benn, my steady and reliable hand. When I am gone, go to the family records hall. Retrieve the family codex." He spoke haltingly, then had a coughing fit that set off numerous medical alarms, but the automated monitor stayed in standby mode. When he recovered, he continued.

"Pull the cylinder on Arin. In there you will find all the proof you need to rule fully in my name." The cough came again, and Karina comforted him until it passed. Benn and Karina exchanged looks of confusion.

"I don't understand," said Benn. The grand duke nodded.

"You will. Arin . . . Arin . . . was . . . never my son. Your mother was already pregnant with him . . ." He coughed again. ". . . on the day we were married."

"What?" said Karina, shocked. The duke waved her off. I moved closer to her for support.

"It was not your mother's doing, Karina. Her honor was intact. Someone—we don't know who—doctors . . . someone . . . they insem . . . insem . . . inseminated her artificially . . ." Again the coughing came, but less this time. "It wasn't her fault." His eyes closed then; he was fading, his physical strength to fight waning along with his will. Karina touched his forehead gently, and he opened his eyes again.

"I am so glad you are my daughter," he said to her with a weak smile. "You are so smart, so beautiful, so loving . . . like your mother . . ." Tears came to her eyes immediately. "Keep Benn here honest. Don't let him become too much the politician."

"I won't. I promise," Karina said, looking across to her brother with tears in her eyes. The duke's eyes started to close again, then he opened them one last time and looked directly at me.

"Peter . . ." I swallowed hard at the unexpected sound of my name.

"Yes, Sire?" I said, my voice cracking as I fought back my own tears. I took a step closer to the bed.

"Lightship Captain . . ." His eyes started to close again.

"Sire—"

"Find Arin . . . Find him, and . . . kill him. He was never . . . our blood." He said the final words with surprising strength. I wasn't prepared for that.

"Yes, Sire," I said softly. "I promise."

Then he closed his eyes and said to Karina, "Keep those doctors out of here. I want to die in peace."

She did as he asked, locking the doors to the bedroom herself. The three of us sat together on the sofa, none of us saying a word, and waited.

An hour later he was gone, both of his children holding his hands as he passed. Karina went back to the sofa, sobbing. Benn was stoic but much more physically supportive of Karina than I expected. They shared close hugs and quiet words, as a brother and sister should. I stayed out of the way. Benn left to make arrangements, or more likely to set plans in motion that had already been prepared. Karina stayed an hour longer with her father, then signaled me that it was time to go. I took her by the hand again, and we walked slowly back to our apartment.

And in my mind I was focused on only one thing: carrying out the grand duke's last command to me.

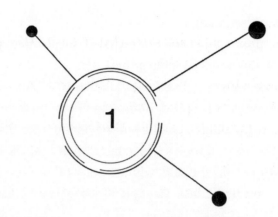

At Candle Aboard
H.M.S. Defiant
Six Months Later

I circled the fencing cage as I had many times before, my sword extended in a defensive position. My opponent circled as well, looking for an opening. We tapped swords numerous times, her taking my measure with each parry and riposte. We danced like this for several seconds, back and forth, my thrust followed by her parry. The game was tenuous for her. I had her down 2–0. Another victory and I would win the match.

She made an awkward lunge at me, and I countered her thrust, then reached out and grabbed her sword hand by the wrist. She tried to do the same to me, but I held her off, my superior size and strength being more than a match for her. I had her now, and the only question was how I was going to finish it. I swung her around and then pulled her toward me, rolling her over my thigh and then dropping her to the mat. Gently, I hoped. I whipped my foil into her rib cage, and the scoring bell sounded.

Game, set, match.

She dropped her foil and exhaled deeply, then pulled her mask from her face and looked up at me.

"I'm never going to get this," she said.

"Nonsense," I replied, doffing my own mask and then reaching down and grabbing her hand, pulling her up from the mat with a firm tug on the arm. "It took a while, but *I* finally got the hang of it."

"As I recall," she said, wiping sweat off of her forehead with her sleeve, "you never beat Captain Kierkopf, and I have never beaten you."

I smiled down at my wife of half a year, Karina Feilberg, Princess of Carinthia, Countess of New Queensland, fencing rival. Though it was hard to call her a rival. We had been at this almost six months, and she'd never really come close to beating me. It wasn't her fault. Dobrina Kierkopf was an excellent athlete, Karina far less so. She was small and petite and no master with a foil for sure, nor would she likely ever be, but she humored me on the mat. I liked to think she made up for her wants as a swordsman with other more favorable attributes.

She reached up and wrapped her arms around my neck. I was a bit over six feet one, she almost a foot shorter. She went to her tiptoes, then kissed me. It was a wet and sweaty embrace, but not altogether unpleasant. As I said, she had her favorable attributes. Still, I wasn't much for public displays of affection on the ship I commanded, *H.M.S. Defiant.* After all, I was the captain, and married or not, we couldn't be seen "eating bread in front of the poor people," as she liked to say. Not a good example.

"I'm heading back to the stateroom to shower. Will you be joining me?" she asked impishly. It was an advantage to have your wife aboard ship, no doubt, especially one as enticing as I often found Karina. But I had business to attend to first.

"Regrettably, madam, I will have to pass. All captains staff at

0830 in Maclintock's office. I'll just catch a shower in the men's locker room."

"Are you *sure* you can't be a bit late for that? It is a Saturday, after all," she said. Now it was my turn to smile. We had both found solace in each other's arms the last six months in the aftermath of the attack on Carinthia and the death of her father, Grand Duke Henrik. We were learning to love each other, and it was a good thing for both of us.

"Duty calls, madam," I said, "and it sounded like serious business." Which I was sure it was. I looked around the gym quickly to make sure we were alone, then gave her a another light kiss on the lips. Again I got the impish smile.

"Your loss, Captain, sir," she said.

"May I remind you, *Lieutenant*, that I am captain of this vessel and you are merely my astrogator and a junior officer. I can order you to do what I want at any time," I said.

"Oh, you can," she acknowledged. "But there are certain orders a wife can refuse that a junior officer never could." With that she swatted my butt, picked up her mask and foil, and made for the ladies' locker room. I watched her go and smiled again, counting myself lucky. She turned back to me at the locker room door and gave me *that* smile one more time. I laughed, hoping that the staff meeting would be over with quickly so I could get back home to where I really wanted to be, with her.

Thirty minutes later I crossed the glass umbilical corridor that would take me from *Defiant* to High Station Candle proper. I had a great deal of trepidation about the staff meeting I was about to attend: an "all hands," which meant all Lightship captains plus Admiral Wesley. No doubt something was up, something big.

A small group of techs was setting up the longwave connection to the Historians' ansible network when I entered the conference room. This would allow the Lightship captains to link up and converse with their fleet commodore and Admiral Wesley in real time. It wasn't a technology I understood, provided by the Historians of Earth, of course, but I knew how to use it, and being able to communicate across many light-years instantaneously gave us a great advantage.

I was the only captain in attendance in the conference room, as both Maclintock's ship, *Starbound*, and mine, *Defiant*, were docked here at Candle in our home system of Quantar. The other captains were spread out far and wide across Union Space, a bubble about forty-eight light-years across, centered around Sol, which the Union Navy had declared they would defend as home space. There were only about sixty G-type spectral stars, humanity's preferred type for colonization, within that bubble. Of those systems, only a few had been colonized in the early days of Imperial growth, since many had no planets with the right climate conditions and atmosphere. We knew of nineteen historical colonies and a handful of industrial bases within that bubble, and our Union, at the moment, represented only five.

I looked at the massive star display on the far wall. Beyond Union Space, the stars identified as yellow dots, the G-type stars of the Imperium were identified as red. That red bubble extended out from about fifty light-years to a hundred light-years from Sol. While it seemed the Empire and Union areas of space were nearly identical in size, the fact was that there were some 448 potential stars with habitable worlds within that Imperial red bubble, nearly eight times as many as in Union Space. The stellar topography greatly favored our enemies in terms of potential numbers of colonized worlds. That was an advantage they could use to crush the Union if we didn't get stronger and more numerous, and soon. The Historians told us that there were some 350 known colonies in the old empire at its peak, before the war, and as we now knew, fewer than twenty of those were on our side of the line. Whether the old empire had ever colonized beyond that hundred-light-year bubble was an unknown.

I turned away from the star display and back to the conference monitors, which were slowly flickering to life. We were now at eight operational Lightships in the fleet, if you counted *Vanguard*, Pendax's ship, which was near enough to ready. I feared that wouldn't be enough ships, despite my confidence in both our Lightships and their captains.

Valiant, commanded by Wynn Scott of Earth, was conducting the long-delayed First Contact mission at Jenarus, which I had previously visited when I was third-in-command aboard *Starbound*. *Resolution*, commanded by Devin Tannace, Maclintock's former number two, was on-station in her home system of Levant. *Avenger* was captained by Mehzut Ozil, a man I had met briefly on Carinthia during the recovery operations there. *Fearless*, commanded by Dietar Von Zimmerman, son of Carinthia's Air Marshal Von Zimmerman, was stationed in her home system. Neither *Fearless* nor *Avenger* had ventured very far from Carinthia since the attack.

Impulse II, captained by my former lover Dobrina Kierkopf, was at High Station 3 in the Carinthian system, prepping for a survey mission to a system called Skondar for possible First Contact. Skondar had been a robust mining colony in the old Imperial days. It was unknown if the colony was still inhabited, but it was known that she had been a treasure trove of metals such as lithium and magnesium, not to mention less exotic but nonetheless valuable gold and silver repositories.

There would be one addition to our virtual table; Captain Lucius Zander, my first commanding officer aboard the original ill-fated *Impulse*, was joining us today as the future captain of the Lightship *Vanguard* from the Union's newest member world, Pendax. *Vanguard* would be joining the fleet in another month or so as our eighth commissioned Lightship.

As the techs finished up their work, I took my seat at the conference table next to Maclintock. We faced a broad, curved plasma in the office's conference work area, just a part of the massive facility the commodore had at his disposal. One by one, the six Lightship captains' faces appeared on the big screen hanging above us. When the last connection was made—that of Grand Admiral Jonathon Wesley in his office on High Station Quantar —the techs departed the room, leaving Maclintock and me alone with our virtual group.

"Ladies and gentlemen," Wesley started, "I hope all is well where you are." There were nods and general acknowledgments all around. "Good," he continued. "Let's get on with it, then. First order of business is new deployments, of which I have three. Captain Ozil, I'm uploading an order packet to you that outlines your new mission, which is a first survey of the Ceta system."

"Thank you, Admiral. We're anxious to get back out," said Ozil, an odd-looking man with short dark hair and big bulging eyes.

"I'm sure you are. This one will be standard stealth-running survey protocols: observe and catalog, but do not engage or participate in any activity that might arouse interest in *Avenger*. And at any sign of Imperial forces in the system, you are to bug out and return to station immediately, no exceptions."

"What are our rules of engagement?" asked Ozil. Wesley looked up sharply from his desk display, staring right into the camera.

"There are none, Captain. You are to bug out, period," he said. The fact was that the Lightship fleet had had no interactions with the old empire since the battles at Levant and Pendax almost a year ago. Wesley apparently wanted to keep it that way.

"Understood, sir," replied Ozil. I could see he was disappointed, but Wesley's orders were probably prudent. The Union was looking for as many allies as we could find, but if a system was already under Imperial influence, our orders were to leave that system alone, regardless of proximity to Union space.

"Admiral," came another voice, this one from the other Carinthian captain, Dietar Von Zimmerman. "*Fearless* has been passed over twice now for missions away from home. Can I ask why?" His Carinthian accent was lighter than most, and I hadn't found communicating with him a problem at all, as his Standard English was very good. Wesley nodded to Commodore Maclintock, who had operational command over deployed Union forces, for an answer to the inquiry.

"The facts are, Captain Von Zimmerman, that I would like to send you out and get your feet wet. Unfortunately, Carinthian Navy Command has insisted that at least *one* Lightship remain in-system at all times until *Bismarck* is commissioned next year. As of this time, that ship has been designated as *Fearless*," replied Maclintock.

What he was really saying was that Von Zimmerman's father, the Air Marshal of Carinthia, was keeping his boy close to home. It didn't sit well. Von Zimmerman got a sour look on his face, then said, "So, Ozil and Dobrina get to have all the fun again, and *Fearless* and I get to go back and forth between High Stations, never leaving our home star."

Maclintock shrugged. "Captain Kierkopf does have battle experience with the Empire, Dietar, and the Carinthian Navy Command is requesting that you stay in-system. There's really nothing I can do about that, except in an emergency. And I think we should all be thankful there have been no recent emergencies. Using any quiet time we have in this conflict is to our ultimate advantage, Captain."

"Aye, sir," Von Zimmerman said with more than a trace of resignation in his voice.

"Next up: Captain Tannace of *Resolution*," said Wesley, comfortable with overseeing if not running the meeting.

"Aye, sir," replied Tannace. He was an agreeable man in his mid-forties, a bit old for a Lightship command, but he had been Maclintock's loyal number two for many years. His appearance was always spit-polish clean, and I was told that's the way he ran his ship. He was a by-the-book commander, and every fleet needed its cache of those to balance out the more risk-friendly types, like me.

"Afraid it's the milk run to Carinthia again, Devin," said Maclintock. "There's another shipment of food goods from the bazaar at Artemis. Even live goats, I've heard—part of the rebuilding efforts. It's not glamorous, but if you manage to pick up some Carinthian schnapps on the way back through and drop them off here at Candle, well, I'm sure you'll get a good evaluation on your next rating."

Tannace laughed and responded with an "Aye, sir." Then we were on to the next issue at hand. Wesley cut in and asked for a report on the Jenarus negotiations by *Valiant*'s Captain Scott.

"The Jenaurians are real shits to negotiate with, sir," said Scott frankly. He was a tall, sinewy, Earth-born African man, darker than any I had ever met. We had our share of aboriginal descendants from the Australian continent on Quantar, but none like him. When he spoke, it was with authority and experience. "They want massive concessions from the standard Concord Agreement, and I'm not of a mind to give in to them. The biggest hurdle is establishing a representative democracy. They have an authoritarian bent to their planetary government, and there are three or four other nation-states that also want a seat at the table, so negotiations may take a while. Still, whenever I tell them we'll come back at another time when they're in better moods, they rush to give in on things. It will take time, Admiral, but I expect they will eventually come to an agreement with us."

"Good news, Wynn. Please keep me informed of your progress, and remember that the Union Council has the Jenarus system at the top of their list for expansion," said Wesley.

"Will do, Admiral," said Scott.

Wesley nodded, giving the floor back to Maclintock, who turned his attention to Zander's report on *Vanguard*'s progress. Zander's transformation over the last eighteen months, since the attack on his shuttle at Levant, was nothing short of miraculous. He now had two eyes again, his skin was a smooth pink, and he even had wisps of white hair hanging down to his shoulders, Bohemian style. It was a far cry from the charred face I had pulled into *Impulse*'s Downship that day at Levant.

Vanguard was officially one month from being commissioned, but Zander already had her crewed up and ready to go. In a pinch, I suspected she could be ready for a fight in days. In fact, I figured Zander could launch her in twenty-four hours if he wanted.

"My intent is to take her out next week on a traverse run to Minara. It's forty-two light-years, so that should be a good test of the traverse drive system," said Zander in his gravel-rough voice.

"Sounds good, Lucius. No contact with the locals, if you please, but you might find your way clear to leave your IFF signal beacon on for a while. The tech survey team said the Minarans seem to have a high level of technology and may have even detected our probes. So don't be afraid to let them know you're there and friendly," said Maclintock.

"Aye, Commodore," replied Zander.

"Captain Kierkopf," said Maclintock. "All ready for the Skondar mission?"

"Ready as we'll ever be," said Dobrina. "Skondar is close to the borderline with empire space. Based on our Historian's longwave probe reports, I have my doubts that we'll find any kind of functioning colony or camp there. But we'll investigate it thoroughly. We've added another thirty marines to our complement and dropped our Downship in favor of the two reinforced marine gunships the Earthers offered. If anybody is alive down there and wants a fight, they'll get one."

Maclintock looked up at her image, unsmiling. "The mining operation is on Drava, the moon of the fifth planet in the system. We need to find out if that operation is still intact and can be exploited.

In Imperial times there were valuable minerals there. They may not be valuable to the empire today, but likely it's different for us. That's my way of saying don't blow anything up you don't have to, Captain." That set off a round of low chuckles.

"Understood, sir," she replied. I could see from her stone-faced look on the display that she wasn't amused. At all. I could still read her moods.

Then Maclintock turned to me.

"Lastly, Captain Cochrane and *Defiant*," he started.

"Ah yes, the golden boy," chimed in Zander. This drew another round of laughs from the other captains.

"Thank you, Lucius," I said, to a few more chuckles.

"Well, he *has* drawn the plum assignment," said Maclintock, turning to me. "You're ordered to take *Defiant* to High Station Pendax, there to rendezvous with a certain merchant named Admar Harrington. The mission is First Contact with the government of Sandosa. They are already in contact with our survey team and anxious to meet us face to face. And since your ship carries both a duke of Quantar and a princess of Carinthia, it seemed to the Admiralty that you were the best option for this mission, diplomatically speaking."

"Understood, sir, but why will we be taking Mr. Harrington?" It wasn't that I minded the man; he was a likable enough chap and a great negotiator who had helped me escape Carinthia at the height of the conflict there. I just wasn't sure I wanted his company aboard my Lightship.

"Pendax and Sandosa had a very strong trading relationship under the old empire. Harrington would like to get first shot at cracking the market. And since Pendax is our newest member, the Union Council had a hard time saying no to him."

"Understood, sir," I said again, but I didn't really like it. Still, diplomatic missions had their bonuses. They tended to be full of state dinners and lots of merrymaking. The negotiations were more tedious, but I found I was able to distance myself from the hardcore horse trading more easily as time went on, using both my royal standing and my position as a Lightship captain to avoid the tough work.

"Full contact protocols will be sent via communications packet, along with a history of Sandosa and any relevant information from the survey teams. Departure from Candle will be at 1000 hours on 02.19.2770. Understood, Captain?" Maclintock finished.

"Yes, sir," I said. That was the day after tomorrow. More than enough time to prepare my crew and go. We hadn't been out in nearly a month, so the space time would be a welcome break from our leisurely port schedule.

When Maclintock was finished with me, he turned things back over to Admiral Wesley. "Last orders, Captains," the Admiral started. "The criminal Prince Arin is still at large. The Empire is out there, also a threat, but we don't know how big anymore. Until the prince is brought to justice and the Empire's intentions are fully known, we are on a war footing. If you encounter empire forces, disengage, contact the Admiralty, and we will organize a response. If you sight Prince Arin or the *Vixis*, your rules of engagement are shoot to kill. No mistakes, Captains, and no mercy for our enemies."

"Aye, sir," I said, as did all the other captains.

At that the formal portion of the meeting broke up, and we proceeded to break into side conversations. I found myself wandering over to Dobrina's large image on the plasma display.

"Looks like we got the plum assignments," she said.

"That's the way I arranged it," I joked. She laughed at that.

"So, I take it you'll be coming through High Station 3 on your way to Pendax? Maybe we could have dinner—you and your lovely bride, of course," she replied.

"I'd love to. I'll have to make excuses to Maclintock about the layover, but that shouldn't be a problem, as long as I bring him a case of your best schnapps," I said.

"I can deliver on that," she said, smiling. Then I thought of something else.

"One more thing," I said. "I'm looking for a qualified astrogator, and I'd like it to be a Carinthian. Right now Lena Babayan and Karina are the only Carinthian senior officers aboard. I'd like to move Karina from astrogator, as I'd much rather have her on longscope for experience reasons."

Dobrina tilted her head at me. "Actually, I have someone in mind. He's very talented but kind of blocked here as a senior lieutenant. If you were willing to offer an eventual promotion to lieutenant commander, I could see my way clear to letting him go."

I crossed my arms in mock angst. "What's the price going to be? And don't say a fencing match," I said. She laughed.

"We can negotiate that over dinner," she replied.

"It's a date. Karina and I will see you on Monday night." She seemed to hesitate. "Yes?" I prompted her.

"Just so you know, I'll be having a guest for dinner," she said.

"Oh. I see," I replied. The possibility that she had moved on from me romantically wasn't something I'd really thought about much, nor was I really sure what my feelings were on the subject. But it was here, and I'd have to face it. "I'll look forward to meeting him, then," I said. Her very large face looked down at me from the display, eyes fixed, her features giving away nothing.

"And I'll look forward to seeing the both of you Monday evening," she finally said. I acknowledged with a silent nod, and she broke the connection. I lingered a bit to see if there were any more casual conversations to be had, but as the meeting dwindled away I said my goodbyes and headed for my stateroom. I eagerly anticipated what was waiting for me there.

I wasn't disappointed.

I entered our rather spacious stateroom and could only see Karina's bare legs and feet beyond the partition that separated our personal space from my work station. I had a desk big enough for six to sit around, a small dining table, bookcases, and a sofa in my office, and then came the partition and our bedroom area, plus the full private bath with a tub. I had insisted on that feature, and I'd never regretted it—what with being a young couple and all, we needed the extra bit of luxury for our more romantic moments together.

As I watched from behind the partition, Karina kicked her legs back and forth slowly, enticing me into the bedroom.

"How was your meeting, *dear*?" she asked, with mock emphasis on the last word. I said nothing in response, but instead walked up and leaned against the partition to get a full view of my wife.

She was stark naked on the bed, her long dark hair still wet from her shower, swiveling her legs back and forth playfully. I had an excellent view of one of my favorite features of her body, and as always, the sight aroused me. She teased me, twisting curls into her wet hair as she read the local tabloids from a tablet plasma, seemingly oblivious to my presence. But I knew better.

"My meeting wasn't nearly as interesting as *this*," I said, quickly unbuttoning my shirt.

"Oh, really?" she replied, turning to me and giving me that practiced, impish smile that always melted my defenses. I hurried out of the rest of my clothes, discarding them all on the floor, and was quickly on the bed next to her, running my hand up and down her body. I gently rubbed her smooth skin, then rolled her onto her side and kissed her deeply. I soon set myself to exploring her other God-given gifts. Our passion accelerated quickly, and we found ourselves fully engaged in lovemaking in a matter of just a few brief moments. From there, one thing led to another and, well . . .

Soon enough we both fell into a peaceful slumber, but mine didn't last, not like I wanted.

I woke up some time later with a start, my heart pounding, my breath shallow and jagged, my side of the bed covered in sweat. I'd had the dream again.

The warped ships. The warped bodies. Young men and women I'd never met, their lives crushed out of them like the yolk from a raw egg. They said you never completely got rid of guilt, and I believed them now. Thousands had died on the Imperial dreadnoughts at Pendax and Carinthia, all of them at my command. Hell, at *my hand*. Their souls haunted me in my dreams. Not every night, but enough that it disturbed me, distracted me, took me off my game. And I couldn't afford that kind of distraction. Not now.

I rolled off the bed in the dark, trying not to disturb Karina. I settled onto my exercise mat on the floor and started the deep breathing exercises the doctors had told me to use in order to clear my mind. They worked—most of the time. I did this six times through as instructed, breathing in deeply, holding it for a count of four, then exhaling. I hoped I could get through them without waking Karina. When I was done I went back to the bed, then felt her soft touch on my neck and shoulders, gently rubbing me. She pulled the bed sheets around me, wiping the sheen of sweat off my back, then slid across the bed and pressed herself against me from behind. It was comforting.

"You had the dream again, didn't you?" she asked. I nodded.

"I hoped I wouldn't wake you."

"Not much chance of that, Captain. It's almost like I can feel it when you're dreaming, the way you struggle. Even when I'm sleeping, I'm constantly aware of you," she said. I put my hand over hers.

"I appreciate it. More than you know," I replied. It was true. We all needed someone to watch our backs, and Karina had mine, always.

"Have you given any more thought to what the doctors recommended?"

I shook my head. "No. Not really," I admitted.

"It's not a sign of weakness to ask for help."

"I know. I just want . . . I want to resolve things myself," I said. She kissed my neck.

"Sometimes that's not possible. Guilt and post-traumatic stress are not easily resolvable. Our minds are . . . complicated things."

I sighed. "Like I said, I want to work it out myself. As long as it doesn't interfere with doing my job—"

"It already has, Peter. At best you sleep five or six hours a night. You're not as sharp as you were before. Sometimes you miss things, both on the bridge and with me," she said. I knew she was right. She almost always was. I had a mind to have her checked out on the intuition scale. I turned back to her, and she put her arms around my neck again, first rubbing my temples and then clasping her hands together behind my head and pulling me in to kiss her. She was demanding in this way, in the showing of affection. It was something she insisted on, and I had to admit she was right about it. It did make our relationship stronger.

"So, what happened at your meeting with Maclintock?" she asked.

"We got our orders," I said flatly. Her lips curled into a mock sneer.

"I know that. I want to know what they *are*," she said, insistent. I sighed.

"We're going out to Sandosa, First Contact mission via Carinthia, or at least High Station 3, anyway. Plus a stop at Pendax to pick up Admar Harrington and a diplomatic team," I said. The fastest way to Pendax was to make the instantaneous jump to Carinthia first, make our way through normal space to Carinthia's egress jump point, and from there make another jump to Pendax, which was thirty-two light-years distant and well inside our Hoagland's instant jump range. That way we avoided traverse space and the unnecessary (and seemingly random) thirty-four-hour journey through an unknown dimension.

The stop at High Station 3 was a bit out of the way, but I found as a captain that courtesy calls were sometimes necessary.

Karina's voice brought me back to reality. "That sounds exciting," she said, without any real enthusiasm in her voice. She knew full well whose Lightship was stationed at High Station 3.

"It is," I said. The next thing was more delicate. "I was hoping we could have dinner with Dobrina Kierkopf aboard *Impulse II*. She's docked at the station for now, and, well, I haven't seen her or her ship since we left Carinthia. And I'm negotiating with her over a placement."

"I thought our crew manifest was full-up?" she said.

"It is," I admitted, "but she has a very talented astrogator who's stuck behind several senior officers." She sat up at this.

"But I'm your astrogator," she said rather forcefully.

I sighed.

"I've been thinking, and I think I want you at the longscope. Right now it's just Ensign Lynne Layton, George's sister, and she's not nearly as experienced as you are."

Karina let out a displeased sound and rolled away from me on the bed, lying on her back to stare at the ceiling. "Do you not trust me?" she asked.

"I trust your skills implicitly. That's why I want you in the best position for the ship and for me," I said honestly. She looked back over her shoulder at me briefly.

"I'm supposed to coordinate our social schedule, you know," she said, apparently conceding the position change. "I know who Dobrina Kierkopf is and what she represented in your life. Probably more than you realize." I leaned over her and kissed her forehead.

"That's why I asked about it first," I replied.

"If I'd known you'd taken over all of my social duties, I wouldn't have been so kind just now," she said in mock protest.

"Oh yes you would have," I retorted. She smacked me hard on the shoulder.

"Men!" Then she was up to dress for the day, and I joined her. It was these small moments as much as the sex that made our life together such a pleasure for me. I found her fascinating in every way, and I loved just *being* with her. Had I not chosen the life of a Lightship captain, I could easily see myself spending my days with her at court as prince and princess with nothing but idle time on our hands, raising a family together.

As she put on her makeup, using her vanity mirror for guidance, she caught me by surprise again. "Have you given any more thought to my proposal?"

"Proposal? I thought it was just an idea. Now it's a formal proposal?" I asked, trying to rebutton my shirt collar.

"I believe anything exchanged between a princess of Carinthia and a duke of Quantar rises to the level of a formal proposal," she said, then turned from her vanity toward me. I had to smile at that. The truth was, though, that I hadn't thought about it.

"No," I said, as I finally finished buttoning my uniform shirt.

"Both our families will need an heir eventually, and I know the news would do Carinthia a world of good," she said, seemingly innocent of the pun she had just made.

I couldn't disagree with her. Carinthia had been brutalized by Arin, and good news was in short supply there these days since the grand duke's passing. It was just that I saw no practical time to have a child while we were both serving in the Union Navy. I took her by the hand and sat down with her on the edge of the bed.

"Karina, you know I want this as much as you do. But we've been married less than a year, and there's so much uncertainty out there—"

"There will always be uncertainty, Peter. The only certainty we're guaranteed is what we make ourselves. You should know that."

She was right on that point. If the last two years had taught me anything, it was that you couldn't rely on things working out as you'd planned in any way.

"You'd have to leave the service," I said.

"I know that," she replied. "But perhaps you should consider that our greatest value to both of our worlds is to serve, united, as an inspiration to the future we all hope to make with the Union." I thought about that.

"Or perhaps our greatest value to the Union is to be seen defending her together, fighting for what we believe is right," I said.

"Perhaps," she said, hesitating. We sat there for a moment in silence, a princess and a duke of the realm, trying to decide our fate together.

"I still have unfinished business out here. Arin—"

"Arin is a ghost hanging over us all, Peter. We can't let him determine our actions or what's best for us—or for that matter, for our people. Both our worlds need this. But you won't give up your quest for the great white shark," she said. I smiled at her.

"I think you mean the great white whale," I said, remembering my *Moby-Dick*. She pulled her hand back.

"Shark, whale, whatever. The point is that we both have a higher calling, a higher duty, than the Union Navy. It's going to come soon enough, so why not now?"

I looked at her, the determination in her. I wondered if it was a trait common in all Carinthian women. I admired it, just as I had in Captain Dobrina Kierkopf. But I wasn't ready to concede my navy career just yet.

"I know that I want to stay in the navy, that that is where I'm best able to serve for the moment. The question you have to answer is where will you be serving the Union best: here at my side, fighting with me, or at home, raising our children?"

"I think we both agree that having me on Carinthia raising our children while you're in space is not a workable option," she said.

"On that we agree," I said. She returned to her makeup mirror and resumed applying her makeup. "So then our only two choices are to stay on Quantar or Carinthia raising a family or stay in space together."

"Yes," she said, applying a modest amount of eyeliner. Then she stopped and turned to me again, right hand at her hip. "You may have to accept the fact that your path changed when you married me. Both of our lives did. My father is gone, and yours won't live forever, even if you don't want to accept that. Life goes on with or without your participation, Peter. You have to decide what's best for *everyone* now, not just for Captain Peter Cochrane of *Defiant*."

"I understand that," I said, and I did. I always thought I would have a number of years yet to serve in space in the Union Navy before I was forced to take on the role of a prince. My decision to marry Karina in the midst of the Carinthian crisis had accelerated all of that exponentially, and now I was facing that accelerating agenda. But deep down I had to admit to myself that I didn't want to give up my dreams of commanding a Lightship so soon.

"I think we should talk about this again when we get back from Sandosa," I said. She turned to me one last time, rose to come to me, and put her arms around me.

"Carinthia and Quantar need us now, Peter," she said.

"They do need us, Karina. But right now they also need trained military commanders and experienced Lightship captains. Unfortunately, I'm one of a rare breed, a rare few, that can provide that," I said. She shook her head.

"I need an answer, Peter. And I want us to make it together," she said, appealing to my love for her. I didn't want us to be bickering about this for the whole length of our mission. I cared about her and respected her too much for that.

"I have a proposal, then," I said. "If we have another six months as quiet as the last six have been, I promise I will give retiring from the navy and starting a family the most serious consideration."

Her eyes flickered back and forth, like she was searching my eyes for the truth. "I'll hold you to that, Peter, and pray that things stay quiet," she said. Then she kissed me. "I love you, and I want us to be happy. As happy as we can be under these circumstances."

I kissed her in return and then made my way to my bridge, visions of imploding dreadnoughts still haunting my thoughts.

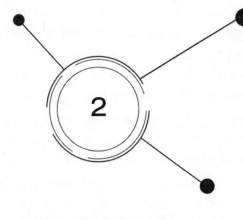

Underway

The journey Monday morning to Quantar's egress jump point was a leisurely one, interrupted only by the sudden frenzy of the quarter-hour prep to spool up the Hoaglands and make the jump to Carinthia. We flashed into Carinthian space microseconds later—or microseconds earlier, as some scientists argued—at exactly 1015 hours ship time.

We were docked at High Station 3 by noon. I gave my crew full liberty with only minimal staff required until 1000 hours the next morning. More than enough time to hit 3's famous beer halls and still sleep off the hangover before we departed for Pendax.

I noted that *Impulse II* was docked in one of the other six operational station ports, but I decided against going over to her right away and causing a ruckus. Dobrina had left Karina and me an invitation to dinner at 1800 by com message, and I decided it would be best to leave the good captain to the running of her ship without distractions for the day.

The last two days had been a bit rough for Karina and me. She had made her feelings known, and I respected that, but I was still only twenty-five, and I wasn't willing to give up on my navy career just yet. This had strained our conversations and personal time, and I for one wanted to be past it. I cared for her far too much to want to fight or have this upset in our lives. Coincidentally, she buzzed in to my bridge com a few minutes after we'd locked *Defiant* down for the day.

"I'm going over to the station to shop for a bit," she said.

"Who with? I hope you're not going to spend all of my bonus," I replied. She laughed.

"No. It's lady things mostly and some local fare. Your Quantar food isn't all that it's cracked up to be, unless you like beef, beef soup, and roast beef," she said. I smiled.

"You left out dried pork and beef jerky. All right, then. But please conduct your business without tromping on my world's dignity," I said. She laughed again. "And you never said who you were shopping with. I know ladies don't like to do these outings alone."

"I didn't say, did I? Anyway, it's not the kind of thing that a man would enjoy, so you'll just have to trust me on this," she said. What could I say to that?

"I understand. Have fun, but please avoid the tabloid press as much as possible," I cautioned her.

"Of course. I'll see you back aboard in a few hours."

"That's fine. Just leave time for dinner prep," I said.

"As you command, Captain," she said. Now it was my turn to laugh. We said our goodbyes and then hung up. I felt like the conversation was more hopeful than those we'd had the last few days. Personally I hoped dinner would go a long way toward bringing us back to being of the same mind about things. We'd had precious few disagreements in our time as husband and wife, and I hoped to keep it that way.

I stood and surveyed my bridge, looking for anything out of sorts that I could complain about. When I found nothing, I gave the con to a junior rating named Watson, much to his youthful delight, then headed for the lifter. Liberty on a foreign station wasn't something a Lightship captain commonly took, and I found myself wistful for the days when I could semi-anonymously crawl around a High Station with Layton and Marker, drinking our way from pub to pub. Those days were gone, I decided, and many others like them would likely come to an end soon as well. I sighed as the lifter doors shut and pressed the button for the gym deck, hoping there might be someone there to give the captain a fair game of squash.

There was, and I was soundly beaten by a Carinthian marine named Verhunce. She was a co-survivor of the battle at the Jenarus Founder station. She was tight and wiry and ultracompetitive, and she reminded me more than a bit of Dobrina Kierkopf, I decided. We didn't talk about Jenarus at all, and I made a mental note to peruse Marker's latest Fitness for Duty report on her, just in case. I knew full well about my own problems and wanted to make sure she wasn't experiencing the same things. It was obvious she was tough as nails though, as she drove me around the squash court relentlessly, seemingly at her whim.

After the drubbing I received, I licked my wounds back in my stateroom and waited for my wayward wife to return from her shopping. She did, but in barely enough time to dress for dinner aboard *Impulse*.

"So, how did it go?" I asked innocently enough as she freshened her makeup.

"Oh, quite lovely. We raided the stores of all the local food I could find. Even had time for a quick pedicure. Dobrina knows her way around the station, and that saved a lot of time," she said. I sat up at this.

"Dobrina? As in Kierkopf?" Karina turned and gave me the impish smile.

"What, I didn't tell you? The good captain of *Impulse* and I have had a standing date for an outing for quite some time. She was very helpful in *so* many ways," she said. The smile got more devious.

I jumped to my feet and grabbed her from behind, and she let out a mock squeal. "And what did this help entail?" I asked, refusing to let her go back to her makeup preparations.

"None of your business! Now let me go!" she demanded. I refused and held onto her.

"I think I have a right to know," I said.

"Oh no you don't," she said, then turned and kissed me quickly on the lips. "Girls have secrets." I let her go then and sat back on the bed, astonished.

"So you two have had this planned the whole time?" I asked. She turned back from the mirror again.

"Uh-huh."

"And what did you talk *about*?"

"We're going to be late if I don't hurry, dear."

"We're already late. What did you and Dobrina talk about?"

She turned toward me one last time. "Things we have in common," she said. She rushed through the rest of her preparations, making innocuous small talk about her shopping spree. For my part, I just kept checking my watch. She was presently in order, with just enough time for us to make for *Impulse II* and be on time to our dinner.

We walked through the station together, attracting paparazzi, well-wishes from businessmen and women, and firm salutes from Carinthian and Quantar sailors alike. This caused the five-minute walk to stretch to fifteen, and I had to answer plenty of questions about where we were going (*Impulse II*), what our mission was (classified), and, of course, when we were having children (no comment).

Once we were cleared to board *Impulse II*, we gladly made our way to her service lifter, which ran a direct line to and from officer country. When we were inside the lifter and the doors were shut, Karina turned to me and took me by the arm.

"I want you to know that I am over my disagreement with you," she said. "I won't bring up the idea of having a child again until it's time. You offered a year, and I will take that year."

I smiled, then bent down and kissed her, which I loved doing. "I'm glad," I said, then took her by the hand as the lifter doors opened. We walked down a short hall to the captain's stateroom. The door was open, and servants greeted us at the threshold. I glanced inside. It was every inch the marvel Zander's cabin had been aboard the original *Impulse*, done in the heavy baroque style the Carinthians favored, but it was different in that it had a distinctly feminine touch to it.

"Captain and Mrs. Cochrane," announced the head servant. At that we stepped through the door.

Dobrina greeted us both with a hello, handshakes, and a smile. She seemed different to me. I had known her primarily as a tough-minded commander, as competitive as any man I'd served with in the line of duty. She was more settled now as a full-rank captain—more tempered, it seemed to me—and the change was both encouraging and enlightening. I wondered how much this new man in her life had to do with the change.

"Please, let's have a drink before dinner," she said as she gestured to matching sofas near the stateroom's fireplace, where a servant held champagne glasses for the three of us. We each took a flute and clinked glasses, then drank. The Carinthian champagne was surprisingly good, and I complimented her on it, then got on to other things.

"So, I understand you and my wife had a bit of an outing today?" I asked casually. Dobrina and Karina exchanged glances and then laughed together—or more precisely, giggled. "I'm sorry if I don't get what's so funny, and my guess is this isn't the first drink you two ladies have had today."

"You'd be right," said Dobrina with a wink. I sighed.

"So, what did you do besides shop? Exchange notes on me? Tell secrets at my expense?" I asked. They drank and giggled together again without answering. "What? What's so funny?"

Karina took me by the hand. "There are secrets, dear, and then there are *secrets*," she said. This only made me more curious. I decided to change tactics.

"I was wondering when I get to see this new man in your life?" I asked, anxious to meet Dobrina's new beau for a variety of reasons. They both laughed full-on this time. Then Dobrina stood up and nodded toward the closed door to her private quarters.

"In just a moment now, I think," she said.

At that the door to Dobrina's private apartment opened, and a beautiful but very familiar woman stepped out, smoothing her dinner dress and smiling as she came.

The Princess Janaan of Levant.

I looked to Karina, who looked up at me and smiled. Then I looked to Dobrina, who smirked and took another sip of her champagne. Janaan took the offered champagne from the servant as she passed and came to join us.

"I'd make introductions," said Dobrina, laughing again, "but I think we already all know each other."

"If only for a brief time today," finished Karina, reaching out a hand in greeting toward Janaan. "A pleasure again, Princess." The two princesses shook hands while I watched, feeling helpless. Then all three of the ladies laughed, no doubt at my expense, and drank again.

I drained my champagne glass and motioned the servant over for another drink. This had the makings of a long night.

"Pleased to see you again, Princess," I said, taking Janaan's hand from Karina and trying to change the direction of the evening. She turned to me and smiled back, her dark eyes still showing that smoldering fire I had experienced on her home world.

"And you, Captain," she replied, briefly taking my hand before releasing me. At Dobrina's suggestion we all sat down, Janaan next to Dobrina on one sofa and Karina next to me on the other.

"Surprised?" Dobrina asked me, still smirking. I should never have underestimated her.

"Of course," I said. I hadn't considered that Dobrina's new "man" could be a woman, and certainly not a princess of my acquaintance from a very conservative world.

"Disappointed?" Now she was probing me.

I shook my head. "You know as well as I do that the Union Navy regards personal relationships as personal and not the Navy's business. I just . . . I didn't expect that the two of you would find each other in . . . such a way."

"It's really your fault," said Janaan, smiling. "I came to Carinthia to lead an aid team from Levant. The good captain and I found ourselves consoling each other over something we had in common. Losing you, of course."

"Of course," I replied. Karina slid her free hand into mine.

"*I* was surprised when Dobrina told me about their relationship," said Karina. "Mostly in that I expected a princess of Levant would have had a difficult time carrying off such a relationship, especially with the more conservative societal elements you have to deal with back home."

"I find that the farther out in space I go, the less influence those elements seem to have. But really, Peter, you should be flattered. Here you sit with three beautiful, accomplished women who spent the day together, and none of us has had cause that whole time to complain about you as a lover," Janaan said. I blushed at that and laughed uncomfortably. What could I say to that? I quickly asked for more champagne.

"Well, thank God for that," I said. "Perhaps, ladies, this isn't the best time for these discussions? *Defiant* does have a First Contact mission beginning tomorrow with a trip to Pendax," I reminded them.

"The captain is right," said Dobrina, standing abruptly. "This is not the time. And at any rate, dinner is served." She motioned us toward the finely set table.

Janaan and Karina walked off together, chatting quietly, but I wanted a private word with the captain of *Impulse II*. I trained my eyes on Dobrina as we lagged behind the two princesses. When I got her isolated enough, I opened fire.

"For God's sake, Dobrina, why?" I asked her quietly. She laughed just a bit as the servant handed me my new drink.

"I'm sorry, Peter. I had no idea any of this would happen, but the fact is that the princess and I found each other on Carinthia, and as often happens, one thing led to another. I find her company enthralling, frankly. She's a renaissance woman trying to reform her world, and I found that compelling," Dobrina said.

"And as a lover?" Dobrina smiled and put her hand over my mouth.

"Dinner," she said, and she gently pushed me toward the table and my wife. I went, resigned to my fate.

Dinner was formal and polite with no further discussions of private matters, to my delight.

Afterward, Dobrina and I needed to get down to business, and so we did. Janaan and Karina wandered back to the fireplace with glasses of sherry firmly in hand, conversing quietly.

"And so we meet to negotiate, Captain," I said. Dobrina smiled.

"And so we do."

I leaned back in my chair. "So, what do you want for this talented but nameless astrogation officer?" I asked. She leaned forward, all business now.

"Three cases of Quantar shiraz. And your junior Propulsion officer. What's his name again?" she asked.

"Ensign Mancino," I replied. "I hate to lose him. Graded out A-1 at the academy in the class of 2769."

"I know. He was on my list until you stole him out from under me. Fact is that I need more Quantar sailors to balance things out. He'll do just fine," she said.

"And what's your hotshot astrogator's name?" I asked.

"Lieutenant Ezhil Arasan. One of the best I've got in any department. But he's blocked from advancing. Too many young senior officers aboard."

I nodded. "I can offer him a straight transfer as a lieutenant with an upgrade to lieutenant commander in six months, once I have Layton's promotion paperwork complete," I said.

She smiled. "I will convey those terms. I'm sure he'll accept."

But I wasn't finished.

"There was also a case of schnapps for Maclintock involved, if I remember correctly," I said. "And that shiraz will be half my stores."

"The schnapps was delivered an hour ago. It should be in your stateroom by now. As for the shiraz and Ensign Mancino, just the cost of doing business, my friend."

I smiled and we shook on it. "Just don't get him killed," I said of Mancino.

"I won't," she replied, "and I expect the same consideration for Arasan."

"You've got it," I said, and went to get up. Her hand on my arm moved me back to my chair.

"There is one more thing," she said.

"As always."

Her face got grim. "The Princess Janaan. I don't know whether you know this or not, but she's accepted a position as Admar Harrington's Special Secretary for Union Negotiations. She'll be joining you on your mission to Sandosa, and she'll need a lift to Pendax."

I had a ready reply. "Please inform the princess and Lieutenant Arasan that they must be aboard *Defiant* by 0800 hours tomorrow. We leave at 1000 hours. A suitable cabin will be provided for the princess, but I ask that she remain discreetly out of the way until her duties call for her to be seen aboard ship. Will you convey my instructions?" I said.

Dobrina nodded. "I will," she said. And with that we shook hands, and I joined Karina by the fireplace. We quickly said our goodbyes to Dobrina and Janaan, with a reminder for the princess to be prompt tomorrow, and then we made our way once again to the lifter.

In the brief quiet of the service lifter, Karina turned and kissed me firmly on the lips. "Let's go home, Captain, sir. I have a bit more than a case of schnapps to surprise you with," she said. I smiled.

"Why, Lieutenant, I do believe you were shopping for more than just sauerbraten and rauchkäse," I replied, returning her kiss.

"Umm," she said, smiling at me. "You may be right."

Then I had to convey the news about Janaan coming along for the ride.

"I'm fine with it if you two are. We're all adults here, I believe," she said. With that she reached out and hit the stall button on the lifter, then turned to face me.

"I want to ask you something very important," she said. I nodded assent but said nothing. "Would you have made a different choice than marrying me if you'd had the chance? I mean, about Janaan." She was asking me the question I had been dreading. There was no good answer.

"I'm happy with the choice I made," I said to her.

"That's not an answer," she said, shaking her head. I thought about that for a second.

"Karina, the circumstances under which we were married weren't ideal, obviously. But in the last year I have come to love you, respect you, and admire you, and I realize now how important you are to me and to *Defiant*. You're my wife, my confidante, the future mother of our children. No woman could give me more than that," I said.

"She could. She's everything that I am and more. We both know it. She's statuesque, more beautiful, dark, and exotic. Everything I'm not. The fact is that I was just the right girl at the right time, and by pure luck she was out of the picture. I have no doubt you would have chosen her if the circumstances had been different," she said, pulling back from me. I thought about what she had said very carefully before answering.

"You're right," I replied. Her face quickly flushed with anger. "I would have chosen her if I had never met you. If we had never been put together by circumstances beyond our control. If I had never known you or kissed you. But the fact is, being here with you now is all I want, all I could think of wanting, and my future with you is all I can hope for or dream of." It was a gamble, a high-stakes one for sure, but I meant every word of it.

She looked up at me, her face still flushed red. I didn't know if I had quelled her anger or enflamed it. Then she came at me, pushing me back against the lifter wall and kissing me passionately before pulling away again.

"You're mine, Peter Cochrane. And don't ever forget it," she said. Then she covered my mouth with hers one last time before setting the lifter to resume its descent path.

And with that the lifter doors opened, and we faced the onslaught of paparazzi again all the way home.

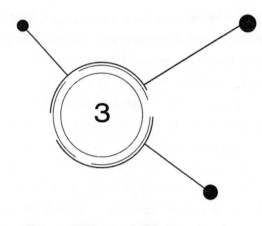

To Pendax

I called the staff together at 0900, and Lieutenant Arasan was there on time. He was a dark-skinned and lanky lad, likely of predominantly Indian descent. I introduced him to the group around the table, which included my XO, Babayan, my master chief, John Marker, George Layton, Duane Longer, Ensign Lynne Layton (George's younger sister), Karina, and *Defiant*'s resident Earth Historian, Gracel. She had joined us just as we were commissioned, coming over from her former assignment with Dobrina and *Impulse II*. She was a matronly woman in what appeared to be her late forties (though actual age was always up for debate with the Historians), with shoulder-length, predominantly gray hair and a pleasant face. She seemed to favor little to no makeup, and her tone was almost always all business. This would be our first mission outside of the local Union worlds, and her presence would be essential if we ran into any sort of Imperial trouble. I hadn't gotten a good feel for her yet, at least nothing like the rapport I'd had with my former mentor Serosian, who had chosen to remain ship's Historian aboard *Starbound*, serving with Maclintock. He and I had had a falling out during the Battle of Pendax, and it was a rift I didn't see healing any time soon. In any case, I felt my relationship to Gracel was better off as formal and distant, and that's how I tried to keep it.

After the introductions, I started right in on the day's business. "XO, would you please give your morning update?" I asked of Commander Babayan. She cleared her throat.

"All systems green. Ship's telemetry is topping out near 100 percent," she said. I turned to my second-in-command.

"*Near* 100 percent, XO?" I asked.

Babayan gave a slight shrug. "Two of the hybrid drive plasma inducers are running at about 97 percent efficiency. It's not a major issue and shouldn't affect performance in any significant way. We do have fourteen other inducers topping out at 100 percent. All in all it's less than three percent anomalous on overall impeller systems, sir," she replied.

"We have one hour to launch and almost two hours travel to the Carinthia egress jump point, Commander. Let's see if we can get them *all* to 100 percent?" I said. She seemed annoyed at this, but she gave me an "Aye, sir," and we moved on to Duane Longer of Propulsion. Longer held the field rank of Super-Lieutenant, which George Layton formerly held aboard *Starbound*. I liked Duane, but I wanted to see him operate a bit more under pressure before I made his rank upgrade permanent. If he continued to improve he would eventually be the senior department head reporting directly to Layton, who was filling the role of third officer that I formally held on *Starbound*. The one thing I had no doubt about with Longer was his stalwart work at the Propulsion station.

"Duane?" I prompted him. He was ready with his report.

"All propulsion systems are at max preparedness, sir, sparing the hybrid drive plasma inducers, but all the drives themselves are working fine. Chemical impellers, sub-light HD drive, Hoagland hyperdimensional drive, traverse jump generators, all at full max, sir. Give the orders, and we'll get you where you need *Defiant* to be, sir."

"And this trouble with the hybrid drive infusers?" I asked. He looked to Babayan and then shook his head.

"Negligible, Captain. The XO and I will have the bugs worked out within the hour," he said. I smiled at his confidence.

"Thank you, Duane," I replied, then turned to the other side of the table and our new Lieutenant Arasan. "Astrogation?" He looked down to his plasma, then addressed the table in general rather than me directly.

"Carinthia egress point and Pendax ingress jump points calculated and locked per the latest readings from the Historian ansible network. The jump should be uneventful," he said.

"And the traverse jump from Pendax to Sandosa?" I asked. This time he turned to me.

"Also calculated. I estimate 34.2 hours in traverse space, sir," he reported. And there it was again, the seemingly random time in traverse space between two star systems. No two places were the same, and none of the times seemed to relate to the normal space distances between any two stars. The time required to travel between one star and another in traverse space changed with every trip, and calculating it was tricky, but from what Dobrina had told me, Lieutenant Arasan was up to the task. The Historians could never quite explain the time anomaly adequately. I supposed it had something to do with the constant movement of planets, stars, and galaxies throughout the universe. You were never truly in the same place twice in this space-time dimension, no matter that the distances seemed to be constant to the untrained eye.

Now I turned to Gracel. "What do we know of Sandosa, Historian?" I asked. She leaned forward and addressed the room in her usual formal manner.

"The colony on Sandosa was founded in the First Colonization Wave of the 2150s, primarily by colonists from the Iberian Peninsula of Earth. Mainly Spanish, Portuguese, Catalan, Basque, and Andalusian settlers with small minority groups of Moroccan Muslims and Sephardic Jews. The colony thrived mainly on a maritime economy richly seeded from Old Earth and supplemented with biomodified indigenous ocean species. After a century, though, the colony stagnated, and population was stuck at around two million. Just as the Second Wave of Colonization opened up on Earth, a discovery was made of large-scale mineral deposits in the high mountains, 2400 meters above sea level. This set off a second colonization period that brought in mine workers recruited from various other colonies looking for financial opportunities. Within two decades the new immigrants outnumbered the original colonists. This led to an imbalance of power between the ruling founding families and the working-class minorities. This tension has persisted for centuries, and from the communications we have received, there was an open revolt—probably not the first—about twenty years ago, following a planet-wide famine. The government there now wants their world known as the People's Republic of Sandosa, according to our survey teams."

"Were they loyal to the Empire or the republicans during the Imperial Civil War?" asked John Marker, my master chief, from down the table.

"Officially neutral," replied Gracel, "but behind the scenes there is strong evidence they were loyal to the Empire. The founding families wanted to maintain the status quo, essentially cutting the new colonists out of the planet's prosperity."

"If they were loyal to the old empire, then why are we going there?" followed up Marker. "Aren't there more promising systems out there waiting for us to come?"

"Perhaps," Gracel said. "But Sandosa and Pendax were beneficial trading partners before the war. Pendax merchant interests are anxious to reestablish those trading routes."

"Well, that explains it," said Marker. "What Harrington wants, Harrington gets." There were chuckles around the table at this. It was a common saying on Pendax itself and one heard many times before in the Union services.

"True enough," I interjected. "There isn't a more important merchant than Admar Harrington on Pendax. But he will soon be a guest on this vessel, and regardless of what you may think of Pendax's political system, I expect you all to treat him and his team with respect." The fact was that Pendax was having trouble converting to a democracy from a merchant economy, and Harrington was the most likely cause of the trouble. He was an influential man there, but he had also been instrumental in providing crucial technology for the rapid cleanup of Carinthia after the atomic attack by forces loyal to the regent, Prince Arin. For that, the Union Council was grateful and gave him much leeway in conducting his own world's business. Pendax was a full member of the Union now, and we would back them, and Harrington, in any way asked of us. He had also been instrumental in my escape from Carinthia after my trial and near execution there, and I personally owed him a great deal.

I moved down the table to Ensign Lynne Layton, the younger sister of my third-in-command and *Defiant*'s com officer. I'd plucked her from Maclintock's staff on *Starbound* as a favor to George so he could "keep an eye on her," as he liked to say. "Com status report, Ensign," I requested. She straightened in her chair and delivered her report confidently.

"Com systems are linked with the Historian's ansible network at 100 percent efficiency, sir," she stated. I nodded to encourage her to go further. She was still a bit reserved in staff meetings with her peers, and I attributed that to her relative youth at only nineteen. But to make it through the Lightship Academy at that age, she had to be very talented. She cleared her throat before continuing. "The Historians have upgraded the com systems so that they can link through the ansibles in real time using the longwave system, no delays with the signals traveling through normal space. Anywhere the ansibles are active and Historian Gracel has tied us into the hyperspace longwave network, we can communicate in real or near-real time to any planet or ship within our instantaneous jump range."

"What about ships or systems that require us to use traverse space?" I asked.

"A minimal delay, sir—usually a few hours. Nothing like we experience with the ship. A hyperdimensional longwave apparently carries much less 'baggage' than an actual Lightship. I've tested these systems myself both on *Defiant* and *Starbound*, and they seem to work flawlessly, sir."

I turned back to Gracel. "Care to comment on this new technology, Historian?" I asked, smiling. I received a pleasant if reserved smile in return.

"Only to say that the network is not yet complete, and I haven't been authorized to link you into all possible outlets yet," Gracel replied.

"I'm clear on the network. I was more inquiring about the technology itself," I said. She shrugged.

"Let's just say the principles are similar to the hyperdimensional drive, but without its accompanying limitations for traverse time, and leave it at that," she said.

I wasn't quite willing to let it go yet, though. "I think we're all curious how messages and telemetry can travel such great distances with no time delay," I said.

She looked annoyed but answered nonetheless. "Perhaps it's your perspective that needs adjusting. The messages and data don't actually 'travel' the distances between ansibles. They enter a higher dimension at one point and exit at another, similar to the hyperdimensional drive. That's the most I can tell you, I'm afraid. I'm not a trained physicist."

I nodded to her. "Indeed." Satisfied for the moment, I turned to Karina. "A report on your new assignment on the longscope, please,

Lieutenant Feilberg?" I asked. She had kept her maiden name for her Navy duties and for most of her royal ones as well. Only on Quantar was she referred to by my last name, Cochrane.

"Fully operational, sir," she said, all business. "She has the latest upgrades, and Historian Gracel and I have spent two hours daily training on her. I feel I'm ready to take over the station as your number one on the 'scope, sir."

"I concur," piped in Gracel.

"Well then. If all goes well on this mission, I may have to put you in for a promotion, Lieutenant," I said.

"Thank you, sir," Karina replied. She tried to suppress an embarrassed smile but wasn't completely successful.

With that I turned to George Layton, my helmsman and third officer. "Commander?"

Layton opened his plasma reader at my prompt and began his intel report.

"As Historian Gracel reported, the Sandosa system seems to have undergone some significant social upheaval in the last few decades. Most of the contacts the Union has established there report that the ranking government officials are almost all from the second wave of colonization, so much so that there were some concerns expressed in the early reports that the minority founding ethnicities weren't included in any of the original contact discussions. The Sandosa government corrected that by producing some originalist representatives, and it has since gone out of its way to extend every courtesy to our survey teams. They are said to be extremely enthusiastic about the pending arrival of a Union Lightship and the delegation from Pendax and opening full negotiations," she said.

"So they know we're coming in?" I asked. He nodded.

"They know generally, sir. Last reports from three days ago indicate they are anxious to receive us at our earliest convenience."

I tilted my head at him. "Is three days our last report? I thought forty-eight hours was the maximum protocol between contacts with the survey teams. With the enhancements to the Historian's ansible network, I shouldn't think getting clear communications would be a problem."

Layton ran his hands over his plasma, checking data and searching through files. I didn't want to put him on the spot for circumstances beyond his control, but I didn't want to go into an unknown system with stale intel either. It was the third officer's responsibility to keep his captain fully informed at all times.

"Seventy-four hours since the last survey team report, sir," he admitted after reviewing the files. Well overdue.

"I can help reestablish contact with the survey teams," offered Ensign Layton. George looked pensively down the table at his younger sister, clearly not wanting to be shown up by her.

"Let's do that," I said to them both. "Work together and get me an update. And if you need help you can also bug the Historian."

"Thank you for volunteering me, Captain," Gracel said with mock cheerfulness.

"Oh, you're welcome," I replied. This set off a round of chuckles. At that, it was time to close the meeting and get on to business.

"XO, prep the ship for the jump to Pendax. Mr. Marker, have your marines trained and ready. I don't know if we'll need them on this mission, but I expect top form regardless," I said.

"Aye, sir," said Marker. I stood then, and the staff stood with me.

"Call me in my cabin with fifteen minutes to go before the jump, XO," I ordered. That timing meant that I expected them to be ready when I got there. "I expect updates from all of you on my arrival on the bridge. You're dismissed." And with that they all scrambled to their duties, and I made for my stateroom to prep for my first active duty mission as captain of *Defiant*.

We flashed into Pendax space with extreme precision, so much so that we were actually fewer than five hundred meters from the jump point's designated "center." This achievement was worthy of a public compliment, and I duly gave one to the ship's astrogator, Lieutenant Arasan.

From there we made the two-hour trek from our ingress jump point to High Station Pendax. The purpose of having a deep space station so close to the jump point was to be prepared in case of any hostile arrival. The two-hour distance, accomplished at a standard sub-light cruising speed of .005 light, which would obviously vary with the speed of any approaching craft, was to give a time cushion to any forces scrambling to deploy to face a potential enemy. So you always wanted a High Station close to the jump point, but not too close. Pendax was busy building a second High Station in orbit around the planet, something the Union had recommended and for which it was happy to provide the skills and materials.

We docked the ship without incident, and upon arrival I received two invitations: one for dinner from Captain Zander of the under-construction *Vanguard*, and the other for a late evening cocktail reception with Admar Harrington. I accepted both on behalf of my wife and myself.

After running the crew through standard post-docking procedures, I announced on the shipwide com that all non-duty personnel had liberty until midnight. With the changing of shifts, that meant almost 70 percent of the crew would have at least a few hours to knock around on a new High Station in a new system and sample her wares.

The dinner with Zander went by quickly with his usual grousing about this and that, but the upside was that *Vanguard* really was ready for commissioning at any time. The Lightship fleet was getting stronger, and that was important news. I begged off of further conversation on account of the 2100 hours cocktail reception. Zander understood, even if he didn't like it. He knew how persuasive a man his new boss could be.

Karina and I arrived a few minutes early, both of us in our formal navy attire, and were quickly ushered into an already crowded receiving room. This was clearly to be a combination business and social event. We spent a good few minutes meeting and greeting dignitaries of various rank, all of them no doubt important on Pendax itself. After a few minutes of this, Harrington made his entrance.

He was certainly a man comfortable with the pomp of office, being the richest and most powerful merchant prince on a world full of them. He was a large, balding man with an oversized winged mustache and a gray military uniform complete with dozens of sparkling service medals on his chest. He sported an unlit pipe in one hand, probably as an affectation, and an ornate walking stick in the other, with a pair of wire-rimmed glasses thrown in to make his appearance complete. By every measure this was a man who wanted for nothing, and he was in his element. He made his way across the room, greeting numerous dignitaries as he came. Karina and I waited patiently by the room's fireplace, making conversation with lower-level merchants and their companions.

When he finally arrived, he bowed graciously to my lady. "Princess," he said, then turned to me and repeated the bow. "Sire." I extended my hand in greeting, and he shook it.

"Captain will do just fine for me, Mr. Harrington," I said.

"My friends call me Admar," he said. "I would be pleased if you would do the same."

"Thank you, Admar," said Karina, smiling. He waved us over to a set of chairs around a low wood coffee table. We were escorted over by a cadre of Harrington's assistants, both male and female, and sat down with our drinks and hors d'oeuvres. The women in his employ, I noted, were strikingly beautiful and impeccably dressed.

"I'd like to discuss the Sandosa trip, if we might," he started in.

"I'm pleased to do so, Admar," I replied. It seemed a bit informal to call him by his given name, but even as the richest man on Pendax he had no official title except "Chief Merchant," which was bestowed on him by Union negotiators during the admission agreement negotiations.

I explained the latest intelligence from Sandosa and that he could probably expect a different culture than the one Pendax and Sandosa had shared prior to the war.

"That's a disturbing note. If the government there has become paranoid socialist, they may not desire the mutually beneficial trading agreements we had before," Harrington said.

"What were the details of those?" I asked.

"Mainly meat, livestock, coal, and timber from our side. Precious metals and magnesium ore for manufacturing from their side, plus other exchanges on smaller scales. As I recall from reading the records, arable land is somewhat scarce there, and they couldn't keep livestock very well because of the lack of grazing land. Plus the planet is mainly limestone, not very conducive to farming and the like," he concluded. Then he looked up at me.

"This is why the Merchant Council has authorized me to bring along a Special Secretary for Union Negotiations with Sandosa. We may need to offer them the full benefits of Union membership to make this work."

"Seems logical," I said, taking a sip of my drink. "So tell me, Admar, what progress have you made with fulfilling the Union Concord agreements?" At this Harrington got a sour look on his face. The Concord agreements were certain social contracts required in order to receive the full package of benefits from the Union Council. Failure to comply could even result in economic or technological penalties.

"Things aren't progressing as fast as we or the Union would like," he finally admitted. "It's difficult, converting from a merchant-based oligarchy to a representative democracy. In some ways, the way we have things, with the Merchant Council running affairs, is far more efficient than your Union proposals."

I smiled. "Quantar has a strong merchant class tradition as well, none more rich and powerful than the Cochrane family. But we've managed to adapt to a local parliament and having only a single seat on the Union Council. The first step is often the hardest."

Harrington's sour look didn't dissipate. "It may sound easy to you, Cochrane, but your family always had a working parliament, even in Imperial times. Pendax has been run by the merchants for so long . . ." He trailed off.

"Change is difficult, Admar, but in the end it is beneficial. Sharing a bit of your wealth with the people of Pendax will reap its own rewards," I offered.

He eyed me askance, as if sizing me up. "Spoken like a man who is the heir to the wealth of two worlds, not just one," he said.

"True," interjected Karina, smiling. "But isn't this mission about opening up interstellar trade routes again, to make you even more rich and powerful than you are now? And isn't a tidy little democracy for the common welfare worth the economic and technological benefits you will gain from the Union?"

Admar smiled, and I could see he was charmed by her. "Yes," he said. "That it is. But still, when you've run things one way your entire life, change is not easy, even in the face of greater profit. Especially at my age." Then he turned back to me.

"Which brings up another point. As I sit here with you I am the most powerful man on my world, but I have no title to back my great wealth and success. Both your and your wife's family's wealth and status are secured by your adherence to the old Imperial peerage system. You are prince and princess, but I sit here as merely a common man. The Imperial system on our world was abandoned long ago." I considered this for a moment.

"I'm not authorized to offer any such standing, as I'm sure you know. But I could see my way clear to present a case for your entitlement to your council, *if* things proceed as planned on Pendax. When we complete this mission, and if my father and the new Duke Benn agree, the Union Council could move to approve such titles and sub-gentry classes," I said. This seemed to please him for the moment.

"And now you see why I needed a Special Secretary to negotiate such things. I understand you've already met."

"That we have," said Karina, smiling again. Harrington nodded.

"The Princess Janaan came to my attention during our ascension negotiations with the Union. She has a fine mind for both business and diplomacy, and she's a master negotiator. Having her is an enormous asset, Princess," said Harrington.

"I understand, sir," Karina replied. Then Harrington looked to me for affirmation.

"You'll get no argument about your business decisions from me, Admar. They're yours to make as you see fit."

"I'm sure," he said with a nod. And then we drank to the success of the mission.

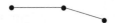

Twelve hours later, I was happy to be underway out of the Pendax system. I'd arranged to have Janaan quartered a deck below us, and I put Harrington in a spare stateroom right near the service lifter. Janaan could come and go as she pleased, and neither Karina nor I would have to have any contact with her, our main duty lifter being on the exact opposite end of the deck.

Harrington and I had several informal meetings, but he was saving his big briefing for the last few hours before we dropped out of

traverse space near the end of our thirty-two hour journey to Sandosa. In the meantime, I kept myself busy on the bridge and in my
own stateroom with my wife.

If I was being honest with myself, this whole mission made me
uncomfortable for a number of reasons. The upset with Karina, Harrington's lack of enthusiasm for meeting Union Concord guidelines,
Janaan's mere presence on my Lightship, and the whole "People's Republic of Sandosa" thing. I couldn't help but think we were heading
into troubled waters. Troubled, but in the end not dangerous, or so I
hoped.

With eight hours of traverse time left in our journey, Harrington
called his briefing at 0900. Present in Harrington's stateroom were
Harrington, Lena Babayan, and of course Janaan. I'd left George Layton at the con. Harrington cleared his throat before beginning.

"The main city on Sandosa is the capital, known as New Seville.
It has a population of about 1.3 million. The rest of the planet is a
collection of small cities and fishing villages, all connected to the
original seafaring industries. Only about thirty of these cities have a
population in excess of one hundred thousand, almost all on the
main continent and most of them located on or near the sea. The
mining plateau on the main continent is where the true riches lie:
gold, silver, platinum, copper, magnesium, and uranium, along with
precious gemstones and the like. The plateau is mostly inhabited by
the second-wave immigrants. There are no cities there to speak of,
and most towns are just small camps built around the resources. The
place is a miner's paradise, but the living conditions outside the fishing towns and the main cities are primitive." He paused before
continuing.

"At some point in the Imperial past, the second-wave population
grew so fast that the camps couldn't hold them. The uneducated
worker population started coming down out of the mountains and

onto the plains seaports looking for other opportunities. The First Settlers didn't take kindly to having so many mouths to feed. Some
second-wave colonists were taken on as indentured domestic servants,
and the wealth generated from the metals trade made the First Settlers
immensely rich. The second-wave colonists eventually took over much
of the industrial work as the First Settlers retired to lives of leisure.
This was well known and well documented in Imperial times, but after
that things get sketchier, of course. There were obviously social pressures with a population of haves and have-nots at odds in a two-class
system. We know the second-wave population eventually overthrew
the original Sandosa government, but we don't know how long ago.
And without Interstellar trade, the planet struggled to survive during
the Great Separation, before Reunion Day. We believe that in Imperial
times the population was close to nineteen million. Today, our scout-
ing parties estimate it at closer to eleven million. Understandably, they
are very anxious to resume trading with other worlds."

"Understandably," I said. "But I'm still unsure what Pendax hopes
to gain from trade with Sandosa. It doesn't seem like they have much
to offer either Pendax or the Union beyond their minerals, which are
available on other worlds." Harrington looked uncomfortable. When
the silence dragged on, I got very direct with him. "What do you hope
to accomplish with this agreement, Admar?"

He looked at me, then pulled off his glasses and rubbed his eyes
before continuing. "As we discussed earlier, Captain Cochrane, my
government is having difficulty transitioning to a democratic form
that the Union will accept. In exchange for many of the things we
used to sell to Sandosa, it is my hope that my merchant Wasps will
come home with many of the precious metals I mentioned," he said. I
was curious about this.

"Why? I mean, you're already a wealthy man," I said.

"Yes, but not so wealthy that I cannot be challenged. Like it or
not, Pendax is run on a currency system that is based on gold, silver,

and other precious commodities. If I can import enough of these materials from Sandosa, I can increase my position exponentially. Then no one can challenge me, and my power in the Merchant Council will be such that I can push through your precious Union reforms. Isn't that what you want?" he said, more than a bit testy with me.

"I am not a politician, Admar. I'm a Lightship captain, nothing more." I glanced from him to the Princess Janaan. She seemed uncomfortable with this exchange, and then the two of them exchanged a look which made me curious again.

"And what's the part you're not telling me?" I asked. Harrington shook his head.

"I've heard about your damned intuition!" he said. "Annoying trait." He slapped both hands down on the table. "Very well. I'll tell you, then. The other thing we need from Sandosa is . . ." He looked to Janaan one more time. "Women."

"What?" I said. Harrington sighed heavily, swept some papers off the table, and looked away from me as if he were embarrassed. It was Janaan who ultimately answered.

"Pendax has agreed to exchange its advanced technology and political support for Sandosa's Union membership in return for immigrants. *Female* immigrants," said Janaan. I looked to Babayan, but she said nothing, so I nodded for Janaan to continue. "The war was hard on Pendax. They were bombarded by both sides. The upshot is that on a planet of twenty-four million people, there simply aren't enough women. Many of the men fought off-world, and frankly, when they returned, much of the original population was gone, killed in the war or the aftermath. They've fought a shortage of women in their population for decades."

"I see," I said. "And Sandosa?"

"Just the opposite problem. More women than men by as many as three million. They've promised a million female immigrants over the next decade. It would be a huge boon to Pendax," she finished.

"And to you personally, no doubt," I said, turning back to Harrington. "They'll probably make you president for life if you pull that off."

Harrington shrugged. "So now you know it all."

"Thank you for being honest with us, Admar," I said. Then I turned to my XO.

"What updates do you have for us, Lena?"

She opened her plasma and spread it out on the table top. "We've had no further updates from the survey teams," she said, "and that's disturbing. Of course we can't expect contact while we're in transverse space, even by longwave, but the teams were well overdue for reporting when we left Pendax."

"I'm not comfortable with this lack of information, Commander. I expect you to reestablish contact with your survey teams within an hour of us flashing into Sandosa space. I will see any failure to do so as a sign of potential hostility toward our survey teams by the Sandosa government," I said. Then I turned my attention to Harrington once again. "I won't put this ship in harm's way for the sake of an economic mission, Admar. Any irregularities will have to be sorted out straight away, or I'll turn this ship around at a moment's notice."

"I don't expect any such problems, Captain. My contacts on Sandosa should be able to sort out any problems. I'm sure it's just the vagaries of an antiquated communications system," he replied.

"And just what is it that the good captain fears?" asked Janaan, cutting in. "You have the most powerful ship within fifty light-years at your disposal. Certainly a small backward planet like Sandosa can be of no worry to you?"

I stared at her for a second or two, trying to decide if she was seeking to embarrass me. Whether she was or not, I found I didn't care for her implications.

"Perhaps the Special Secretary should keep to her areas of expertise and let the Lightship captain keep to his," I said in reply, then turned again to Harrington.

"My guidelines stand, Admar. I want to hear directly from the survey teams within an hour of dropping out of traverse space, or this trip will be over before it begins."

"I don't foresee that as a problem," he said.

"As you say." I turned back to my XO. "Commander Babayan, please have Mr. Marker prep his marine teams for planetary Search and Rescue. If we don't have clear contact from the survey team by my deadline, I will be authorizing the marines to go in and get them."

"Aye, sir, I'll have the plan on your desk within the hour. But I must ask, how will we find them on the planet?" she asked. I tapped a spot on my left arm.

"Historian tracker technology. Standard now on all pre-contact survey teams. I could tell you the details, but then I'd have to kill you," I deadpanned. Babayan smiled.

"Understood, sir," she said. "I'll also talk to Gracel about receiving any possible traverse space telemetry updates. She may have some special trick she's willing to share."

"Thank you, XO," I said. "I prefer that you oversee the marine plan first. If there's nothing else?"

With that I was up out of my chair and went quickly out of the stateroom, heading to the far end of the deck and the lifter to the bridge as my XO followed behind me. The deck was busy, and I saluted lower ratings more than a few times on my way. Babayan peeled off to head to the marine quarters on the hangar deck, and I dismissed her.

Presently I arrived at the lifter and pressed the call button. After waiting a few seconds, the doors parted silently, and I stepped inside. As I turned to close the doors, a hand reached in and held the door back. To my great surprise, the Special Secretary swept into the lifter and then shut the doors behind her.

"Princess, if I've given you the impression—" I started.

"Stop," she said as the lifter accelerated up the conning tower toward the command deck. The lifter obeyed her command, stalling between decks. I turned to her.

"Madam Secretary, this is a surprise—"

"Surprise is what I want to avoid. I must share with you my concerns, Captain, not as your former fiancée but as the Special Secretary," she said seriously. Now I was intrigued.

"State your concerns, Madam Secretary," I said. She turned and faced me directly.

"Harrington has me worried, Peter," she said. I was uncomfortable with her using my proper name under the circumstances, but I decided to ignore it for the moment.

"Why?"

"This trading in women, it seems out of place to me. I worry about the conditions these women will be sent into on Pendax. It is a fairly wealthy world, but it is a completely male-dominated society. Women do not even have the right to own property in their system unless directly granted permission by their husbands," she said.

"So your concern is that they'll essentially become servants to their husbands?"

"Yes. And I don't trust Harrington on the mining operations, either. I think he would like to completely take over and make the miners trade one form of indentured servitude for another."

I thought about what she had said, and I had to admit that I had my own reservations about Harrington. "The most I can promise you, Princess, is that I will make sure any formal agreements have to be approved by the Union Council. I will make a full report to them myself and include all of your concerns in my report," I said.

"I appreciate that," she said.

I nodded, then turned to the lifter controls and said, "Resume." We had barely started up again when she said, "I do have one more question." Something about her tone gave me pause.

"Stop," I said to the lifter control. "What do you need to know,

Princess?" Again she faced me directly. We were separated by a few feet inside the lifter.

"If you hadn't met your princess, your Karina, and if there hadn't been a crisis on Carinthia, would you have kept your promise to marry me?" she asked. I didn't hesitate to answer.

"Without a doubt, Janaan. But the fact is that I did meet Karina, and we did marry, and it has now become much more than a marriage of political convenience. I love her, and I intend to keep all my promises to her," I said. She smiled wanly, disappointment on her face.

"Then I am resigned to that truth. I could have made you a wonderful wife, Peter."

"I know." We stood there in silence for a moment, and then I once again said, "Resume." I thought for a moment as we rose toward the bridge, then uttered another command to the lifter. "Stop next deck," I said. It did, three decks below the command deck. The doors opened, and I looked down the hall and called to a female midshipman. She came at a run, holding an armful of plasma tablets.

"Yes, Captain?"

"In the lifter, if you please, middy," I said. She looked back down the hall.

"Sir, I was just running these reports down to—"

"I understand, middy. But please step aboard the lifter," I insisted. She did as instructed, and I strategically placed her between Janaan and I. "When you get to the bridge, you are to walk around for a few moments, make some conversation, then proceed back down to your assignment. Understood?"

She looked to the princess and then to me and nodded.

"Yes, Captain," she said, though she was obviously confused. Janaan raised an eyebrow to me.

"Appearances," I said in response. She smiled. I said nothing more as the lifter doors closed and opened a few moments later onto the command deck. I walked down the short hallway to the bridge and then to my station. The middy followed me in, then the princess, who made for the Historian's station and struck up a quiet conversation with Gracel. Karina was at the longscope and turned to smile at me, then noted the princess and the female midshipman. She nodded to me, and I winked back at her as I took my chair.

"Report, Mr. Layton," I said, as casually as I could.

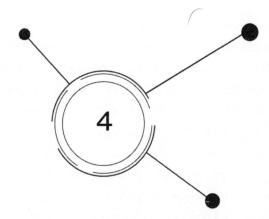

In the Sandosa System

We dropped into the Sandosa jump point right on time and within a dime's distance of dead center. Lieutenant Arasan was good at his job.

"Excellent drop, Lieutenant," I said to him. It was no false praise. Jenny Hogan had been a great astrogator aboard both *Starbound* and *Impulse*, but Arasan was every bit her equal. "Chemical impellers until we clear the jump point, Mr. Longer. Then I want the sub-light HD drive engaged, .0002 light if you please."

"Aye, sir," said Longer from my right. He leaned down to his Propulsion ensign and gave the orders. I stood up, and Babayan stood to my left, observing the bridge operations. At that moment Admar Harrington decided to join us on the bridge.

"Mr. Harrington," I said.

"Captain," he replied. "I trust all is in order, or soon will be."

"One would hope. Ensign Layton," I called to my com officer. She rushed up to me, short blonde hair bobbing as she came.

"Here, sir," she said.

"Report, Ensign."

She looked pensive. "No intel updates waiting for us on arrival, sir, either by packet or longwave communiqué," she said.

"That's disturbing, Ensign." I looked to my wife at the longscope station and nodded in her direction. "Work with the longscope officer to broaden your search. Feel free to bring in Historian Gracel if necessary. We need answers. Understood?"

"Understood, sir," she snapped. I waved her off and got a perturbed look from my wife before she turned back to her work. I suppose she found the gesture disrespectful, and she was probably right. I made a mental note to not repeat it. I turned back to Babayan.

"I want an update from our survey teams, XO, and I want it yesterday. Use the teams from Intel section if you have to, but make sure you get it to me by 1900. I'll be here on the bridge waiting for your full report," I said. That gave her an hour.

"Aye, sir," snapped Babayan, and she was off to the Intelligence section on deck eleven, no doubt to push and prod my new Intel officers for her report. My statement that I would be waiting for the report on the bridge indicated to my senior officers that our formal nightly dinner would be put on hold until further notice or even canceled. These ship routines were important, and I felt it was necessary to stick to a strict schedule whenever possible. It aided discipline, in my view. Waiting for those routines and working under stressful conditions were also part of the job, and that was necessary, too.

I called down to Marker to get an update on our Marine Search and Rescue plan. Marker answered the call. "We're ready when you are, Captain. Do you think we'll need to rescue the survey teams?"

"I hope not, John," I said, then told them to prep for launch on a fifteen minute clock.

"I have one shuttle ready to go now, sir. We can be off the landing deck in sixty seconds. The second shuttle can follow ten minutes after that," he said.

"Understood, Master Chief. And good work."

"Sir," he said. I cut the com, as usual getting more than I expected from my head marine.

At that I ordered Longer to slow our speed by half, just to give my Intel and com teams time to do their work, and then I left him the con while I went to my captain's office to brood. This wasn't a promising start. Harrington joined me.

The office was a small work area, not even technically off the bridge but separated by an energy field that could drown out any conversation or go opaque for privacy. Karina nodded to me as I passed, but I felt I couldn't acknowledge her now. When the captain was on the bridge, everyone was expected to maintain their stations regardless of relationships, shift times, or normal rotations. This crew had been on duty for ten hours already, but no one would be getting a break anytime soon. At least not until I knew what was happening with the survey teams on Sandosa.

After activating the aural privacy field, I sat in my chair while Harrington sat down heavily across the desk from me. "The longer this goes on, the more troublesome it becomes," he said to me.

"Tell me something I don't know." It came out a bit harsher than I wanted, so I set the office screen to opaque and offered Pendax's chief merchant a drink. He favored our Quantar Shiraz, so I was more than glad to share one with him. Then I got down to business.

"Where are my survey teams, Mr. Harrington? What do you know of this Sandosa government?" I asked.

Harrington sighed. "All I really know is what we've been able to communicate by com and visual longwave up until now. They are interested in trade, surely, but how much they really have to give—besides female immigrants—is unknown. From your own survey team's early reports, they have nothing close to hyperdimensional technology resembling ours or First Empire utility. That should make the system safe for our negotiations," he said.

"'Should' is an imprecise word that I have never liked, Mr.

Harrington. The survey teams are now nearly a week overdue to report, and Sandosa shouldn't have anything that could detect, deflect, or block a longwave signal or packet or disable a Historian network ansible. In short, unless they have been taken captive and their communications devices disabled or destroyed, they should have reported by now." He had nothing to say to that.

We drank for ten more minutes, making small talk, when the breakthrough came.

Karina called me on my desk com to report they had picked up a signal. I dissolved the office screen, and Harrington and I rejoined Karina, Layton, and Gracel at the longscope station. Lena Babayan followed a few seconds later.

"Report," I demanded of my longscope officer.

"Gracel found a packet embedded in some low-level telemetry. The ansible was knocked offline about twelve days ago, probably by a collision with a small meteor. They've been using an embedded longwave packet in something known as radio frequency radiation signals to try and contact us. Since this is an archaic technology, we didn't even know the signals were being sent," Karina said.

"Thank you, Lieutenant," I said. "That explains the technical side of things. Now what about the signals themselves? What do they say?"

Babayan jumped in. "All conditions normal on Sandosa, sir. They remain anxious to greet us and begin negotiations at the first opportunity," she said. "They have even provided us a preferred vector to approach the planet, sir."

"Thank you, XO," I said. "Hold status." Then I headed off to my office with Gracel without giving any further orders, expecting my crew to wait. Once we were in private, I gave the Historian my instructions.

"Plot us a variant course that follows their preferred path as closely as possible. I want us to avoid any moons, space stations, or asteroids that might house weapons that could be used against us," I said.

"You don't trust them?" Gracel asked.

"I didn't say that, Historian. I just want options. Arrange a coded signal that I can transmit to you to overtake the helm onto that variant course in an emergency. Understood and agreed, Historian?"

She nodded, but I said nothing more.

"Understood and agreed, Captain," she finally said.

"Thank you, Gracel." With that I disengaged the privacy screen and returned to my bridge while she departed for the lifter to begin her work.

"Helm," I called to George Layton.

"Aye, sir," he responded.

"How long to Sandosa using their preferred path at our current speed?" Layton looked at his display readouts.

"I make it approximately twenty-one hours, sir," he replied. I nodded.

"Set our speed to make planet fall in fourteen hours," I ordered.

"Sir," cut in Duane Longer. "We can get there much faster if we use—"

"I'm aware of our propulsion options, Lieutenant. Please carry out my orders precisely," I said. I turned to Babayan. "XO, call up second shift personnel immediately. All senior bridge personnel are on a twelve-hour break. No more than four hours of R&R, and no less than eight hours of sleep. I want us to be top-shelf ready when we arrive at Sandosa. All senior officers and department heads should stay on yellow status during the rest period. First shift resumes at 0800 tomorrow," I finished. That would give us two full hours before arrival at Sandosa.

"Aye, sir," replied Babayan as she began calling up the second shifters and dismissing the senior staff. Harrington nodded to me as I made one more trip to my office. When full security was engaged again, I called back down to my marine commander on the voice com.

"Marker here, sir," came his gravel-rough voice.

"I want you to prep one of the gunships we loaded at Candle with a tech crew and make for that damaged ansible. I want a full assessment of how and why it became inoperative," I ordered.

"Yes, sir. Do you suspect sabotage, sir?"

"I suspect everything, John. If the damage is a natural malfunction, as the reports say, then I want the report by 0800. If it's anything less than fully natural, I want to be notified immediately by longwave com. Now get that crew out there. They have four hours."

"Yes, sir. Anything else?"

I hesitated for a moment.

"I want all of your ships fully outfitted for combat operations by the time we arrive at Sandosa. No less than ten minutes to clearing the deck of all vehicles after any distress call," I said.

"You expecting trouble on Sandosa, sir?" asked Marker.

"Expect? I don't know. But something tells me we should be prepared for any eventuality on this trip."

"Intuition, sir?" Marker pressed.

"If you like," I replied. Then I cut the com and headed off the bridge for my stateroom.

I woke a full ninety minutes before first shift started in a raging sweat and with a pounding heart. My dreams had been fitful and once again full of imploding dreadnoughts and the screams of dying people I had never heard and that I had never met nor even seen. The PTSD I had denied existed for so long was still there, heightened by my unease over this Sandosa mission. I slipped out of bed and put on casual fatigues, stopping only to brush my teeth and take another look at the bottle of pills the doctors had prescribed back on Carinthia. I shut the drawer, slipped on my boots, and quietly shut the door behind me as I made my way out of officer country and down to the private observation lounge near the stern. I rang once and got no response, so I opened the door and went inside. The lounge was empty. I set the privacy lock for thirty minutes, the maximum, and then found a single-seat enclosure, turning the view to the beautiful passing stars.

I took the lotus position, as Serosian had trained me to do so long ago, back on Quantar. I went through my mind, clicking off my concerns for the day one by one on a mental checklist, then throwing those thoughts outward to the passing stars to let them go. I gave special attention to the fate of the dreadnoughts and their crews and my still-strong guilt about my actions, actions which I believed to be right but which had cost me my mentor and friend.

Then I turned to receiving, to quieting my mind and opening myself to my meditations, breathing deeply and regularly, slowing my heart back to its normal, healthy rhythm, and discarding the anxiety. Once I was free of my concerns and found myself literally floating along in space, inside the vessel I commanded, a thought came to my mind.

You are a very lucky man.

I smiled at that, and a few seconds later the quiet two-minute chime rang. I stretched my body and filled my lungs with deep breaths, then came back to my world and my ship.

As I exited the lounge, others were waiting outside, some for morning prayers, some no doubt for meditation, others for a last bit of intimacy before the day began. As they greeted me I nodded to them all but did not reply; I wasn't on duty yet, and neither were they. It reminded me—and them, I hoped—that we were all equal, just simple men and women navigating the massive waters of the universe in the tiny boat we all shared.

I slipped quietly back into the stateroom and heard the sound of Karina running the shower water. I slipped out of my fatigues to wait my turn, laying down on the bed. But she was having none of that.

She peeked her forehead, soaking-wet hair, and eyes over the glass door of the shower. It reminded me of how tiny she really was. "Get in here, Captain. That's an order," she said.

"I thought I'd wait until you finished," I replied. She shook her head.

"No chance. Move it, mister."

With no possibility of talking her out of it, I slipped into the shower next to her, but instead of giving me room under the showerhead, she spun around in front of me and gently bit me on the shoulder. It was curious foreplay.

"Karina, I've got no time for play this morning," I protested.

"And you didn't last night, either," she said, clearly disappointed. "You're salty. Were you dreaming again? The sweats?" I pushed myself under the showerhead and let the water run over my head and face.

"Yes, if you must know."

"And?"

"And I did my meditation."

"Did it work?"

"For now," I said, then handed her the shampoo. "Now if you don't mind, the captain needs his hair washed and his back scrubbed."

"Oh, now that it's *your* needs, it's a priority," she said.

"Just wash, woman," I said. "I've got less than an hour to be on duty."

"Same here," she said, then gave me a smack on the ass that I probably deserved.

I was on the bridge ten minutes before the day shift officially began. I'd left Karina in my wake, as she was still messing with her makeup for the day. It made her mad that I'd left without her, as we usually came to the bridge together as a show of unity. But today I had more serious things on my mind. I went straight to my office after acknowledging the last of the night crew and put up the aural shield, but I left the visual mode open to the bridge so that I could watch the comings and goings and everyone could see me. I checked my message coms on my desk panel and found nothing out of the ordinary except an acknowledgment by Gracel that she had corrected our course three times during the night, each time to avoid a potentially threatening object. But in each case her scans had come back negative for hyperdimensional activity, meaning no Imperial presence, at least for the moment. I voice-commed her a thank-you, but when I looked up from my display she was already on the bridge at her station. She gave no acknowledgment of receiving my message, so I just assumed we were on the same page. I scrolled through the messages on my monitor and found another com from John Marker stating "ANSIBLE SURVEY NEGATIVE" in the subject line and nothing else but his usual sign-off. Normally I would let it pass, but today was not going to be a normal day.

I tapped my ear com and said his name out loud. He came on the line a second later.

"Good morning, Captain," he said, a bit smug. "Did you rest well?"

"As well as could be expected under the circumstances, Chief," I replied.

"Good to hear, sir." Now that the phony pleasantries were over . . .

"I'd like some more details on the ansible run, if you please," I said.

Marker cleared his throat. "Of course, sir. The tech crew got to the ansible in about four hours. It didn't take long for them to determine what the problem was. There was a cricket-ball-sized hole in the thing, sir. Went right through the central processor unit."

"Coil rifle fire?"

"Negative, sir." I could almost see him shaking his head at that. "There were no discernible traces of energy weapons fire, sir. They reported back to me, and I had them swap out a replacement CPU. Took them some time to get it properly calibrated, but once they did it fired right up, and now it's purring like a warm kitten on a cold winter's day, sir."

"I take it they're on the way back now?"

"Yes, sir, about two hours and forty-five minutes out at three-quarters speed." I thought about that.

"Tell them to take it up to full burn. I want them back here before anyone on Sandosa can get a full look at one of our gunships. And I want that ship turned around in thirty minutes for full marine operations, just in case," I said.

"Yes, sir. If I may ask, what is it about this situation that concerns you so much, sir?" I pondered that for a moment before responding.

"The fact that there was no coil fire residue doesn't mean that the ansible couldn't have been disabled from its primary function with intent. Someone could have used a kinetic weapon on it to simulate a natural malfunction," I said.

"You mean like a rock or some kind of grapeshot, sir?"

"Or a cricket ball, John. Are we running our standard in-system debris screens?" The debris screens were a low-level electronic field designed to clear a ship's path through normal space. Not high tech or high-powered, but useful enough to take out anything smaller than a two-person ground car.

"Aye, sir, we are," Marker said.

"Relay to the XO to raise the sweep level to max. I don't want any surprises."

"Will do, sir," he replied. I thought about having him up on the bridge at his weapons station when we arrived at Sandosa, but then I decided that if we did need marine help at any point, I wanted him as close to his shuttles, gunships, and men as I could get him.

"All as ordered, Master Chief," I said by way of signing off.

"All as ordered, sir," he echoed, then cut the line.

I looked out to my bridge and then to my watch. The day crew were all at their stations, waiting for my call to make the shift change. I still had forty seconds. I shut down the aural screen and made my way down to my chair, which sat empty at all times except when I was present.

I sat down. "XO," I called to Lena Babayan. She came up.

"Sir."

"Day shift begins."

"Aye, sir." Then she repeated my words to the bridge crew and again on the shipwide com. The bridge became a bustle of noise and activity as the night shift crew was relieved by the day shift and relinquished its stations. The change was done in less than two minutes. Babayan took her station next to me.

"Day shift underway, Captain," she stated. "Debris screens at full as requested."

"Acknowledged," I replied. "I think it's going to be an interesting day, XO."

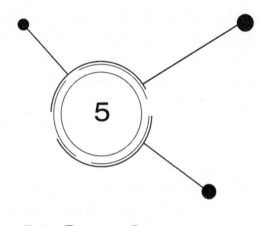

At Sandosa

Ninety minutes later, the gunship was neatly tucked away in our Landing Bay being prepped for full marine missions, including combat operations, and we were on final approach to Sandosa. At twenty minutes to our designated orbit point above the capital city of New Seville, the Sandosans got hold of us via a standard com wave. Not very advanced. Usually a longwave signal would be appropriate protocol, but they had what they had.

In a very formal manner and with some broken Standard, the message very politely invited us down to New Seville at our earliest convenience. It was 0400 local time there, but they seemed eager to meet regardless of the hour.

I had Babayan send a message informing them we'd like to make one run around the planet for a geological survey to match historic records, but it was also a chance to scan their satellite network, space defenses, and level of technology. I made her promise them we would be down at the capital at their designated coordinates in three hours max.

They politely and excitedly accepted.

Admar Harrington called up from his stateroom and asked permission to talk with his trading contacts. I agreed, as long as my Intel team got to monitor all communications. He was a bit put out at that but agreed to my conditions nonetheless.

Next I called for a senior staff meeting to discuss final strategy. Fifteen minutes later we were all in the command deck briefing room.

"John," I said, looking down the table at Marker. "What's our passenger capacity for this first trip?"

"I wouldn't be comfortable with fewer than a dozen marines going down fully geared, sir, and that doesn't count me," he said.

"Light arms on your person, please, Master Chief," I said.

"Sir," he responded quickly. I could see from his face that he wasn't pleased, but he was my marine commander, not one of the grunts.

"So that leaves twenty-four seats, then. Myself, you, Harrington, and the Special Secretary. Gracel is five, and I don't want you flying, John," I stated.

"Private Verhunce can fly her, sir," suggested Marker.

"I can fly a damn shuttle," said George Layton from the end of the table. I considered his request, and it made sense. He was our best pilot.

"Okay, Commander Layton, then," I said. "But make sure Verhunce is one of your twelve marines. It doesn't hurt to have backup."

"What about me?" interrupted Karina with some force. "I'm not needed on the longscope now that we're in orbit, and I am still a princess of Carinthia."

I looked around the room, sizing up the mood before I spoke. Everyone was dead still. They knew this was a personal issue as well as a professional one. "You're also my wife. And I don't like risking you so soon," I said. "If you could wait until we can assess the situation on the ground?"

"You know how I hate waiting," she responded, more on a personal level than a professional one.

"Captain," piped in Babayan. "I assume you're leaving me in command in this scenario. But may I remind you that if you do, you won't have a single high-ranking Carinthian among the diplomatic contingent to make first contact."

"She's right!" piped in Karina. I put my hand to my forehead and sighed. There was a round of laughter. Everyone was jockeying for position.

"Lieutenant Commander Layton, you're staying for now."

"But—"

"No buts, George. The ladies are right. Commander Babayan will join the diplomatic contingent. Private Verhunce will fly the shuttle. The rest of the seats will be filled with the Science, Intel, and Economic teams. And that will leave you at the con, George. Thirty minutes after we land I want a second shuttle deployed. Make an excuse and say it's an agricultural survey or something. But I want it ready at any moment to land and lend assistance if necessary," I said.

"And me?" asked Karina, indignant. I looked down the conference table to her.

"You'll have to stay put until we've had a chance to evaluate the situation on the ground. I'm sure there will be some sort of diplomatic dinner or some such thing. When that happens, I will have you down for it." I said it with a finality that left no room for argument. Karina was still ready with a response.

"May I remind the captain that he and I both represent Union worlds in our royal capacities? Our greatest value to this mission is to be seen together, presenting a united front to the government of Sandosa."

"Noted, Lieutenant," I said. "But for now, the plans remain the same. All named staff is to be ready in the landing bay in two hours. Pack a bag for at least one overnight, if not two. All day shift bridge personnel are relieved and will be replaced with junior officers and night shift for the duration of our stay. Marines will be in full combat dress, excepting Chief Marker. Mr. Harrington and the Special Secretary will each have one accompanying marine wherever they go. Science, Intel, and Economic teams will get one marine escort per team or subteam, up to a max of six total marines. Two guards at the shuttle at all times on two-hour rotations. The relief shuttle will cycle through every six hours, and for now, keep the gunships out of sight in the landing bay," I ordered.

"Will we just be replacing the twelve marines during the shuttle rotations, sir?" asked Marker.

"On the rotation cycle, yes. But the backup shuttle should be fully prepped and outfitted with thirty-six combat marines at all times."

"Yes, sir. That only leaves two marines for the command party, sir."

"Plus you, Mr. Marker. I'll feel plenty safe," I said.

"Aye, sir."

"Captain, what about arming the command party?" asked Babayan. I thought about that for a second.

"Holstered honorary sidearms only. Is that clear?" There was a chorus of "Yes, sir" to that. The honorary coil pistols were usually reserved for military displays, and each one had just six shots worth of plasma in the small chambers. In this instance, though, I thought some sort of personal precaution was appropriate.

With that I ended the conference. The personnel lucky enough to go on the diplomatic mission headed back to the bridge and handed off their stations. Karina left the briefing room well ahead of me, and by the time I got back on the bridge she had relinquished her station to Ensign Lynne Layton and was gone from the bridge. I finished my final preparations in my office, then handed off the con to George Layton and made my way back to my stateroom, where I was sure I would face some angry words from my wife.

For once, I was wrong.

She was there all right, but she was sulking while I packed my bag with personal items.

"Don't forget your toothbrush," she said idly while flipping through a plasma magazine, lounging in her reading chair and already out of uniform. I didn't take the bait, though, and just kept packing quietly, including the aforementioned toothbrush.

When I was finished I called up a yeoman to take my bags down to the Landing Bay. After he came and went, Karina and I sat together in silence for a few minutes, she in her chair and me across the room in one of the dining chairs from our small table, the bed between us. Finally she put her magazine down.

"I should be going to represent my people," she said without looking at me. "The Special Secretary gets that privilege."

"But that's precisely why you're *not* going," I replied. "She *has* to be there for the working meetings as part of her job, and you don't. I've always been a bit uncomfortable with this mission, and I don't want to risk you when it's unnecessary. The Sandosans have forwarded a day's agenda to us: two hours of introductory talks, then six hours of formal talks, then a state dinner at 2000 hours in the premier's palace. If you come down two hours before that on the 1800 rotation shuttle, then you can be formally presented at the dinner as my wife and a princess of Carinthia. Right now I've no need for a longscope lieutenant to fill one of only twenty-four available seats on the first shuttle," I said.

"I've seen the list of formal meetings. I could help with the immigration negotiations." It was actually a good point—she could—and I felt I had to give her something as a concession.

"Contact the Special Secretary and have her hook you up to the negotiations via a visual longwave, or whatever system they have. But

I don't want you to leave the ship until the dinner. I need to know you're safe," I said.

She accepted this concession with a nod, but, then she said, "Are you sure that you'll need a princess of Carinthia at 2000 hours? You already have a princess with you, plus your Carinthian XO." Her ego was bruised; I was smart enough to see that.

"I'll need my loving and supportive wife, who just happens to be a princess of the realm. Will she be there?" I asked. She made me wait a long time before answering.

"She will," she finally said. "Shall I pack a bag, or will you only require me for dinner and drinks?"

I thought about the answer to that question long and hard, then made the decision that was best for the mission.

"It will be safer if you spent the night aboard *Defiant*. And I would sleep better knowing you were here," I finally said.

She was quiet for a long time, then replied, "As you wish, Captain."

When there was nothing more forthcoming, I resigned myself to the impasse and got up to leave. As I opened the stateroom door she said one last thing to me.

"Be careful, Peter."

"I will," I said, then hesitated. "Karina, I know it seems like I'm leaving you out, but please know that it's because I love you and want to protect you from danger."

She looked at me. "I know that, and I know that you know how much I care about you and want you to be safe as well," she said.

"I do," I said. When there was nothing more to say, I made my way to the Landing Deck.

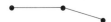

I had a medic from the sickbay staff inject the Historian's longwave transponders into the entire landing team before we boarded. I ordered the Intel section to monitor the entire party at all times and report every thirty minutes to George Layton on the bridge. He was unhappy about being a glorified babysitter, but he'd drawn the short straw, along with Karina.

"George," I said into my ear com from the Landing Bay, "I know you want to be down there with us, but you are performing a vital role. You'll be down soon enough. And make sure you get a longwave off through the ansible to the Admiralty that we are commencing full First Contact protocols with Sandosa."

"Understood, sir," he replied. I could tell he wasn't happy, but he was down my priority list a ways. Lots of people were unhappy about not being selected for this mission.

I cut the line with Layton and turned to Marker. We were the only two not on board the shuttle.

"Shall we, sir?" he said. We made our way up the steps and into the pilot's nest, where we each strapped in next to Verhunce, our marine pilot. She greeted me with a hello, and I returned the pleasantry. She'd been one of the survivors of the station battle at Jenarus, and I respected her greatly for how she had conducted herself there. She was a corporal now, and she'd earned it.

"Take us out, Corporal," I said.

"Yes, sir," she responded, and we moved smoothly off the deck of *Defiant* and into space over Sandosa.

"How long will the descent take?" I asked Marker. He looked at his watch.

"About twenty minutes, sir, if we take the slow route. If you want to make it exciting . . ." He trailed off.

"Let's just stick to slow and dull," I said. "No need to scare the passengers or our hosts."

Marker just smiled at that. Then he leaned in and whispered to me.

"I hope they have beer at the socials," he said. Now I smiled. "Me too."

Precisely on time, Corporal Verhunce brought us down on a large landing field at the New Seville capitol complex. There was a military honor guard and a pair of decorated grandstands full of people waving colored streamers, the blue, red, and gray of the People's Republic of Sandosa. The center of the complex was taken up by a bright red dais where numerous dignitaries awaited us.

It would have been an impressive sight, had it not been obviously staged. The PRS had all the hallmarks of a despotic twentieth-century socialist state. No matter how many times that model had been tried on different planets, it had always failed as a governing philosophy. I remembered reading a quote in school from a famous woman whose name I had forgotten, who said, "The problem with socialism is that you eventually run out of other people's money." That rang true in my experience, and it seemed to ring true for Sandosa. As I glanced out the shuttle's side door next to the pilot's nest, I noticed a capitol complex of gray marble, mostly dirty gray marble. The main thoroughfare was clear of cars, but the road was dusty with dirt and grit, and a few unimpressive military vehicles stood watch. Over the dim gray skies of New Seville the Sandosa star shone meekly. I guessed it to be early morning of what was certain to be an unimpressive day, weather-wise.

"Sir?" asked Marker as we stood at the door threshold.

"You first, John, then Verhunce, then I'll follow. The marines can deploy out the rear, but weapons are to be kept down, and they are to assume parade rest immediately. The rest of the dignitaries can follow me out the pilot's nest door," I said.

"Aye, sir." With a nod to Verhunce, he unlatched the shuttle door, opened it, and let the staircase slide down to the tarmac. Then the impressive marine walked calmly down the stairs and stood to one side, and Verhunce followed and deployed to the other side. I took the five short steps down to the tarmac and waved to the adoring crowd, which cheered loudly, then stepped forward to allow the rest of the entourage to follow. Once we were set on the tarmac, a military band played music that sounded like a funeral dirge to me, hopefully not the planetary anthem. The crowd stood still and stoic as it played itself to a dismal end, none too soon for me. That was followed by more cheering and streamer-waving from the grandstands. A loudspeaker voice yelled out at the adoring crowd, no doubt introducing us in some sort of Asian-variant language. After a few minutes of this, things were brought to a halt by a pair of soldiers bringing up a podium and microphone for a man in military garb to come up and speak to us. He spoke again in Asian, as if we would understand, but I got the general gist that he was welcoming us to the PRS.

Soon we were approached by groups of children, who pinned plastic flowers to our uniforms while giving the ladies full fake bouquets. Janaan caught my eye, and I smiled at her. She seemed as amused by the phony display of affection as I was.

"Think they'll let us go inside now, sir?" asked Marker. I smiled again.

"It is a bit brisk out here, isn't it?" I deadpanned, keeping my formal smile pinned to my face.

"I've had warmer days in a space suit," he replied.

Eventually the spokesman came up and introduced himself to us with a salute, which I returned. I didn't retain his name, though, as he spoke poor Standard. Everything about him screamed "elder statesman," and he eventually called up an honor guard, which escorted us to cold steel benches in one of the grandstands.

I clicked over to my private com line with Marker as the wind howled through the marble square. "Looks like you're shit out of luck with the beer, Chief," I said.

"My ass is sticking to this bench," Marker replied through the com. I tried not to laugh.

Over the next twenty minutes we were presented with a parade of low-grade military equipment that likely would not have impressed the North Palace Guard back on Quantar. Everything was polished, but nothing was new, and most of it seemed like it was for policing the populace, not fighting. I smiled and returned soldiers' salutes, and blissfully, we were finally taken inside to what seemed to be the main administrative building.

Once there we met military attachés who finally spoke some decent Standard, if haltingly, and after being warmed up with tea in a reception area, we were ushered to the second floor, where we were seated around a long rectangular table which could easily accommodate forty. At the head of the table was a podium that was adorned with the Sandosan flag, the same colors as the streamers but with a single red-and-gold-piped star in the center. We were invited to use the restrooms and then were refreshed with more tea and some small snacks, which were surprisingly sweet-tasting. After a few more minutes of this, the room started filling up with Sandosan representatives, who staked out their seats and began chatting informally with our representatives, especially Harrington and the Special Secretary.

"What do you think so far, sir?" asked Babayan, who was flanking me on my right. I looked at Marker and we both smiled, and then I turned back to her.

"Not impressed so far. They must know who I am, yet except for that elder statesman and a few of the attachés, no one has even formally greeted me yet," I said.

"Maybe it's possible they think Harrington outranks you," said Marker. "They've been communicating with him exclusively for the last year."

"Could be," I said.

"Actually, sir, I was wondering what your first impressions were of them as potential allies, or as Union members," said Babayan. I was a bit chagrined by her reminder that there were priorities other than me on this visit.

"Of course," I started. "First impressions are that the time between the Imperial Civil War and today has not been kind to Sandosa. It doesn't look like a developing society. In fact, it looks to be just the opposite—declining, and possibly failing."

"I wouldn't let my marines use that military equipment for target practice," piped in Marker.

"Your impressions, XO?" I asked Babayan.

She shrugged. "Based on what we've seen, which admittedly isn't much, I'd say they were about a five on the societal scale, maybe a three on the industrial," she said.

"Not exactly top of the list for Union admission. It's more likely they'd only get a trade agreement, if that, but that depends on the Union Special Secretary," I said, glancing across the table at Janaan, who was engaged in a smiling conversation with a Sandosan woman in military uniform bearing the rank of captain. "Anyway, it depends on what they truly have to offer. And right now Quantar and Carinthia don't need women." We all laughed.

A few minutes later things finally began to get going.

A man in a civilian suit gray as the skies over New Seville entered from the rear of the room through some simple French doors. He was the first dignitary I'd seen in civilian garb. He was a grim-looking man, never smiling, talking to a couple of flunkies in his own language. I'd have guessed him to be about fifty, but it was hard to tell. His face was lined and his skin pale, like everything here. I wondered if this was the premier, a man whose name I couldn't quite remember from Harrington's briefings. Just at that moment I got a touch on my elbow from Harrington.

"Just in time," I said, standing to greet the merchant. "Is that the premier?"

Harrington shook his head. "No. That's the vice premier, the man who runs day-to-day operations of the government, Kay Jen Kho. He prefers to be referred to as just Kho, with his title first, of course."

"Of course. Vice Premier Kho," I repeated for practice.

"The first premier is Uto Kim. You probably won't meet him until the state dinner tonight."

"Good to know."

"Things should be getting underway here soon. I caution you not to take these people at first appearance. They may be far more sophisticated than what they've shown us so far," Harrington said.

"I'll take that under advisement," I replied. Harrington nodded and started to move off, but I stopped him with a hand on the arm.

"One more question. I haven't seen a single one of the original immigrants, the Iberians, not even as a servant. What's the story there?" I asked.

Harrington looked very uncomfortable at my question, but then he nodded at the podium as the vice premier moved toward it, preparing to speak. "Later," he said, then made his way back across the table.

"Problem, sir?" asked Babayan. I shook my head as I sat back down.

"Not sure yet, XO," I said.

At that a man began pounding a gavel, and the entire room came to order quickly. He stepped up to the microphone and spoke in Standard to the room.

"On behalf of First Premier Uto Kim and his Glorious Wife, Lady Mae Zhen Kim, I call this meeting to order. We are here to greet the first interstellar visitors to our world of Sandosa in many years. We are excited about the possibilities these talks hold and look forward to discussing how we can all work together in the future to the benefit of Sandosa, Pendax, and the other members of the Union of Stellar

Republics," he said. That was the first time I'd heard that title used in a long time. Most of us just called it "The Union." The man banged on the gavel a couple more times and then introduced Vice Premier Kho, who approached the podium and began speaking in his native tongue. The second man now sat to one side of the podium, and as Kho finished a statement, he translated into his own microphone for the rest of us. His Standard was by far the best I'd heard from anyone here so far.

"We welcome you to Sandosa," stated Kho through the translator with little to no real sincerity, his face never breaking from its solid, stoic look. "Chief Merchant Admar Harrington of Pendax and his party will be negotiating bilateral agreements with our Ministry of Economics, which should be beneficial to both our worlds, and we look forward to those agreements being concluded in the coming days. We also wish to acknowledge Captain Peter Cochrane of the Union Lightship *Defiant* and his party, who will be discussing possible military exchanges between his Union Navy and our military forces." That was news to me. "We hope these first discussions will be fruitful ones."

These kind of statements carried on for ten solid minutes, and we all applauded after Kho concluded. None of us was offered an opportunity to speak, which was fine with me since I hadn't prepared anything.

The spokesman came to the podium again after Kho left the room and informed everyone (in both languages) that we could continue informal talks for another ninety minutes, after which we would receive a two-hour break before segregated formal talks began in several other rooms. Anyone interested in getting acclimated could go with an assigned escort to staterooms on the third floor. Since I had no one specific to meet with, I opted for the latter, as did most of my command crew. Gracel informed me she was going to stay and work diplomatic angles, to which I agreed. As we headed up an ornate flight of stairs to the third-floor staterooms, my mind turned back to my wife. I planned on checking in with her on a longwave and perhaps even bringing her down early, if she agreed. So far, Sandosa seemed harmless and quaint enough.

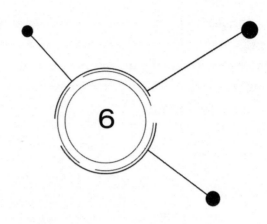

On Sandosa

After resting and chatting via longwave with Karina, who was anxious for the formal negotiations to begin so she could contribute, I ventured downstairs, where I met up with Marker.

He and I weren't included in the formal negotiations, and we were both fine with that. Personally I didn't think I'd make much of a diplomat. I was too impulsive, and frankly I was much better suited for the Union Navy, in my opinion.

We were met by a military colonel named Lee-Ten Ho, who offered to take us to the local airfield and show us Sandosa's best military equipment. The drive in a military ground car took us about thirty minutes.

Colonel Lee, as he asked to be called, was by far the most Caucasian-looking man we had met so far on Sandosa, and he commented on it.

"My family was a mix of the original colonists and the later immigrants, and Lees have served in the Sandosan military going back to near the planet's founding," he said in near-perfect Standard, by far the best we'd heard anyone speak since we arrived, as we rolled on in the ground car. I was tempted to ask another question and decided to take the risk.

"We've seen none of the original population of colonists since we've arrived, Colonel. Is there a reason for that?"

He looked distinctly uncomfortable with the question. "I am not at liberty to discuss government policies with you at this time, Captain," he said. "Please do not press me on this point." I wondered if our conversation was being monitored, as I had to assume it was everywhere we went.

"It is a question your government will have to answer at some point if it wants military and technological assistance from the Union, Colonel," I said, raising the ante but not pressing him too hard.

"That is understood, Captain," was all he replied. I shared a glance with Marker, who did not look happy with that answer. We went on in silence until we arrived at the airfield.

We got out of the ground car and went to a firing range, where a host of soldiers were lined up and waiting for us. "These are some of our best marksmen," said Colonel Lee. With a command in his own language, a series of shooters lined up to take standing sniper shots at targets about two hundred meters away. The ordinance was conventional ammunition, bullets, and the marksmen were near perfect.

"Could I try one?" asked Marker. The colonel barked an order, and the nearest marksman handed over his rifle to Marker. Marker stepped up and aimed the rifle. His first shot was wide left and low of the target. "Hmm," he said, checking the barrel for true sighting.

"Is there a problem, Master Chief?" asked the colonel. Marker looked down at the rifle.

"It's awfully heavy," he said, then re-aimed and ripped off six straight shots that blew the center of the target to dust.

"Impressive," said the colonel.

"He's one of my best marines," I commented.

"Undoubtedly."

Marker gave the rifle back and reached for his sidearm, then looked at me. "May I, sir?"

"That's up to the colonel," I said. Marker looked to Colonel Lee.

"Of course," the colonel said with a sweep of his hand toward the shooting range. Marker stepped up and unholstered his pistol. He aimed with one arm casually and fired a single shot at the target, which disintegrated in a shower of debris and flames.

"A most impressive demonstration," said the colonel.

"This weapon is a ceremonial sidearm, Colonel. It's nothing like the standard marine-issued weapons that we have. You don't have energy weapons on Sandosa?" I asked. He shook his head.

"Not at this level of proficiency," he said. "It is something we're desirous of."

"I understand that, Colonel. But Sandosa will have to prove she is . . . mature enough to handle such weapons," I said.

"You think of us as children?" asked the colonel with a passive face that gave away no hidden anger, if there was any.

"We think of Sandosa as a developing society that has not fully recovered from the Great Conflict, as I have read you call it here," I said.

"Yet your planet was chosen by the Earth Historians to receive just such technology," Colonel Lee said. I nodded.

"That is true. Quantar and Carinthia have both been lucky in that respect," I admitted.

"But poor Sandosa, we were not chosen, and so we are looked down on."

I decided to be as diplomatic as I could. "Sandosa's turn will come, like it did for Levant and Pendax, if she opens her society to change and works with the Union and not against her," I said.

"That's what this mission is all about for us, Captain. Seeing if we have common ground from which to work together," Colonel Lee replied.

From there we went to a grandstand to watch several unimpressive armored vehicles perform maneuvers, both with and without accompanying infantry. After the show we got back in the ground car and headed back to the government complex. I found Colonel Lee engaging enough, and I felt he was an honest soldier, but I wouldn't give my trust to anyone until he proved worthy of it. He tried to raise the question of military assistance with me, but I replied with a blunt question asking whom Sandosa was fighting.

"We have the right to protect ourselves from those who would seek to dominate us or even invade us. Your Union is fighting such forces now, isn't it?" he replied.

"We are," I stated. "But things have been very quiet on that front for some time. I think Sandosa is safe from the Empire at this point." He stayed stoic and looked unhappy with my answer. I decided to take a chance with my next question.

"Are you worried about falling under the influence of Pendax?" I asked. He nodded.

"Exactly, Captain, and that man Harrington. We do not trust him," he said. I leaned back and shared a glance with Marker before replying.

"It seems, Colonel," I said, "that you are in good company."

I picked up Karina from the landing strip at precisely 1800, two hours to spare before the banquet. She was happy to see me and happy to be on Sandosa, which made me feel better about excluding her until we could assess the safety of the situation on the ground.

Once back in our stateroom Karina unveiled a beautiful Asian-style silk dinner gown of deep blue and gold with dragons and flowers inlaid in the fabric. She said it was a gift from Premier Uto Kim's wife, Lady Mae Zhen Kim. I confessed to having difficulty keeping track of all the names of officials here. It certainly seemed as foreign a culture to me as I had ever seen, but the dress was beautiful.

I left Karina the massive bath and boudoir for her dinner preparations while I went back out to the salon area of our stateroom to meet with my senior staff: Marker, Babayan, and Gracel plus Harrington and the Union Special Secretary, the Princess Janaan.

I shut the door behind me, then removed my navy jacket and held court from an overstuffed chair. "I assume we have privacy protocols in place?" I asked Marker. He nodded.

"Our longwave security field should block any unwanted surveillance," he stated.

"So, what's our report on the negotiations?" I asked, looking around the room. Gracel started in.

"I would say things went well. We do have some commonalities. They are willing to take on our economic and technical advisors in exchange for improved communications tech, and we sold them on some consumer technology that will help the urban population. Transportation and agriculture will also likely lead to agreements, but we didn't want to rush in over the top of Mr. Harrington's bilateral deals. And they are unwilling to go back to what they see as a corrupt social and economic structure that they believe caused suffering under the old rule of the original settlers," she finished.

"Merchantism?" I commented. "That could be a sticking point with the Union council." Then I looked to Harrington. "And the status of your bilateral agreements, Admar?"

Harrington shuffled in his seat. "We have agreement on 1.5 million immigrant women over the next ten years, as well as the precious metals deal I discussed earlier. The Special Secretary will oversee the immigration program. In exchange for all that, we're offering agricultural equipment, training, seeds, and stock, the hardiest stuff that can survive and thrive in this climate. Imports will go way up, so the average Sandosan's life should improve immensely," Harrington said.

"And what about giving them Wasps?" I asked.

"Two initially, then one every two years for trade only—no weapons systems, if the agreements are fulfilled," he said.

"Just make sure they are the downgraded commercial models," I said. He nodded.

"That is the plan."

I looked to Janaan. "Can you guarantee that the women immigrating to Pendax will be treated fairly? Not like slaves but with guaranteed educational opportunities and the like?" I asked. She smiled.

"That wording is in the agreement, Captain, and your wife was instrumental in making sure it got in there. It will not be hard to find volunteers from the local populace. Five women from amongst the trade delegations have already asked me to be in the program. They will get a fair chance at a new life with new men on Pendax," she said with just a hint of a sparkle in her eyes. I turned away from her quickly to Babayan and Marker. She still had a hold on me, I had to admit.

"Military assessment?" I asked. Marker snorted.

"As we suspected, the military is mostly used to patrol the urban centers and control the populace. There is a 2000 hours curfew, and most residents are inside an hour before that hits. It is an oppressive society, but the military is underdeveloped, at least from what I've seen. Not an outside threat to anyone," he said.

"One thing is disturbing, Captain," cut in Babayan. "There seems to be a sizable portion of the military disbursed to the high mountains, to the mines and such. No real explanation for it, as there doesn't seem to be any internal or external threat to the mining operations."

"So why would they be there?" I asked. Only Gracel answered.

"It could be that the work is dangerous," she said.

"Or it could be that the military is there to ensure the mines are worked via forced labor camps," I said. "Which brings up the question of the day: where is the original Iberian population? Has anyone seen one person who would fit that description?" I looked around the room. No one answered. I continued.

"So we may have a situation where ethnic cleansing has occurred and the Iberian population is now enslaved in the mines." Again, no one responded. "We'll do their state dinner tonight, but tomorrow John and I will fly a shuttle up there and see for ourselves. And if we find what I suspect we might, then there are going to have to be immediate and drastic changes on Sandosa one way or another. Even if I have to impose them myself."

"Do you believe your position gives you that power?" It was Janaan, challenging me.

"I do," I said immediately. "And no discussion to the contrary will change my mind once it's made up."

"I would advise caution, Captain," said Gracel.

"And I take that advice seriously, Historian. But don't forget I also have a royal title and my family has a seat on the Union council. I've been given broad powers not only to evaluate and recommend action on Sandosa but to take such action if I deem it necessary," I finished, then looked around the room. There were no more challenges.

"I'll see you all at the banquet," I said, then got up and went back to the bath to make my own preparations.

An hour later I was just finishing dressing for the banquet, freshly showered and shaved. I'd chosen my formal princely regalia for the evening: my blue tunic and orange sash. It went nicely with my wife's formal dress, which I could now see had been closely matched to the deep blue of Quantar's royal colors. Karina came around the corner of the dressing room, dangling her second earring in her hand as she tried to hook it into her ear.

"Stop," I said as she tried to pass. "Let me."

"No," she protested. "I've got it. You zip up my dress." She turned her back to me, and I did as instructed. She took one last look at herself in the mirror, twisting and turning, before picking up the matching clutch the Sandosans had provided, then turned to me, arms spread wide.

"Am I finally presentable for a Lightship captain's wife?" she asked. The dinner gown was beautiful and form-fitting. It had a high collar with a gold diagonal line running out and around her right breast and small open panels on the front, well clear of her breasts, though, for modesty's sake. I saw that the back had a small oval opening as well as she spun for me. I thought she looked stunning.

"You're far more than presentable. They sure seemed to get your measurements correct," I said.

"Asians are a bit more petite. Their sizing seems to suit me," she said with a smile.

"Indeed it does," I said. Then she got a cross look on her face.

"I believe you're leering, Duke Peter. That will be impolite in the high company we're dining with tonight, I believe."

"You're probably right," I said, giving up my carnal thoughts for the moment and offering her my arm. "Shall we?"

The walk down to the Banquet Hall was short, and we quickly picked up an escort, a military guard and, thankfully, the translator we'd had in the first of the meetings. His Standard was by far the best I'd seen on the trip, excepting Colonel Lee. He followed us into the hall and showed us to our seats. We were next to the head of the table, where First Premier Uto Kim and his wife would be sitting. I noticed that Harrington would have the premier's right side, while Karina and the Lady Mae Zhen Kim would be seated next to each other. Janaan would be placed next to Harrington—I wondered if they thought she was his mistress—and then Vice Premier Kay Jen Kho and his wife. I seemed to be very much an afterthought, and that suited me fine. It seemed the Sandosans didn't like me much, and quite frankly I didn't like them much either, so we were even.

I arranged for Babayan and Marker to switch seats so that Marker and I could sit together and drink if things got too boring. He flashed me a flask of what I was sure was some of his precious stock of scotch. I leaned close to him and said, "Only in an emergency, John."

"Right, sir," he whispered in reply.

The banquet, of course, took its normal route with public introductions, starting at the back of the table. Karina and I were privately introduced to Uto Kim and his wife, but I was greeted with nothing more than a simple handshake and bow from the first premier. Karina and Lady Mae Zhen were soon engaged in close conversation—in Standard, no less, and without an interpreter. They were having a great time as the different courses of food were introduced. Something called "Peking duck" was the main meal. I had to confess it was tasty. There were many champagne toasts during the course of the evening, done in both Sandosan and Standard. Once the meal and dessert were done, however, they served out a small white ceramic bottle to each of us that had red Asiatic characters on it. The small bottles were capped for us, and we were encouraged to drink toasts (all in the Sandosan language) from teacups. The first toast was from the First Premier, so we all had to stand and drink.

The first shot had me thinking I'd been poisoned.

I sat back down and choked out a whisper to Marker.

"My god . . . what is this stuff?"

"Tastes like shuttle fuel," he said in reply. Suddenly the servants were refilling our teacups. This time it was Vice Premier Kho giving the toast. This was quickly followed by Lady Mae Zhen, who spoke hers in both languages and said very nice things about Karina. By the fifth toast, I was feeling much the worse for wear. Marker finally rescued me by grabbing my bottle during one of the toasts and dispensing with the contents under the table while pretending to cough, taking one for the team as the Sandosans chuckled a bit at him. When they poured again and I drank, it was thankfully scotch, but the damage had been done.

The rest of the evening was a blur. All I remembered was Marker helping me back to my room, confirming our 0600 private mission, and then setting my own alarm for 0530. The last thing my wife said to me was a reminder to take my hangover medication. I remembered looking in my hand and seeing the two small pills . . .

When my alarm went off at 0530 they were still in my hand. I stumbled off to the bathroom to be sick, then swallowed the pills quickly with some water. I hated this planet.

Marker arrived precisely at 0600 as I struggled to get into a pair of casual marine fatigues. Karina came out of the bedroom in a bathrobe, rubbing at her weary eyes. I remembered that I'd wanted her up on *Defiant* for the evening, but she had obviously made other plans and stayed with me.

"Christ, it's not even light out yet," she said. "Where are you two going?"

I made a "hush" gesture, index finger to my lips, then said, "Up the coastline. We're going to watch the sunrise, check out the fishing industry, that sort of thing. It might be helpful to Sandosa if we can find some useful industries to add to their application," I said, lying.

"When are you coming back?" Karina asked. I shrugged.

"Midday, hopefully. I'm not helping in the negotiations anyway, so I'll probably be heading up to the ship after that," I lied.

"I'll wait for you to get back then," she said. I shook my head no.

"The transfer shuttle will wait for you. Marker and I will take the one that's already on the ground. I want you back aboard *Defiant* pronto. Lots to do today," I said. "And tell Layton all is well down here." That last part was military code for heightened readiness. Basically I was ordering Layton to prepare the ship for a potential conflict on the surface. I wondered if Karina was awake enough to catch the code.

She hesitated a second, cocked her head at me, then said, "I'll pass your message along, Captain." I nodded at that, finished strapping my boots up, then stood to leave with Marker. Karina came up to me. "I'll be home within the hour," she said. That was code for message received and understood. I kissed her cheek, then headed out the door. Out in the hall I randomly picked two of our marine guards to join us on the flight for protection, leaving two for Karina. Then we made our way down to the shuttles.

"Forget to take your hangover pills, sir?" asked Marker as we headed for the tarmac.

"More like I passed out before I could take them. What is it we used to say at the Academy?"

"I feel like two bags of shit warmed over," said Marker.

"Accurate," I said.

"Well then, we'll try and keep it a smooth ride," he said, smiling.

I was just trying to hold down whatever I had left in my stomach.

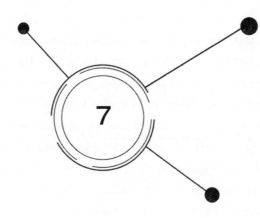

7

Corporal Verhunce flew us out of New Seville and up along the coast, and we filed a flight plan indicating the same and got confirmation from Sandosa flight control. I guess we were too big as dignitaries for them to deny us.

"So, when do we deviate?" I asked Marker, finally feeling the positive effects of the hangover pills after another trip to the shuttle loo. Marker checked his watch.

"I've planned us to hug the north coast, then turn inland where the coast nearly touches the mountains. It's about a sixty-kilometer run inland and then upward to what appears to be a heavily populated camp at about twenty-four hundred meters. We can probably safely survey from there, sir," he said.

"No offense, John, but I didn't come on this flight to observe from a distance. If we can get over the camp or even down into it, can we defend ourselves against their military?" I asked.

"Aye, sir, if that's what you need us to do. Right, Verhunce?" he asked.

"That's affirmative, sir. I can fly this bucket anywhere past their defenses. I doubt they can lay a finger on us," she said.

On that note, I lay back on my flight couch in the pilot's nest and closed my eyes. "Then wake me when we start the climb," I said.

Forty minutes later Marker shook me gently awake.

"On our way up, sir. And we've increased our speed, and we're running quiet. I'm betting they don't have anything that can track us," he said. I sat up from my couch and checked the controls. We were only thirty kilometers from our target. Marker had let me sleep some extra minutes. I turned to Verhunce.

"What are our defenses?" I asked.

"None at the moment, sir. I can run a kinetic energy screen all the way up to a full Hoagland Field," she said. I looked to Marker.

"The Hoagland's not needed, sir. The screens will stop any conventional ammunition plus most missile warheads. We haven't seen any evidence they have anything close to advanced weapons available." I looked to Verhunce again.

"The screens should be enough, sir," she said with a smile. I liked her. She rather reminded me of Dobrina Kierkopf, which wasn't too surprising, as they were both of Slovenian descent.

"Then we'll go with the screens," I said. "How long until we're at the camp?" Marker looked at his watch.

"Six minutes, sir."

"Take us up another thousand meters, Verhunce. I want a good look at this operation before we drop down on our friends," I ordered. She gunned the shuttle engines and took us up to a flat thirty-five hundred meters, likely well out of their conventional weapons range.

"Think we'll be pissing them off having a look from up here, sir?" asked Marker. I shrugged.

"I could care less about their feelings, John. We're here to evaluate them as potential future partners, not make friends."

A minute later I was at the shuttle's limited longscope, using a long-range viewer and looking down. It only took a few more moments to find the camp.

"Hold it here, Verhunce. We're right over them," I said. She did as instructed, and the shuttle went to station-keeping over the camp. I zoomed the 'scope. What I saw appalled me.

What looked like thousands of people, men and women wearing gray-and-white-striped prisoner's garb, were shuffling back and forth from ramshackle barracks to a massive mine entrance. Those who came out were hauling small railed cars full of black ore, likely coal, and depositing it on conveyor belts, either with shovels (if they were lucky) or by hand. The second outgoing line had much smaller cars on a separate rail-and-belt system. I ran a spectral scan and found this second line contained metals, primarily copper with some others mixed in. The cars on this line were much smaller and run exclusively by women. They were all unloaded by hand. What we clearly had here was one line going into the mountain hole and two separate lines coming out. No doubt the two lines diverged somewhere deep inside the mountain. I guessed, based on the volume of workers and the size of the barracks, that there were perhaps twenty-five thousand people involved in the operation. The whole area was fenced in with defensive turrets spread around and plenty of armed guards on display. I turned to Marker.

"Chief, please confirm my findings," I said. Marker took to the longscope for about thirty seconds, then stood back up.

"Looks like an enforced labor camp to me, sir," he said.

"Are you getting a recording of everything from the 'scope, Verhunce?" I asked.

"Yes, sir. Fully recording, sir," she said. I locked eyes with my Master Chief.

"Under Article Two of the Union Code, any and all forced labor camps encountered during any mission, First Contact and beyond, are to be neutralized immediately. The victims are to be treated as refugees, the oppressors as enemy combatants. Do you concur with my conclusion that this camp meets those criteria, Chief?" I said.

"I do, sir," he said. I turned to Verhunce.

"Corporal, take us down as fast as she'll go, right over the camp as low as you can, and then back out to open air over the valley. If I don't see the guards all crapping their pants, I'll be writing you up," I said.

"Aye, sir," said Verhunce enthusiastically. I turned to Marker.

"Chief, man the weapons console. We'll make a warning pass, and then we'll swing back out over the valley, give them a chance to decide if they're going to make a business decision or not. Then we'll make our run in. If they fire at us, take out every tower on the first run. Second run I want those fences down." Then I hesitated.

"Third run, sir?" asked Marker. I thought for a second.

"If they shoot at the laborers, take them all out."

"Civilian casualties, sir?" asked Marker, taking his station. I took my safety couch and strapped in.

"Likely can't be avoided. Do your best, Chief, but saving as many as we can is the priority," I stated.

"Understood."

I swiveled to our two marine escorts in the shuttle personnel bay.

"Strap in, boys. Likely to be rough from here on in."

"Yes, sir," they said in unison. I turned back to my pilot.

"Call *Defiant*, Verhunce. Use the longwave. Tell them I want every marine they can spare crammed onto the reserve shuttle, and I want them down here in less than ten minutes. And call the rotation shuttle in New Seville. I want them off the ground immediately with my wife aboard if they haven't already left."

"Yes, sir," she replied.

"Start our run in two minutes," I ordered.

"Yes, sir," they both said in response. And so we waited the time out in silence, Verhunce forwarding my orders via longwave text com.

The shuttle descended at a frightening rate, straight down, right on top of the camp. As I watched on the display, the roar of our engines terrified them, and both prisoners and guards went scrambling for cover. Then Verhunce hit the jets, and we went from VTOL mode to flying over the camp and out into open air over the valley as Verhunce turned us back to face the mountaintop camp.

"Station keeping," I ordered. "Let's give them a minute to decide what to do." I watched on the longscope viewer as the workers all scrambled for cover, some in the barracks, some under the mountain. It was chaos. The guards were trying to keep the workers away from the fences by firing warning shots. None were firing at the workers so far. I watched for a few more seconds, then said, "Let's make our run."

"Aye, sir," said Verhunce. We closed in on the camp at about half the speed we'd gone out at, letting them know we meant business this time.

"Towers targeted, sir. I count eight," said Marker. "Easy to take out with the forward coil cannon, sir."

"Confirmed," I replied. We were within about fifteen hundred meters of the camp when they made their decision.

The shuttle shook from an impact on our kinetic energy shielding, then sputtered and began to lose altitude.

"Verhunce!" I yelled as the engines strained to stay in operation.

"Some kind of advanced microwave weapon, sir. Invisible to the naked eye and no warning, either. Kinetic energy shield is completely gone, and they've damaged the engines with some sort of disruption beam, sir," she replied frantically, struggling with the controls.

"Hoagland Field!"

"Already up, sir," Verhunce said. "A few more seconds of that and they'd have had us."

"Weapons? Communication?" I asked Marker as we shook from side to side.

"All out, sir. If that's the best they've got—"

He was cut off by an alarm klaxon.

"Incoming missiles!" warned Verhunce. "Plasma-tipped warheads detected."

"Two of them, sir," reported Marker. I turned to Verhunce.

"Get us down on that plateau, Corporal!"

"Aye, sir!" She pushed the shuttle forward as the missiles approached.

"They can't get through our Hoagland with those," said Marker.

The missiles hit a second later, and the shuttle shook violently. The plasma breached the hull in the personnel bay, burning a hole about a foot across in the hull and starting a fire as melted metal dripped to the floor. One of the privates unstrapped, jumped up, killed the fire, and sealed the hole with a single foam canister. I turned back to Marker.

"I thought you said—"

"A microwave burst from the warhead disrupted the Hoagland Field, sir. The plasma ignited on impact. They can't shoot us down, but they can punch holes in us like a tin can," yelled Marker over the blaring klaxon.

"We're not space-worthy with that hole in the fuselage," chimed in Verhunce. "And the starboard engine is on fire." I looked out the window to confirm the fire.

"Thank you, Corporal." I slid over to the longscope viewer again and looked down, seeking an advantage. "I've got a fix on a ridge they appear to be firing from. Can we hit it with anything?" I asked Marker as a second round of plasma missiles fired at us.

"Railgun's out, all I have is anti-personnel grapeshot, sir," Marker said.

"Do it. Don't wait for my order," I said. Marker just nodded and fired. The grapeshot was a collection of small metal balls like ball bearings, ranging in size from a centimeter across up to cricket-ball-size. Very effective against unarmored soldiers or fast-moving targets that carried their own kinetic energy. In this case they found their perfect match in the incoming missiles. They exploded in a bright red fireball a few hundred meters from the shuttle. We passed through the dissipating warhead plasma with minimal new damage.

"Again," I ordered Marker. "This time at the ridge." He nodded and fired a second time.

We all watched as the scene played out before us. Marker's grapeshot scattering against the ridge sent bodies and parts of bodies falling from the rock. Verhunce let go of the useless shuttle controls as we glided in and hit the plateau on a fairly flat plane, then slid through the camp's fences, taking out one of the guard towers before skidding to a halt right in the middle of the damn camp. All I could do was watch.

I unbuckled and jumped up out of my chair. "Weapons!" I said as I grabbed the nearest coil rifle, charged it, and went straight to the view window in the pilot's nest door.

About a hundred Sandosan soldiers were slowly closing in on our smoking hulk of a shuttle.

"I'd say we've got about two minutes," I said.

"And then what?" asked Marker.

I looked back at him but didn't say anything.

The second shuttle I'd called down for backup took out the ridge weapons position a few seconds later, then sent all the Sandosan soldiers scrambling as they pummeled the camp's towers and blew out large gaps in the fencing. At that point many of the prisoners began braving the fracas and ran out of the barracks, heading for the open fences. The second shuttle hovered about ten meters above the middle of the compound and quickly released her cargo of thirty marines on tether lines before ascending again to continue the barrage. The marines spread out to cover our position, taking out many of the scattering Sandosan soldiers as they advanced to protect us.

"Out!" I ordered, pushing the cabin door open, and we were all on the ground in seconds. Our jobs, though, seemed confined to mopping up. The marines were fully armored, and the Sandosans were no match.

Marker came up to me ten minutes later, the middle of the camp full of hundreds of Sandosa soldiers sitting disarmed with their hands on their heads. Now they were the prisoners. Sporadic fighting continued around the camp.

"Those were sophisticated weapons, sir. Nothing the Sandosans have shown us up until now," he said. I nodded.

"They didn't develop them, so where did they get them?" I replied. I think we both knew the answer. Confirmation came seconds later.

"It's Commander Babayan, sir. *Defiant* is under attack," Verhunce said, handing me a portable longwave com.

"What's the situation, XO?" I demanded.

"Suicide drones, sir, lots of them. Nothing we can't handle, but this is not Sandosan technology. They date to late Imperial War days. They're disruptive, keeping us busy," Babayan replied.

"Take them out as swiftly as possible," I said. "Something is up here, XO. And I don't mean just on Sandosa. This mission has been in the works for several months, so it stands to reason intelligence could have gotten out about us coming here. This is a distraction. The question is from what."

"Yes, sir. Expediting clearing the space over Sandosa, sir," she said.

"Do we still have the ansible link to the Admiralty?" I asked.

"Yes, sir. Drones are not targeting it."

"Expedite a message to Wesley. Tell him we need reinforcements ASAP. Wasps, troop transports, administrative officers. Sandosa is going to need a new government."

"Sir," she started to protest, "*Defiant* can handle any and all required military contingencies—"

"I'm very aware of that, XO, but I need *Defiant* ready to move on at a moment's notice. I don't believe this attack is isolated. The question is, where's the next one they're trying to keep us from?" I said.

"Aye, sir," she replied. "Anything else?" I hesitated for a second.

"Is my wife back aboard?"

"Yes, sir, along with Historian Gracel and the whole diplomatic team."

"Good. Call down to the Sandosa government. Give them fifteen minutes to evacuate that Administrative Hall and government complex, then burn it to the ground. Can you do that and fight the drones at the same time?" I asked.

"Aye, sir!"

"You have your orders, XO. I'll make contact with you when I'm back in space. Secure longwave frequencies only."

"Acknowledged," she said, and with that I signed off and handed the com back to Verhunce, then turned to Marker.

"Can your marines handle the cleanup here, John? I need to get back to *Defiant*."

"Aye, sir, we can. Just got word a gunship is on its way with the rest of the marines. What shall we do with the prisoners, sir?" he asked.

"Standard POW protocol. Take anything, down to their underwear, that might be a weapon. Turn their rations over to the prisoners, then tell them to get the hell off this mountain. I want you finished and off-planet in two hours. Can you do it, Chief?"

"Sure as hell can, sir. What about the damaged shuttle?"

"Fix it," I said as I turned and walked away. "Verhunce." I waved to my marine pilot. "You're with me."

We made our way to the working shuttle, and Verhunce took over from the pilot, whom I ordered to oversee the repairs to our damaged shuttle. We were locked in and in the air five minutes later as our incoming gunship circled, waiting to land and take our place.

I used the shuttle com to call Babayan again on the longwave.

"Status, XO."

"Sandosans are scrambling to exit the government buildings, sir, and they've been warned it's going to be a pile of ash soon. Suicide drones have been neutralized within one hundred clicks of *Defiant*. There are a few more scattered throughout the system, but not close enough right now to cause us any trouble," Babayan said.

"Is it safe for us to come up?" I asked.

"Safe enough, sir. If one of the drones comes after you, it will never get close enough to get a whiff of your tail, sir."

I smiled. "I'll hold you to that," I said, then signed off.

"Take us up, Corporal. Full burn on the engines. I miss my captain's chair," I said. Now Verhunce smiled.

"It's a pleasure, sir," she said.

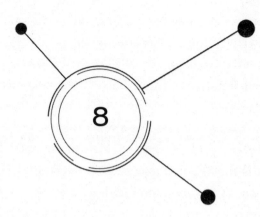

8

The next morning, after numerous protests, I agreed to meet with Harrington about the Sandosa situation. He, Janaan, Karina (because she represented Carinthia's vote on the Union Council), Babayan, and I met in the command deck briefing room. To say that Harrington was steaming mad was an understatement.

"Every bilateral agreement we've made with the government of Sandosa has been abrogated by your actions, Captain. Do you know what that will cost?" he said, storming out of the gate at me. I sat back in my conference chair, eyeing him, trying to keep my emotions under control.

"There is no government of Sandosa, Chief Merchant. As of this moment Sandosa is under Union protection for her own safety and will likely stay that way for quite some time," I said. Harrington slammed his fist on the table.

"That's precisely what I mean! Who gave you the power to upend a whole culture at your whim simply because you have such great military power at your disposal?" he demanded of me. I was having none of it.

"The power doesn't come from me or my ship but from the Rule of Law, Mr. Harrington. Specifically the Union Code, which your Special Secretary should be very well aware of," I said, glancing at Janaan, who seemed perturbed that I'd brought her into the discussion so quickly.

"I'll have you know I've already filed a protest with the Union Council about your actions. They're indefensible," Harrington said.

"So is making a whole ethnicity slaves, Chief Merchant," I replied. I wasn't in the mood for this today, so I pressed on, trying to draw things to a conclusion as quickly as I could. "As for the Union Council, I've already filed my own brief. Commander Babayan has the details." Babayan cleared her throat before starting, reading from a tablet plasma.

"We estimate that more than 1.25 million ethnic Iberians were being used as full-on slaves. Now that we've released them, they are all asking for asylum, which it seems likely the Union will grant. You might note that about two-thirds of the Iberian population are women, and we've recommended they all be relocated to Pendax immediately," she said.

"But we can't handle that many refugees!" protested Harrington.

"You can and you will," I said. "It meets the need of your population for immigrants, as outlined in the agreements the Special Secretary negotiated with Sandosa."

"But what about my precious metals as compensation? Will those agreements still go forward?"

I looked to Karina. She spoke up.

"Mr. Harrington, my husband and I represent two votes on the Union Council. Earth and Levant represent the other two votes. As an associate member, Pendax *may* be allowed a vote on these matters *if* the council can't agree unanimously. I can guarantee that at least *one* of our worlds will not allow you a vote if everything goes just the way you want it. In short, you're going to have to earn your status, and aiding Sandosa in becoming a suitable member to join our Union will go a long way toward getting you what you want," she said. I smiled at her adroitness with Harrington. Harrington started calming down immediately, apparently accepting his situation as unavoidable.

"Please continue, Captain," he said. "We are anxious to get to work."

"As I was saying, the first priority will be relocation of healthy members of the Iberian population, especially those with important technical skills who wish to leave. Any women from Sandosa who indicate a preference to emigrate will also be allowed to queue up in the initial stages. So that will meet or most likely exceed your initial desire to increase the number of marriageable women on Pendax," I said.

"But—" I held up my hand to silence the Chief Merchant. At this, Karina stepped in again.

"These women will not be taken from one kind of slavery into another, Mr. Harrington. You will set up a program, and perhaps the Special Secretary can help here, that will place these women into safe and economically viable relationships, preferably marriages. To get to your point about your precious metals, they will be under Union control, but if you *hire* the local populace to work the mines at fair wages, allow union organizing, and provide proper housing, health, and safety protocols to be followed in the mines, then that control may be released back to you, as long as the trade benefits both Pendax and Sandosa. You can also enhance your position with the Union Council by guaranteeing the safety and security of the immigrant women once they reach Pendax," she said.

"I've already drawn up a plan to implement just such an immigration program, Chief Merchant. You've had it on your desk for a month," said Janaan.

Harrington looked at her, irritated, then shrugged toward me. "Why is immigration such a big issue with you, Captain?" he asked. Karina answered for me.

"Because Pendax's inheritance and divorce laws favor males very strongly, Mr. Harrington. It's an antiquated system that does not promote property equity, which is one of the stated goals in the Union Council charter."

"It's also one of the reasons you're having so much trouble getting your full membership approved by the council," I added. "So it's in your best interests to reform. I'm sure the Special Secretary will be more than happy to review her plan with you at your earliest convenience, which should be soon, since we plan on relocating the first batch of asylum-seekers immediately."

Harrington looked chagrined but said nothing. I continued.

"There are many other individual issues, but they will all be included in my full report. The main points, though, come down to this." Now Harrington brightened up. "As part of its final steps to becoming a full member of the Union, Pendax will take Sandosa under administration, with help from the Union, of course. But primarily they will be *your* responsibility."

"What specific responsibilities would I have?" asked Harrington, eyeing me as if he were waiting for the other shoe to drop.

"Everything from the sewers to the health care system to the roads and pension plans," Karina said. "The full monty." I wasn't sure she knew what that actually meant. "How well Pendax performs in this role will determine how much gold and silver you receive as compensation and how quickly your status as a full member will be granted by the council."

"And of course, how capable a leader you will be seen as by the council. It may seem costly now, but in a year or two Pendax will be thriving and Sandosa will be rising up the scale toward full membership herself," I said. Then I reached into my brief folder, pulled out a formal Letter of Agreement from the Union Council, and slid it across the table to Harrington. "If you agree to the terms laid out in this agreement and you help both Sandosa *and* Pendax flourish, Pendax will be granted full membership, and you personally will be named Head of State, with full hereditary royal titles for you and your gentry classes. All you have to do is sign."

Harrington looked inside the brief, thumbing through the pages, then stopped and looked to Janaan. "You've read this, I assume?" he asked.

She nodded. "Yes."

"And you think I should sign it?"

Again she nodded. "Yes." At that he pulled out a pen and signed the first page. Janaan signed it as well, and I let Karina sign for both Carinthia and Quantar. Then the paper went back to Janaan.

"We've done good business here today," she said with a smile.

"We have," I agreed. With that Harrington stood.

"I'll have to go prepare a speech to the people of Sandosa, something to give them confidence that we are on their side," he said.

"We should urge as many as possible of the skilled Iberians to stay," said Janaan. He nodded.

"That would be a positive. I don't pretend it's going to be easy—"

"Well, it's not," I said. "At least the speech-giving part."

"What do you mean?" asked Harrington. I looked to Babayan.

"We destroyed their entire satellite communications array while we were fighting off the suicide drones," she stated.

"You what?"

I shrugged and stood up myself. "That may well be the first thing you have to fix."

"But how will I communicate . . ." he trailed off. I smiled.

"Perhaps you'll find some old planet-bound digital communications networks. I believe they called it 'broadcast radio' or something. Either way, I'm sure you'll figure it out," I said. With that I gave a nod, and everyone started to leave the room, save for Harrington and Janaan.

"What have I gotten myself into," I heard him say as we got into the hallway. Karina started to laugh, and then Babayan, and soon I was joining them as we made our way back to the bridge.

Six hours later, *H.M.S. Vanguard*, commanded by Captain Lucius Zander, late of Carinthia but now of Pendax, burst through the dimensional barrier and arrived in-system, accompanied by half a dozen Wasps. It was the first group sent through by the Union to provide supplies, skilled workers, and military reinforcements to Sandosa. Harrington had requested that *Vanguard* deploy even though she was technically still a few weeks from her formal commissioning. It seemed Harrington wanted me and *Defiant* out of his system as soon as possible, and I couldn't blame him, but I was also very comfortable with what we had accomplished here. Sandosa was on its way to modernization and Union membership, and we had freed more than a million slaves from hard labor and ethnic cleansing. I counted that as a good week's work.

About an hour through the gate, *Vanguard* was hailing us, or more specifically Zander was hailing me. I took the call in my bridge office with the sound barrier on to prevent eavesdropping. After our formal greetings, Zander jumped right into it.

"Why is someone always trying to kill you?" he asked. I laughed.

"I wish I knew."

"Well, if you're done mucking about on that dismal planet, you could get your arse in gear and get out here and meet me," Zander said.

"I was planning on leaving soon anyway. What's the rush?" I asked.

"My boss wants you gone—you're a 'polarizing figure,' it seems—and Wesley wants you back in the hunt," he said.

"The hunt for what?"

"Our girl is forty-eight hours overdue to report from Skondar," said Zander. I knew what he meant by "our girl."

Dobrina and *Impulse II*.

"That's troubling," I said.

"But not altogether definitive. Wesley wants to conference via ansible about it at 2200 hours, after we rendezvous and make your upgrades."

"Upgrades?" I bristled. "*Defiant* is the best trimmed Lightship in the fleet."

"Well, maybe so, but our Historian has codes to present to your Historian, Gracel, to activate certain systems that might be of use in the near future, as I understand it."

I was again taken aback by the fact that my ship had weapons systems and capabilities I knew nothing about but that the ship's Historian knew of. I decided that in the future, perhaps Lightships and the Union fleet would be better off without the Earthmen and their hidden agendas and oversight.

"What time do you want to rendezvous?" I asked.

"1600, lad. That will give the two Historians time to trade codes and make their adjustments before we have to talk to the grumpy old man," Zander said.

"Just a minute," I replied. I put Zander on hold, shut off the aural shield, and made my way onto the bridge deck.

"Mr. Layton," I asked, "how long until we can rendezvous with *Vanguard*?" Layton scrambled, looking at his dashboard for a quick answer.

"All our shuttles are still down on the planet, sir. I'd say about forty minutes to get our people off the ground—"

"I asked how long until we can rendezvous," I stated, interrupting him. He silently scanned his board again.

"I'd say about four hours at best speed, Captain," he finally said. That would put us at rendezvous at about 1545 hours.

"I'll hold you to that, Mr. Layton," I said, then turned to Babayan. "Button us up to bug out, XO. No slipups," I ordered. She stiffened.

"Aye, sir," she said, accepting the challenge in her stoic Carinthian way.

"So ordered," I said to the whole bridge crew. Then I went back to my office and re-engaged the aural field.

"We're on for 1600 hours, Captain Zander. Dinner at my place, nothing formal," I joked. Inside I wasn't laughing. This Dobrina business was what I had feared earlier. Occupy us here at Sandosa, then strike on two or three other fronts . . . It was a solid strategy.

"I'll see you then, Captain," said Zander, then signed off. I did the same, then sat back, watched my now very busy bridge crew, and worried.

Out of the frying pan and into the fire.

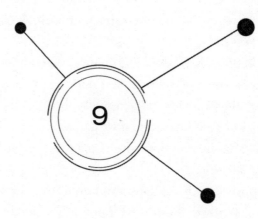

9

We were in shuttle range of the rendezvous point fifteen minutes early, just like Layton had promised. Zander requested permission to drop in on my landing deck, but that would use up all the time we'd saved en route, and I wanted to get to the bottom of this Dobrina business as soon as possible. Instead, I ordered Layton—whom I regarded as the finest helmsman in the Lightship fleet—to take us into umbilical range, which would save precious minutes but would require some tight flying within thirty meters of *Vanguard*. Zander was put out when I denied him landing privileges, but he couldn't argue with the efficiency of an umbilical tie. I had other reasons to request the umbilical; I wanted some of his marines.

I watched from my bridge chair as Layton decreased our speed relative to the stationary *Vanguard*. By the time he shut the propulsion drives down and started flying us in on reverse thrusters, slowing our speed as he locked *Defiant* to *Vanguard*'s relative station, we were less than a kilometer apart. Three minutes later the distance was a few hundred meters. A minute after that he shut us down with twenty-eight meters between *Vanguard*'s Landing Deck and ours. He started extending the umbilical to establish an airlock connection between our two vessels.

"Well done, Mr. Layton," I congratulated him.

"Thank you, sir," he replied. I nodded to Babayan and Karina to join me, and we quickly made our way down to the umbilical airlock. Gracel was already there when we arrived.

"I'll expedite the upgrades, Captain, then brief you once we're finished," she said.

"I appreciate that, Historian. But all this secrecy about what my ship can actually do has me a bit put out," I said.

"I understand your reticence about us, Captain. It seems to run high among Lightship captains," she said.

"Yes," I replied, but gave no further comment. The airlock doors parted, and the first person through was *Vanguard*'s Historian, an incredibly tall and lanky man that Gracel introduced as Lenkowsky. I couldn't tell if that was a first name or a last name. After the introductions, the two Historians went off together, and I stepped up to the threshold.

Lucius Zander always surprised me. This time he came through the umbilical with a series of technicians trailing him, but he walked in front without any assistance and stepped up to shake my hand.

"Captain Cochrane," he said.

"Captain Zander," I replied. Then he greeted Babayan and shook her hand. Finally, he stepped to the side and gave Karina a head bow.

"Highness," he said.

"I'm having none of that," she replied. "Give me a hug." He looked embarrassed, but he complied, then turned back to me.

"Fine bit of flying by your pilot," he said. "Any closer and I'd have had your arse for the meat in my sandwich."

I laughed; I couldn't help myself. "Yes, well, that's what I pay him for," I said. "Lots to discuss. We can eat in my stateroom."

"Indeed. I hope your cuisine has improved," he said.

"Markedly," said Karina, smiling and taking credit. She took Zander by the arm, and they headed off chatting while I took care of business with Babayan.

"You have the con, XO. We'll only be locked for a few hours, so get as much done as you can, trading technical equipment and the like. And just so you know, I'll be asking Zander for more marines."

Babayan looked surprised. "How many?"

"At least thirty," I replied. "No point in having two heavy shuttles and two gunships with only sixty marines. Besides, I know he left dock with a double squad. Make sure we have the bunks and other facilities to make them at least marginally comfortable."

"Aye, sir," she said and went on her way. Then I headed up to the galleria to catch up with Karina and Zander.

We had a quick meal before digging into the business at hand. Karina served Zander some of his favorite Sumatran coffee from a small stash we had onboard.

"Thank you, Princess," he said as she poured.

"You're supposed to stop calling me that. On *Defiant* I'm just a lowly lieutenant," she complained in mock anger.

"Sorry, uh, Lieutenant. Old habits die hard."

Presently Karina sat, and we got to it.

"So, what do you expect from this conference with Wesley?" I asked.

"I expect it to be a communiqué," he replied between sips of coffee. "I doubt he'll risk sending anything vital over the longwave ansible network. Most likely it will be an encrypted packet with new orders for you. I'm merely a bystander in these events."

"I doubt that," said Karina.

"You may be right, Prin— Lieutenant. I'm sure *Vanguard* will be under orders to bug out of this rock at the first sign of trouble." I thought about that for a moment.

"I hate to say it, but I've expected this. The weapons the Sandosans used on us were far more advanced than they had any business having, so I presume they had help. Imperial help," I said. Zander nodded.

"It seems likely they made a deal with them for improved technology, and likely the trade for that was your and the princess's lives," he said.

"But they failed," Karina commented.

"Indeed," said Zander. "I've analyzed the Imperial attack strategy. Very unusual. They didn't commit a single living, breathing man or woman, just the suicide drones. And those things aren't very effective at taking out sophisticated weapons like the ones Lightships have. I think this attack was aimed at you and your wife specifically. The Sandosans were just pawns they trusted to do the dirty work."

"I agree. But that's just one part of it. If they'd wanted to take out *Defiant*, they would have needed a dreadnought at least. These other weapons seemed designed to catch us in our shuttles, when we were vulnerable," I said. "If we hadn't taken the initiative with the attack on the camp, I think those drones would have taken us both out on our way back to *Defiant* at the conclusion of negotiations."

"Seems a logical strategy. For assassination, anyway."

"You're both so casual about this," said Karina.

"We're both military men, Princess"—he missed that one—"and your husband is thankfully the suspicious kind." I stood up and paced at this.

"What?" asked Karina. I turned back to them but addressed Karina.

"I want you to stay with *Vanguard*," I said. She stood to her full five-foot-one height, seething.

"No!" she said. "My place is on *Defiant*, with you."

"You're a princess of Carinthia and the most valuable thing in the galaxy to me. The odds are that Wesley will order us to Skondar in search of *Impulse II*. That will be very dangerous, and the Empire just tried to kill you through agents on Sandosa," I said.

"But my place is with you," she repeated. I shook my head.

"Karina, Sandosa was only the first move. Likely Skondar is second, and God knows what is coming after that. *Defiant* is on a war footing, and I don't want a princess, especially when she's my wife, to be in the middle of a war zone," I said.

"I trained for this mission," she said, much more calmly. "And I won't let you take me out of it. I'm staying, and as a fellow sovereign, you can't order me to leave this ship." I looked to Zander, who shrugged.

"I think she's got you." I turned back to my wife, unwilling to give in where her safety was concerned.

"Yes, but as a lieutenant in the Union Navy, I can *order* your commission transferred to Captain Zander's command," I stated.

She looked at me, not challenging me, but furious that I was trying to kick her aside. She mulled over my proposal for a moment, then said, "Very well. I will resign my commission in the Union Navy and hereby relinquish all rights and privileges bestowed upon me by my rank. I will stay aboard *Defiant* as a princess of the realm and as your wife. Just try ordering me off your ship now in either one of those roles," she said. Then she sat down on our sofa and crossed her arms, fuming, and refusing to meet my eyes. I sat back down.

"Well, that's settled," I said, but Karina wasn't finished. She looked at me, eyes burning in anger.

"Did you really think I'd let you go rescue your old girlfriend without me to watch over you two?" she asked. I shook my head.

"No, I didn't, and I was foolish to even try."

"You were," she said. Then she got up and left the dining area for our bedroom, slamming the door behind her.

"Well, I think that went well," Zander deadpanned.

"Finish your coffee," I said. "And let's go visit our Historians."

On the way to the Historian's quarters I broached the subject of adding another squad of thirty-two marines from *Vanguard*. It took some horse-trading, but eventually Zander agreed, seeing as the six Wasps he had brought carried more than two hundred troops each besides the cultural and technical personnel.

When we arrived at the Historian's quarters, Gracel and Lenkowsky didn't look happy to see us—but then, most Historians never looked happy. The style of Gracel's public rooms was much different than Serosian's had been. It was a much more minimalist style on what was essentially another spacecraft within *Defiant*. The room was mostly white with black trimmings with four club-style chairs laid out around a central table. Presently Zander and I sat down with the two Historians.

"What's our status?" I asked Gracel.

"Upgrades are installed and calibrated, Captain," she said, then stopped.

"And . . . what are those upgrades?" I prodded her. She sat forward.

"Generally, frequency modulation disruptors for your coil cannon arrays, enhanced jumping capabilities, and a weapon known as a torsion beam."

I tilted my head at her. "Well, *generally* that certainly sounds formidable, but what specifically can you tell me about each one?" I wasn't here to dally. The call from Wesley was coming up in another few hours, and I wanted as much information as I could get before then.

Gracel stayed silent for a moment, contemplating me, then proceeded. "The frequency modulation disruptors are keyed in through your coil cannon arrays. Essentially it's a carrier wave that rides piggy-back on your coil plasma. This wave rotates its frequency every few microseconds. This will allow it to disrupt any similar technology, like the kind the Empire has been using lately with their warheads, allowing you to shoot their incoming missiles out of space before they get near you. It could also be used against a Hoagland Field, or some such similar defense, to bore holes in their energy shield and allow your weapons to penetrate to their hull," she said. "Your weapons officer will not have to engage this system; it will simply be a new component of the existing coil and antimissile defenses of *Defiant*."

"That is an enhancement. Thank you, Gracel," I said. "I'd like that capability to be available in some of our missile warheads as well, just as a backup method of delivery."

She nodded. "Will a hundred be enough?" she asked. I smiled.

"It will." I looked at Lenkowsky, but he said nothing, so I turned back to Gracel. "What can you tell me about the drive enhancements?" I asked. Gracel continued.

"Simply put, point-to-point jumping will now be available to you, Captain. *Defiant* won't need to waste hours after a jump to navigate to a High Station or an enemy target. With our enhanced ansible and probe network, we've now mapped out in detail every star system within a more than fifty light-year sphere around Earth. We can place you in nearly any position within a system, as long as we have about half an AU barrier around you when you jump in. This jump system displaces a lot of normal space with jump space, but it dissipates rapidly. Still, the effects of a displacement wave can be uncomfortable even on shielded ships."

"So I guess what you're saying is don't jump in too close to a friendly," said Zander.

"Exactly, Captain," replied Gracel.

"What about jumping out?" I asked.

"The same general rules apply to proximity," she said. "The ship's drives will generate a hyperspace bubble around the vessel using the Hoagland Field as a limiting barrier, and once you press the go button, you'll be gone in microseconds."

"And how is this system accessed?"

"Through the longscope, of course. Your astrogator will bring up spatial coordinates from our network, and the 'scopeman will verify, integrate, and execute," she said. That reminded me that I'd just lost my most experienced 'scope officer, a relationship I would have to repair in more ways than one.

I looked to Lenkowsky again. So far he had said nothing, so I asked him directly, "Tell me about the torsion beam."

Lenkowsky merely stared at me as Gracel stepped in again.

"There was much debate about giving you this weapon, Captain, about whether you were even trustworthy enough to be given this much power. In the end your Admiral Wesley convinced the Order to release it for use on *Defiant* and *Defiant* only," she said.

"What's this?" said Zander, practically growling at her.

She snapped around at him with a quickness that reminded me of a snake striking at its prey. "Your Admiral agreed to these terms— in fact, he was the one who proposed them—so complain to him, Captain Zander, not to me."

Zander let out a rough grunt of derision, then quieted as Gracel turned back to me.

"The torsion beam is the most powerful weapon we have ever entrusted to the Union, Captain Cochrane, and also the most dangerous," she said.

"How does it work?" I asked.

"It's not important how it works, Captain," said Lenkowsky, finally speaking. "It's how you learn to use it in battle."

I thought that was a very stark statement, and his tone made it feel like a warning. I found that I didn't like him much. Gracel certainly had more charm going for her, even if she was much more distant to me personally than Serosian had ever been.

I waited for Gracel to continue.

"I won't go into too many technical details, because quite frankly, I don't know them. Torsion is essentially the energy created by the rotation of a highly magnetized object. We use these rotating magnetic cores in all of our interstellar drives and our energy weapons; even the guidance systems for our missiles and torpedoes have magnetic cores in them. When a Lightship spins up the Hoagland Drive, essentially what we're doing is rotating a magnetic core and energizing a magnetic field. The crystalline structure of the drive components acts as an energy conductor for the magnetic field energy, which can then be channeled to either the drive components or to generate a field around the ship. This magnetic field, the Hoagland Field, is then extended around the ship, creating a 'bubble' of normal space in our dimension that protects the ship. Eventually, as I understand it, the energy created by the torsion becomes so great that the drive opens a singularity to a higher dimension, a hyperdimension, and we can jump through it."

I nodded for her to continue.

"The torsion beam is generated the same way, by our own magnetic drives. Because it uses the internal singularity to pull in energy from the hyperdimension, its power is essentially limitless, but it does have other limitations. It's not an energy weapon, so it can't be used to, say, have a shootout with another ship. Rather, it is a field generation device that can focus that field on a specific target, as long as that target has a rotating magnetic core," she said.

"Missiles, torpedoes, HuKs, drones, dreadnoughts, and the like," said Zander.

"Yes," cut in Lenkowsky, "or even other Lightships." I didn't miss the obvious implications of that statement.

"Or planets," I said. I looked directly at Gracel. "What would happen—"

"If you used it on a planet?" she interrupted. "You could accelerate the spin rate of the planetary core. The target world would be ripped apart from the inside out in mere minutes."

The room got silent then.

"That is not the intended purpose of this weapon, Captain," said Lenkowsky in a much softer tone. "Your Admiral Wesley requested a weapon so that you could hunt Prince Arin. This is what we gave him. Its other potentialities will hopefully never have to be used."

"How will it be integrated through *Defiant*'s weapons systems?" I asked Gracel.

"It will be an additional option on the gravity weapons display. It can be charged and queued up on the longscope, then firing command will be transferred from there to your console. Only you can use this weapon, Captain," she said.

"I understand. Will you be regulating my access to the weapon?"

"No," she said. "It will be available to you at any time. The power, and the responsibility of using it, will be solely yours."

I thanked her and Lenkowsky, and then Zander and I departed. As we silently walked down the galleria together, I was deep in thought. Then Zander spoke.

"Looks to me as though you'd better get your longscope officer back in the fold," he said.

"It's my top priority before we hear the communiqué from Wesley," I said. Zander looked at his watch.

"Two more hours, laddie. My boss has already insisted on sitting in on the meeting, along with his Special Secretary," he said.

"I understand. We'll prep the command deck briefing room for the five of us," I said.

"Five? Including your wife?"

"No," I said. "Including my most experienced longscope officer, who also happens to be a princess of Carinthia."

And with that we walked silently together into the unknown.

When I went back to the stateroom, Karina was busy reorganizing her clothes, specifically setting aside her dress and duty uniforms.

"Karina, we have to talk," I said. She turned back to me, garments in hand.

"About what, honey?" she said sarcastically, like an adoring wife. I came in and sat down on the edge of bed, facing her.

"About your resignation," I said.

"What about it?" she replied without looking back at me, casually sorting through her collection of blouses.

"I want you to rescind it."

"Oh, that," she said, then pulled out the blue dress from the Sandosa dinner and turned to me. "I'd rather like to keep this. I know they were awful people, but I think it looks fantastic on me, don't you agree?"

I nodded yes. She turned and put it back in the closet. I took my chance to take her by the arm and sit her down next to me.

"Karina, this is serious business. We could be in grave danger. The Union, I mean. I want to protect you above all else, you know that. I love you. I want you to be the mother of our future children, but right now I need you here on *Defiant* as an officer, not as a princess," I said.

"I'm afraid your actions haven't left me any other role but that of princess," she replied. I stood up.

"There are new weapons, powerful weapons. Weapons that require an experienced longscope officer to manage them. Without that experience, we could all be in great danger."

"You're not just saying this to get me back on your bridge deck, are you?"

"Well, yes and no. I need you. *Defiant* needs you. Hell, all of the Union needs you at your post. Now, will you put on your uniform again or not?"

She looked up at me. "You're serious."

"As much as I've ever been."

She pulled her uniforms closer to her, rubbing the green fabric between her fingers, then hung them up again. "When do I report?"

I looked at my watch. "Ninety minutes. In the briefing room. We're expecting Wesley's communiqué packet then."

She turned back to me. "I'll be there," she said.

"We'll talk about the other issues . . . later. When there's more time."

"There's never more time, Peter," she said. That was true enough. I pulled her in and kissed her on the forehead.

"Thank you. I'll be on the bridge."

"Aye, sir," she said. I gave her a quick smile—all that I could manage—and made for my captain's chair.

I entered the briefing room ten minutes early, expecting it to be empty except for the techs setting up the call receiver. I was wrong. Zander was there. I sat down next to him, at the head of the table.

"Any last words of wisdom?" I asked. He shook his head.

"None I can think of, lad. This is going to be your situation to handle. Wesley will want me to keep station here, oversee the rebuilding of Sandosa while you do the dangerous work. Not three years ago it would've been the other way around. Such is my lot in life," he said.

"Well," I replied, "if this get as sticky as I think it might, we'll see each other again sooner than you might think." He just nodded at that.

Shortly Harrington came in, accompanied by the Special Secretary, and sat down without saying hello. Zander and I both stood as she entered, then repeated the gesture when Karina followed half a minute later. I was glad to see my wife in her duty uniform, at least for now. The truth, though, was that I wanted her off this ship and back to the safety of Quantar as quickly as I could make it happen. She was my wife, after all, and a princess, both roles for which I valued her highly.

Once the techs were done, I ordered them out of the room and locked the door, activating the room's security protocols. Then I called up to Ensign Lynne Layton at the com station.

"Have you received the packet yet?" I asked her.

"Aye, sir. It's ready to decrypt and download to your display," she said.

"Do so, Ensign. And be sure to delete the original packet from your com board once the download is complete."

"Aye, sir." We waited in silence for almost three minutes while the packet downloaded to our secure server and decrypted. Once it reached 100 percent, I activated the communiqué from my dashboard without another word. The Admiralty Linkworks logo appeared on the room's main screen for five seconds before Wesley's image replaced it, sitting at his desk in his office on High Station with Quantar floating above him through his windows. He started with the usual protocols about secrecy, then turned to the business at hand.

"I have read the full reports of Captain Cochrane and his crew and those of Mr. Harrington and the Special Secretary for Union Relations. I find Captain Cochrane acted in compliance with both military Rules of Engagement and within the codices of the Union Code, especially as it pertains to dealing with ethnic cleansing on a subject world. Although I might differ on some of the specifics of proposals made by Captain Cochrane for the oversight of Sandosa by Chief Merchant Harrington in specific and Pendax in general, I find none of the protested provisions to be of merit at this time. The Union will proceed with the makeover of Sandosa's culture with Pendax serving as the responsible party and cultural guide. The protested provisions can be reviewed by the council on a six-month basis at the chief merchant's request." That last part was a bone, albeit a small one, for Harrington.

Wesley continued. "At the moment of the recording of this communiqué, 1820 hours Quantar local time, I am placing all Union military forces at Defense Condition One. The following orders to Captain Cochrane and Captain Zander apply with immediate effect."

"One: Captain Cochrane is ordered to take *H.M.S. Defiant* to the Skondar system, there to assist in the possible search and rescue of *H.M.S. Impulse II*, commanded by Captain Dobrina Kierkopf. *Impulse II* has been off-com for nearly forty-eight hours. All efforts to contact her have been to this point unsuccessful. All methods, weapons systems, and upgrades aboard *Defiant* are available at the captain's discretion for use in combat, should there be any. Rules of engagement are limited only by conditions on the battlefield, if there is one. Traverse time to Skondar is estimated at 10.7 hours, so go loaded and arrive ready. Feel free to use your new point-to-point jumping technology, Captain." I nodded at that. "Coordinates to Skondar are embedded in this packet.

"Two: Captain Lucius Zander is ordered to relieve *Defiant* aboard *H.M.S. Vanguard* and oversee the initial transition of Sandosa from a paranoid socialist system to a constitutional monarchy style of government with appropriate institutions. However, we recognize that under these current circumstances, *Vanguard* may be asked to assume the role of a warship at any moment. Therefore, Chief Merchant Harrington of Pendax will coordinate the transition teams with support from Union Navy Wasp frigates and commercial Wasps from his home world. The Special Secretary is to be in charge of oversight of Mr. Harrington and ensure compliance with Union standards and codices in regard to Sandosa." With that he stopped reading from his prepared script and looked straight into the display.

"Ladies and gentlemen, the entire Union is on high alert for an outbreak of full-scale war. Sandosa was likely the first diversion. Skondar is likely the second. Do your jobs, but be prepared to bug out for the nearest battlefield at any moment. I expect reports as soon as humanly possible." Then he stood and saluted us. "Wesley out," he finished with a flourish. No one saluted back.

I stood and faced the room.

"Mr. Harrington, I suggest you pick a flagship from among your Wasp merchant fleet, but be prepared to lose *Vanguard* and the Navy Wasps at any moment," I said. He nodded.

"Special Secretary Katara, I suggest you stay on the commercial flagship Wasp until the military situation can be sorted out. You can monitor progress on Sandosa from space for the moment," I said.

She was ready with a counter. "You know as well as I do that it's not the same as being on the ground," she said. I looked at her, then checked the look on my wife's face. Karina was staying impassive. I turned to Zander.

"Consider Captain Cochrane's recommendation as an order from me, Princess," he said. Janaan looked frustrated, but that was that. When there was nothing else, I turned back to Zander.

"Captain Zander, I hereby and gladly relinquish all command and oversight of the Sandosa system and the planet Sandosa to you and *H.M.S. Vanguard*," I said. Zander stood.

"Accepted, Captain. Now if you'll be on your way presently out of my system, I'd like you to go get our girl," he said.

I smiled and stood. "Acknowledged, Captain," I said with a salute. "Now get off my ship."

"Aye," he said.

With that Harrington and Janaan stood to leave as well, and Karina hugged Janaan. I merely gave her a nod, then watched the three of them leave the briefing room. I turned to my wife, who remained behind to talk with me privately.

"There are some substantial changes to the longscope system, especially weapons. I suggest you get together with Gracel ASAP to go over the upgrades in detail," I said.

"Aye, sir," she replied, then snapped off a salute. I saluted back and then took a step closer and put my hands on her waist.

"Karina—"

"There will be time for apologies later, Peter. Right now we both have work to do." Then she kissed me lightly, just once, and was off. I followed her across the command deck to the bridge and took my captain's chair.

"Commander Babayan," I called. She moved quickly to my station.

"Yes, sir?"

"Button down the ship for an interstellar HD jump, XO. You have thirty minutes from the time the umbilical rolls up to get us underway," I said.

"Underway to where, sir?" she asked.

"At least one AU minimum from any station, rock, or planet in this system, XO. We're going to use point-to-point jumping. Have Mr. Layton plot the course, get Longer to give you all the sub-light speed he can, then get back to me with a timing estimate."

"Aye, sir. And then?"

I looked at her.

"Then we jump into the Dragons' domain," I said.

She nodded, then started barking orders to George Layton at the helm.

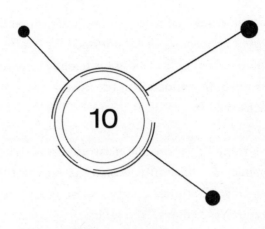

To Skondar

We were in position to use the point-to-point jump drive to Skondar for the first time forty-eight minutes later. Lieutenant Arasan provided the coordinates and fed them through to Layton at the helm. I had no doubt they were accurate and would place us in a prime spot in the Skondar system.

A roughly ten-and-a-half-hour journey awaited us in traverse space, and then it was another hour and a half to Drava, based on Arasan's calculations. *Impulse II*'s last reported location was near the mining colony, but ninety minutes was a long time when your friends might be in peril. I intended to get there faster if we could.

Lena Babayan sat down at her station next to me. "Point-to-point jump coordinates loaded into the helm, sir, and verified by the long-scope officer," she said. I looked to Karina, who gave me an affirmative nod. I noted that Gracel was with her at her station, on the bridge for a major event for once. I turned my attention to Duane Longer at Propulsion.

"Mr. Longer, are you in receipt of the proper jump coordinates?" I asked.

"Aye, sir, I am," he said. "Hyperdimensional drive spooled and ready at your command, sir." I motioned for Gracel to come over and join me at the Third Officer's station, usually reserved for George Layton, but he had his hands full at the helm.

Gracel took the seat next to me. "Where will we jump in, Historian?" I asked.

"According to the ansible network, about 1.5 AUs from the gas giant Skondar-5. The mining colony is on the third moon of S-5, known as Drava. Estimate eighty-six minutes from the arrival point to reach the Drava colony," she said.

"Thank you, Historian." I nodded to Longer again. "You have the wheel, Mr. Longer."

"Aye, sir," he responded, then counted down from five, and once more we were in a tiny universe of dense gray barely bigger than our ship, traveling through dimensions unknown.

I checked my watch, then turned to Babayan. "Another ninety minutes max for the main bridge crew, and then I want them all off duty and resting for at least seven and a half hours, XO," I said.

"Aye, sir," she acknowledged, then began the process of bringing replacement crew members to the bridge again for transitions.

I spent another thirty minutes in my bridge office before signing off and heading down to my stateroom to kill off the remaining time in traverse space and to rest. Karina joined me a few minutes later, heading straight for the bath. I undressed in silence and went to bed to get some sleep while she soaked quietly in the tub. Some while later as I dozed, I felt her warm and very naked body slide in behind me, nuzzling my back as I lay on my side.

Her body's warmth against mine drew me back from the brink of oblivion. Once she was sure she had my attention, she started whispering softly in my ear.

"I want you to know that I believe in you, even if I don't always agree with you. You're a good husband, a great Lightship captain, and the man I want to spend the rest of my life with. Don't ever for a moment think that I don't love you just because I disagree with you. I want us both to be safe in whatever lies ahead. As safe as I feel in your arms."

The next few moments were full of kisses and passionate embraces as I tried to show her just how much I loved her and she did the same for me. When we both settled down again, I held her close as she drifted off, but my mind stayed active, relieved that we were on the same page again but worried about what awaited us at Skondar.

Our alarm went off a full hour before we were due to drop out of traverse space and into the Skondar system. We both prepped for duty, Karina spending most of her time wrangling her unkempt hair that had been unleashed during the night. Once she got everything under control, we both made our way to the bridge with a full fifteen minutes to spare.

The rest of the crew arrived presently, and I checked my watch again: 0640. It was going to be a long day. With five minutes to go, I turned the final process over to Babayan. She had been an excellent choice for XO and made sure everything happened according to schedule. Right on the dot she signaled to Longer, and he made the call. On our main plasma screen the dark gray of traverse space dissipated and normal space returned. An orange-brown gas giant was visible as a coin-sized dot in the upper left of the display.

"Focus and magnify," I ordered. The screen zoomed in and refocused on S-5. There were two moons visible. I looked for Gracel, but her station was empty, so I changed tacks.

"Longscope officer: system report, please," I said. Karina stepped out from her station.

"Eight planets, none habitable, but the third moon of S-5 is marginally within habitable ranges. Nicknamed Drava after a river in the Carinthian province of Old Austria on Earth. She's home to a former Imperial mining colony, though little is known about what was mined there. She's currently occulted on the far side of S-5 from us, but we have plotted a course which will place us in orbit over her in—" She looked up to check the bridge clock. "—eighty-three minutes."

"Thank you, Lieutenant," I said. "XO, reset the bridge clock for eighty-three minutes." Then I turned to George Layton. "Lieutenant Commander Layton, get us underway to Drava."

"Aye, sir," he said, then ordered Duane Longer to activate the sublight HD drive. I turned to Karina.

"Send our Union IFF signal toward Drava, Lieutenant. Use the longwave frequencies. Let me know immediately if we get any kind of response," I ordered.

"Yes, sir," she said, then pivoted to her station with military precision. Sometimes I forgot how well trained she was. I turned back to George Layton.

"Make sure we intersect with *Impulse II*'s last known location, Commander. I want us to go straight at her."

"Aye, sir," he responded. Now it was my XO's turn again.

"Commander Babayan, prep all the marines, gunships, and shuttles. I want them on a five-minute turn from the moment I give the order," I said.

"Yes, sir," she said, then got on the com. A five-minute turn meant that they had to be ready to be spaceborne five minutes after the issuance of any "go" command from a superior officer. I didn't know if I'd need them, but I wanted to be prepared in case I did.

I stood then and activated the shipwide com, which set off a brief alarm klaxon. "All hands," I started, "this is the captain, calling battle stations. From this moment on, we are on combat footing at all times until relieved of such status by me. Personal weapons and sidearms are to be worn at all times. Highest security protocols from this moment forward. Off-duty personnel will proceed to security stations. I repeat, this is the captain, call to battle stations." With that I disconnected, and the alarm klaxon sounded again. There was a flurry of

activity as two guards with coil rifles came in and positioned themselves on either side of the bridge entrance. Unnecessary rooms like
the command deck briefing room were shut down and locked. An
armory officer came through and delivered personal coil pistols to the
entire bridge crew. I went to my office, unlocked my safe with the
biometric key code, and pulled out my own personal pistol, securing
it to my holster before returning to my captain's chair.

"Time to Drava, helm?" I asked George Layton, not bothering to
look at the bridge clock. I liked keeping my bridge crew involved.

"Seventy-six minutes, Captain," he replied. I nodded.

Now all we had to do was wait.

"Com officer," I said to Ensign Lynne Layton when we were fifteen
minutes out from Drava. "Any response to our IFF signal?" She shook
her head from her station a half deck below me.

"Negative, sir. No response on any standard com channels," she
said.

"Longscope officer?"

Karina turned to me to deliver her report. "Longwave frequencies are clear as well, sir. Nothing to report." I stepped up to the
guardrail, looking down on Ensign Layton.

"What about low-definition bands?" I asked quietly.

"You mean like broadcast radio?" she asked. I nodded. "Give me
five minutes to check, sir," she responded.

"You have two, Ensign." She nodded affirmative and turned back
to her board. Babayan came up next to me.

"If *Impulse*'s longwave and standard coms are out, what are the
chances she could broadcast on a low-band radio wave?" she asked,
low enough so that only we could hear.

"Small," I said. "But it is something we practiced at the Academy."

"Disaster beacon?" she asked. I nodded.

"When it's all you have . . ."

"But that would mean she's disabled at best."

"Yes, but a signal would at least indicate that she is alive." Babayan looked at me quizzically. "By 'she' I mean *Impulse II*," I clarified.

"Noted. I still think that's a big hope, Captain." I turned to face her.

"I'm aware of the situation, XO," I said, then walked a few paces away from her to be alone. If there was nothing on the low-band radio, then it meant one of two things: *Impulse II* and Dobrina had been destroyed, or they were no longer in the Skondar system. Each had heavy implications.

It was nine minutes from intersect when Ensign Layton nearly jumped out of her chair.

"I've got something on the low-band radio, sir. It's a repeating signal, unclear as to the meaning."

"Let's hear it, Ensign," I said. She switched the audio to the main bridge speakers. A series of pops and beeps followed.

"Could that be natural or something coming from the mining colony?" asked Babayan, doing the job of a good XO, always questioning.

"It's not natural, ma'am," said Layton with confidence. "But it's hard to pinpoint. Could be coming from somewhere near the mining colony, but it repeats regularly."

I listened again, then smiled.

"It's an SOS in what used to be called Morse code. She's sending us a signal!" I said.

"It could be from the old colony, sir. Perhaps it's been repeating for hundreds of years," warned Babayan, playing devil's advocate.

"Ensign Layton, respond with the same signal. Match signal strength and frequency."

"Aye, sir," she said and carried out my orders. The incoming signal stopped for one cycle, then started repeating again. Everyone on the bridge looked at me.

"Now send our call, LS-474," I said.

"Sir, I just recorded their signal and broadcasted it back to them. I don't know how to actually—" I jumped down to her station.

"I'll do it," I said, then keyed in *Defiant*'s call sign using her com board. The transmission from *Impulse II* stopped again for one full cycle, then resumed. I listened closely.

"LS-452," I said. "It's *Impulse!*" The next few seconds were a flurry of activity as I ran back to my station. I put Karina on locating the signal, but the colony was on the occulted side of Drava, turned away from us so we couldn't get an exact fix. I ordered the five-minute turn for the Marines, which would put them at launch-go when we were directly over the colony. I ordered all weapons and defense systems to high alert. Then we all saw it.

The colony had come into view on the main display, which automatically magnified and enhanced the image. Next to the colony, stuck on the surface of Drava, was *Impulse II*.

"She's been taken to ground, sir," said Babayan.

"I can see that. Is she—"

"Hull integrity is still intact, and her forward sections are protected by an active Hoagland Field," cut in Karina, telling me what I needed to know. She may have been forced to the surface, but *Impulse II* was still in one piece.

"Anything else I need to know, Lieutenant?" I asked my wife.

"Yes. There is an ongoing battle—energy weapons discharges and the like—going on aboard *Impulse*. But . . ."

"But what?" I said.

"The only active life signs I can detect are behind the Hoagland Field, sir. Therefore the other combatants must be—"

"Automatons," I said. "Robots, like the ones we faced at Jenarus."

I hesitated only a second. "Activate search and rescue protocols," I ordered. "Let's get our marines down there now!"

Babayan came up to me in the bustle that followed my new orders. "Captain, I request permission to lead one of the marine shuttles down there on any search and rescue or combat mission," she said.

"Granted," I replied. "And I'm right behind you."

"What?" That came from Karina's station.

Babayan stepped swiftly between me and the lifter. "You're the captain, sir. You belong on the bridge," she said evenly.

"Yes, I know. But I'm also the most battle-tested command-level officer on this ship in Marine excursion duty, next to you and Marker. And besides—"

"This is personal." That came from Karina. I looked over at her. She was mad at me again, but . . .

"I'm waiting to hear another name with my level of experience," I said, looking around the bridge. There were no answers to my challenge. I activated my com link.

"Mr. Marker, let's get those marines off the deck. Commander Babayan and I will be down in three minutes."

"You, sir?" Marker said. "You personally are going on this mission?"

"I am, John," I said. "So I think you'd better get used to the idea."

With that I put George Layton in command, then made straight for the lifter, purposely not looking back.

We were off the landing deck as planned three minutes later, both shuttles and one of the gunships. I was still crawling into my EVA suit when Commander Layton relayed that *Defiant* had taken up synchronous orbit over the colony and *Impulse II*. "Keep your head up, George.

These things can be deadly. But if you see anything that's not alive come out of that hole in the ground"—I meant the colony—"you have my permission to blast it to infinity."

"Aye, sir. But atomics—"

"*Impulse* is shielded by her field, Commander," I said.

"Yes, sir, but only half the ship—"

"Yes, George, but it's the half our people are in. Carry out my orders," I finished.

"Aye, sir," he said. I cut the line, then slid into my seat next to my shuttle pilot, Corporal Verhunce.

"Fancy another crack at these bronze bastards?" I asked. She nodded.

"I do, sir, but it won't bring back those we lost at Jenarus."

"It won't," I agreed. "But I still want the shot at them." Verhunce said nothing more to me, so I quizzed her. "I take it you don't agree with me being aboard this mission either."

She shook her head. "Not my call, Captain."

"I'm asking your opinion."

"I have none, sir, unless you're ordering me—"

"I am." She cleared her throat before continuing.

"It's true you are one of the three most qualified officers to lead this mission. But it is also true that you are a Lightship captain, and you shouldn't be out here, exposing yourself to danger. At some point, sir, you'll have to stick to your bridge and let the rest of us do our jobs," she said. That was sobering.

"ETA till we're on the ground, Corporal?" I asked by way of deflecting the conversation.

"Two minutes, sir, and we'll be coming in hot," she said. I switched off my ship com and started up the longwave com back to *Defiant*.

"Lieutenant Feilberg here, sir," came Karina's voice.

"Karina . . ." I said.

"Don't start. I know what this is about. She was your lover and your friend. Go rescue her. The rest doesn't matter now." I resigned myself to the fact that she was right. This wasn't the time.

"Patch me through to Commander Layton and keep the channel open," I said. She did so without another word.

"Layton here, Captain."

I looked down at my watch. "George, in less than ninety seconds we'll be on the ground on Drava. If you see anything moving on the ground or in the sky that's not human, take it out. If these are the same automatons that caught us at Jenarus, their weapons emit a disruption field, like an EMP. It will likely knock out our communications, but whatever you do, don't break off from this engagement until either we have *Impulse* back or . . ." I trailed off.

"Or what, sir?"

"Or we're dead."

"Captain, you don't have the benefit of a Hoagland Field defending you against these things," Layton warned.

"I know we don't. But this time we do have the localized fields protecting the shuttles and our personal shielding on the EVA suits, which we didn't have before," I said.

"I hope that's enough, sir."

"It should be. Keep this channel open via longwave at all times. And keep *Defiant* safe," I ordered him.

"Aye, sir," he responded. I went to my wrist com and switched back to the shuttle channel.

"How long?" I demanded.

"Forty-four seconds, sir," said Verhunce. I switched again to the personnel channel.

"Forty seconds, ladies and gentlemen. Charge your coil rifles and ready your concussion grenades. Anyone with disruptor-tipped RPGs?"

"Four of us, sir," came a private's reply.

"First two squads hit the ground with suppressing fire. RPGs follow and target anything made of amber metal that moves. Squads three through six, suppress, advance to *Impulse* as fast as you can go, and set up a perimeter within the shuttle's field. Last squad will bring the explosives," I said.

"We don't have an explosives engineer," replied the main RPG private.

"That's why it will be my job to blow the hull and your job to cover me," I said.

"The hell it will!" came Marker's voice.

"You have your orders, Chief," I replied. I looked down at my watch. "Fifteen seconds," I called out over the main channel, then switched back to Verhunce. "Set her down less than fifty meters from the hull of *Impulse*, if you please, Corporal," I said to her just as we started to rock from incoming ground fire.

"You don't ask too much, do you, sir?" Verhunce replied.

"Only what I know you can do, Corporal. Only what I know you can do." Then I looked out the cabin window, green automaton rifle fire crisscrossing our path as we sped to the ground. This was going to be fun.

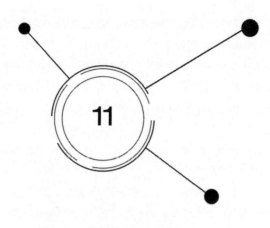

On Drava

We hit the ground hard and skidded a good distance on hard-pan rock. Pieces of amber automaton went flying past the window. Verhunce must have taken out as many as she could while still following my orders.

"Forty-eight meters from the hull, Captain," she called out as we unstrapped our safety couches. I didn't have time to respond, but I made a mental note to commend her for her skilled landing.

"Go marines!" I ordered. The rear hatch flew open, and the first two squads poured out, laying down suppressing fire and then hitting their bellies hard. The five marines in the RPG unit were next, and they laid out a volley that hit so close it rocked the shuttle. Then the next three squads vaulted past them as they reloaded and volleyed again. I looked to Verhunce. "Our turn, Corporal." I checked my C-19 explosive charges one last time, and then we were through the hatch and into an open, bright plain full of Union marines and at least fifty golden-amber robots of the deadly kind. The shuttle's Hoagland Field protected us for about a twenty-meter radius around the ship, but the hull of *Impulse II* was far beyond that range. I looked around: two men wounded but thankfully not dead.

"I need three squads to get me to that hull," I yelled. Fifteen marines came up, including Verhunce. I waved her off. "Negative, you're the pilot," I said over the din.

"Squad two lost a man. I volunteered," she replied.

"But—" I started to object. She just gave me that hardheaded Carinthian look. "All right, then. RPGs and suppressing fire, spread out, don't be predictable in your movements, and get me to that hull. Once it's blown, I want everyone inside," I said. "We go in five." I counted off from there, and we made our end run under a volley of RPG and coil rifle fire from our marines near the shuttle. I was almost embarrassed that I had four marines sticking to me as I ran, green death flying all around us. Our new personal EVA shielding would help, but there was no guarantee against the automatons' powerful weapons. I saw a flash as one of my escorts fell. I kept running until we hit *Impulse*'s hull hard and took cover. My best guess was that we were somewhere near the Intel section, five or six decks below the galleria. I quickly set the charges for a thirty-second delay, then ordered a retreat back the same way we had just come. I helped pick up my fallen escort as we ran. When we got back under the protection of the shuttle's limited Hoagland Field, we laid the marine out under cover of the wing. I looked down.

It was Verhunce. There was a large dark wound in the middle of her chest. A medic came and took her inside with the other wounded, but she had been outside the shuttle's field range when she'd been hit.

"Marker, Babayan, report!" I called through the command com channel.

"Holding our own, sir," said Marker.

"Same here," replied Babayan.

"The charges go off in nine seconds. After she blows I want a full spread of concussion grenades at those devils and then all units to advance on the automatons. I want to finish this," I said.

"Aye, sir," they both confirmed. Right before the charges blew I saw a coil cannon blast, no doubt from *Defiant*, hit about half a click away. Layton was doing his job and keeping the automatons at the mining colony from reinforcing.

The C-19 explosives' blast against *Impulse*'s hull was spectacular, hot metal flying all around us. When the smoke cleared, the concussion grenades followed from my marines, blowing amber robot parts everywhere. The next volley of RPG ordnance mixed with coil rifle fire seemed to put the robot threat down for good.

"Advance!" I ordered, and we charged with a loud battle cry. As I ran I saw the upper quarter of an automaton firing its green death ray randomly, trying to target marines, which was difficult without eyes or a head. I pulled my pistol and charged it, then blew the thing to pieces. I hated them, and with good reason. They'd killed thirty-three of my comrades at the Jenarus station.

We gathered at the hole in the hull of *Impulse II*.

"Where to now, sir?" asked Marker.

"Inside and up," I said. "To the galleria."

We used hooks and metal rappelling wire to climb up to deck sixteen, three decks below the galleria. From there we ran up utility corridors to the rear entrance of the galleria. The ship was wide and baroque, much like the first *Impulse* had been. But something was different. About thirty meters in front of us was a shimmering silver field of energy, like a wall of lake water. Behind it we could see amber figures, distorted though they were, moving back and forth.

"Defensive field," said Marker. "They never used one at Jenarus."

"How do we break it?" asked Babayan. I looked around.

"I'm open to suggestions," I said.

"Maybe we can draw them out," said Marker. "The shuttles carry electrostatic charges for disrupting enemy electronics, kind of like an EMP burst. They can be fired from the RPGs."

"Get them," I said. Marker ordered two privates back to retrieve the static charges from the marine munitions officers. Two minutes later we had our five RPG marksmen loaded and ready.

"Spread out your fire across the field," said Marker. He looked to me, but I just nodded for him to give the firing order while we all took cover.

"Fire!"

The static RPGs shot out at the energy field and exploded quite spectacularly. There was an unexpected recoil as the field absorbed the static energy and bulged in our direction before returning to normal a few seconds later. We'd succeeded in "denting" the field but not in penetrating it.

Obviously, we'd alerted the automatons to our presence as they started coming through the field unobstructed. We'd succeeded in getting their attention. I counted five.

"Take cover and return fire!" I ordered. As I brought my rifle up to my hip to unload, the RPG private next to me exploded in a hellfire of green energy. I gave them everything I had.

"Concussion grenades!" I heard Babayan order. Six of them hit the deck as we all scrambled for the safety of the access hallway and its protective bulkhead. When they blew, amber robot parts went everywhere.

I took one look and yelled, "Charge!" We rushed back in again with full-throated battle cries, filling up the remaining open galleria area. A second later another group of five automatons came through the field, firing at will. We quickly retreated behind the rear wall bulkhead again under their heavy fire. I saw more marines fall as I came.

"Suppressing fire!" Marker ordered as he, Babayan, and I gathered for another strategy session.

"What now?" asked Babayan.

"There's too many of them," said Marker, then looked to a marine private.

"Concussion grenade, private!" he demanded. The private complied.

"What are you going to do with that?" I asked him as he set the charge to two seconds.

"We've got to get that field down. It must have projectors on the walls, blanketing the area. I'm going to shove this thing right through that goddamn field, break up those projectors. I damn well didn't give up a professional rugby sevens career just to shoot robots from a distance in the Navy. I'll need all the fury of hell from you two to get past those things," he said, looking at me and Babayan in turn.

"I could order you not to," I said.

"Don't," Marker replied.

"Give me the grenade, John. I'll do it," I said.

"No, you won't!" said Babayan, pushing me back. "You're the captain, and captains don't take risks. You stay back. You shouldn't even be down here."

Marker looked at me with an intense stare, the kind I'd only seen from him in battle. "Remember, Peter, *Impulse* was my first Lightship, too. And I'm the tactical commander on the ground here, not you, captain or not. I'll get this grenade past that field somehow. Just make damn sure you take out the rest of those golden devils once I do."

"John—"

"My mind is made up, sir," he said. "We've got to break this deadlock." It was suicide, or nearly so, and he knew that. But he wouldn't have any of my protests.

"You have five seconds, sir," he said, then made for the galleria entrance, clutching the concussion grenade. I stood and switched to the main com channel.

"Five seconds, marines! All hands to rush the galleria deck and provide suppressing fire! Concussion grenades once the field is down, and don't stop shooting until everything that's not alive is in pieces!" There were many grunts of agreement at that. I had nearly ninety able men and women behind me, minus the wounded, ready to charge to their deaths. Their bravery, and that of John Marker, shamed me.

On the count of five, a dozen marines swept out ahead of Marker, coil rifles blazing. A volley of concussion grenades followed. More robot parts scattered, replaced by reinforcements coming through the field. Then Marker made his move. We stormed out of the hallway, all of us, Babayan and I taking up defensive positions on the left flank. Marker ran like the wind, blazing his coil rifle, firing from the hip at a dozen automatons while he clutched the concussion grenade in his left hand. He barreled through three of the toasters, sending them flying like so many bowling pins. As I watched, I could see the concussion charge blink red. He'd activated the two-second delay, but he still had a good five meters to go. I stood up from my defensive crouch.

"No!" I said out loud.

Marker dove for the field barrier. He stretched out the grenade in his left hand, and it penetrated the field. The grenade exploded, shattering the defensive field like ten thousand fragile pieces of glass.

John Marker disintegrated.

I wanted to puke. I wanted to scream. Instead, I found myself giving an order.

"Charge!" I yelled with rage and fury, then ran out in front of the entire unit firing everything I had, my rifle in one hand, my pistol in the other. Concussion grenades rolled across the deck, dangerously close, blowing automatons into tiny pieces. Marines swept all around me, past me. I saw one man get his arms ripped off by a robot. It was two minutes of hand-to-hand fury.

In the end, the galleria was ours, and the evil, the golden devils, were gone.

I pulled off my EVA helmet, hyperventilating, and then vomited. A second later I pulled my helmet back on as a low-band radio signal, likely blocked previously by the energy field, came through.

"This is Captain Dobrina Kierkopf of the Lightship *Impulse II*, calling Union marine units in our galleria. Are you receiving me?" came a scratchy voice. I clicked on my com and switched to low-band.

"Aye, Captain Kierkopf. This is Captain Cochrane of *Defiant*. We're receiving you loud and clear."

We swarmed up the galleria to near the Historian's quarters. The toasters had reinforced the bulkhead and basically built a wall of something like concrete around the doors. Whatever it was, it went from floor to ceiling. We tried laying grenades right on it and detonating them, but we got nowhere. It was impervious to grenades, coil rifles, anything we had, like it was indestructible. Analysis showed it was made of some high-tech carbon nanotube material.

Five minutes later a group of Carinthian marines, led by Captain Dobrina Kierkopf, came scrambling down the galleria from the bridge side.

"Sorry we're late to the party," she said. "Once you knocked that field down, it shattered on our side as well. We were able to get down the lifter shaft and take out our unwanted guests."

"How many do you think are in there?" I asked, nodding toward the concrete material.

"No telling," she replied. "We kind of lost count of how many we destroyed."

"How long have you been fighting here?" I asked.

"Most of three days. Mostly hand-to-hand. That mining colony has advanced gravity weapons. Those automatons broke through to our landing deck the first day and set up a beachhead, all while a gravity beam was hauling us down to the surface. They wanted the Historian's quarters, the yacht, and we couldn't hold them off. I ordered everyone we had left up to the forward decks, behind the bulkhead protecting officer country and the conning tower. We were able to stabilize the Hoagland Field inside the ship and cut off their advance, but we've been just holding our own while they set up shop here. Hard to tell what they're up to, but they certainly want the yacht intact at a minimum, maybe all of *Impulse II*," she said.

"That won't happen," I said confidently. She smiled just slightly at my bravado.

"I've got my engineers working on extending our Hoagland Field around the whole ship again. They told me twenty minutes, but that was twenty minutes ago," Dobrina said, checking her watch. At that I got a chime on my com.

"Hold on," I said, then switched on the longwave channel to Layton on *Defiant*. "What's your status, Mr. Layton?"

"Situation is worsening, sir. We're unable to pick off all of the robots coming out of that mine shaft. If I were guessing, I'd say it was a fricking factory," he said. Dobrina took a separate call from her engineers. I listened in as they reported that the full Hoagland Field was going up now.

"Can you scan *Impulse II* and confirm her field is operating fully and protecting the ship and our shuttles?" I asked Layton. It was Karina's voice that came on the line and answered.

"I can confirm, sir. According to longscope readings, *Impulse II* has a fully functioning Hoagland Field," she said.

"Layton," I said into the com, "how many robots advancing on our position?"

"Hundreds, sir," he said, disconsolate. "Too many to take out individually. And there's another complication. They're hitting us with a gravity beam as well, trying to bring us down to the surface. And it's all coming right out of that mine shaft."

"Status of that situation?" I said, concerned about *Defiant*.

"We're holding our own but losing ground a bit at a time, sir," Layton said.

"That's just like us," said Dobrina. "They wear you down."

I had to make a decision. I looked back to Dobrina. "Did you try using atomic weapons on the mining colony?" She shook her head.

"We never got the chance. The goddamned Historian cut off our weapons and tactical systems," she said, fury in her eyes. I turned back to my conversation with Layton.

"What's our lowest-yield atomic?" I asked Layton.

"Twenty kilotons, sir."

"Effective range?"

"For full destruction? About 1.6 kilometers, sir."

"How far from us to the mine entrance?"

"Just over two clicks. Pretty damn close," he said.

"Twenty-kiloton warhead delivered dead-center in that mine shaft. You have two minutes, Commander Layton," I said.

"Aye, sir," Layton said, then cut me off to get to his duties. Since our weapons systems were operative, I could at least assume that Gracel was still loyal to the Union. For the moment.

"That's too close," said Dobrina.

"I know," I said. We had too few choices. The field would protect us from the blast, but the land area around *Impulse II* could be devastated, making it impossible for us to get her off the ground again. What was certain was that as long as those gravity weapons were working, neither of our ships were going anywhere.

"Get your crew locked down," I said to her. She nodded acknowledgment and started to move. I stopped her with a hand on the arm.

"We lost John Marker," I said. She looked sad at that.

"I've lost a lot of good men and women in the last three days," she replied. Then I let her go. I turned back to my marines.

"Prep for atomic detonation. Follow all safety protocols," I ordered. We scrambled back down the galleria, hunkered down near the rear bulkhead, and waited.

I watched the warhead come down from *Defiant* on my watch's tiny display screen. We called them watches, but really they were multifunctional coms, environmental trackers, and remote devices. I could even set a grenade charge with mine. Command-level clearance, of course. Babayan huddled close to me, watching the warhead descend on her own watch display. We were set in place behind the bulkhead wall, where we had originally come into the galleria.

"Ten seconds," I called to the marines. "Detonation protocol." At that they all tucked their heads in close to their chests as best they could. Babayan and I kept watching the displays.

The detonation was too bright for the small display to track. It tried to break down the flash by using darkening shades of contrast. Eventually it just gave up, and the display went blank.

Even through the active Hoagland Field, the ground beneath *Impulse II* shook and rattled. We were rocked for several seconds—so severely, in fact, that I thought we might end up sinking into the ground, which would make getting spaceborne again a nearly impossible task. Lightships were meant to function in space, not on planets.

Eventually the shaking stopped. I ordered five squads out to clean up any surviving robots. The rest of us made a break for the Historian's yacht again.

"Report, Layton," I demanded over the longwave as we ran.

"We got 'em, sir. Direct hit. All gravity-suppressing fields are de-activated. *Defiant* is free."

"Good work, George. Keep scanning the rubble for any signs of activity. Alert me immediately if you see anything not human moving down there. We're going to get *Impulse* off this rock, then we'll all be going home," I said.

"Aye, sir," he acknowledged.

When we got to the Historian's quarters, which contained the yacht, nothing had changed. The impenetrable wall of carbon nano-tubes was still intact. Captain Kierkopf arrived presently.

"They're still in there," I said.

"Yes," she replied, "along with that goddamned Historian." Her hands went to her hips in a familiar gesture I'd seen many times.

"Do you think they captured him, or was he disloyal?" I asked.

"A traitor," she snapped. "They never would've gotten through our defenses if he hadn't shut down the Hoagland Field. Luckily, I had my own safety protocols installed last year, after Carinthia. I'll never trust a Historian again, and that goes for your friend Serosian."

I shook my head. "He's not my friend anymore. At any rate, you won't find me defending the Order. They clearly have their own agenda," I said. She sighed.

"Yes, as you warned me almost two years ago. I should have lis-tened to you then." She stood there, looking at me. I wanted to allow her to vent her anger, but there were pressing items on the agenda.

"Can you get *Impulse* off the ground?" I asked. She nodded.

"My engineers say so, even with that hole you blew in my hull," she replied, sounding annoyed.

"I was trying to help."

"That you did. I think we can be ready in thirty minutes. But what do we do about *them* in the meantime?" she asked, gesturing to the wall of nanotube goo.

"Once we're in space, you'll have to eject the yacht," I said.

"That will require us to drop our Hoagland Field. It will also eliminate our redundant drive backups."

"*Defiant* will cover you," I insisted. She pursed her lips at that, thinking.

"I guess I have no other choice." I cocked my head at her.

"I guess you don't."

"One other request. I lost a lot of people in the battle. Can I borrow some of your marines as backfill?" she asked.

"I can spare five squads," I replied. Twenty-five of my original crew of ninety-six. And I realized I didn't even know how many we'd lost in battle yet.

"Thank you, Captain." She nodded an acknowledgment to me and then to Babayan, and then she was gone back to her bridge. I turned my attention to my XO.

"Five squads, as I promised. Get the rest to scramble back to the shuttles and then up to *Defiant*, posthaste," I said.

"Sir, we're down a pilot," Babayan said. I stopped for a moment, thinking about that and the shot I saw Verhunce take to the chest while protecting me.

"Is Corporal Verhunce dead?" I asked. Babayan looked at me with more than a bit of concern in her eyes.

"If she's going to live, we have to get her to intensive care on *Defiant* as fast as we can," she stated.

"Go," I said. "I'll fly my own shuttle back."

"Aye, sir." And like that she was gone, yelling at squad teams to assemble and report to Dobrina's marine captain for temporary reassignment. As I watched her go, I realized how lucky I was. I'd had so many good people in my crews the last few years, but now one of them was gone. I walked back to the spot where John Marker had broken the robots' energy barrier. There was no trace of him, not even a spot on the floor.

Good people indeed. But now one fewer than before.

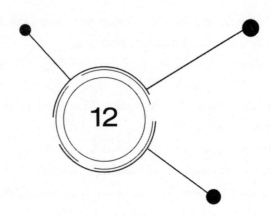

12

True to her word, Captain Kierkopf had *Impulse II* spaceborne again in thirty minutes. We shadowed her from above, five clicks over her all the way up to a safe orbit. Once she seemingly had her space legs again, I went to Babayan.

"Sitrep, XO," I demanded. She snapped around to me quickly to answer.

"*Impulse II* is operational, sir. Not sure if she's battle-ready, but all her systems that were under control of the Historian have been bypassed, and she now has weapons, propulsion, and full com available again. She reports that the automatons and the Historian believed to be inside the yacht have been isolated by an internal Hoagland security field," she said.

"So she's ready to eject the yacht with the command override?"

"Captain Kierkopf reports ready, sir."

"Good." I'd deployed my shuttles and gunships with ample missiles and torpedoes to deal with any threat from the yacht. The yacht itself was a powerful ship-within-a-ship, but it was not impregnable.

Dobrina's insistence on built-in safeguards around the Historians and their activities were about to pay off big time.

"Order our gunships into close proximity range of *Impulse II*. Remember that when she initially drops the yacht, it will still be protected under *Impulse*'s Hoagland Field. Once they cut the field, all bets are off, and I want a clean kill," I said.

"Aye, sir," said Babayan. I looked to the weapons console, where John Marker should be. It was empty.

"Commander Layton," I said. He popped to his feet at the helm.

"Here, sir."

"Take the weapons station. I'll have a job for you," I said. He looked across the bridge rather sadly, then took the empty station and brought her online.

Lena Babayan came up behind me. "Covering your bases, sir?" she asked. I turned to her.

"I trust the gunships to do the job, but I don't trust those fucking robots or Historians," I said. Babayan looked to the empty Historian's station.

"And Gracel?" she asked. I turned my attention to the main view display.

"Caution is advised, XO."

"Understood, sir." That meant our resident Historian would be under constant surveillance and given a discreet escort. I'd already determined my answer if she complained: her continued presence on my ship was a privilege, not a right.

Dobrina signaled her readiness to eject the yacht fifteen minutes later. I ordered my shuttles and gunships into close proximity range to blast the Historian's ship, then went up to Layton at the weapons console.

"George, the coil cannon arrays have an enhanced frequency disruptor capability. This will allow us to punch holes in any defensive field the yacht might put up so that our missile warheads can penetrate and destroy the ship. Once the yacht is ejected, she'll be protected under *Impulse*'s Hoagland Field for about five seconds. To disconnect the field from the yacht, *Impulse* will have to shut the field down and then refire. It will take about five to ten seconds before the contracted field is back up to protect *Impulse.* During that time I want *Defiant*'s coil cannons on that yacht. Then we let the gunships launch their missiles. I want this thing completely destroyed, and I want *Impulse* kept safe for those ten seconds. You get me, Commander?" I said.

"I do, sir," said Layton.

"You have my full confidence, George." Which was my way of saying "I think you're as good as the man who used to occupy that station." A man who was our friend and was now dead.

"Thank you, sir," said Layton. I started back to my chair, switching over to Babayan's com channel as I went.

"Tell the good captain of *Impulse* we're ready when she gives us the go sign," I said.

"Aye, sir."

I sat back in my couch, watching the main view display, a tactical grid overlaying the main visual. We were about five clicks from *Impulse II*, close enough to get there in seconds and assist if something went wrong. I watched as our gunships positioned themselves, then waited.

It only took a few more seconds for the yacht to be ejected. It reminded me of a whale birth I had seen once as a child at the New Briz Aquarium.

The yacht floated free, completely covered with the white nano-goo the automatons had used. *Impulse* began to back away on chemical impellers, and then she shut down her Hoagland Field and left the yacht—and herself—exposed.

"Now, Mr. Layton!" I ordered. Orange coil cannon fire leapt out from *Defiant*, but as I suspected, the yacht immediately activated her own defensive field. It had probably been on the whole time the yacht had been attached to *Impulse*. The coil fire hit the field, and a blaze of swirling energy danced around the ship, as if the two energy sources were fighting each other tooth and nail across the hull of the yacht. Our gunships were triangulated on the yacht's position, and they fired their missiles, which contained enough power to flatten a city, right on the ten-second mark. As the coil cannon arrays rotated and fired their second volley, the missiles began to impact the yacht's Hoagland Field. The frequency disruptor waves in the coil cannon fire did its job, punching holes in the yacht's protective field. The warheads began to explode against the field, at first to no effect, but slowly the atomic plasma broke through in places and caused secondary explosions against the vessel's hull. Soon the yacht began to drift into Drava's atmosphere, burning as she went and leaving a vapor trail.

"Got her, sir!" said Layton. "She's going down!" I checked the tactical. The yacht's Hoagland Field was gone, but the display showed her hull was still 75 percent intact. That nano-goo was something else.

I got on my tactical com quickly.

"Gunship commanders, pursue and destroy. I say again, pursue the target and destroy it," I ordered. Babayan touched her ear, close to her private com implant.

"Gunship pilots are reporting strong resistance to their weaponry," she said. "Hull still—"

"Understood, XO." I turned to Layton. "Another blast from the coil cannons, if you please, Mr. Layton," I said.

"Aye, sir," Layton said. He fired three full volleys.

"Still 60 percent hull integrity, sir," reported Babayan. I stood, angry.

"Begin pursuit," I ordered. "Prep the high-yield torpedoes. And get those gunship pilots off their asses, but continue to fire missiles at the yacht."

"Sir!" said Babayan. I watched as we pursued our prey. It took every missile the gunships carried to get the yacht's hull integrity down to 35 percent. I finally ordered them out of the way as we loaded a set of eight torpedoes with a combined yield of eight megatons. I watched as the torpedoes lanced out, waiting as they streaked inward on the slowly descending yacht. She had maintained her structural integrity despite contact with Drava's weak atmosphere. Oh, she was burning all right, just not fast enough. Then the torpedoes hit.

"Nothing bigger than two percent mass of the yacht left, sir," said Babayan. "Tactical AI is reporting it as destroyed." I slowly sat back down, and she took her station next to me. "That was much harder than it should have been," she concluded.

"You can break anything if you have a big enough hammer," I said, and she smiled just slightly at that.

"Sir!" came the overeager and stressed voice of my com officer, Ensign Lynn Layton. "Distress signal from *Impulse II*, sir. She's reporting that the gravity weapon from the mining colony has reactivated!"

"That's impossible!" said Babayan. In our rush to judgment on the yacht, we had left our damaged sister ship all alone. I jumped up again and turned to Karina at the longscope.

"Can you confirm that, Lieutenant?" I asked her. She stepped out from under the hood.

"Confirmed, sir. The gravity weapon from the surface of Drava has got *Impulse* again, and she's pulling her in," she said.

"Get us moving, Mr. Longer," I demanded. "Max sub-light speed. What's our ETA to *Impulse*?"

He turned from his station. "Six minutes, sir," he said.

"Make it three."

"Aye, sir," he said, then hesitated. "Should we wait to get the shuttles aboard?" he asked.

"Negative. They can catch up later." With that Longer put us in motion back the way we had come. Then Babayan came up next to me.

"What was that you said about needing a bigger hammer?" she said. I shook my head.

"How many of the Mass Destruction Weapons do we have aboard?" I asked.

"Two," said my XO. "Two-hundred-and-fifty-megaton yield each." I nodded.

"Get them ready."

"Both of them?"

"Both," I said.

"Aye, sir."

This wasn't going as planned. At all.

"Ensign Layton, get on the com and have Historian Gracel report to the bridge immediately," I ordered.

"Yes, sir," the young ensign replied. I looked at her. She was petite, with blonde hair and the same blue eyes as her brother. And I thought, *This is who we're fighting for.* The next generation of Lightship crew would be the ones who would take us back out, deep into the galaxy, into the realm of the old empire. *If* we could finish the business at hand, taking out the threats to the Union.

Presently Historian Gracel stepped onto the bridge.

"What can I do for you, Captain?" she asked almost casually. I motioned her over to my office and turned on the aural shield so we could speak privately. I leaned toward her from my side of the desk as she sat down.

"I assume you've been observing our combat situation?" I asked.

"Of course."

"Those automatons have *Impulse II* in their grip again. They seem relentless. I need to know how we can stop them," I said. Her answer was cryptic, as Historians often were.

"You have ample weapons at your command to stop them any-time you want, Captain," she replied. "The question is, do you have the will to use those weapons?"

I stood up then and spoke more pointedly. I didn't have time for puzzles.

"Cut the bullshit. *Impulse* is only in this situation because one of your Order betrayed her captain, who happens to be my friend. A lot of lives were lost, including John Marker's, and it's safe to say there won't be any more of *you* serving on Carinthian Lightships anytime soon. So how about you stop talking in circles and give me some in-formation I can use?"

She cocked her head to one side. "Ask your questions, Captain," she said.

"First, what *are* those things?"

She responded, her voice quiet and her tone suddenly very seri-ous. "Just what they look like. Self-perpetuating automatons, built for combat, run and controlled by a distributed AI consciousness."

"So there's no central control AI running all of this?" I asked. She shook her head.

"Not in the way you would perceive it. There is a certain amount of communication that can take place between the many distributed AIs under the right circumstances, allowing them to strategize and exchange intelligence. But each group you encounter is essentially au-tonomous from the larger whole. That way there is no single point of failure for the whole system and only individual risk is assumed," she said.

I contemplated that. "Who built them?"

She didn't hesitate. "The Founders, over four hundred thousand years ago. They were originally intended as a defensive military to keep the Founder civilization safe from outside aggressors. Until, of course, the aggression came from within."

"So they destroyed the Founders?" She shook her head.

"No. There *was* a war, but the Founders built in safeguards, and for the most part those safeguards worked. But the cost was high. So very, very high . . ." She trailed off, her eyes glistening red. It was almost as if she took it personally.

"What happened?" I asked. She swiveled her chair toward me.

"The Founders cleansed their empire of these machines as much as they could. They set up a safe zone of planets—Earth was among them—and then they left. Their culture, their arrogance, were crushed by their failure of judgment and the mass destruction of their civilization. Essentially, they went away and left us, their children, to our own devices. When we rose to the stars five hundred years ago, it was the first time humans had gone into interstellar space in one hundred and fifty millennia," she said.

"So, that's why there were no alien races ever discovered in the First Empire's sphere of influence, even at its height," I stated.

She nodded. "And the First Empire only inhabited a portion of the area the Founder civilization encompassed. We believe the Founder civilization was almost ten thousand light-years across, not even one tenth of the entire galaxy."

"And the First Empire was just one hundred light-years across, give or take." Again the nod. "You said the Founders left, but where did they go?"

"Again, we believe—and it is only a belief—that they went 'home,' to the source," she said.

"The source?"

"That's what we call the Beta Lyrae star cluster, their original home system, which is about 960 light-years from Earth."

"And you think they're there now?" I asked.

"Possibly. Or possibly they went much farther. We don't know," she said.

I thought about the situation again, now that the history lesson was over. "So how do I fix this current mess?" I asked.

"That," she said, "is up to you."

At least I had one answer. *Defiant* did have the weapons to defeat the automatons. Gracel's answers had raised almost as many questions, but they were questions for another day.

"XO, what's *Impulse*'s situation?" I asked as I retook my captain's chair.

"She's bucking the gravity waves, sir, but losing ground as you would expect. I don't know how those damned things survived the atomics," she said.

"The nano-goo," I said. "It's something else altogether. Look how much weaponry it took just to crack the yacht. Obviously the mining colony is hardened against just such an attack, and my guess is that our first nuke didn't even scrape the dust off that stuff. It did clear the robots out of the open area, but I'm betting that mine has been transformed into an automaton factory."

"But why?" asked Babayan. I thought about that for a second. There was really only one answer that made sense.

"They're building an army, XO. And you only need armies if you're planning an invasion. We've got to stop this one before it starts. That's why they wanted *Impulse II* and *Starbound*: transportation to their first target," I said. Babayan sat back in her chair. I looked over to Gracel, who had taken the Historian's station again. She sat quietly, just watching.

"Range and time to *Impulse II*, Mr. Layton." He swiveled toward me.

"Thirty seconds to intercept, sir," he replied. At that moment we were hit full-on with a gravity wave ourselves, which shook the ship until the inertial dampers kicked in and stabilized us.

"They've got us in their grip again, sir," said the XO.

"Acknowledged," I replied. "Status of our MDW, XO."

"Both cued up in our torpedo bay, sir."

"Pick one and transfer firing control to my console."

"Aye, sir," Babayan snapped. I hit the shipwide com.

"All stations, prepare for launch of atomic weapons. Full protection protocols until I give the stand down. All stations, all departments signal compliance," I said. We waited another two minutes for the compliance signals to come in. Then I got a personal com call from *Impulse II.*

"What's your strategy to get us out of this?" Dobrina asked.

"Two-hundred-and-fifty-megaton MDW atomic right down their throats," I said. There was a second of silence.

"And if that doesn't work?"

"There are other options, Captain Kierkopf," I said. "The main thing you have to do is start creating some distance from Drava as soon as you're free of the gravity field. I'll take care of the rest."

"You sound very confident," Dobrina said. I turned to look at my Historian one more time.

"I have some reason to be, Captain. Now if you don't mind, I have a two-hundred-and-fifty-megaton missile to launch."

"*Impulse* out," she replied. I turned back to Lena Babayan.

"Weapons control at your console, Captain," she said. I looked down at the weapons control, primed and targeted.

"Let's get this done," I said out loud, then pressed on the firing icon and launched hell at the mine.

The missile arced out over Drava, pinging as she went, right on target for the mining colony. It was safe to say that any structure on the surface or even several kilometers deep would be wiped out, but my fear was that the factory was much deeper in the mine than that, below a protective nano-dome.

The three minutes it took our missile to complete its arc seemed to take an eternity. Finally she hit the mine, dead on target. The tactical showed an incredible release of radiation, heat, and light, enough power to vaporize a small continent. Then we waited. Karina scanned through her displays on the main viewer—infrared, x-ray, heat signature, longscope radio wave—looking for some kind of definitive result. Five minutes later we got it.

"Detecting movement, Captain, below the dome crown. From the energy outputs . . ." she trailed off.

"Lieutenant?" I prompted her. She turned to me, a distraught look on her face.

"From the readings, Captain, it looks like there is movement and power at full operational ranges for a factory or similar facility below the dome," she said, "but I can verify that both Lightships are free of the gravity weapons."

"Thank you, Lieutenant," I said, then stood up. "Mr. Longer, get us out of here. Full impellers. Take us out to a hundred thousand clicks from Drava." I turned to my XO. "Commander Babayan, contact *Impulse II* and have her rendezvous with us at Mr. Longer's coordinates. Mr. Layton, Historian Gracel, in my office, please."

Once they were both seated in my office, I turned on the aural field again. I looked at Gracel. "I take it hitting them with one of our gravity weapons would be useless?" I asked her.

She nodded. "They have effective countermeasures in place," Gracel replied.

"So it's the torsion beam or nothing," I said.

"The what, sir?" said Layton.

"A new weapon, George. I'm authorizing you to prep it for me. Gracel here will provide you with the display icon to activate it."

"It will use most of your ship's power. You'll have to recharge your battery reserves after you fire it," Gracel said.

"How long will that take?"

"Approximately eighteen minutes to regenerate full power through the ship's interdimensional singularity."

"So we'll be vulnerable during that time," I said.

"Obviously," she replied. I looked to Layton.

"Prep the weapon, George. Don't worry about what it does; I'm the only one with firing control. Just make sure you target the magnetic core accurately," I said.

"The magnetic reactor core of the mine, sir?" Layton asked. I shook my head.

"No, George. The magnetic core of Drava itself." He stood and nodded.

"Aye, sir," he said, and then he was off to the weapons station. I looked at Gracel.

"You said I had the weapons to stop them," I said.

"And now I see that you have the will to use them, Captain," she replied. "Good luck." And with that she was back to her station, leaving me alone in my office.

We were powered up and ready to go ten minutes later. On my display console the icon for the torsion beam had appeared: a red phoenix. I tapped the icon, and the display came to life with an array of data: distance to the target, spin speed of Drava (about eleven hundred clicks an hour), an estimate of the time it would take to run the weapon and at what energy cost, etc. I chose the most rapid scenario, which would take five minutes. I wanted this over with now. Once I had queued up the weapon and set my parameters, the phoenix icon reappeared, larger and in the center of the display. I had the power of the gods in my hands. I hit the intraship com again.

"All stations, this is the captain. We are about to fire a new weapon. This weapon is very powerful, but it should be safe for us to use. I hereby order all nonessential stations to stand down to safe mode. We'll be turning off the Hoagland Field to fire the weapon, and the only technical units on full alert will be the forward coil cannon teams. Once again, all other nonessential systems are to stand down in safe mode. This is the captain; it is so ordered." I looked to Gracel for any further insight, but she remained a blank stone wall. I felt strange leaving the ship essentially defenseless in such a recent war zone with the enemy still active, so I added one more order before signing off. "All stations maintain standard radiation protocols during the weapon engagement," I said. I looked back to Gracel again after shutting off the com.

"Not necessary, Captain. The weapon produces no radiation," she said.

"Thank you, Historian. But those automatons are still active, and I simply felt . . . better safe than sorry." Then I turned my attention to Babayan. "A ten-second countdown, if you please, XO."

"Aye, sir, ten-second countdown." She turned on the intraship com and began the count. When she hit the mark, I pressed the icon on my display and activated the torsion beam.

The effect was odd. I felt a bit of dizziness, but it passed in a second. There was no beam to see in visible light, so I asked Karina to switch to infrared. Then we could see the beam spinning and swirling, resembling a DNA strand as it swept out of our coil cannon arrays and streamed toward Drava.

"Close-up on Drava, Lieutenant Feilberg," I said. Karina quickly switched to a visible-light close-up display of the moon. I could see its spin rate accelerating as the torsion waves penetrated Drava's surface and impacted the moon's magnetic core. It turned ever faster, second by second, like a child's toy top spinning out of control. The pressures exerted increased exponentially. At the three-minute mark, the helpless moon started to break up, large chunks of its surface breaking off and floating into space as the power tearing it apart grew stronger than the gravity holding it together. Seconds later it was moving so fast that its surface started to glow a bright red-orange, which grew darker as the seconds passed. As this continued, the bridge stayed silent. I wanted to swallow, but my mouth was dry as a desert. *Dry as Drava*, I thought. Then the beam shut off as it hit the five-minute mark. Slowly Drava's spin rate started to decline. What was left was billions of rocks a fraction of the size of the original moon. In the center glowed the molten magnetic core, the only thing left of the moon, surrounded by a massive cloud of dust and rocks dispersed over ten times the area of where Drava had originally been.

"Now I am become death, the destroyer of worlds," I said quietly. It was probable only Babayan heard. I felt strangely empty at what I had just witnessed, but I was confident that the outcome was a worthy one.

"Order stand down from all extreme conditions, XO. Plot a course to the jump point, and make sure we stay close to *Impulse* all the way," I said.

"Aye, sir, but where are we headed next?" I shrugged my shoulders.

"The nearest Union system with repair facilities, Commander," I said.

"That would be back to Pendax, sir. A twelve-hour ride in traverse space by our latest estimates," she said. I looked at my watch.

"Announce that a wake is to be held in all departments to honor our dead. Day shift personnel first, starting at 2000 hours, then the other shifts as they come off duty. Have the command briefing room prepped for the bridge crews. Encourage them to bring remembrances of their lost comrades," I said.

"Aye, sir," Babayan responded. With that we both stood, and I walked off the bridge to retreat to my stateroom.

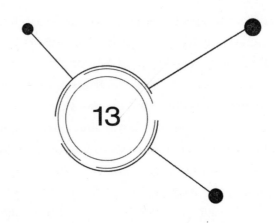

Back to Pendax

Going through John Marker's things was difficult. As captain of *Defiant* I could have had someone else do it, but it felt right to do it myself, and I wanted company. I asked George Layton to join me after he got off shift at 1800.

We went through Marker's things mostly in silence. I found his service medals and awards, things we could display at the wake. Layton, his best friend on the ship, found his stash of aged scotches.

"Should we bring these?" he asked me.

"Of course," I said. "I'm pretty sure he'd want us to share it on an occasion like this." Layton sat down on Marker's bed, staring at the bottle collection.

"I can't believe this is all we have left of him. Not even a body," he said. I brought over a pair of glasses from the bookcase and cracked one of the bottles, pouring one glass each for Layton and me, then handed Layton his glass. He took it without really moving his gaze, almost like he was in shock.

"I believe the unofficial marine motto at times like this is, 'May we fare as well when we die,'" I said, then raised my glass.

"May we fare as well when we die," responded Layton. We clinked glasses and drank. The scotch was hot in my throat and bitter, much like I felt. I looked at the table: three scotch bottles and half a dozen military awards. The sum of a man's life.

"Is this enough for a proper memorial?" I asked. It didn't seem so. Layton looked at the paltry assortment on the table.

"Wait. There's one more thing," he said. He got up and went to Marker's small closet, shuffling through the clothes until he pulled out an all-black rugby shirt with Marker's name and the number three on the back.

"He wore this when he played in the Rugby Sevens Grand National Final. New Zee versus New Queens. He was an eighteen-year-old amateur. Had a promising career if he'd wanted to go pro, but he gave it up to enlist in the Union Navy," Layton said. That struck a chord.

"Just like me. Only my game was soccer. All this time and I never knew that about him," I said. I wanted to pour another shot of the scotch, but Layton handed me the jersey instead. I looked at it closely.

"It still has grass stains on it," I said. Layton nodded.

"He never washed it. Claimed he never would. He said the ground at National Stadium was holy." He was right about that. I had never been lucky enough to play there, but John had.

I said, "Bring it, George. It's something everyone deserves to see."

With that we started to pack up. Layton promised to take the items to the briefing room, where Lena was going to set up a display. I thanked him, then headed off toward the lifter. My next stop was the sickbay.

I entered the sickbay, buried in the depths of *Defiant*, and nodded to the doctor on duty, who nodded back. His name was Samkange, and he was a large man of African descent. I wondered absently how he operated with such big hands. Rumors were he was the most skilled surgeon aboard.

"Yes, Captain, may I help you?" Dr. Samkange asked.

"Doctor, thank you. I'm looking for Corporal Verhunce. Is she able to speak?" I asked. He nodded.

"She's doing well, sir. Recovering nicely. And fully able to express her opinions," he said. "Bay Five." I smiled and thanked him, then started down the hall.

"Captain," said Samkange. I stopped and turned back.

"Is there something else, Doctor?"

"Yes, sir. Her injuries were significant, at least in the area she was hit. Much of her rib cage was disintegrated, and her left breast will have to be regenerated," he said.

"That is severe," I said. "What can we do for her?"

"Well, we're keeping her lightly sedated so that the regeneration process can do its magic, but I'm afraid with that bone damage . . ."

"Just spill it, Doctor," I said. He sighed.

"It's just that she won't be able to serve in the Union Marines as a combat officer with an injury like that, I'm sorry to say. I can't certify her," he said.

"Ah," I replied. "I see. So what *can* she do?"

"Administrative work. Strategy and tactics. She can even teach if she wants to, but she can't fight again," said Dr. Samkange.

"That will probably hurt her worse than the rifle shot," I said.

"I understand." I thought about the situation for a second.

"Can she fly?" I asked.

"What?"

"Can she fly a shuttle?"

The doctor eyed me, stuck between what I figured was probably the truth and loyalty to his captain.

"I could approve that level of duty status. But if she gets transferred or reexamined by another doctor, I can guarantee they'll ground her, sir," he said.

"Thank you for that, Doctor," I said, then made my way down the hall to Bay Five. I knocked on the door.

"May I come in, Corporal?" I asked. Verhunce tried to sit up, and a maze of tubes and wires descending from the ceiling moved with her. She looked very good, I decided, for a woman who had been shot in the chest by a killer robot while protecting me. She scrambled to find a more dignified pose.

"Sir," she said.

"At ease, Corporal. May I sit with you?"

"Of course, sir," she said. I sat in a chair next to the bed.

"Well, you're getting the full treatment, aren't you? Please tell me you're not in any pain?"

"No, sir. They keep me plied with the best stuff they have."

"That's good," I said. Then there was an awkward silence. "I just wanted to thank you for protecting me and apologize for you having to take that laser shot."

"No need to apologize, sir. Just doing my duty." I smiled. Marines always said that.

"I know you were, but protecting me was out of the ordinary. You took a shot for me, and I can never repay that," I said.

"It's done, sir. Don't give it a second thought," Verhunce said. "I'm just anxious to get back in the fray, sir."

I cleared my throat. "About that—"

"Doc says I'll be good to go in a week, sir."

"That's true, Corporal. But it's not that simple." She looked away from me.

"Don't take me off active duty, sir," she said, her voice quavering and going quiet. It was a statement, not a plea of any kind.

"Corporal, normally in these situations—"

"Sir, I'm asking you, as a woman who saved your life—"

"Wait," I said, holding my hand up to stop her. I took a deep breath before continuing. "Normally in this situation you would be grounded from active duty and we would have to drop you at the next official Union Navy outpost. But this isn't normal. I came in here to tell you that I've negotiated limited field duty terms with the doctor. You'll stay active as my shuttle pilot, but no more hand-to-hand stuff," I said.

"So I can still fly?"

"Yes."

"And shoot the coil cannons?"

I smiled. "If required."

"And I can still carry a coil rifle?"

I nodded. "But only in situations where you'd be guarding the shuttle. Do you understand these limitations, Corporal?" She smiled and nodded affirmative.

"I do, sir," she said. I stood.

"Then when you get out of here, I'm ordering you to do a week of physical therapy before I return you to limited duty," I said.

"Thank you, sir!" she replied. There was a moment's hesitation. "Sir, about the battle—how many did we lose?"

"Twelve dead, nine more injured. But . . . one of the dead was John Marker." I watched as all of her health monitors started to rise out of the safety zone.

"I'm sorry to hear that, sir," Verhunce said, looking away from me again. "He was . . . a great Marine commander."

"He was," I agreed. "Did you . . ." I wanted to be delicate here, "Did you know him well?" She looked up at me again and smiled.

"Not that well, sir. He . . . he wasn't my type." I smiled back, knowing exactly what she meant.

"I get you, Corporal," I said. At that the doctor came in, no doubt having been alerted by the spike in her vital signs. After some brief checking, he reclined her bed flat and pumped up her pain meds to allow the medical machines to do their work. Her eyelids started to droop, and I knew I would lose her soon. The doctor stepped out of the room again, and I went up to her and kissed her on the forehead before I left.

"Thank you for saving my life, Corporal," I said.

"You're welcome, Captain," she said, then drifted off to sleep.

As I left I stopped to shake the doctor's hand. "Thank you, Dr. Samkange," I said. "I owe you one." He smiled as we walked back to the doctor's station.

"Yes, sir, I believe you do," he said.

The command deck briefing room was decked out to honor John Marker. Lena Babayan had done an excellent job. Marker's Marine portrait was hanging on the far wall with the rugby shirt underneath, and a large table had been set up to display his medals. Many people had dropped off personal mementos on the display table. His scotch was also set out with hors d'oeuvres and finger food from the galley. It was a nice layout, and well attended. Almost all of the first shift bridge crew was there, along with many of his marine comrades. Karina came up to me and took me by the arm.

"Should the captain make a speech?" she asked.

I looked around the room. "He should, but he should also show leadership." I went over to the untouched scotch at the table and poured it into one of the glasses, then another and another. Karina started pouring as well until everyone in the room had a glass. I took a fork and tapped on my glass for attention. I looked around the room at the young faces, realizing that in many ways, I had their lives in my hands. Then I began.

"John Marker was a friend of mine for more than three years. I took my Marine training with him at the Lightship Academy and quickly decided that I would stay in the officer's corps." There was a small laugh at that. "He saved my ass aboard *Impulse*, and I don't know how many other times. What he did for all of us, sacrificing himself, was something only true heroes do. John Marker was a true Quantar hero, and I will always be grateful to have known him . . . and to call him my friend." At that I could feel the water forming in my eyes, and I couldn't stop it, so I decided not to. I raised my glass.

"To John," I said in a weak and cracking voice.

"To John," the room replied. And then we drank, and the room grew silent. I felt the tears run down my cheeks, but I did nothing to stop them. Neither did anyone else. The silence lasted for a long while, broken only by the occasional sob. Then I spoke again, my voice breaking.

"Enjoy this time. Tell your stories about him. And by all means, finish his scotch," I said, then raised my glass one more time. At that Karina came up to me, took my glass, and set it on the table.

"Let's go home," she whispered in my ear, "and let them celebrate him." I nodded and led her by the hand out the door to the lifter, wiping my eyes free of tears.

My meditations didn't help at all this time. Karina slept quietly beside me, but I tossed and turned for half the duration of my allotted sleeping period. I was restless, both over the heavy loss of my friend and for being stuck in interdimensional space while god-knows-what transpired in the greater universe around me. I felt helpless, powerless, and then the anxiety came. The doctors had diagnosed me with posttraumatic stress disorder after I'd killed—there was no other way to put it—more than thirty thousand people on board the Imperial dreadnoughts while fighting at Levant, Pendax, Carinthia . . .

I washed with warm water in our sink basin, then wiped my face dry and soaked up the sweat around my neck. I opened the medicine drawer and once again had my standoff with the medications the doctors had given me. This time I opened a bottle and took two pills in my hand, clutching them tightly as if they were precious jewels.

Karina's soft and loving hands covering my own stopped me. "I've watched you fight taking this medication for months now, Peter. If this was the solution for you, you would have taken that route long ago," she said. Slowly my hand opened, revealing the two yellow pills I had been holding onto so tightly. She took them and put them back into the bottle, leading me by my free hand back to our bed, where her gentle breathing and soothing touch released a heavy weight off my chest. I drifted off in her arms, surrounded by love, light, and visions of my friend as I would forever remember him: young, strong, and vital.

And with my sleep finally came peace.

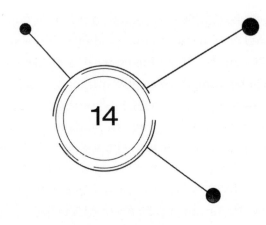

At Pendax

After a few hours of sleep I was back up and on the bridge with Karina and the first-shift day crew. We were due to come out of traverse space and back into our own reality in just a few minutes' time.

"XO," I called to Lena Babayan. She came up to stand next to me at my bridge console.

"Sir," she said, sounding eager and ready to go.

"We need to be prepared for any eventuality when we drop in at Pendax. If Zander kept to his schedule, he should be docked for resupply at High Station Pendax, but we're going to have to push him out to get *Impulse II* into the repair dock as fast as possible," I said.

"You're expecting more trouble, sir?" I nodded.

"Much more, XO. This has the feel of an endgame move by the Imperial forces. Trying to take down not one but two Lightships at Skondar, building a ground army of robot fighters. On the surface, it couldn't be worse circumstances," I said honestly.

"Do you think they're attacking core Union worlds, sir?" she asked. I nodded again.

"I would; try and create as much destabilization as possible, make us question our every move. Our first job will be to get *Impulse* to the repair dock. After that, our options are wide open, and I want us to be ready to move," I said.

"Possible direct jump, sir?" Babayan asked.

"You read my mind. Prep us now, XO. We could have to move fast."

"Aye, sir." I turned my attention to George Layton, walking up until I was standing over his helm station, looking down at him from the railing. He turned and looked up at me.

"Ready to go, George?" I asked.

"Anytime, sir. Just give the orders," he said. I smiled and gestured toward his console.

"Keep the steering wheel hot. I want us ready for action the moment we're in normal space again."

"Aye, sir," he said. My next stop was Propulsion.

"Duane, make sure we hit the ground running. Full impellers the moment we hit normal space," I said.

"Aye, sir. Should I prep the hybrid drive as well, sir?" Longer asked. The hybrid drive, a mix of chemical impellers and a sub-light hyperdimensional drive, was still occasionally unstable, but it had saved our bacon more than once. It was reliable enough for my tastes.

"As you said, Mr. Longer," I replied.

My last stop was the longscope and my wife. "Preparations, Lieutenant?"

"Ready and able, sir," she replied with a snap to her voice.

"I'll want a tactical assessment and longwave coms in place when we arrive at Pendax," I said. She nodded affirmative.

"Understood and prepared, sir," she said. I gave her a smile and walked away, past the empty Historian's station. One more call to make. The ship's clock showed we had twenty-two minutes until the drop out of traverse space, if Lieutenant Arasan at the navigation station was correct in his estimates, and he usually was. I went into my office and activated the aural shield before calling down to Gracel.

"Sitting this one out, Historian?" I asked when she answered my call chime.

"On the contrary, Captain. I'll be on the bridge presently," she said.

"Any thoughts on what we might expect when we arrive?" I queried.

"I can't give you any specifics, Captain, because I don't have them. But I can monitor the level of chatter along the ansible networks while we're in traverse space. I will only characterize it by saying it is extremely active," Gracel said.

"Thank you, Historian," I replied, then switched our com link off. I stood and made my way to my station, observing each of my junior officers in turn one more time as they conducted their business. Finally I turned to Babayan.

"Are we ready, XO?"

"Ready, Captain." I sat in my chair.

"Then let's get this show on the road."

We jumped back out of traverse space precisely on time and at the standard Pendax jump space coordinates. *Defiant* came under almost immediate fire, as did *Impulse II*, which followed us out by only a few seconds. Luckily for both of us, by standard protocol we had our Hoagland Fields activated until we cleared the jump space area.

The attackers were unmanned Imperial HuKs of varying sizes and displacement, lined up in a staggered picket formation at the jump point.

"XO, call battle stations!" I declared from my safety couch.

"Aye, sir!" Babayan replied, then took to the shipwide com to make her call. I turned to Karina.

"Longscope officer, get me a view of *Vanguard*. I need to know how many ships we're facing in-system and what displacement," I said.

"Aye, sir," she replied. I looked over at the weapons station. I was missing John Marker already.

"Propulsion, full reverse impellers. Give us some distance from those HuKs," I said to Duane Longer. Instead of streaking in-system as originally planned, we now had to change tactics and back away from the HuKs. Longer gave an "Aye, sir" in response, and I moved on to my helmsman. "Mr. Layton, plot us a course out of this battle-field."

"Where to, sir?" asked Layton.

"Inbound, toward the star and High Station Pendax. I don't want to fight these HuKs out here. Let's use our speed to outrun them."

"What about *Impulse*, sir?" asked Layton. I checked her out on the local tactical display. Dobrina was firing missile volleys every few seconds.

"She's fit enough to fight. Pass your best course on to them and tell them to follow us in."

"Aye, sir," Layton said. I turned back to Babayan.

"XO," I said, "take the weapons station."

"Aye, sir," she said, and she made her way without hesitating to the weapons console.

"Longscope officer, report," I demanded of my wife.

"Transferring tactical situation to the main display, sir," Karina said. Then she stepped out from under the hood and began narrating as she flipped through her visuals. "There are six HuKs in the general vicinity of the jump point, sir. We are bigger, faster, and better trimmed than any of them by a long way. Against two Lightships, it's a terrible mismatch."

"Irrelevant, since I am ordering us to ignore them and proceed in-system," I snapped at her.

"Yes, sir," she replied, obviously trying to ignore my tone. "From a tactical standpoint, they were probably left here to confront any incoming Wasp reinforcements, sir."

"What's the tactical situation near High Station and *Vanguard*?" I asked. She switched displays to go in-system by about a dozen AUs. High Station Pendax and the Lightship *Vanguard* appeared on the display.

"They're being kept busy by about a dozen automated ships, sir. Eight HuKs with heavier weaponry and at least four suicide drones, although I can see enough evidence in the battle debris to account for at least two more destroyed drones. They're facing off against *Vanguard* and three Wasp frigates, sir, as well as the High Station," Karina said.

"That's a containing force, not an attacking one, unless they didn't expect *Vanguard* to be here, which from their recent exhibitions I highly doubt. Are the High Station's armaments up and running yet?" I asked my wife. Karina nodded.

"To a degree. Hoagland Field is active, coil cannon arrays are in use, but no torpedoes or defensive missiles installed yet, sir," she said.

"And no dreadnoughts?"

"None sighted in-system as yet, sir," she concluded.

"Thank you, Lieutenant."

"What's their tactic?" It was Babayan, calling in on the private command com line.

"Most likely to take out the High Station, make resupply of Sandosa more difficult from here. Probably just a chance that *Defiant*, *Impulse*, and *Vanguard* all showed up at once," I said. But now they were heavily outgunned and likely to change strategy.

"Keep your eyes glued to your console, 'scopeman," I said to Karina. "Any hint of dreadnought-sized displacement, and I want to know immediately."

"Aye, sir," responded Karina.

"Helmsman, take us into the battlefield. Propulsion, best estimate of our arrival time?" I asked Longer.

"Eleven minutes and fifteen seconds at best speed, sir," Longer replied.

I sat back in my chair and said, loud enough for all of the bridge to hear, "Let's hope Captain Zander leaves us something to blast." There were nervous chuckles at that, but inside I was worried—not at what we faced, but at what might come now that the battlefield had tilted so strongly in our favor.

I had Layton "slam on the brakes"—a metaphor for our extreme deceleration—three minutes from the battlefield. We came about and turned in on the HuKs buzzing High Station Pendax. *Impulse* followed our line, though she couldn't match our maneuvers or speed, needing the repairs that she did. On her trail were the remaining six HuKs, who had given up their picket line defense of the jump point and were pursuing, hoping to at least catch the wounded *Impulse II*. *Vanguard* was dug in at the High Station, pounding away at the HuKs with her pulse coil cannons as they swept past. I was almost embarrassed at how much firepower I had at my disposal, even if most of it was massive overkill against such light attack forces.

We had so much speed to our advantage that I relied on this as my first tactical weapon. Foregoing missiles and torpedoes, I ordered us to make a pass straight through the battlefield, broadside, firing our coil cannon arrays at will. When we were done with the maneuver two minutes later, five destroyed HuKs lay in our wake. Zander's Wasps eagerly moved in and finished off the drones. Then *Vanguard* started to move, pounding at the remaining wounded HuKs to finish them off. I had Layton turn us again, still at high speed, so we could intercept the trailing HuK flotilla. Dobrina had the same idea and was already engaging them with long-range missiles.

I pushed *Defiant* into the battlefield again, crossing between *Impulse II* and her targets, her missiles' smart warheads thankfully avoiding our path so we didn't get caught in a friendly crossfire. I had Babayan target three HuKs in a stack formation, our attack angle extreme but just acute enough to get them all. She didn't miss. When we were done, there was HuK debris everywhere. I sent a quick congratulatory signal to Dobrina for her three kills, then turned my tactical attention back to *Vanguard* and High Station Pendax. There was no need. Zander and his Wasp frigates had cleaned their zone of enemy combatants as well. The whole battle had taken seven minutes.

I ordered Longer to complete our deceleration and then went to the briefing room with Babayan to conference with the other captains.

"Good work, Captains," I said. Zander grunted.

"Good work yourself," he said. "Seems to me some of our ships have been left off the upgrade list."

"I second that," said Dobrina. Both of them were speaking from large UHD projections hovering over the conference table.

"Do either of you have a problem with me taking command of battlefield operations in this system?" I asked as I sat down. They both shook their heads.

"I don't know what we did to end up working for *you*, but it seems to be our lot," said Zander. I smiled, then started in.

"First order of business, what's the communications situation? Does the Admiralty know of this attack?" I asked.

"Likely not," said Zander. "Those HuKs jumped right on our tail, almost like they knew we were coming. The first things they took out were the longwave ansibles and the Historian network probes."

I nodded. "Which is what I would do. Pick one of your Wasps, Captain Zander, and send it through the singularity to Carinthia. Let them know about the attack and that we have Pendax secured. And I want reports on any ongoing action in other Union systems. Tell them I recommend that the entire Union Navy go to high alert status," I said.

"As you say," replied Zander. I looked up at Dobrina's image.

"Captain Kierkopf," I said. She had a tiny hint of a smirk on her face. I couldn't help myself; I still loved rattling horns with her.

"Captain Cochrane," she replied.

"Since your ship needs repairs from the battle at Drava, I think *Impulse II* should replace *Vanguard* as the primary defender of High Station Pendax. But keep a loose lock on the station. If Imperial units come back here with more firepower, we're going to need you quickly," I said. "Any estimates on how long you'll need to be in dock?"

"Well, you blew a pretty big hole in my ship. Having said that, we're fully operational with suspension fields, and I've put the damaged sections on life support until repair crews can get working. Repairing the ship's mechanical and electrical systems will be more difficult to give an estimate on, depending on what High Station Pendax has on hand," she replied.

"She's fully stocked with spares and replacements, and there's no shortage of good technicians. I'm sure you'll be back on track in hours, not days, Captain," interjected Zander.

"Thank you, Lucius," said Dobrina. The next part was going to be a tougher sell.

"Lucius," I said, looking up at Zander, "I'll need you to guard the ingress jump space in case more Imperial units come through." Zander bristled a bit at that suggestion.

"My boss won't like me straying too far from home," he said, referring of course to Admar Harrington, still ensconced in the Sandosa system.

"I understand the political situation, Captain. But the fact is that *Defiant* is faster than *Vanguard* in normal space and able to jump at will without needing interdimensional jump space to do it. If you're needed elsewhere, I want you close to jump space so you can get to the battlefield in a hurry," I said.

"Understood, Captain. And where will you be?" Zander asked. I thought about that for a second.

"Near Pendax itself. Any attack now could come from dreadnoughts equipped with the same jumping capability *Defiant* has. Now that they know where our defenses are, they could jump right over this position and attack the planet directly. We can't allow that," I said.

"We certainly can't," Dobrina agreed quickly. No doubt the attack on Carinthia was playing on her emotions. I looked to Zander for confirmation, or at least grudging agreement.

"It's the opposite of how I'd do it, but I let you have field command, so I'll have to live with it," he said.

"Thank you, Captains. Let's get that Wasp out to Carinthia and back so we can get our tactical update," I said.

"Aye," said Zander, who was looking offscreen at a console, obviously giving the order to the Wasp. I turned to Lena Babayan.

"Have Layton plot us a course inbound to the planet, and tell Longer I want best possible speed. We have the advantage for now, and I want to keep it," I said.

"Aye, sir," came her reply. Then she was up and gone to the bridge.

"I'm signing off," said Zander. "I've got to haul my scow out to jump space."

"Of course," I said with a slight bow of my head, a sign of respect to my more experienced comrade. At that I stood, looking up at Dobrina. "Was there something else, Captain?" She smiled down at me.

"I just wanted to formally thank you for your assistance at Drava," she said.

"I blew a hole in the arse of your ship." Now her smile grew deeper.

"I seem to remember a similar injury on the fencing court," she said. Now I smiled.

"I do remember that."

"You keep cutting holes in my behind. Some would say that's a pattern." My smile got wider.

"Perhaps it is," I said. Then things got silent between us. She spoke much more softly this time.

"If you were here, I'd kiss you to give you a proper thank-you." I looked down at the conference table.

"I don't think my wife or your new woman would appreciate that," I said, looking up at her again. Dobrina took a deep breath.

"I'm sure they wouldn't. Until next time then, Captain."

"Until next time," I agreed. Then I shut off the display, hoping there wouldn't be a next time.

The trek inbound to Pendax proper was uneventful, taking just over two hours. I placed us at Pendax's L2 Lagrange point, facing outward toward the jump point and High Station. Pendax's large but surprisingly light (in terms of mass) moon orbited at about four hundred and fifty thousand kilometers from Pendax itself, and we were well positioned for any incoming attack from a dreadnought—or any other vessel—that could direct-jump into the system. Trying to jump in closer than either an L1 or L2 Lagrange point would take serious balls on the part of a ship captain or some of the most precise astrogating ever seen. I was confident we were positioned well enough to defend the planet.

I took us down from battle stations to high alert status while we waited for word from Zander's Wasp or for some other action. Frankly, it was boring work, but I made sure *Defiant* was ready.

After four hours of just sitting in my captain's chair or walking from station to station reviewing things I had no business getting involved with—that was XO Babayan's job—I went to my office and activated the aural shield, then called up Zander and Dobrina on my desk display.

"I was just about to com you," said Zander. "My Wasp captain just called in. She says it's chaos out there. Imperial drones and HuKs jumping into every system. Then we scramble and they scurry back through the jump point."

"Testing our defenses, trying to draw us out," I said. Zander nodded.

"Or wear us out," said Dobrina. "Constant alerts like that will take their toll on ship crews."

"It could be one flotilla of smaller vessels doing the jumping from an uncataloged system, then jumping straight back home and into another system. The flotillas always vary in size and makeup, so there's no telling if it's a single unit or not. Smallest incursion has been three ships, the biggest fourteen," said Zander.

"How many HuKs?" I asked.

"The most they've seen is nine. Wesley has ordered all his Wasps and a good many of the local navies out to the jump points in the three systems: Quantar, Carinthia, and Levant. Each has a single Lightship defending the planet. The problem is that our Lightships can't move away from their home planets because of the threat of dreadnoughts jumping in behind them and hitting their home worlds," Zander said.

"And here we sit with three Lightships and no activity at all," Dobrina said.

"Essentially, we're immobilized by our own tactics," I said. "All of our mobile firepower is stuck in one system. What's the current Lightship distribution, Lucius?"

"Well, the three of us here, of course, *Resolution* at Levant, *Starbound* at Quantar, and *Fearless* and *Avenger* at Carinthia. *Valiant* has even been recalled from Jenarus for backup," he said. I contemplated the situation. Staying where we were was no good, but they were obviously trying to antagonize us into making the first tactical move.

"Lucius, prepare *Vanguard* to move in-system and swap positions with *Defiant*," I said.

"And then where are you off to?" This time it was Dobrina asking.

"Home," I said, "to Quantar via Carinthia. All this sitting around . . . They're obviously waiting for us to make the first move, so I'm going to make it. Levant will be the least defended system once *Defiant* has jumped. If we can force an attack there—"

"You can't guarantee that's how it will go," Dobrina said. I looked up at her image.

"You're right, I can't. But sitting here isn't doing any of us any good. So ordered. Thank you, Captains," I said, then cut off the communication.

I stepped out of my office and ordered Lena Babayan to get us moving again.

"Back to the jump point, sir?" she asked. I nodded.

"My mistake, XO. We can't just sit around and wait forever. Time to get *Defiant* into this scrap."

"Aye, sir," she said, then made the call on the shipwide com. I took my chair again, anxious to get home to Quantar, balance the scales, and hopefully force our enemies' hand.

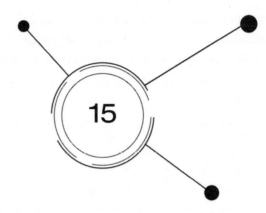

15

We cruised past High Station Pendax at a considerable speed, passing her just closely enough to wobble our tail at *Impulse II*. Repairs and replenishment of her weapons stock were ahead of schedule, and Captain Kierkopf estimated her operational ability at 85 percent. That was good enough for me. I had confidence Dobrina and Zander could defend Pendax more than adequately. It did leave our First Contact team at Sandosa exposed, but they had no real value as a strategic target just at the moment, saving the value of Admar Harrington or the Princess Janaan as hostages, which was high to me personally but minimal to the Union overall.

We made for the egress jump point space of Pendax, there to make our first transitional jump to Carinthian space, then home to Quantar, where we would join up with *Starbound* and I would fall under the command of Commodore Maclintock again. In many ways it would be a relief to turn situational command over to someone else for a while. I'd had my fill lately.

We could have used our instant jump capability to make the transition to Carinthia, but Gracel had informed me this technology could be tricky, causing us to miss our targets by considerable margins, and thus she had asked me to use it sparingly. I complied, ordering us to the jump point to make the transition, which had already been well defined. It was tricky to cut new pathways through space, where planets and star systems were always moving, and jump space allowed us to keep our bearings consistent rather than risk calculating our own new pathways from star to star.

Twenty-eight minutes from jump space, the battlefield shifted under our feet.

An alert klaxon sounded throughout the ship, echoing in my ears. "Hyperdimensional displacement, Captain, 1.3 AUs astern of our current position," reported Karina in a calm and professional manner.

"Identify," I demanded of my longscope officer.

"By mass and configuration . . . it can only be a Lightship, sir."

"We're the only Lightship that can jump without using jump space," said Babayan.

"No," I said, "there's one other."

"*Vixis*?" said Babayan.

"*Vixis*," I replied, then quickly got to my feet. "Call battle stations, XO!" Babayan made her call as I ordered us to turn back the way we had come, toward our enemy. Toward a man I had promised my wife's father, the grand duke, that I would destroy.

Prince Arin of Carinthia.

"How long until we're within firing range?" I asked Karina.

"At current speeds relative to each other's movement and inertia, about seven minutes, Captain," she said.

"Next time just give me the number, Lieutenant," I said without looking at her. She was trying to do her job, perhaps better than it needed to be done. I just needed the raw data. I wanted this man badly. I turned as Gracel entered the bridge and took her station.

"Have we engaged them yet?" she asked me.

"Not yet," I replied, then looked at the tactical clock. "In six minutes and thirty seconds." At that Gracel motioned me closer. I went to her station.

"You must be aware that Prince Arin will have many of the same weapons at his disposal that you have," she said.

"I suspected as much."

"He may also have weapons that you do not, and you may have some that he doesn't."

"Noted, Historian. Any tactical advice before we join the battle?" I said. She shook her head.

"No more than this, Captain: he wants your hide as much as you want his, and he'll do anything to win, short of suicide," Gracel said. I thought about that.

"Then we'll have to be prepared for anything," I replied, then went back to my chair and the tactical display.

"Recommendations, XO," I said. Babayan came and sat next to me.

"Highly suggest a proactive posture, Captain. Don't let him take the first shot. Use anything we can to take him out," she said.

"My thoughts exactly. Prep the weapons station for conventional, atomic, gravity, and torsion weapons. Stock the launch tubes with tactical atomic missiles and torpedoes. I want as much firepower as we have on hand ready to go by the time we engage *Vixis*," I said. I watched as Babayan went to the weapons station and keyed her tactical plan into my display. Basically it was an ever-accelerating use of weaponry. Tactical missiles first, mixed with the enhanced coil cannons with their Hoagland-Field-busting properties, then heavier-yield torpedoes, all in the first thirty seconds. I added in a push-pulse from the gravity weapons array just to throw *Vixis* off guard, followed by a volley from the anti-graviton disintegration weapon to test her Field, then rinse and repeat, escalating the yields as we hammered each other. I hit send to update Babayan's tactical plan as we hit the one-minute mark.

I took to the shipwide com.

"All hands, we are preparing to do battle with the Lightship *Vixis*, once one of ours but now under the command of the Butcher of Carinthia, Prince Arin. We will be facing an enemy unlike any that we've battled, with a ship at least as well equipped as ours, as we can assume the disloyal Historians have provided the prince with everything we have. It will be a battle to the death, if need be, and my goal is to completely destroy *Vixis*. But because of our relative balance of power—a balance of terror, really—we have no guarantee of victory. Man your stations, do your jobs, and follow your orders, and I believe we will be victorious. Captain out," I said.

"Thirty seconds, Captain. Shall I give a countdown?" That came from Karina. I smiled very slightly at her. I was putting her life on the line, too.

"No countdown, please," I said, then turned back to my primary tactical display.

"Captain," called Babayan, "they've fired early!"

"Hold stations and hold to the timing of the battle plan," I said back to her.

"Aye, sir," Babayan replied.

"What have we got incoming?"

"Tactical atomic missiles, sir, but they fired early by at least thirty seconds. Perhaps they have greater range than we have?" she said.

"Or more confidence," I replied, watching the incoming volley of ten missiles as it closed in on us.

Five seconds.

The missiles impacted our Hoagland Field, and to my horror, they didn't explode. Instead they used some improved form of the vibrational wave weapon, then imploded, leaving a hole in our field. Not large, mind you, but the detonation of an atomic weapon against our defenses . . .

A second volley hit us, then a third.

"They're cutting our field open like Swiss cheese, sir," reported Babayan.

"Fire all our missiles and torpedoes," I ordered, trying to remain calm in the center of the storm. I swiveled to face Gracel.

"Why doesn't our field close back up and protect us?" I asked her.

"Unknown at this time. Most likely scenario is that they've matched frequencies with our field. In other words, the field thinks it's a closed system, but it isn't. They're fooling our defensive AI," she said.

"XO, can we recalibrate, adjust the field frequency?"

"Aye, sir, but it will take time—up to two minutes—and we'll have to bring the whole field down to do it," said Babayan.

"That's what they want," I said. "Death by a thousand cuts or drop our shielding completely and be exposed. What's the status of our missiles?"

Babayan shook her head. "Ineffective so far. Their defensive field seems to be adjusting to the coil cannon volleys, and our atomics are detonating against her field but causing no damage, sir. Sir! *Vixis* is accelerating!"

"Evasive, Mr. Layton. Mr. Longer, engage the hybrid impeller drive, get us out of here—" I was cut off by the impact of tactical missiles against our exposed field. The nuclear energy seeped through our shielding and impacted the hull, boring holes in our sides. A second explosion rocked us again seconds later.

"Atomic impacts, numerous locations, Captain. Some of our missiles detonated in the launch tubes. There will be casualties," reported Babayan. Atomic weapons going off in our launch tubes was a disaster. Despite the hardened protections we had in place, there were going to be losses. Big losses.

"How many did we lose, XO?" I asked, not really wanting to know the answer.

"Three of our launch bays are gone, sir, full loss casualties. Their atomics detonated ours," she said. Three of eight gone—fifteen men and women. Only our internal Hoagland Field barriers had saved the ship. They were designed to do that, to separate potentially destructive weapons from the bulk of the ship and crew, but still . . . I had to do something, and quick.

"Understood, XO. Mr. Longer, prep the hybrid drive for overload," I ordered.

"What, sir?" said Longer. "That could—"

"Cause an explosion. I'm aware of the hybrid drive specs, Mr. Longer. I ordered you to get us out of here. A short-range jump via the hybrid drive might just do the trick," I said. An overload, flooding the system with antiprotons, would cause the drive to explode.

"We'll lose the drive until it can be repaired," warned Longer.

"You've got twenty seconds to execute, Lieutenant." I watched as *Vixis* launched another round of implosion missiles, followed by high-yield atomic torpedoes. "Pick off as many of those as you can, XO," I ordered.

"Even the battle AI can't guarantee we'll get 100 percent of them, sir," she replied.

"You have your orders, XO. Mr. Longer, are you ready?"

He looked up at me. "Ready, sir."

"On my command," I said. When the countdown clock got to ten seconds, there were still twelve implosion missiles and half a dozen high-yield atomics incoming. I made eye contact with Longer, who looked up nervously at me, his hand hovering over the hybrid drive button, ready to flood the system. At five seconds he was sweating. At three seconds I gave the order.

The ship bucked and shook as the hybrid drive overloaded and exploded, sending a shockwave out of our impeller thrusters, a shockwave that moved us a considerable distance from our previous position in less than a second. The ship was rattled and the inertial dampers had to work overtime, but in the end we were still there, still together, and *Vixis*'s missiles missed us. I figured I'd bought us maybe twenty minutes.

"Damage!" I demanded.

"Hybrid drive is gone, Hoagland Field is down, and the chemical impellers are gone, sir. But we still have the sub-light HD drive, sir," said Longer. The sub-light HD drive was much faster than the chemical impellers we had in normal space anyway. It operated on an ancient technology called an EmDrive that used electromagnetism as a propulsion mechanism, essentially bouncing microwaves back and forth inside an enclosed vacuum chamber to generate thrust. Now that we had access to the wonders of higher dimensional energy, the drive was robust to say the least.

"Bring us about, Helm. Close on our target. What's our distance, Longscope officer?"

"They're 111,550 kilometers out, sir," Karina said.

"Too far for missiles or coil cannons. XO," I called down to Babayan, "prep the gravity weapons and load them onto my display and refire that goddamned Hoagland Field." The reset of the field would take us a few seconds, but it would come back up fully functional. *Vixis* would have to punch holes in us all over again.

Presently we were accelerating toward our enemy. I sat back down in my chair, and the gravity weapons display icon came up on my console. I activated the system and moved through to the gravity beam option. The gravity beam would act like a lance in a joust, pushing a highly concentrated beam of gravitons against the defensive field of *Vixis*, pushing her off course and hopefully leaving her vulnerable to other types of attack.

"Captain, *Impulse II* is inbound to the battlefield, sir," said Karina from her longscope station. That was unwelcome news.

"I don't have time for this," I said, turning to Ensign Lynne Layton at the communications station. "Send a longwave and order *Impulse* back to her station. Her job is to defend High Station Pendax.

Inform her that you are acting with my authority, and copy Captain Zander as well. We could be facing a fleet of dreadnoughts at any moment, and our primary responsibilities haven't changed. Make that clear," I said angrily.

"Aye, sir," she replied, and she turned back to her station to send the messages. I went back to my console, called up the anti-graviton plasma weapon, and powered it up. We'd need to get inside of twenty thousand clicks to use the gravity weapon, but after that we'd be well inside the safe range to use the plasma weapon. My hope was that multiple hits by such powerful weapons would overload *Vixis*'s defensive fields. I might just get lucky, if I added one more element to the mix.

"XO, do we have any frequency-modulating warheads available?" I asked. She quickly checked her inventory.

"We have six left, sir. But they weren't effective during the first skirmish, and neither was the coil cannon modulator," Babayan said. I looked to the ever-placid Gracel at her station, then walked up to her.

"If we use the frequency-modulating warheads after the push-pulse weapon, and then fire the anti-graviton plasma . . ."

"I see your strategy, Captain. It just might work. But you'll have to get close to use the push-pulse cannon and the missiles, and it will take considerable time to power down the cannon before you bring up and fire the anti-graviton plasma. Remember that they use the same gun ports," she said.

"How long?"

"As much as two and a half minutes," she replied. During which time we'd be vulnerable to attack. I thanked her and turned back to my console, plugging in my new tactical strategy and forwarding it to Babayan.

"Load the warheads and have those missiles ready for my order, XO," I said.

"Will do, sir," she replied.

"Captain." This time it was Karina trying to get my attention. "*Impulse II* is still closing in on the battlefield."

Goddamned Dobrina Kierkopf.

"How soon until we're in firing range of the gravity pulse cannon?"

"Six minutes and ten seconds to twenty-thousand-kilometer range, sir," she said. I nodded to her.

"I'll be in my office. Get *Impulse* on the longwave com," I said.

"Aye, sir."

Ten seconds later I was behind my desk with the aural shield up. Dobrina's fuzzy image appeared on my desk monitor, then began to clear up. It didn't clear my anger.

"What do you think you're doing?" I demanded.

"Defending the Union against these thugs," she replied.

"That's *my* job. Your orders—and I remind you that you agreed to my taking field command in this system—are to defend the High Station. A dreadnought jumping in behind our lines could destroy the station," I said more calmly.

"I'm aware of that. But I—"

"You couldn't pass up the chance to get revenge against a man who devastated your world. I get that. But you're making an emotional decision, not a logical one. I'm ordering you back to High Station Pendax."

"I . . . resist that order, sir," she said.

"Now, Captain Kierkopf," I said firmly. That sparked her anger.

"I'm not your woman anymore, Cochrane, and you can't protect me from my own decisions. My mind is made up. Orders be damned," she said, a look of grim determination on her face.

"Then you're on your own, Captain. I have a battle to fight," I said.

"But—" I cut the com line then and went back to the bridge.

"Status," I demanded of my crew.

"Four minutes fifty-three seconds to gravity pulse cannon range," reported Babayan. "All weapons charged, and strategic battle plan is programmed into the AI."

"Belay that. I'll handle everything but the missiles from my own command console."

"Sir," confirmed Babayan, then went to make her tactical adjustments.

"Mr. Longer, set our forward momentum to engage the battlefield at twenty thousand clicks on time with the clock. Speed isn't as important as accuracy in this maneuver," I said.

"Yes, sir. Matching the countdown clock to the twenty-thousand-click range," said Longer.

"At ten thousand the AI will launch the missiles. I want all our forward momentum cut at that point. Once those missiles hit I want us dead stopped to fire the anti-graviton plasma."

"Aye, sir," replied Longer. I sat back in my chair and pulled up the tactical console.

"Sir, *Impulse II* will reach the battlefield less than two minutes after us," said Karina. "Should we coordinate—"

"Negative, Lieutenant," I said, looking up from my console. "*Impulse II* is not part of this attack. We will not coordinate with her, nor change our strategy for her, nor come to her rescue so long as the battle with *Vixis* is engaged. Am I understood?" The bridge got quiet then.

"Understood, sir," replied Karina. I turned back to my tactical display, counting down the minutes until I could reengage with *Vixis*. The bridge stayed quiet except for the general banter required of battle operations.

"One minute, sir," said Karina from her longscope station, breaking the silence. I checked the position of *Impulse*. At her current speed she would blow past our position relative to *Vixis* when we decelerated after hitting the ten-thousand-click mark. She didn't have many of the same weapons enhancements that we had, so she would have to get much closer to engage the rogue Lightship. I doubted Captain Kierkopf cared about that; she was out for revenge and revenge only. That worried me on a personal level, but she was disobeying my orders, and if she wouldn't follow my commands, then there was really nothing I could do. At thirty seconds my board was green to fire the gravity push-pulse cannon.

"Countdown if you please, Longscope officer," I said. Karina counted us to zero, and I waited a few more seconds just to be sure. Then I hit the fire button.

The gravity pulse was invisible to the naked eye. In the infrared spectrum it appeared as a tightly coiled scalar wave, technology once thought to be mythical in nature. The wave lanced out at *Vixis* and in mere seconds crossed the vacuum and impacted against her Hoagland Field. The result was spectacular—*Vixis* was bounced nearly ten kilometers from her original position and thrown completely off her ecliptical plane, which was necessary to maintain contact with an adversary on the battlefield.

"Nailed her, sir," declared Layton from the helm station. "She's spinning out of control. I think we knocked out or at least damaged her inertial dampening system."

"We'll know in a few seconds," I replied. If we had indeed knocked out *Vixis*'s inertial dampers, her crew might even now be mere spots on the wall of her interior. But that seemed too easy. *Defiant*'s inertial damper system was robust, and I had to assume *Vixis*'s was as well.

"Her spin rate's starting to slow," reported Babayan from the weapons station. "Thrusters activated."

"She's still with us," I said. I turned to Longer. "Progress of our deceleration?" I demanded.

"Ninety seconds to missile range, sir," he replied. It was the longest ninety seconds of my life, watching as *Vixis* slowly righted herself, as *Impulse* closed on the battlefield. She was dangerously close to being in range of our missiles, even if they were programmed for

Vixis's Hoagland Field frequency. I couldn't sit by and watch this any longer.

"Ensign Layton, contact *Impulse II*. Warn her one last time that she is entering an active battlefield and will soon be in danger of friendly fire. See if that gets her attention." The young ensign replied with an "Aye, sir" and sent the message. I waited as the seconds ticked off to the ten-thousand-click range and the automated launch of our missiles.

"Should I put the battle AI on hold, sir?" asked Babayan from her station. I surveyed the tactical display: nineteen seconds to our missile-firing range, *Impulse II* thirty seconds from the same status, *Vixis* quickly righting herself to face us again . . .

"Negative. *Impulse* enters the battlefield at her own risk. The AI proceeds as planned," I said. And then there was nothing to do but watch as the scenario played out. Dobrina was going way too fast in *Impulse II* to fire her missiles or torpedoes. It was obvious she was going to make a sweeping run past *Vixis* and engage her with coil cannons, hopefully just seconds after our missiles hit. Then she would effectively be out of the battle for a solid twenty minutes while she decelerated and turned back to us. It was a one-shot strategy—not one that I advocated—but if *Vixis* was pockmarked with holes in her Hoagland Field, it could be very effective, even produce a kill.

If.

I watched as our missiles streaked out and accelerated toward the still-reeling *Vixis*. The only question was how much damage we had done with our gravity-pulse cannon. The missiles closed quickly as I powered up the third leg of my attack plan, the anti-graviton disintegrator. She warmed quickly and was at my disposal with more than twenty seconds to spare.

Then the unthinkable happened.

The missiles started to veer off, away from *Vixis* and toward the rapidly closing *Impulse II*. With safeguards placed in the missile guidance systems, what we were witnessing just wasn't possible.

"Babayan, what's happening?" I called from my station.

"Unknown, sir!" she replied, feverishly swiping her hands over her weapons console, looking for an answer.

"I know," said Karina from behind me. "*Vixis* has swapped shield frequencies with *Impulse II*, probably using her disaster field codes. For all intents and purposes, the missiles now recognize *Impulse* as *Vixis* and *Vixis* as *Impulse*." A quick look at my tactical board proved she was right. The missiles were still locked onto the same frequency they were originally programmed to recognize, but that frequency now resonated from *Impulse II*.

"Warn off *Impulse*! Now, Ensign!" I yelled at Lynne Layton.

"Too late," said Gracel from behind me. She was right.

I watched as the missiles impacted against *Impulse II*'s Hoagland Field. They had the desired effect but not against the desired ship. *Impulse*'s Hoagland Field became riddled with holes, and in that instant, *Vixis* began moving toward her. I looked down to my board, only once chance left.

I fired the anti-graviton plasma. Babayan came running from her post.

"You could hit them both!"

"Unlikely," I pointed to the tactical display on the main viewer. The two ships were far enough apart that the enveloping plasma would hit *Vixis* before she could reach *Impulse*, but not by much. My bridge crew and I watched helplessly as the plasma closed on *Vixis* while *Vixis* closed on *Impulse*.

"Detecting a power surge from *Vixis*, sir," said Karina from her station.

"What kind?"

"Uncertain, sir," she replied.

"XO, how long until—"

"Seven seconds, sir," said Babayan. Then we saw it. The same sickly colored green energy weapon that the automatons used streaked out from *Vixis* and through *Impulse*'s damaged Hoagland Field.

The green energy beams impacted against *Impulse*'s hull. Then she broke in half amidships, and her stern twisted away and exploded.

Our anti-graviton plasma arrived seconds later and enveloped *Vixis*. We watched the blinding white-and-silver shimmer of the plasma exploding as it impacted *Vixis*'s Hoagland Field. Then the screen adjusted for light, and the plasma faded.

Vixis was still there.

"Her field is down!" exclaimed Babayan.

"Enter a firing solution! Use the mass-destruction warhead we have left and fire the torpedo!" I commanded.

"Forward torpedo bays took a big hit during the first volley, sir. They say they can't comply for seven minutes if they are to meet minimum safety precautions," replied Babayan.

"Damn the safety precautions!" I said.

"Captain." The voice came from behind me. From Gracel. It was all I needed to hear.

"Belay that. All ahead toward *Vixis*," I ordered. I went to the Historian's station.

"We won't catch her," I said. She shook her head no.

"But you wounded her," she said. I turned back to the tactical display. *Vixis* was accelerating now and pulling away from us. I had a decision to make.

"Longscope officer, status of *Impulse II*?" I said.

"Forward hull is drifting, sir. Many escape pods in the vicinity, sir," Karina said soberly. "Her stern aft of bulkhead seventeen is completely destroyed." My decision was made for me.

"Mr. Longer, reduce speed to .00003 light. Mr. Layton, reset our course to rendezvous with *Impulse II*. XO, alert search and rescue teams," I said. I sat back down, watching as *Vixis* sailed away from us and *Impulse II*—or what was left of her—grew closer.

"Captain." It was Ensign Layton's voice. "Captain, receiving a communication. It's from *Vixis*, sir. Audio only."

I stood to attention. "Let's hear it."

"Captain Cochrane, this is Prince Arin, commander of the *Vixis*," the voice said. I had no doubt it was a legitimate com from the prince.

"What do you want?" I asked in an annoyed tone. There was a chuckle at the other end.

"Just to tell you that today was only your first defeat. There is more to come, power you cannot even conceive of. Tell your Union Council to surrender now, and your ships and your worlds will be saved from the same decimation that befell Carinthia. If you continue this conflict . . . well, very little of what you are and what you cherish will survive. Do you understand me?" Arin said.

"I have always understood men like you, Arin. Men like you must be destroyed at any cost," I said. Now there was open laughter on the channel.

"Brave words, but pointless, as you'll soon see. I look forward to our next meeting," he said.

"And I look forward to pulling my sword from your throat, Prince," I said, and I meant it. The laughter came again.

"Indeed, Captain. I'll look forward to you trying." Then the signal was cut, and a few seconds later *Vixis* vanished from the Pendax system with a hyperdimensional flash.

The bridge crew were all looking at me. I sat back down in my command chair.

"Let's get our comrades back," I ordered, and the bustle on the bridge resumed as the crew switched their duties from battle stations to search and rescue.

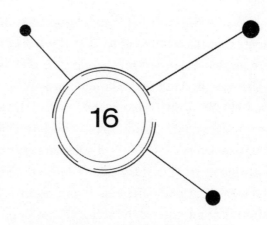

To Carinthia

Search and rescue took five hours to complete. We pulled in more than thirty lifepods with seventy-six survivors aboard. On one of them was Captain Dobrina Kierkopf.

I met her face to face on *Defiant*'s shuttle hangar deck with a security team in tow. She was directing her surviving crew to assist with getting the injured to sickbay when I interrupted her.

"Captain Kierkopf," I said, calmly but with force. She spun around and glanced at the security detail on either side of me.

"Captain Cochrane," she said.

"Have you identified your surviving second-in-command?" I asked.

"My XO, Kaaren Treblont, survived," she said.

"Call her over." After a few seconds a tall, dark-haired woman came over and saluted me. I saluted back.

"Commander Treblont, I am placing you in field command of the surviving members of *Impulse II* as of this moment. I want a manifest of all surviving crew members, their physical condition, and their assignments aboard *Impulse*. Get that list to Commander Babayan on the bridge ASAP. She will help you to match your healthy crew to assignments that need filling aboard *Defiant*. As of now you will report as requested to any of my senior staff and assist them in any manner they see fit. Am I understood?" I asked.

"Yes, Captain," said Treblont, then looked to Dobrina.

"Captain Kierkopf," I said, turning back to Dobrina. "I am confining you to quarters for willfully disobeying my orders as field commander of this mission and for killing more than half of your crew. You will have a security detail outside your doors at all times until the grand admiral or another such higher authority can determine your fate. Do you understand and accept my orders?"

"I do," she said. "But I want the captain to know—"

"Save it for Wesley," I said. "I lost fifteen of my own in this attack, and you lost a great deal more, including most of the marines I loaned you. Those losses are on your head, Captain. And I don't want to hear from you about it again." Then I waved the security guards—one man and one woman—forward, and they marched Kierkopf off without another word.

I turned one last time to Treblont. "Carry on, Commander," I said, then strode quickly away from the deck.

My longwave conference call with Zander was quick and uncomfortable. He didn't try to defend Dobrina, and I made it clear early on that I wasn't willing to listen if he tried.

"I've recalled all my free Wasps save one at my boss's orders," said Zander. "He'll be coming home in the remaining Wasp with the Princess Janaan. I guess Sandosa can wait for now."

"It can," I agreed.

"There are still three in each system to assist your local navies, but we're going to have to make more, it seems, and soon." I shook my head at that.

"I don't think there's time. This has the feel of an endgame move by Arin and the Empire," I said.

"Is that what your intuition tells you?" I nodded.

"That, and it's also the only logical play. I'm heading home to Quantar immediately via Carinthia. Anything you want me to convey?" I asked. Zander shook his head.

"No. But I do have one request. Let me bring Dobrina and the survivors of *Impulse* aboard *Vanguard*."

"No."

"Why not?" I looked at Zander intently, barely able to contain my fury at what Dobrina had done to her ship, her crew.

"Because the only place I'm dropping her off is at the admiral's doorstep," I said.

"What about her crew? I could use trained spacers—"

"No, Lucius. Your job is to defend Pendax with what you have. Mine is to get out of this system and back to Quantar as quickly as possible. We'll decide how to proceed from there."

"So there's no moving you?"

I shook my head again. "No."

"Very well, Captain."

"There's one more thing," I said. Zander raised his eyebrows at me on the monitor. "The wreck of *Impulse II* will have to be destroyed to keep her from falling into enemy hands. The Empire could learn much from what she contains."

"They already have *Vixis*," protested Zander.

"Standard scuttle protocol, Captain. Now, do you do it, or do I?" I asked. He sighed.

"I'm not sure I could be the one to destroy another fair lady with her name," he said.

"Fine. I'll do it. I hope to see you again, Lucius, in better times," I said.

"The feeling is mutual, laddie."

With that I signed off and went to my bridge, there to plan the destruction of one of my sister ships.

High-yield torpedoes would normally be the order of the day to scuttle what was left of *Impulse II*, but I wanted to save my remaining ordnance. I ordered up the gravity weapons display and selected the anti-graviton plasma. It would disintegrate the hulk of *Impulse* down to the molecular level—probably even good enough for Admiral Wesley.

I ordered us closer, and we took up a position ten clicks from *Impulse*. Then I ordered full stop while I powered up the weapon. Lena Babayan came up to me then.

"We haven't completed a full rescue survey. There is still a tiny chance there might be survivors aboard who couldn't make it to the escape pods," she said.

"I'm aware of that risk, XO," I said, trying hard not to be annoyed. The last thing I needed was more guilt on my conscience. I turned to Karina, who had yet to yield her longscope station to her relief. We'd been at work for more than twelve hours, and none of the primary bridge crew had left even though I had given them leave to do so more than three hours ago.

"One final longscope scan for bio signs, if you please, Lieutenant," I said to her. She nodded acknowledgment and started her scan. She forgot to "Aye, sir" me, but I wasn't going to hold it against her or nit-pick. We'd all been through too much today.

After a few minutes she came back to me with a negative on bio signs. I looked to Babayan. "I'm satisfied, XO. Your opinion?"

She shook her head. "No opposition to carrying out the scuttle, sir," she said. I went back to my console and sat down, and Babayan joined me. I went to the display and looked at the firing button for a few moments, thinking about the men and women who had been lost in the battle.

"Rest in peace, *Impulse*," I said in a soft voice.

"Rest in peace," repeated Babayan in a whisper that only I could hear. Then I fired the weapon. The plasma enveloped the cold hulk of *Impulse II* in a matter of a few seconds. With no Hoagland Field to protect her, she went quickly and quietly, the silver cloud sparking for only a moment before she vanished from history forever.

I stood. "Mr. Layton, how long to the jump point to Carinthia?" I asked.

"Ninety minutes at max cruising speed," he stated. Max cruising speed was .005 light-speed. We were half an AU away.

"And how long to High Station 3 at Carinthia after that? I want a reload on our missiles and torpedoes."

"Roughly two hours at that speed, sir," Longer said.

"So ordered. All primary bridge crew are to complete their duties and hand off their stations for a minimum rest period of three hours. I don't want to see any of you on the bridge until then. That includes you, XO," I said.

"Acknowledged, sir," Babayan replied. Then she called the relief shift to the bridge, and everyone scrambled to leave as quickly as possible. I waited a few minutes longer than the rest as Karina handed off the longscope station to her understudy, and then we went down to our stateroom together, hand in hand.

I didn't bother to undress when I got inside, just removed my boots and duty jacket. Karina took a couple more minutes, then slid into bed next to me wearing only her body suit top and underwear. She was warm and inviting, but I was too tired to even let my mind go there. I wrapped her in my arms, took in the deep scent of her hair, and then we both fell asleep without another word.

Sleep provided me no relief from my discomforting dreams once again. I was glad when the alarm chime sounded: thirty minutes to High Station 3. I roused Karina gently, kissed her once tenderly, then was up and out of our room while she was still dressing. We'd hardly said a word to each other the whole time.

We jumped into Carinthian space, and to my surprise, both *Fearless* and *Avenger* were closely positioned near High Station 3. I called Dietar Von Zimmerman, captain of the Lightship nearest High Station 3, *Fearless*, as members of the day shift slowly started taking up their positions again. Many had eyes still red with fatigue. That included Karina, who looked much the worse for wear. I doubted she'd ever let herself be seen as she was now—messed hair, little makeup, red, tired eyes—in a social situation.

Captain Von Zimmerman chimed back to my request, and I took it in my office.

"I hear you had quite an ordeal at Pendax," said Von Zimmerman.

"And at Skondar, Captain. We've lost many good men and women, and *Impulse II* was a major casualty. I had to scuttle her," I replied.

"My god, the reports didn't say that," he said. "I'm sorry to hear. Did Captain Kierkopf survive?"

"She's confined to quarters pending a review of her actions in the battle," I stated. Von Zimmerman looked shocked.

"Captain, are you sure—"

"The Admiralty will decide her status, Captain. Now, if you don't mind, I'd like docking clearance at High Station 3 for a reload of my atomic ordnance. We lost three launch bays in the battle, and I'd like to replenish my other bays before we go on," I interrupted. I wanted no part of a discussion about Dobrina's actions or her fate.

"Granted, Captain. Where are you ultimately bound for?"

"Back to Quantar. She needs two ships defending her at the moment, just like Carinthia."

"Understood."

"That brings up one more question, Captain. Why are you and *Avenger* deployed so close together?" I asked. Von Zimmerman looked uncomfortable with the question.

"Let's just say I had a disagreement with Captain Ozil, sir," he said. I tried to repress my emotions, especially my anger. Carinthia was too important a system for trifles like this, and she would undoubtedly still be a major target for the ousted regent, Prince Arin, who craved the throne there.

I put Von Zimmerman on hold and signaled Captain Ozil onboard *Avenger* to join the conversation. Once I had them both on the screen, I lit into the young captains.

"You two have to stop this bickering, this quest for glory. Neither of you have seen battle before. Well, I've seen enough in one day to make my stomach turn. I am not your superior officer, but I *am* your senior in battle experience, so you will follow my orders. Captain Ozil, since you are closest to Carinthia, you will take *Avenger* to the L2 Lagrange point and defend your home world until you are relieved. Captain Von Zimmerman, once *Defiant* has been resupplied, you will make the jump to Pendax and relieve Captain Zander and *Vanguard*. You will send them here to Carinthia to take up your position, and you will take up station defending Pendax until you are relieved. Am I understood?"

"You are, sir," said Von Zimmerman. Ozil also gave his verbal agreement. I wasn't satisfied.

"I will report your behavior to the Admiralty when I arrive at Quantar. This is not a game, gentlemen; it's dead-serious business, and many millions of lives are at stake. I want you both to think about that while you are defending all Union worlds, not just your own. Now, I am going to walk a few meters to my command chair, and by the time I get there I want to see you both underway, or there will be more repercussions. Am I understood?" This time the "Yes, sir"s were in unison. I shut off my monitor without another word and made for my chair. A quick glance at the tactical display showed that both ships were already moving. Babayan came and sat next to me.

"New tactics, sir?" she asked.

"I want Zander one quick jump away from Quantar or Pendax in case of an attack. These two kids don't seem to know what they're doing," I said.

"They're both twenty-seven, sir. You're only twenty-five," she pointed out. I stood.

"Battle experience can age you greatly, XO."

"I agree with that, sir," she said.

Once the two remaining Carinthian Lightships were in position, *Avenger* at Carinthia proper and *Fearless* at the jump point, I ordered us into dock at High Station 3. Since the restock and the trek back to the jump point would take four to five hours, I ordered the bridge crew to take another rest period, and I joined them. Babayan insisted she wasn't tired and requested to stay on the bridge through the transition, so I let her. She was tough as nails, that was for sure. My orders were to wake me up thirty minutes from jump space, which I planned on using instead of our mobile jump capabilities. No sense in using it until we had to.

This time Karina and I both got undressed and sank fully into our temperfoam bed. I was almost out when she touched my arm.

"Are you still awake?" she asked softly.

"I am now," I replied without moving. She rubbed her hand across my chest.

"Is there anything I can do to relieve your stress?" she asked.

"No," I said instantly. If she was hinting at recreational sex, it was the furthest thing from my mind. I felt like I'd been up for four days. I rolled onto my side, and she wrapped an arm around my abdomen in a comforting way.

"What are you going to do about Dobrina?" I was even more uncomfortable with that topic. It was true my relationship with her was complicated, but her actions at Pendax were not.

"She's lucky she's not in the brig," I said. "What she did was irresponsible, careless with the lives of her crew. She wanted revenge on a personal level. She let that get in the way of following orders, and she got a lot of talented young people killed."

"So, she won't get any special treatment from you?" Karina asked.

"I already said she's lucky she's not in the brig. Once we're in Quantar space I'll refer her to the Admiralty with my report. They can decide what to do with her."

"So that's it for you?"

"It is for now." At that I stopped talking, and she let me. After a few minutes she rolled back over and was soon asleep. After our conversation, though, I found myself tossing and turning for almost thirty minutes. Once I was sure she was asleep, I got up and quietly went to my medicine cabinet in the washroom. I took out a timed sleep capsule that was set at three hours, poured water from the sink, and drank it down.

Then sleep came, and I drifted off, dreaming pleasant dreams for the first time in weeks.

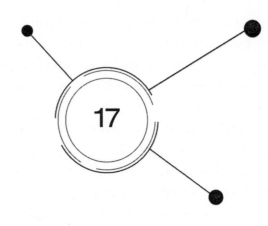

To Quantar

The entire first shift bridge crew was back on duty a good ten minutes early. My timed sleeping pill had worked perfectly, and I woke up feeling refreshed and ready to go, despite our current circumstances. Karina had tried once again to raise my spirits as we showered together, and this time I let her. The experience left me more than ready to take on the challenges of the day.

I read through my status report that I planned on submitting to the Admiralty upon our arrival in Quantar space. It seemed like ages since we had left, and I would be very happy to get back to Candle and conference with Maclintock again, or even Wesley. But there were things in my battle reports—the destruction of *Impulse II* and the confinement of Dobrina—that I wasn't looking forward to explaining to either of my higher-ups. I'd disobeyed orders myself plenty of times, but my choices had never directly cost the lives of 172 of my fellow crew. That was an action that I couldn't reconcile with my personal feelings for Dobrina, and I'd be glad to let the command structure above me figure out what to do with her. I was certainly in no position to judge.

Presently we cut the umbilical to High Station 3 and were on our way to the jump point to Quantar. Everything proceeded smoothly, and twenty minutes from jump space I ordered Dietar Von Zimmerman and *Fearless* through to Pendax. Zander would no doubt follow along presently. I wasn't a betting man, but if I were a gambler, I'd bet that the next Imperial attack would occur at one of the Union's core systems—Quantar, Carinthia, or Levant—and not at an outlier like Pendax or Sandosa. We still had seven functioning Lightships in the fleet and more than thirty Wasps, plus the local navies, which were slower but still packed a considerable punch. That would (theoretically) allow us to concentrate our Lightship assets on the main systems.

Prince Arin, though, was a wildcard. His ship had clearly received upgrades from Imperial sources, and a fleet of automated HuKs, suicide drones, and manned dreadnoughts led by him would be formidable. It seemed they were trying to force an endgame conflict by design, but on their own turf and under their own terms. The only remaining questions were where and when.

Via longwave probe sent through the jump singularity, Zander signaled *Vanguard*'s readiness to jump into Carinthian space, but I replied that he should wait until after we made the jump to Carinthia. I was anxious to get home.

Babayan signaled all green, and we made the jump. It was a relief to see the stars of home again on our displays. I ordered Duane Longer to take us to Candle at best speed, then called ahead to Maclintock and transferred my report packet. To my surprise, he signaled back within five minutes. I took his call in my office.

"Commodore," I said.

"Captain," he replied. "I've read your report on the battles at Skondar and Pendax. Pretty hairy stuff. I want you to know that both *Starbound* here at Quantar and *Resolution* in the Levant system have received most of the same weapons upgrades from the Historians that *Defiant* has. Looks like we're going to need them."

"I think so, sir," I agreed. Maclintock looked pensive for a moment.

"Peter, we should talk about the issue of Captain Kierkopf and her confinement aboard your ship," he said.

"Yes, sir," I replied. I was prepared to defend my principles on the matter.

"Please explain," he said straightforwardly. I straightened up a bit in my chair, conscious of the fact that I was under the gaze of my direct superior officer.

"Sir, *Impulse II* was damaged in the battle at Skondar. After taking field command of the three Lightships stationed at Pendax—with the other two captains' agreement, I might add—we were faced with an attack by the Lightship *Vixis*. I had ordered *Impulse II* to dock for repairs at High Station Pendax. Once *Vixis* was engaged, Captain Kierkopf violated my field orders and brought her ship into the battlefield, unauthorized by me," I said.

"I can think of many times you've violated orders, Captain," Maclintock said to me. That stung. I decided to accept his version of my behavior for the moment.

"Yes, sir, I have. But in those instances I took what I believed was the only course of action to save lives. Captain Kierkopf's actions, which were in direct violation of my field orders on multiple occasions, resulted in the deaths of 172 of her shipmates, including many marines I had loaned her after the battle at Skondar. I found her actions reckless and destructive, but even so, sir, I did not have her arrested pending charges. I merely confined her to quarters," I finished. Maclintock got that pensive look on his face again.

"Captain Kierkopf is an experienced Lightship captain, Peter, a vital asset. They are hard to find and even harder to train. And we are at war, Captain. That merits some consideration. *Defiant* arrives at Candle in ninety minutes. I would request that you release Captain Kierkopf from confinement until such time as we can conference with the grand admiral and determine our next move. Will you agree to such terms, Captain Cochrane?" Maclintock asked. I shrugged in response.

"There's nothing to agree to, sir," I said. "You're my commanding officer. I'll release her immediately. *Defiant* out." With that I shut off the two-way com. I didn't really care if that pissed him off.

I called down to the security team posted outside Dobrina's cabin and ordered them to release her, with the caveat that she was to stay off my bridge. I waited to see if Maclintock would call back to chastise me, but he didn't, so I shut down my desk com and went back to my command chair to fume over a decision I greatly disagreed with.

The docking at Candle was uneventful, and after a few minutes Maclintock called me to his office for a conference. I was informed that Captain Kierkopf was invited also. I made for my stateroom to freshen up a bit. Karina was there, waiting, as usual, to pick my brain. She sat down on the bed as I swapped out my casual duty jacket for my formal one.

"What do you think he'll do with Dobrina?" she asked.

"I'm sure I've no idea. But it will undoubtedly be different than what I would do," I said.

"Why do you say that?"

I looked at her before turning to check myself in the mirror. "We're very different people, Maclintock and I. He's almost exclusively by the book. I rely more on my intuition," I said. Karina leaned back on the bed, one arm propping her head up.

"Some would say you rely entirely too much on your vaunted intuition." Now that one pricked my ego, and I didn't like it much. I turned back to her.

"My intuition told me to marry you. Should I have considered all the facts and taken another course?" I asked in none too friendly a manner.

"That was mean," she said. I shrugged.

"You started it," I said. "Are you ready to go?"

"Ready to go where?"

"I think it's likely the overall geopolitical situation will be discussed. I thought you might be interested, as a princess of Carinthia." With that I donned my cap and started for the door.

"Now, wait just a minute, Captain. I'll go with you under the condition that you stop being mean to me," she said.

"I'm in a bad mood."

"That you are," she responded. We stood there at an impasse. I finally gave in.

"I'll stop being mean if you will," I said. She looked at me, head cocked to one side.

"Fine," she finally said, then donned her formal jacket and cap, and we were off. The lifter down to the umbilical level took a long time coming. When the doors finally opened, we were both in for a surprise.

Inside the lifter were Captain Dobrina Kierkopf and her XO, Commander Treblont.

"We'll take the next lifter," I said automatically.

"We certainly will not," said Karina, and she dragged me inside. I went to one corner, Dobrina to the other, leaving Treblont and Karina between us. It only took seconds for my wife's patience to be exhausted and her noted Carinthian temper to kick in. She reached out and stopped the lifter between decks.

"All right, goddamn it, I've had enough of you two!" she said, looking to Dobrina first and then back to me. Treblont was smart enough to step back and get out of the way. "You've been comrades, friends, and lovers for more than two years." I noticed a look of surprise cross Treblont's face. "You," she said, pointing at Dobrina. "I'm a princess of the realm, and I could order you to talk this out." Dobrina's head snapped around at that. Then Karina turned her wrath on me. "And you. You're my husband, and although I am inferior to you in rank on this ship, I can make your life most unpleasant, and I think you know what I mean. I've had enough of this shit between you. I command you *both* to work it out." With that she stepped back to the rear of the lifter and joined Treblont. I said nothing for a few seconds, until she kicked my boots from behind. It was a very immature gesture, but it was effective.

"She disobeyed my direct orders and got 172 of her crew killed," I finally said. "As far as I'm concerned, there's nothing more to it."

"And you disobeyed my orders aboard *Starbound* and convinced Maclintock to let you explore that Founder station at Jenarus when you *knew* there was trouble ahead. All those dead Imperial marines. But your decision only got thirty-three people killed. Or do the men and women who died under your command count less than the ones who died under mine?" asked Dobrina. I whipped around to face her.

"You lost your command. Your ship was cut in half, and I had to scuttle it," I said.

"And you destroyed my first command without any orders to do so!"

"I also saved *Starbound*!"

"At the cost of the first *Impulse*!" she retaliated.

"So you've both made mistakes. Huge, costly mistakes. Lives were lost. Which one of you is the worse commander?" cut in Karina. "Go ahead, I'll wait." When neither of us said anything, she started in again. "Just admit that both of you have made poor decisions and let the higher-ups sort it out. You two seem to think this is personal when it's not; it's war. It seems to me that Dobrina is most upset at being judged, and you, Peter, are most upset at being disobeyed, which is something you've been proud of doing in the past."

"But—" I started.

"No buts, Peter. You've both made mistakes. Now, both of you just admit you've been wrong, shake hands, and let's be done with it," said Karina.

I kept my place. I couldn't bring my arm to move toward Dobrina. After a few seconds she stuck her arm out at me, stiff and formal. After a moment's hesitation I reached out, and we shook hands. Then, like two boxers, we went back to our separate corners. Karina stepped between us again.

"Thank god that's done," she said, then restarted the lifter.

Maclintock's conference room was laid out like a war council, which it was. Dozens of officers spread around the room in a circle, with the most important dignitaries taking up the first row of tables and adjutants and lower-ranking officers in the second tier. Dobrina, Karina, and I sat in the first row of chairs, facing the giant display screens. Treblont took up a position in the second row with several other junior officers. I regretted now not bringing my XO, but there was no one I wanted in charge of getting *Defiant* shipshape more than Lena Babayan.

On the conference room displays, all the remaining Lightship captains appeared one by one via longwave visual com, except for Wynn Scott of *Valiant*, who was still in traverse space and bound for Sandosa. As the clock to the start of the conference wound down, the Admiralty linkworks logo vanished and was replaced by the massive image of Grand Admiral Jonathon Wesley on High Station Quantar. Soon my father's image also appeared and those of Duke Benn Feilberg on Carinthia, Admar Harrington of Pendax, and finally Prince Sunil Katara of Levant, who winked at me. I waved back.

The last to enter the room was Commodore Maclintock, accompanied by my old mentor Serosian, who was still *Starbound*'s Historian of record. He hadn't volunteered to come with me to *Defiant*, and in the end I hadn't asked him, feeling the need to move on in more ways than one. Still, he nodded to me as he sat down on the dais next to the commodore, and I returned his acknowledgment. Presently Wesley called the conference to order.

"Ladies and gentlemen, this conference is top secret and of the highest importance. Nothing said in here is to be repeated to anyone outside this room, including those of you on the longwave visual displays," he said, then cleared his throat before continuing. "Obviously we are here in a time of crisis for the Union. The Lightship *Vixis* has reappeared in the Pendax system and was confronted by the Union ships *Defiant* and *Impulse II*. As all of you know, *Impulse* was heavily damaged and had to be scuttled in the battle. We will not be discussing the circumstances of that loss this meeting," he said, looking down on me from above as mighty Zeus might look down on a puny human.

"In addition to the return of *Vixis*, we've had several incursions into Union space from other types of Imperial craft: HuKs and suicide drones, but no dreadnoughts. This begs the question of where they are. I'm going to solicit thoughts on this matter, and I'll begin with the captain who has fought two battles with Imperial forces recently, Captain Peter Cochrane of *Defiant*."

I was a bit surprised to be up first, but I reached out and activated my microphone. "Actually, Admiral, *Defiant* has been involved in three recent battles with Imperial forces: the attack on us at Sandosa, the rescue of *Impulse II* from Skondar, and our battle with *Vixis* at Pendax," I started. "Each of these conflicts had its own unique setting and outcome. Sandosa showed us that the old empire had the will and the capability to influence a culture reemerging from the old Imperial Civil War era. Although the Sandosans did not use sophisticated weaponry, the Imperial forces had upgraded them to types of weapons they wouldn't normally have had. We can no longer assume that any prewar culture we come in contact with has not been previously influenced by the Empire.

"At Skondar we encountered something I found extremely chilling. Not only did the enemy there have automatons similar in design to the ones *Starbound* fought at Jenarus, but we found what we believe was a manufacturing base, an old Imperial mining colony from which an army of these automatons was being constructed."

"An army? By whom? For what?" It was Duke Benn Feilberg. I turned to my right to face his image on the display screen.

"The only sound military conclusion, Your Highness, is that someone was building an army in order to invade a Union world, or worlds," I replied. "I don't think I need to emphasize to this council what that could mean. The power of these automatons is considerable, greater than anything we have in terms of soldiers. An invasion by these things could lead to massive casualties on any planet unfortunate enough to be invaded. And lastly, I think it is safe to assume that Drava was not the only facility where they are conducting such activities," I finished. Then Wesley jumped back in.

"And how was the battle at Drava concluded in your favor, Captain?" he asked. I looked down, as if intent on boring a hole in the desktop with my gaze. Wesley knew full well the answer to that question. It was in my report packet. I didn't want to answer, but I had to.

"*Defiant* deployed a new weapon—one only we possess—called a torsion beam. It was given to us by the Historians. The weapon has the ability to magnify the spin rate of any highly magnetic object, like a ship's drive system or even a planetary core," I said. The room stayed silent.

"And?" prompted Wesley. I took in a deep breath before continuing. This wasn't something I wanted to talk about.

"And we used it on the magnetic core of Drava to tear the moon apart. A full analysis is in your report packets," I concluded. But Wesley wasn't finished with me.

"Would you please share with us your conclusions regarding the battle at Pendax?" he said. I leaned forward again and looked at each of the leaders of the Union in turn, ready to tell them the truth.

"The fact is that even with our upgraded weapons, the best we could manage with *Vixis* was a draw, if you call losing a Lightship and

172 of her crew a draw." Dobrina stiffened next to me, but I wasn't here to candy-coat anything for the sake of her feelings. "*Vixis* has sophisticated weaponry, analysis of which is in all of your reports. She's a match for any of our Lightships, and she displayed an energy weapon, similar to what the automatons use in rifle form, that was powerful enough to cut *Impulse II* in half, even through her defensive fields. This coming battle will be extremely difficult, and all we can do is guess where they might strike."

"Where would you strike, if you were them?" The voice came from my left, the deep baritone of my former mentor, Serosian. I turned to address him directly.

"I'd strike at any core world of the Union—Quantar, Carinthia, Levant, even Earth. Whichever is perceived as the weakest. It's clear that they want to draw us onto their battlefield, to ground they know well, and that they know they will have an advantage there."

"Are you suggesting we take the bait? Attack where they attack us? Play their game?" asked Serosian.

"We've always been playing their game, Historian. You know that," I said. I couldn't read his thoughts by the look on his face, but if I were guessing, I'd say he was irritated by my reply.

"So your recommendations are?" This time it was my father chiming in from the display panel.

"This is an endgame scenario for the Imperial forces, sir. They want this over, and they want it done quickly, and their way. From what I've seen these last few days, I don't think there's a thing we can do about it except take the fight to them as best we can," I said.

"Your director asked you for a recommendation, Captain, not your opinion," said Wesley rather curtly.

"All planetary fleets and defenses to maximum. All Lightships and Wasps moved to instantaneous jump point range of any of the four primary worlds," I said.

"Of which Pendax is not one," said Admar Harrington. The other council members made noises of conciliation to Harrington, but no promises. I continued.

"When we attack, we must attack with everything we have. No holding back, or we're likely to have nothing to come home to," I concluded. Again it was Serosian who challenged me.

"And what if they lure us to one core system, then attack another?" he challenged.

"Then we go there," I said. "If our planetary defenses and local navies can't defend our worlds for a few hours while we get to the battlefield, then we're doomed already anyway."

"So that's the best plan you have?" said Duke Benn.

"It's my only recommendation, Highness. We go in full-strength or not at all," I said.

"And fight on their terms?"

"In my opinion, we have no other choice, Highness. Otherwise it will be a war of attrition, and they overwhelmingly have the numbers."

There was so much debate and crosstalk at that point that Wesley had trouble maintaining control of the room. When he got everyone quieted down, he asked all military personnel except Maclintock to leave the room. We all shuffled out to the lobby, waiting to be called back in. To my surprise, the only one who dared approach me was Dobrina.

"You always did have an art for stirring things up," she said.

"And you always had the common sense to stop me. But not this time. Why?" I asked.

"Because this time," she said, "I agree with you."

We were out in the lobby for more than thirty minutes. I found it irritating and a waste of time, but it did give me a chance to com in with Babayan on *Defiant*.

"We're ready to go, sir. Fully stocked and resupplied. We even picked up another marine detachment, though we're still down on that count. We can go the minute you give the order," she said.

"I'm not sure there's going to be an order," I replied. "The politicians have been in there alone for half an hour. My guess is that they'll break soon for shrimp cocktail and table military action until tomorrow." Babayan laughed at that.

"You should try humor more often," she said. "You're good at it."

"Thanks. I don't get— Hold on." The doors to the conference room swung open again, and there was quite a commotion accompanying it.

"Only command and executive-level officers are to return to the council room," announced a captain wearing diplomatic bars. "The rest of you are dismissed and asked to return to your assignments." There were murmurs of discontent at that, but I quickly rounded up Karina and Dobrina and headed back in, dropping the line with Babayan. It took us another minute to settle in before the doors were shut and locked and Wesley started in again.

"Decisions have been made," he announced in his gruff Newfie accent. "The Lightships *Starbound* and *Defiant* will be sent through to Levant immediately, where they will join *Resolution*." That was the ship commanded by Maclintock's former exec, Devin Tannace, a man I didn't know at all. "It has been determined that Levant is the most likely Union world to be attacked for two reasons. The first is that she has only a single Lightship with a crew that has never seen battle, and second is that she has control of the reconstructed jump gate, which allows for travel to the inner empire, specifically Altos. From the Altos system, we might have a tactical advantage, and Captains Maclintock, Cochrane, and Kierkopf have been in-system before." I determined from that statement that Dobrina wasn't going to be disciplined for her actions at Pendax, despite my report to the Admiralty. Wesley's next statement confirmed my suspicions in a very big way.

"Captain Kierkopf, since you have no current command but you do have experience battling Imperial units, you are hereby placed in field command of the Lightship *Resolution*. Captain Tannace and his command crew have agreed to step down on a temporary basis until this situation is resolved. It is my understanding that you have eight senior officers, a large number of junior officers and marines, and several experienced technicians available to you from your old crew. You can take those people with you to man as many positions as possible with battle-tested personnel. I expect you to have the list of positions to Captain Tannace by the time you dock at High Station Artemis," he said.

"Aye, sir," she replied. "I do have one request, sir."

His massive image looked down on her from above. "Go ahead," he prompted.

"My request is that the Historian aboard *Resolution* be removed prior to my arrival. I've been betrayed by two of them now, sir, and I think that's as much as any Lightship captain should have to endure," she said.

"I trust Historian Valdere implicitly," said Serosian, cutting into the conversation.

"Irrelevant, since I don't even trust *you*," retorted Dobrina. That elicited an expression of annoyance across Serosian's face.

"Regrettably, I have to deny your request, Captain," Wesley said abruptly.

"But—"

"Captain Kierkopf, the Historian Order has been our greatest ally. There wouldn't even be a Union Navy if not for them. So while I understand your reticence under the circumstances, my order stands," he said firmly.

"Yes, Admiral," she replied, backing down.

"Sir, what about *Vanguard*?" I asked. "Captain Zander is experienced, too." Dobrina's head whipped around at that. She didn't like my implication, but I didn't care.

"*Vanguard* will be protecting Quantar, only an instant jump away. Which brings me to the other assignments. *Avenger* will remain in the Carinthian system and *Fearless* at Pendax. When *Valiant* arrives, I'll have her stay at Sandosa to protect the mission there. That's the best we can do for the moment, ladies and gentlemen. Now you have your assignments, and they are so ordered."

With that the meeting broke up, and we all scrambled our separate ways to fates unknown.

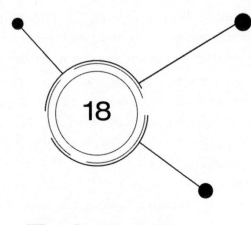

18

To Levant

I called Babayan again and ordered a twenty-minute countdown to breaking dock. We wouldn't waste any time getting to Levant. It would be a ninety-minute run to jump space if we used the regular jump point technology, but after arriving on the bridge I went straight to my office and called up Maclintock.

"Commodore, I suggest that we skip the normal jump point process and use our direct jumping technology once we've cleared displacement range of Candle. My helmsman can put us half an AU from the jump ring and Artemis station without much problem, sir," I said.

"How long until we can rendezvous with *Resolution* once we jump in?"

I put him on hold to switch com channels and asked Layton and Longer the same question, then went back to our conversation. "If we use our HD impellers, my Propulsion officer says we'll be seventeen minutes out, sir," I said.

"Good enough. Let's get these buckets moving."

"Sir," I said, making a final point. "We've navigated this system before. Commander Layton can plot an accurate course that will save us maximum time. It would be best if *Starbound* matched our course and speed and followed us in."

Maclintock thought about that for a second and then agreed. "Confirmed, Captain. We'll follow your lead, but then I'm stationing my ship at the jump gate ring while you dock at Artemis and exchange command crew with *Resolution*," he said.

"Also confirmed, sir. Estimate nine minutes from breaking dock until the jump, sir," I said. Maclintock nodded.

"We'll see you in Levant space," he said, then signed off. I went to my command chair and briefed Babayan.

"We'll need to be at least a hundred thousand clicks from both Candle and *Starbound* to make the jump, XO," I said. She nodded.

"Understood, sir. I've had Layton plot us a course away from Candle and out of the system, and then we'll lay our course back into Artemis Station using Lieutenant Arasan's jump coordinates once we hit Levant, sir."

"I'll leave it in your capable hands, XO," I said, then made my way to the longscope station. Karina turned to me as I approached.

"Anything I can do for you, Captain?" she asked with a slight smile. I gave her one back before getting serious.

"This is likely going to be very rough, Karina. I want you to consider staying here at Candle before we break dock," I said. She eyed me in that strong Carinthian way that I knew meant no before she even spoke a word.

"I've been through two battles and an attempted murder with you just on this mission, Captain. And *now* you're asking me to step aside?"

"I was thinking . . . I want to protect you, our future, perhaps even our children. That's all," I said, and I was serious about it. Her safety was my paramount personal wish for this mission, and I wasn't going to find any peace on that on the battlefield.

"If my husband is to die in this war, I want to be with him, helping him, helping fight the battle. Not stuck on some military station waiting to hear word of his fate. So my answer is, a hundred times no. We live and survive and are victorious together, or we die together. And that, Captain, is final," she said sternly.

"Understood, Lieutenant," I replied. I looked quickly around the bridge to see if we were being observed, then snuck in a kiss on the lips. "As you were, Lieutenant."

"As *you* were, Captain."

I managed a smile then and headed back to my chair.

We broke dock precisely on time and started to make our way to a safe jumping distance. *Starbound* did the same. Everyone was present on the bridge except Gracel, and frankly I was glad she wasn't there. I had all the information I needed from her, and I found that her presence in battle was more of a distraction than a help.

Babayan reported we had reached safe jumping distance from both Candle and *Starbound* right on the dot, time-wise. I sent a confirmation code to *Starbound*, got an affirmative ping back, then took my command chair and strapped in.

"Five-second count, Mr. Arasan," I told my astrogator. He gave the countdown, and then we shifted interdimensional location, and I found myself looking at the inner Levant system. A few seconds later, *Starbound* jumped in a hundred thousand clicks behind us. It took me another few seconds of looking at the visual display to realize something was wrong.

I jumped to my feet. "Tactical," I ordered. The main display switched over and zoomed in on Levant Prime. It quickly identified multiple ships engaged in a firefight. One of them was *Resolution*. Another was *Vixis*. "What the fuck," I said. "This can't be a coincidence. How did they know we were coming? XO, tactical report!" I demanded. Babayan made for the tactical station, which included the weapons console. It took her a few seconds to respond. I used those seconds to my advantage.

"Mr. Layton, get us moving. Target an intercept course to *Vixis*."

"Aye, sir," said Layton as the bridge crew leapt into action. I turned to Longer.

"Full HD sub-light drive, Mr. Longer." He affirmed my orders, and then I was on to my wife. "Longscope scans, Lieutenant," I ordered.

"Already complete, sir. *Resolution* is fully engaged with *Vixis* and three HuKs. There are two dreadnoughts parked near the jump gate, holding at station-keeping. Suicide drones are attacking both High Station Artemis and planetary defenses, sir," she reported.

"Tactical report, XO?"

Babayan swiveled to face me. "Out of range to engage either the dreadnoughts or *Vixis*, sir. *Starbound* could engage the dreadnoughts holding the ring more easily than we could from her position."

"My thoughts as well, XO." Just then Maclintock chimed in on my personal com. I sat down to take it.

"Commodore," I said out loud.

"Captain. My tactical analysis indicates that *Defiant* is better positioned than we are to go get *Vixis*. You are so ordered. *Starbound* is headed for those dreadnoughts. We must control that gate," Maclintock said.

"Agreed, sir."

"How long until you reach *Resolution*?" I looked at my watch.

"Sixteen minutes, sir," I said.

"That's a long time," Maclintock said. I patched Karina and Babayan into the conversation.

"Battlefield status, Lieutenant," I said. Karina replied.

"*Resolution* defenses are down to 63 percent, sir. *Vixis* is using her frequency modulation missile tech to punch holes in *Resolution*'s

Hoagland Field. She's taking a pounding, and she doesn't have the full counterstrike capabilities that we have to take them on," she said.

"Time until her defenses collapse?" I asked.

The line was silent for a second, and then she said, "Seven minutes at best, sir."

"XO?"

"Five minutes best time to missile or torpedo range, sir, but they're too closely locked to use any of our Mass Destruction Weapons with an acceptable margin of safety at this distance," Babayan said.

"Make your best call, Captain," came Maclintock's voice through the line. "Just save *Resolution*. We'll regroup at Artemis once we've run the enemy out of the system."

"Aye, sir," I replied, thinking to myself that he was far too optimistic. Levant's planetary defenses were taking a pounding, and Artemis was just holding her own. We were already on full HD impellers, and the hybrid drive was shot, thanks to my play at Pendax. I stood and looked to my astrogator.

"Mr. Arasan, can you plot us a hyperdimensional jump back to the point we left Quantar, then program another jump back here, putting us closer to the battlefield?" I knew what I was asking of him. It was a dangerous thing and had never been tried before, to my knowledge. I wasn't even sure if it *could* be done. But if we couldn't pull it off, *Resolution* would likely be lost. And these types of skills were why I'd brought Arasan aboard in the first place.

"A double jump, sir?" asked Arasan. "That would be a neat trick. I can program it into the astrogation AI—"

"How long?" I interrupted. He looked at me with grim determination.

"Two minutes, sir," Arasan said confidently.

"Do it." I sat back down and waited. If we pulled off two near-simultaneous jumps to Quantar and back, we'd gain almost three minutes of life for *Resolution* and probably surprise the hell out of Prince Arin and *Vixis*. I focused next on Babayan.

"XO, I want a volley of frequency-busting missiles followed instantly by a high-yield mass-destruction torpedo as soon as we jump back in," I ordered.

"How big on the MDW torpedo, sir?"

"All in. Fifty-megaton."

"I can do that, sir, through the battle AI, but we'll only get a volley of four missiles from the functioning launch bays, saving one for the torpedo," Babayan said.

"Good enough, XO. Make sure the AI doesn't waste a second waiting for my order once we jump back in."

"Aye, sir." She paused then. "What about *Resolution*'s weakening defenses, sir?"

I looked at her. "They'll just have to be enough, Commander," I said.

A minute later, Lieutenant Arasan reported that his calculations were complete, and I called for a shipwide lockdown while he prepped the jump controls. I prayed his calculations were correct and that the space around our previous egress jump point at Quantar was clear of local traffic. An unshielded ship hit by a hyperdimensional displacement wave could be destroyed by our maneuver. It was a risk I had to take. I made a note of the ship's clock—12:26:37—then gave my order.

"Ready, Mr. Arasan?"

"Ready, sir."

"Then push the button, man."

He did. The transformation was as "normal" as could be expected. The first time.

The AI immediately reengaged the jump unit microseconds later, and I felt like I'd been hit on the head with a rock. My vision was blurry, and my head felt like it was spinning faster than a jump core. What seemed like minutes passed, and I was still disoriented, the spinning slowly dissipating, the blurred colors slowly forming recognizable shapes again. Nausea swept over me, but I pushed that down as best I could, trying to take stock of my bridge. I looked at the main display as the others slowly came to their senses. The ship's clock read 12:26:42.

The whole maneuver had taken five seconds, regardless of how long it had *seemed* as we traversed interdimensional space. Then I comprehended what was on the main display screen. There was a Lightship, its defense field glowing purple as it took energy weapon fire. We were close enough that I could read the catalog number on the ship's side: ULS-442.

Vixis.

I looked at the screen magnification; it had reset to 1:1. We were probably two hundred meters apart.

"Babayan, did the missiles fire?" I asked. If they had . . .

"Negative, sir," said Babayan, shaking her head, probably as much to clear it as anything else. "Battle AI was knocked out by the double jump. And frankly, so was I."

I turned to Longer. "Full reverse, Mr. Longer. Get us some distance—"

Before I could finish my order, we were hit broadside by a volley of *Vixis*'s missiles. I tried to call up the tactical display, but it wasn't working. In fact, a lot of systems weren't.

"Shield damage?" I asked.

"None, sir," replied Babayan. "Those weren't the frequency-busting missiles, just standard tactical nukes." If you could call a ten-kiloton atomic warhead "standard," well, then we were doing fine. No way they'd get through our Hoagland Field defenses with those.

"You can bet the next volley will be frequency-busters. We caught them by surprise, XO, but we won't again." I turned my attention to my helmsman. "You need to get us to at least a thousand clicks away to fire our missiles, Mr. Layton," I said.

Layton shook his head. "The HD impellers went offline during the double jump, sir. They're coming back now, as are most systems, but we're running on chemical thrusters, and I make it . . ." He looked down at his console.

"Eighteen seconds to safe firing range, Captain," interrupted Longer.

"*Resolution* is moving, sir, and so is *Vixis*," reported Babayan.

"Where?" I demanded.

"*Vixis* is moving off slowly, but *Resolution* is ramping up speed to pursue her," she replied. "*Vixis* must have been damaged by our displacement wave when we jumped back in."

"But fully shielded, and even at two hundred meters, she's still together. Just surprised and stunned a bit," I said. I turned to my wife. "I need a longwave com, and I need it quick. Tell *Resolution* to back off. We're targeting *Vixis*, and if she stays in range . . ." I said.

"Understood, sir," Karina replied and went to her work. I turned to Babayan.

"XO?" I asked, looking for a second-by-second tactical update.

"Nine seconds to firing range. *Resolution* is now backing off—looks like she got the longwave message," said Babayan.

"That was quick work," I said.

"Five seconds to firing range on *Vixis*," said Babayan.

"Don't wait on my order, XO," I said.

"Aye, sir." A precious few seconds later, the volleys were away. We all watched on the now-functioning tactical as our own shield-busting missiles impacted *Vixis*'s Hoagland Field and detonated, followed seconds later by the MDW torpedo explosion. It was blinding for a second until the light filters on the main display rebalanced. When the screen cleared, we could clearly see *Vixis* limping along, her amidships burned and interior fires registering on our heat scans.

"We got her, sir!" declared Babayan. I ran through the tactical scans on my console. Her weapons and main propulsion were still active.

"Not yet, Commander. Mr. Layton, plot intercept. Mr. Longer, full impellers until we catch her," I said. Longer shook his head.

"We can't catch her, sir. Our HD impeller systems are still coming back up to full capacity from the double jump. I might be able to get you a shot with the anti-graviton plasma, sir. *Might*," he replied.

"Do it. Lieutenant Feilberg, report on the battle at the jump gate ring?"

"Commodore Maclintock reports a standoff, sir. Those dreadnoughts have a new type of defensive field, likely taken from *Vixis*. No progress in moving those beasts off their line," she said.

"And you can't score if you can't get the goalkeeper off his line," I responded. Then Babayan came up to me.

"*Vixis* is pulling away, sir. She's only twenty thousand clicks from the jump ring, and with our sub-light impellers still coming back up, we can't match her course and speed," she said.

"But the plasma weapon—"

"You could destroy everything if you fire it in these close quarters, sir. *Vixis, Resolution, Starbound*, those dreadnoughts, even Artemis station. As XO, I say the risks are too high."

I switched the main display to tactical. *Starbound* was backing away from the dreadnoughts, *Resolution* was halfway between Artemis and the jump gate, and we were in between all of them and *Vixis*, who was rapidly pulling away toward the jump gate ring. "That's twice we've engaged her, XO, and twice she's gotten away," I said. Babayan said nothing to that but stood beside me as we watched *Vixis* activate the ring and slipstream through, followed closely by her companion dreadnoughts.

"Are there any suicide drones or HuKs left fighting?" I asked.

"Two drones and one HuK," reported Babayan, pointing them out on the display.

"Then let's go get them, Mr. Layton. I believe Artemis Station will be able to resupply whatever missiles we use up," I said.

"Aye, sir," said Layton with a smile. Then I sat back in my command couch, frustrated as ever.

Three hours later I had *Defiant* docked at Artemis Station along with *Resolution* and *Starbound*, and Wesley and Maclintock had called for another strategy session. Karina was invited to represent Carinthia's vote, and my friend Prince Sunil Katara of Levant had called in from the surface. It was, after all, his planet we were orbiting.

"This is obviously a trap," I said once the session commenced, not bothering to wait for Wesley to start with any formalities. "We know where the jump gate ring is preprogrammed to take us."

"Unless they found a way to reprogram it," retorted Captain Dobrina Kierkopf from down the conference table. She was sitting in on the conference call along with all the other Lightship captains. Their images were displayed in individual frames on the conference room screen, which was much smaller than the enormous one in Maclintock's office on Candle. "They could be baiting us right into the teeth of their entire navy."

"They're probably doing that anyway," I said. "It doesn't change the obvious. They want us to follow them."

"If it's a trap, we shouldn't go," Karina said. Wesley looked up from his battle reports long enough to comment.

"Regrettably, Highness, this is a military decision, not a political one. Your opinion is noted, but it will not be critical in our decisions about what this fleet does or doesn't do next," he said.

Karina looked perturbed and said, "Understood," then pushed back slightly from the table.

"Opinion, Commodore Maclintock?" Wesley asked.

"As you can see from the reports, Admiral, those dreadnoughts are a match for us with their new defensive fields. They're similar to

Hoaglands but seem to have a slightly less robust design. Probably a field upgrade done on the fly. One thing for sure is if we go after *Vixis*, we're going to need a larger fleet," Maclintock said.

"I disagree," I said. "The fleet we've seen is not that large. It is possible that Prince Arin and *Vixis* are being allowed to run rogue raids on the Union without the full cooperation of the Imperial fleet, the actual size of which we still don't know. And one more thing: we *do* know where *Vixis* went. She could have jumped out at any time, to any system, but she went through the ring. She wants us to follow her to Altos. Or at least Arin does."

"And again," said Dobrina, "if we do so, we play right into their hands."

Wesley looked up at the many faces of his captains on the screen. "Opinion, Captain Zander?" he asked.

Zander cleared his throat. "Captain Cochrane is correct, Admiral. This is a trap. But they know that we know it. My guess is that they're betting we'll send a small force through, and they'll take that force out. We'll send another force to find out what happened to the first, and so on, and so on. Pick us apart by attrition. When they know we are weak, they'll come through and take over. End of the war."

"So, what's your suggested strategy, Captain?" asked Wesley with a hint of sarcasm in his tone.

"We go, but not with a small force. All in, everything we have: Lightships, Wasps, cruisers from the local navies, everything. And we beat them. Then we come back through that damn gate and blow it to hell so they can never use it again," Zander said.

"I agree," I said. "Trap or not, we must go. And with everything we have." Karina grasped my hand while Dobrina shook her head.

"It's too much of a risk," she said.

"Like the one you took with *Impulse II* at Pendax?" I said. She fumed but said nothing back to me.

"It's insanity," said Maclintock. "Leaving the Union worlds defenseless is not an option."

"We're defenseless anyway, Commodore," said Zander, showing anger for the first time. "If we try and wait this one out, we'll get picked apart. They let us grow our fleet up over the last year not out of kindness but because they didn't care. They have overwhelming numbers, and thanks to the fucking prince regent of Carinthia, they know everything they need to know about Lightships. The math is simple. They have the numbers, we don't."

Wesley waved his hand to cut off the debate. "This rancor is pointless," he said. "The Admiralty has already made up its mind on this." By "the Admiralty," he clearly meant himself. "The following orders are final. The Lightships *Starbound*, *Defiant*, and *Resolution* will make the jump through the gate at 0900 Union Universal Time tomorrow. The Lightship *Vanguard* will relocate to Levant, as will all other Lightships and available Wasp frigates. This second flotilla will await orders in the Levant system until battle reports are received from Altos," he dictated.

"And if there are no reports from Altos?" asked Dobrina.

"Then the jump gate ring will be destroyed. You'll have twenty-four hours to get it done and get back," he said with finality.

"And if we're still fighting for our lives on the other side?" asked Maclintock. "How will we get home from some 244 light-years away?"

"The old-fashioned way: point to point. If you survive, Commodore," said Wesley. And that was that. But I had more to say.

"Sir, if I may—why do we have to wait until 0900 tomorrow? That's almost twelve hours from now," I said. "If there's going to be a fight, then let's get on with it." The Admiral looked up sharply at me.

"You have three missile launch tubes that need replacing, Captain, and the other ships need minor repairs. Don't be in such a rush to reap the whirlwind, son. It's coming soon enough," he said.

"There is one more thing, Admiral." This time it was Captain Devin Tannace of *Resolution* speaking up. "I must protest your previous order turning my command over to Captain Kierkopf. You said *Resolution* and her crew was untested on the battlefield, but that is no longer so. We fought against the enemy today, and we acquitted ourselves well."

"I agree," chimed in Prince Katara. "*Resolution* is Levant's Lightship, and Captain Tannace is our leader. I must insist that she be allowed to go on this mission with her own captain at the con, a captain that her crew knows and trusts, rather than replacements from another ship that was destroyed in battle against this very same enemy."

Wesley looked at both men's images on the screen, then simply said, "Denied. We need our most experienced officers on this mission. Captain Tannace will run the Levant Planetary defenses until *Resolution* returns. Captain Kierkopf's assignment is temporary. Now, if there's no more debate?" He looked at everyone with an intimidating stare that I'd seen before. It was well practiced.

"One final question, Admiral," I said, annoying him one more time. He looked at me, his face red, but said nothing, so I continued. "All Union worlds save one are represented here by a Lightship captain, a royal, or both. Where is Historian Serosian? Doesn't he represent Earth's interests in these matters?"

Wesley deferred to Maclintock, who said, "The Historians are holding their own confab, as far as I know. Something about policy decisions to be made."

"What policies?" I asked. Maclintock looked perturbed.

"I'm not sure, but I assumed they were none of our goddamned business," Maclintock said, glaring at me. I said nothing to that but turned back to Wesley.

"Sir, with respect, I propose that we leave all our Historians behind on this mission. We are heading into a battle, and their . . . peculiarities might not be a positive addition at this time," I said.

"I agree," said Dobrina quickly. Her support was welcome but unsurprising. Wesley looked to Maclintock.

"I'll let the Commodore make that decision. This is his mission," said Wesley.

"The young Captain Cochrane may not value Mr. Serosian's presence, sir, but I do. I wouldn't fly *Starbound* without him," he said. "And I insist that they all go. Or perhaps the other captains would like to withdraw from the mission?"

I looked down the table at Dobrina, and she looked at me, but neither of us said anything.

"Then if there's absolutely nothing else, your mission briefs will be downloaded via longwave packet by midnight. Good luck tomorrow, Captains. We are adjourned," Wesley said. And that was that.

I walked back to *Defiant* hand in hand with my wife. Neither of us said a word.

I prayed that my intuition about this mission was wrong.

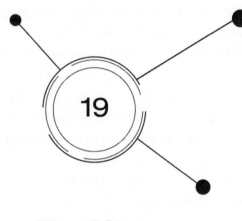

To Altos

Even after a vigorous night of lovemaking with Karina, I didn't sleep well. We never knew, in these circumstances, if each time would be our last time together. She was worried about the mission, but I was more worried about her. This mission was dangerous beyond belief, and I didn't want to risk her at all. But the fact was that she'd earned the right to be here, and I had to respect that, even if I didn't like it much. At all.

I went to meditate in the early hours of the morning and found everything quiet and peaceful. I prayed to the Universe that my ship would remain in the same condition on this mission, quiet and peaceful, but I knew that was an unlikely outcome. I showered early and gently woke Karina, who had slept much better than me. I guess I had worn her out more than a bit.

By 0830 the bridge was crawling with the day shift crew, everyone running down their checklists one more time. I had a feeling this would be the last High Station break we would be seeing for a while.

Precisely at 0900 Maclintock ordered us to break dock, and we did, proceeding in an orderly manner to the jump gate ring for a trip into the unknown. *Starbound* led the procession, followed by *Resolution* in the middle and *Defiant* farthest aft. I had protested this position, as I felt *Resolution*, still nicked up from her encounter with *Vixis*, would be best protected by entering last. But Maclintock thought differently, feeling that she could be best served by being bracketed by the two most powerful ships in the fleet. We all had the upgraded weaponry at our disposal, including the gravity weapons, the anti-graviton disintegration plasma, the local jump point generators, frequency-busting missiles, coil cannons, and advanced atomic torpedoes. *Defiant* alone retained the power of the torsion beam. It was the best we had. I just wasn't sure it would be enough.

Nor was I sure about Captain Dobrina Kierkopf. We had been comrades, friends, and lovers, but my affection for her had come to a breaking point with her actions toward *Vixis* in the battle at Pendax. I wasn't sure I trusted her on the battlefield anymore, and I'd made no secret of the fact that I'd have preferred Zander and *Vanguard* on this mission, even if she didn't have the full upgraded weaponry suite yet.

I tensely watched as *Starbound* slipstreamed through the ring and presumably into the Altos system, the former home of the once-hated Sri, a scientific order that had been reviled under the old empire and whose abuses had led directly to the conflict that started the Imperial Civil War. It was not a place I had ever contemplated visiting, and my only previous experience in that system had been aboard *Starbound*, when I'd used the original, crippled *Impulse* as a weapon to destroy an automated Imperial dreadnought.

Next went *Resolution*, three minutes behind, and I started our own countdown clock.

We were on full alert, locked down tight as a drum and ready for battle the moment we entered Altos space. I expected the Imperial fleet to be there and for our ships to be under immediate assault. I hadn't prepared a battle plan, though. How could I? We had no idea what to expect from the enemy on the other side of that singularity.

I was tense and sweating. I checked all our systems one more time; we were as prepared as we could be. I managed a look at my wife, but she was under the 'scope hood and too involved for me to disturb with a last romantic "I love you." She knew, and so did I, and that would have to be enough.

Ten seconds.

"Field on maximum," I ordered. "All stations: final report."

"All weapons systems ready," called out Babayan from the weapons console.

"Propulsion set to engage at .0005 light on your order, sir," said Longer.

"Jump protocols also engaged," called Lieutenant Arasan.

"Helm active and responding," finished George Layton. I looked down at my friend. Whatever we found on the other side, I was sure George would find us the battle space we needed to respond.

At two seconds I gripped my chair tightly. Then we slipstreamed instantaneously through the jump gate ring and into open, empty space in the Altos system, 240-plus light-years from the Union and Levant.

Starbound and *Resolution* were in their standard formation, IFF signals coming in loud and clear, and the tactical display showing them functioning at 100 percent. There was no Imperial fleet of any kind.

I hit the ship-to-ship com and joined in with Maclintock and Dobrina.

"Not exactly what I expected," I said.

"Nor me," replied Maclintock. "Early scans indicate the system is clear of HD signatures. We will continue to scan and advise, but right now this looks like a dead end."

"I can't believe that, sir," I said. "*Vixis—*"

"*Vixis* could have used Altos as a waypoint to somewhere else, like Corant or god knows where. We did give her twelve hours while we refitted. There's no way to know," said the commodore.

"Perhaps we should wait for confirmation that there are no pending attacks in other systems," said Dobrina. "This could be a decoy."

"It could," agreed Maclintock, "or it could be just as it seems for now: a mystery."

"Sir, suggest we explore the system further and find out," I said.

"You read my mind, Captain Cochrane. Send a longwave probe back through the ring to report initial findings to the admiral. We will proceed in a wedge formation with *Resolution* taking point, dropping in on Altos inclined to the ecliptic of the system at thirty-three degrees. Join the formation at your leisure, *Defiant*. Match course and speed with us."

I did as ordered, as perplexed as anyone by what was—or rather, wasn't—happening here.

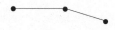

Our deep dive toward Altos would take almost nine hours. Three hours in, after a series of unremarkable scans that showed the system devoid of any hyperdimensional technology we could detect, I ordered my day shift crew to stand down for five hours. I'd need them later, perhaps, when we got close to Altos itself and hopefully found some answers to our many questions. We were dropping HD probes with information packets every hour, reporting back our position, progress, and the surprising lack of urgency in the system to Admiral Wesley.

In return, we were told that plans to destroy the jump gate ring at Levant were being put on hold pending the outcome of our mission or lack thereof. There had been no reports of attacks of any kind on Union systems, commerce and defensive military moves were being conducted routinely and without interference, and life in the Union was proceeding as if all was normal. I even received a letter from my father—the pep talk kind, nothing very personal. I read it on my stateroom monitor, then sat back and wondered what we would do if nothing more happened. Things had been quiet for quite some time before the incident at Sandosa, and I found myself thinking it was possible things could return to that quietness, as much as that perplexed me.

"Penny for your thoughts," came Karina's voice. She was standing at the screened half wall barrier that separated my office from our living quarters, still in full uniform and ready to return to duty at a moment's notice.

"A penny's not worth much these days. And anyway, you should be resting. We still have"—I checked my watch—"three hours and twenty-one minutes before the rest period ends."

"So we do," she said with her impish grin. That always got me in trouble.

"My dear, we are in an enemy star system, 244 light-years from home, a potential crisis ready to explode around us at any minute, and all you can think about is sex?" I said.

She shrugged. "We're young. You're virile. I'm bored. And quite frankly I was thinking something might actually happen once we get started," she said. I laughed.

"So you mean to bring the entirety of the Imperial Navy down on our three tiny ships simply by initiating sex with me?" She put one hand on her hip.

"Women have been accused of worse," she said. I laughed again. "Causing earthquakes, floods, comet strikes."

"I have to concentrate," I said.

"You ordered a rest period, Captain, so come rest with me," she said, extending her hand. I gave her a mock-stern look.

"No, she-devil! Away with you!" With that she took off her coat and started to undo her blouse buttons one by one. It was hard to keep my eyes on the ship's system reports flickering across my monitor. She was quickly down to her underwear, then sauntered over to me and began rubbing my shoulders. They were tight and tense. Soon my uniform shirt was being unbuttoned and she was running her hands across my chest while nibbling on my ear.

"The longscope is nominal," she said.

"What?"

"My station. All nominal. See?" She pointed at my monitor. "Nothing to worry about. Now come and relax with me. We may not get another chance." That much was true, and it could be forever. What choice did I have but to give in?

I swiveled in my chair and pulled her petite figure into my lap, kissing her deeply while she straddled me. She was pleasurable in every way, but I still found myself feeling guilty about taking personal pleasure at a time like this. The fact was, though, that a lot of the day shift crew was probably doing the same thing right now, and how could I blame them? These were stressful times, and we were on a very dangerous mission.

Once Karina had me on the bed, she worked me like it was our last night together. She had grown to be an exquisite lover, and I found myself enamored by every inch of her and by her every move in our bed.

I had no idea how much time had passed as we lay together, her feeling small in my arms. I wondered if I should get up and check, but as I started to break our embrace, she stopped me by grabbing my arm.

"Stay," she said. "I have something to tell you." That made me instantly uncomfortable. It was almost never good news.

"What?" I whispered. She lay there silently for few moments more, breathing deeply. I held her dutifully, as a husband should when something important was about to be conveyed by his wife, but I was also impatient, worrying once again about my command after our long moments of marital bliss.

"I stopped taking my pregnancy repressors," she said quietly. I tried not to react too swiftly.

"When?" I said, equally quietly.

"After Sandosa. It's only been a few days, but . . ." She trailed off.

"But what?"

"If we get through this mission, I'm leaving the navy. And I wanted . . . I hoped . . . to take part of you with me." I understood her desire. I didn't agree with her decision, but I wasn't going to fight it right now. As members of the aristocracy, we had both given the seeds of life to our family repositories so that they could produce an heir if something happened to one or both of us. At the time it seemed like an unnecessary precaution to me, but now I was glad for it. I knew that this mission would only end with either me or Prince Arin dead, and if it was me, I wanted her to have that as a protection, as a last act of love from me.

"You're not saying anything," she said, and I could detect the worry in her voice.

"I have nothing to say," I replied, then waited while I sorted through my thoughts and feelings. "Except that I love you. That I want you to leave the navy too, and that I want us to have a family. And I'll do anything in my power to make that a reality." She rolled toward me then, the gleam in her eyes showing her love for me, a love I was grateful for, a small piece of humanity in the harsh void of space. Then I kissed her, and my thoughts cleared of worries, regrets, vengeance, and guilt and were replaced by nothing but my love for her.

Our flotilla approached Altos with extreme caution. *Starbound* went in first while Dobrina and I waited aboard our respective ships. *Starbound* did a scan of the surface, looking for HD signatures, but found nothing. *Resolution* went next in a reverse scanning pattern to *Starbound*'s, and then finally it was our turn to do the trick.

Nothing.

"What the hell do we do now?" Dobrina asked as we conferenced in the briefing room, each ship captain and their respective Historians on the visual screen. On the main display, Maclintock shrugged.

"We wait. Admiral Wesley has ordered forty-eight hours of surveillance, and that's what we're going to give them. I've forwarded a scanning pattern to your XOs with my orders to commence immediately. In fact, they should have already started. We'll keep sweeping the planet as ordered," he said.

"And if we find nothing?" asked Dobrina.

"Then we count ourselves lucky no one lost their lives on this mission, and we go home," said Maclintock.

"Commodore, there is something in these reports that troubles me," I piped up.

"Captain Cochrane," he said, spurring me to continue.

"Sir, this planet is barely habitable. It's essentially a dull gray ball with a thin atmosphere. There are no mountain ranges, no cities, no rivers or surface water of any kind—in fact, no features at all that we can find. I'm not even sure humans could live there, let alone an advanced culture. Is it possible—"

"It's possible the Sri lived underground, Captain," interrupted Serosian. "This much we suspect from our historical records."

I looked to Gracel for support. "I just don't see how an advanced culture could have thrived here, underground or not," I said.

"There are large gaps in the records from before the war, as Master Serosian has said," replied Gracel. I was taken aback. I'd never heard him called "Master" before. I continued.

"Nonetheless, this seems implausible. We've done underground scans and found no evidence of facilities of any kind. It's almost like this planet is a squashed ball of dirt. I see no way a civilization could have thrived here for half a millennium. But perhaps Master Serosian knows more that he would like to share?" I challenged.

"There's nothing to add to what I've already stated, and Historian

Gracel has already confirmed my statements, Captain Cochrane," he countered. The look on his face was one of annoyance, even anger at me.

"We'll continue our scans of the system. Those are our orders. When our allotted time here is up, we'll leave as instructed. Is that understood, Captains?" asked Maclintock.

"It is," I replied.

"Aye, sir," said Dobrina. Maclintock nodded.

"In that case—" His next words were drowned out by a shipwide alert klaxon.

"XO to Captain," said Babayan in my ear com.

"Go," I replied.

"HD displacement detected four thousand clicks off our bow, sir," she said.

"Is it *Vixis*? Or a dreadnought?" I asked, rising from my chair and heading across the hallway to my bridge station.

"Negative, sir," replied Babayan as she rose from my couch and relinquished the chair to me. "Much smaller."

"HuK? Suicide drones?"

"No, sir." I looked to Karina for an answer.

"Longscope officer?"

"By configuration it appears to be a Lightship yacht, sir. And it's already pulling away from us," she said.

"Away? To where?" She looked up to the main display.

"There, sir. To Altos." I looked at my tactical display, which showed the yacht making rapidly for the surface of Altos. "It's looking as though it will make planetfall in the northern hemisphere of the planet, approximately 19.5 degrees north, sir."

I scrambled into my chair and shut off the alarm klaxon, then linked my personal com into the fleet line with Dobrina and Maclintock.

"Orders, Commodore? Do we pursue?" I asked.

"Not yet," came Maclintock's voice. "At the pace she's descending, we couldn't catch her anyway. Let's wait for her to land and form up over her."

"Aye, sir," I said and gave the order. Eleven minutes later the yacht was on the ground and our flotilla was in geostationary orbit above her.

"Who could be on that yacht? Is it Arin?" asked Dobrina over the fleet line.

"Unlikely," I replied. "The prince is a coward."

"That's your opinion, Captain," said Maclintock. "But if not him, then who?"

"Tralfane," I said. "*Impulse*'s original Historian, and likely *Vixis*'s as well. Where else would that yacht have come from?"

"Status of the yacht?" asked Maclintock.

"Just sitting there on the ground, sir," said Dobrina. "I say we go after it."

"Or bomb it from here," I suggested.

"Neither of those moves would be advisable," said Serosian. "Historian Tralfane is here to negotiate."

"Then let him come up here and do it like a man," replied Maclintock.

"I'm afraid that won't be possible. This meeting must take place on Altos."

"Since when does the Historian Order dictate to the Union Navy?" demanded Dobrina.

"Since now," came Serosian's calm, cold reply. At that, *Defiant*'s systems began to go offline one by one. Propulsion, weapons, astrogation. Only minimal critical systems remained powered. I swiveled around to Gracel's station and found it empty. I knew where she was: onboard her own yacht.

We were betrayed.

"We will not negotiate with our enemies—" started Maclintock.

"And who are your enemies really, Commodore?" said Serosian. "The old empire? The Sri? Robots left by the Founders?"

"I will not participate in any negotiation under these circumstances," said Maclintock.

"Your position is irrelevant, since you are not invited to participate in the negotiation," Serosian said. The yachts from *Starbound* and *Resolution* detached and started heading for the surface of Altos as we watched helplessly on our visual display, the only display system still working. "In fact, the only person invited is the only man who is truly in a position to negotiate for the Union, and that is Captain Peter Cochrane of *Defiant*." Then our fleet com channel went dead, and we lost all communication with each other. The decision was up to me.

I sat in my darkening bridge, a rage building inside me.

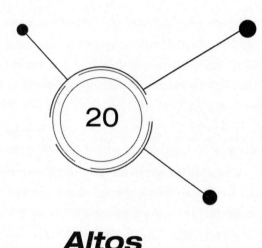

20

Altos

Everyone begged me not to go: Karina, Lena, Layton. But I had to go. Things had changed in an inexorable way, and I was a prisoner to the way the wind was blowing me.

The walk down to Gracel's quarters, which was also her yacht, was annoying—eleven decks of open ladders because she had cut off power to the lifters. When I arrived there were a dozen marines outside her doors. I waved them off and told them to stand down. There was nothing more to it. I stood outside and rang the door chime, which seemed preposterous, but what else was there for me to do?

"Order your men back at least thirty meters," came Gracel's scratchy voice over the intercom. I waved them back and had them drop their weapons for added measure. I was going willingly because I had no choice. The reason didn't matter.

I was going.

The yacht doors hissed open, and I stepped through without incident and into a darkened cabin, the doors shutting quickly and vacuum-sealing behind me. "Proceed to the command deck. You're familiar with the design, I'm sure," came her voice. I did as she asked, going down the stairs from her quarters.

When I arrived she was sitting at the main console, her visual displays showing telemetry and tracking the other two yachts as they descended to the surface, making a triangle of potential enemies.

"One shot with a coil cannon," I said. She turned sharply from the console and looked at me with her steel-gray eyes. There was a coldness and disdain there that I had never seen before.

"You'll never get that chance," she replied, then waved a hand over the console. I felt the yacht detach from *Defiant*, and we started our trip down to Altos. The main display screen quickly switched to a visual display as we descended toward the dead gray globe, a red blinking crosshair showing our intended landing spot. Gracel got up and approached me, stopping just in front of me, close enough for me to physically overpower her if I wanted.

"The console is locked for our destination, Captain. There's nothing you can do to stop it," she said.

"Perhaps not. But I could stop you," I said, and I was angry enough to try it. She smiled wryly.

"You would find that much harder than you think. I *do* understand your anger, Captain. Your power, your potency, all taken away from you with but a small gesture of our ability to control you. But you should respect that power. After all, we gave it to you," she said.

"And now you've taken it away. Why?" She took a step away from me, then pivoted back to face me directly.

"Your own personal actions at the Battle of Pendax, snuffing out human life with disdain—those actions have changed our outlook on your Union, Captain, and on you," she said.

"You mean I've brought this on myself? By defending the people I love?" I asked. She shrugged.

"In a way. We were looking for a leader, a special kind of leader. You were a disappointment."

"A dis— I should never have trusted you," I said, my rage yearning to break free, my fists clenching in anger. Perhaps she sensed the rage in me and took another step back.

"Without our help, your worlds would still be backwaters, your ships stuck in your own star systems, fretting about your petty planetary squabbles. Quantar was merely an experiment, and you were the primary subject. You failed," she said with disdain.

I couldn't contain my rage at her any longer and took a quick step toward her. I barely felt the pinprick of the needle in my arm as she swept her hand across me. Before I could take a second step, my arms and legs froze, and the room began to fade quickly around me. I was helpless. I felt her arms holding me up, then the support of a safety couch beneath me. Gracel leaned in close. I could barely make out her blurred features and her voice came through muddy but just comprehensible.

"You'll get all your answers when you wake up," she said as the room went black around me.

I woke up alone in the yacht. My body had returned to its normal functioning, and surprisingly my head cleared completely within a few seconds of waking up. Whatever Gracel had used on me had worked quickly and efficiently and wore off just as fast. I went to the yacht's console, which was unlocked, and activated the sweeping visual display. Outside, the four Lightship yachts from *Vixis*, *Defiant*, *Starbound*, and *Resolution* were all parked facing each other with their gear down and stairs extended to the surface. There were four EVA-suited figures standing on the barren plain. I had no doubt the closest three were Gracel, Serosian, and Tralfane. The fourth, no doubt from *Resolution*, stood back away from the main party. Obviously he or she wasn't needed for whatever was about to transpire.

I didn't need a gilded invitation. It was obvious they wanted me on the surface with them. I searched for the exterior airlock and an EVA suit and found them in due course. I put on the suit—the highest military grade, of course—then activated it and made my way through to the airlock, taking a deep breath as I opened the outer door. The stairs automatically deployed, and I took five small steps down to the surface of Altos. I could best describe that surface as gray, gritty, hard-packed sand. I looked at the small group standing in between the four yachts and made my way toward them.

The sky was mostly gray and full of flowing dust, propelled by extremely strong winds. Occasionally a dim patch of blue would appear before being blotted out again in seconds by the dust. I was thankful that the balancing force of my suit allowed me to walk and stand in the face of the swirling wind.

Presently I joined my three adversaries: Serosian, Gracel, and Tralfane. Just as I had expected. I switched on my local com.

"Perhaps you'd be so kind as to tell me what the fuck is going on?" I said, not really caring for any niceties. In their own ways, all three of the Historians present had betrayed me, and I hated each of them for it in different ways and to different depths.

Tralfane was the first to step forward. "Follow me," he said. With no other real choice, I did. Serosian and Gracel came behind me, and the last Historian, whom I guessed was Gracel's assistant Lenkowsky, stayed with the ships. We walked several hundred meters, buffeted all the way by the unrelenting wind. Tralfane waved me on into a small depression, where I could see a trickle of water running down a shallow gully barely a meter deep. The water was not more than a few centimeters deep and perhaps a hundred meters long before it disappeared back into the gritty surface.

"Do you see this?" asked Tralfane, clearly in charge of the situation.

"You did all this to show me a trickle of water?" I asked. "There isn't enough here to satisfy a dog."

"Exactly," said Tralfane. "And this is all the water on the entire surface of Altos."

That took me aback. "I don't understand what the significance—"

"The significance is that this is what is left of a world that was once as beautiful and as plentiful in resources as your own. We now stand at the most fertile spot on this entire world. Altos is only two thirds of its original mass. Every mountain, every river, every ocean or lake or city or continent—it is now reduced to this. The winds here are *only* 180 kilometers per hour, making this the most hospitable place for us to meet," he said.

I looked down to the trickling stream, up to the dim sky, and then across the endless barren plain. "I still don't understand the significance of bringing me here," I said. Tralfane shook his head inside his helmet.

"No, you don't. Should you tell him, Serosian, or should I?" he asked. I turned to look at Serosian, who only bowed his head in concession.

"Serosian and I are of different schools, different philosophies of the Historian Order, about how to bring humanity back out of the darkness of the ancient war. What you see here on Altos is what his sect did to the Sri and their world to end the last war."

I looked around. "A weapon did this?" Tralfane stepped up and spoke to me in a tone that I had never heard from him before, almost like sympathy.

"The weapon was called The Press. It was of monumental power, developed by the Historian Order. A gravity weapon so powerful it essentially crushed this world into a cue ball, burned away most of the atmosphere, and left this barren rock in its place." I turned to Serosian.

"Why?" I asked my old friend. Tralfane answered for him.

"The Sri were involved in what you might refer to as transhumanism, trying to make the human race evolve through the use of nanotechnology and the like to push mankind forward. But Serosian's sect believed that they left nothing for the spiritual, the soul, if you will. So they manipulated a rebellion against the Empire in the same way that the Sri manipulated the last three emperors to make war on lesser worlds that resisted genetic recombination, nanite implants, and the like," Tralfane said.

I looked at Serosian. "So the Imperial Civil War was never between two sides, but between your sect and the Sri? And you just used us as cannon fodder?"

"It is more complicated than that, but essentially, yes, you are correct," Serosian admitted without a trace of emotion.

"Do you know how many millions died in that war?" I asked, taking a step toward my old mentor. Tralfane's voice stopped me again.

"He knows. His forerunners left good records," Tralfane said. I jumped back in.

"And now you're repeating that war. Pitting the remnants of the old empire against the Union," I said. "Why?"

"Your beliefs are incorrect. There is no 'old empire,'" chimed in Gracel. I turned back to Tralfane.

"What does she mean?" I demanded.

Tralfane contemplated me for a second, then said, "The weapons you've been fighting—the dreadnoughts, HuKs, drones, and the like—have all been automated," he said.

"What? That's impossible. We detected life signs aboard those ships," I responded.

"Did you? Look around you. Do you think we couldn't fool you when we have technology that produced this? That we couldn't make you think you were fighting men and not machines?" Tralfane said.

"I don't understand. Why would you want us to think—"

"To test you," cut in Serosian. "To measure your empathy, your ability to make choices based on something other than your own interests. In each case you chose your personal relationships, your personal feelings and ideologies, over the greater good of all humankind."

"Bullshit!" I said, my rage rising again. "I chose to save my loved ones and friends from certain death. Do you know how many friends I've lost fighting for the Union?" My hands balled up in fists.

"We know," said Tralfane. "It has been costly to you. But it has molded you and shaped you, haunted and tormented you. And now you've come to this point, this critical decision point."

"What decision?" I demanded, swiveling around to face each of them in turn, my patience growing thin. Tralfane took in a deep breath.

"Our group, our united sects of the Historian Order, have brought you here to make you an offer," he said. I shook my head in disbelief.

"An offer of what?"

"Humanity must unite under one leader, one man. If we don't, we will likely be destroyed by outside forces that are coming even as we speak. If you don't give up your tiny dreams of sovereignty over your own lives, of the Union and the rule of law, then you could doom our entire civilization to extinction," Tralfane said.

"Wait, what outside forces?" I demanded, ignoring for now the broader implications of his statement.

The three Historians exchanged glances. It was Serosian who replied. "The Founders," he said, "are returning."

"The Founders?" I said. Serosian nodded before explaining.

"We've known this since before the first Reunion Day, since before you were even born. We knew that what was left of humanity—dozens of isolated planets scattered all through the old boundaries of the First Empire—couldn't face a threat like that alone. So our sect conceived the Union, led by a single leader driven by intuition and empathy, as the best choice for our future. But Tralfane's sect believed a collective leader, one who could lead mankind with an iron hand—such as Prince Arin—would be best suited for the task. So we went our separate ways, made our separate plans, then pitted them against each other to see who would prevail."

This time I took steps toward Serosian with the full intent of doing him harm. Tralfane restrained me with a strength equal to my own. Suited as we were, neither of us had a physical advantage. I calmed myself and shook one arm free, still confronting my former mentor.

"So this was all just some challenge between you two? I lost a girl I loved, friends, men and women under my command, all so you could prove your pet theory that I was humanity's best option for survival? So you could win *some fucking game*?" I raged at him.

"It was never that simple," said Serosian with what I hoped was a trace of shame in his voice. "The threat to humanity is extremely serious. And there have been many casualties you know nothing about."

"Such as?" Now Serosian truly did hang his head in shame.

"You were not the first in your family to be chosen for this role." The voice came from Gracel and was as cold and emotionless as you would expect. I looked at her, then back to Serosian.

"Derrick?" I said. Serosian stepped forward and faced me.

"This triumvirate—the three Historians you see here—made all the decisions for our Order. Tralfane and I were on opposite sides, Gracel somewhat neutral in the middle. I initially picked Derrick because he had a strong sense of empathy—"

"You mean he had the capacity to love," I interrupted.

"Yes, the capacity to love. And love he did. He fell in love with a young officer named Lieutenant Dobrina Kierkopf. We had put her in his path because we believed she could provide him with comfort and companionship on the journey, the test he was undergoing. But he fell too hard for her, too deeply in love. His empathy for others had not yet matured, and he focused all of it on her." At this Serosian paused, letting his words sink in.

"So he became useless to you?" I asked.

Serosian shook his head. "Not useless. Just not . . . optimal. His emotions had swept him too far to one side, toward empathy and personal love and away from intuition. Without balance, with his empathetic emotions for Dobrina being too strong, he would never make a good choice to lead mankind. And then we began to look at you."

"Your balance between empathy and intuition was even stronger than your brother's," said Gracel. "But Derrick Cochrane was in the way. We put him in a crisis situation. A dangerous one, for sure, but not definitively lethal. He acted to save his lover rather than a whole Propulsion crew. He died a hero's death, but so did the rest of them. And Dobrina lived. And so we were left with you, and all of us agreed that although we would have to wait three more years for you to choose the Lightship service and begin training, your potential, even greater than your brother's, made it worth it."

"So you murdered my brother," I said to her. In that moment I wanted nothing more than to rip off her helmet and squeeze the life from her throat with both hands.

"No," said Serosian, stepping between us. "We gave him a chance to prove us wrong. He chose his lover and died a hero for doing it."

This was all too much for me. I began pacing in a circle, thinking, feeling rage and anger and a burning desire for vengeance. But something stopped me.

"You said that I had failed," I said, facing them all. "I made different choices from Derrick, but I still destroyed those dreadnoughts to save Janaan, to save Levant and Pendax and countless others. I chose my friends over all of humanity every time; you said so yourself, Serosian. And now you want to strike some grand bargain with me?"

"But you forget," said Tralfane. "According to all the reports Serosian filed, you also chose the service over your more pleasurable pursuits. You chose the Princess Karina in a political marriage that was better for the Union over either Janaan or Captain Kierkopf, whom you were drawn to just as strongly as your brother was. You showed the ability to make choices for the greater good. That's why we're here today."

"But why make your offer to me? Why not Prince Arin? You've groomed him from a young age to be your tool of power. Why pick me over him if I have such a spotty record, according to your belief systems?" I asked. I watched as their faces stayed blank, none of them willing to step forward and answer my questions. And then it hit me.

"Arin has gone rogue," I said. "You can't control him any longer, and you need me to take him out because your philosophies, the rules of your Order, won't allow you to after what your Order did here on Altos." I looked to Serosian, who answered for the group.

"Essentially you're correct. The Iron Hand has broken free, and he now controls the AIs that were running the Imperial ships. We could arrange a small party to assist you in attacking him, but our resources are gathering elsewhere," Serosian said.

"Elsewhere? For what?"

Tralfane cut in. "My sect of our Order is leaving human space. We are going on a voyage in short order and leaving you with the gifts, the weapons, we have already given you to survive. But you and Arin must determine who will lead humanity before we depart."

"And where are you going?" I asked.

"To meet the Founders. To join with the remnants of the First Empire, who left here to seek them after the war. They have a three-century head start on us, but we will catch them, face our creators together, and ask the questions humanity has been asking for millennia. But all this will happen half a galaxy away. Someone must remain behind and rebuild human civilization in this 'human' sector of space," Tralfane said.

"So what is your offer?" I asked, finally getting down to it. Gracel stepped forward.

"Become emperor of a new, more just Second Empire, or live under the harsh collective rule of Arin," she said. I shook my head.

"Me? As emperor?"

"This is our compromise," said Tralfane. "Both you and Arin have shown tendencies that we could not control or stop. But if you say yes to assuming the mantle of emperor, we have a way of rendering the prince regent helpless, as we did your ships."

I turned to my former friend and mentor. "And you, Serosian?"

He faced me with courage, and I admired that. "I have nothing to offer except my friendship."

"That's the only thing of yours I don't want," I snapped back at him.

"You should go easy on him, Cochrane," said Tralfane. "Everyone else, every Historian on Earth, has chosen to follow us to seek the Founders. The man standing before you is the only one who believes you have a chance to survive the encounter with our forebears."

I looked at my former friend and pitied him. "An army of one?" I asked.

"It is all I have to offer," he replied somberly. I looked at him, remembering our time as friends, perhaps too optimistically. I doubted we could ever be that close again. But he could be valuable to me.

"Then I accept your help, Serosian. You'll have a lot to make up for," I said. He said nothing, only bowed his head slightly.

"And our offer?" pressed Gracel.

I looked down at the trickle of water that represented what was left of life on Altos and made my decision.

"I made a promise to the grand duke before he died. A promise I intend to keep. Justice for Carinthia, justice for Arin," I said. Tralfane stepped forward.

"And after that? Union or Empire?" he asked. I didn't hesitate.

"Union," I said defiantly. He shook his head.

"A regrettable choice," Tralfane said, and then he handed me a small metal disk.

"What's this?"

"Instructions for how to reprogram the jump gate at Levant and galactic coordinates for Corant. You'll find the prince there. And I can only wish you good luck in defeating him. You'll need it," he said. Then Tralfane and Gracel went to their separate ships and departed along with the other yacht, leaving Serosian and me alone on the surface of Altos.

"I would be honored if you would let me pilot you back to *Defiant*, Captain," Serosian said, looking to me.

"Honor aboard my ship will be in short supply, Mr. Serosian, especially for you. I suggest you keep yours and just get me off this wasteland."

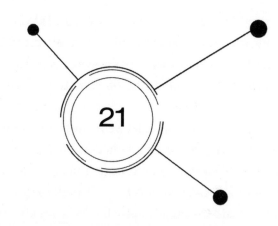

Back to Levant

I called to Babayan from the yacht and told her of our situation and of what had transpired on Altos. Then I called Maclintock and repeated the same. I watched from the yacht's command deck as the three yachts of Tralfane's sect jumped freely away to parts unknown.

"Good riddance," I said aloud.

"They would have made powerful allies," Serosian said. I looked at him.

"Allies in building a Second Empire? No thank you, Historian. One massive failure is enough of a blot on humanity's history," I said.

"So you favor your tiny Union?" he asked. I thought about that.

"I favor a republic of some kind, even a constitutional monarchy, guided by men and women of goodwill over any other structure, yes. And one I'm not prepared to lead. Ever."

"You think I chose wrongly, that I chose totalitarianism over your Union. You feel like I betrayed you. But I didn't, Peter. I was forced to choose between the Union and what was best for all of humanity. I chose humanity," he said. "You have no idea of the powers you will have to face in your lifetime, of the threat to your existence.

My sect used to have as many followers as Tralfane's. But as events played out, the consensus shifted. I was left essentially alone. And now my Order, all that I have ever known, is seeking out the Founders, praying that we have something of value to offer them so they don't destroy us at their whim."

"If they destroy you, at least we'll have three centuries to plan for their arrival," I said. Serosian laughed at that.

"Oh, they'll be here much more quickly than that, young man. You may have a decade, no more." That took me aback.

"But you said the First Empire has been seeking them out for that long."

"And that shows you the difference between their technology and ours. They will be here soon, Peter. Count on it." Those were sobering, unpleasant words.

"Just get me back to my ship," I finally said, then crossed my arms and determined not to talk to him again until we arrived.

Ten minutes later, he skillfully docked the yacht into the port vacated by Gracel. Full power immediately returned to all of *Defiant*'s shut-down systems. I insisted he do the same for the other ships from his console, and he complied.

Once up on the top level again, I opened the yacht's main doors and walked through. Babayan was there to meet me with a security force of thirty very pissed-off-looking marines. Serosian followed me through and was immediately restrained by two marines.

"What'll we do with him, sir?" asked Babayan. I looked at him.

"All systems restored on all three Lightships?" I asked.

"Yes," he replied.

"And all ships' systems once again autonomous from the yacht?"

"Yes," he said again. I looked at Babayan.

"Confine him to a stateroom, but not on the senior officers' deck. He's to have no technology or access to any of our systems, even coms. Four guards on the door at all times," I said.

"Understood, Captain," said Babayan.

"Peter, I can still help you," Serosian protested. I looked him in the eyes.

"I know that. But I don't trust you, nor am I ever likely to again. But you might eventually be useful. I will let you know when and if that time comes," I said. Then I turned back to Babayan. "Eject and destroy the yacht," I ordered her.

"No!" said Serosian. "That would be very unwise. That ship can be another weapon in your fight! You will need all you have in the battle to come."

"Perhaps," I said to him, "but right now it's a risk and a symbol of betrayal, one I need to get rid of." Then I ordered the marines to take him away, and he didn't protest further. My watch beeped in with a longwave notification. "Captains' conference in fifteen minutes," I said to Babayan. "I want that yacht destroyed before then."

"Aye, sir," she said, and then she was off. I sent Karina a com message to let her know I was okay, then agreed to meet her in our stateroom. I didn't really have time for any of this, but I hoped I could reassure her at least a little bit.

Once we were alone she hugged me, and I hugged her back with equal weight.

"Thank god you came back," she said, then kissed me. Just as quickly she broke away again and asked, "What happened down there?" I sat her down on the edge of the bed, holding her hands as I explained.

"They offered me an empire," I said.

"What?" She was surprised. "How—"

"Karina, it will be a lot easier if you just listen. They literally offered me a new Second Corporate Empire with me as the titular head.

One they claimed would be more just and that they would help me to run."

"And?"

"And I turned them down." She tilted her head at me.

"Why?" she asked. I smiled.

"Because what we have, the Union, is better than that."

"But . . . how do you know? I mean, you could be the one to unite humanity again. I can't think of anyone else I would trust more," she said. "Did it come with strings attached? Some sort of poison pill you couldn't accept?" I nodded.

"Many, I'm sure. We didn't get that far into details. But the biggest revelation—and there were many that I can't talk about right now—was that the Founders are returning."

"Returning?"

"Coming back to human space."

She looked perplexed. "From where?"

I shook my head. "From wherever *they* went when their civilization collapsed. Thousands of light-years away, I'm sure. And here's the weird part: there was never any old empire for us to fight against. At least no humans, anyway. It was always those automatons, robots left over from the Founders' time, led and programmed by Arin and his followers. But the Historians lost control of the automatons and eventually of Arin, and now he's waiting for us at Corant with his fleet, and we have to go fight him."

"No," she said, shaking her head and getting up to pace around our stateroom. "No more fighting. I've had enough, Peter."

"This is a fight we have to accept. I promised your father—"

She turned back to me abruptly. "He's dead, Peter, and we're alive. As much as I hate Arin for what he did to Carinthia, you and I should go on living."

"But we'll never be safe until he's gone. This is a job I have to finish," I said. Her hands went to her hips.

"Go, then. Finish the war you started. Finish Arin. Then I want us off this ship and out of this fight forever," she said. I thought about the Founders and how we might have to fight them for our sovereignty or our very survival.

"That may not be possible," I said. She looked at me with that steely Carinthian determination.

"I want a normal life for us and our future children, Peter. And I'm going to have it as best we can manage. Now go to your Captains' conference, and let's get this over with," she said.

So we went our separate ways—me to my conference, Karina back to her station on the bridge.

Neither of us was happy.

The virtual conference filled up again with the images of Maclintock, Dobrina, and their XOs, along with me and Babayan. This time Serosian and Karina were excluded, for obvious but very different reasons.

We were already underway for egress back through the gate to Levant, as Maclintock wanted us out of this system as quickly as possible. I didn't blame him.

"We've all heard your report of what happened down on Altos, Captain Cochrane," Maclintock started. "Now, if you'd please give your opinion of what it really means?"

I leaned forward on the table, thinking. "It's all been very confusing to me, sir, quite honestly. It seems as if the Union was an experiment and Prince Arin of Carinthia and I were pitted against each other during this experiment," I said.

"To what end?" asked Dobrina.

"To determine whether humanity stood a better chance of survival against the Founders if we were led by someone who relied on empathy and intuition or by a dictator, someone with an iron hand. All of these battles over the last few years, all of the conflicts and the casualties, have been orchestrated as part of this experiment. Even my brother's death was part of the plan, to allow me to ascend when the fucking Historians determined he was unfit." I knew that last part would shock Dobrina, but I couldn't hold back vital information from my commanding officer.

"So this fight is all about *you*?" asked Maclintock, an undertone of anger in his voice.

"Myself and Prince Arin, apparently. Yes, sir," I replied.

"So what are we to do with this information? Do you consider it reliable?" he pressed.

"I consider nothing a Historian says reliable anymore. I've always worried they had their own agenda because of the way they doled out technology to us piece by piece, but for want of any other data to conflict with their tale, I'd have to say yes, we have to trust it," I said.

"And what about Arin?" asked Dobrina, cutting back into the conversation. "How much power does he wield?"

"A considerable amount, I'd say. Since the Historians have given us instructions to reprogram the jump gate and the coordinates for Corant, I'd say the battle lines are clearly drawn, Captain. And I would also say the Historians have made it as even a battle as possible. It will come down to will, strategy, and tactics, and a bit of luck, as it always does," I said.

"The question is, does Arin have the power to stop our Lightships like the Historians did? Are we walking into an ambush?" asked the commodore. I considered this.

"We can put that question to Serosian, sir, but I would say he doesn't. With the destruction of the final yacht"—I looked to Babayan, who nodded slightly to confirm—"I would say that ability is off the table. I think it will be a fair fight," I finished.

"You're assuming the Historians want it to be a fair fight," said Dobrina. I looked at her image on the display screen.

"Captain Kierkopf, at this point most of the Historian Order is preparing to evacuate the Earth to go and join the remnants of the First Empire on its quest to find and reconnect with the Founders. I doubt they care much about the outcome of this fight. At least not enough to tilt the field to one side or the other." I turned back to Maclintock's image. "In my opinion, sir, this fight is ours to win or lose, and our immediate future will be determined by its outcome."

Maclintock nodded at me. "Duly noted, Captain," he said. And that was that.

Nothing left to do now but fight.

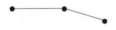

To our surprise, when we arrived back at Levant, we were greeted by the whole Union Navy. Our three Lightships plus *Valiant, Vanguard, Fearless*, and *Avenger*, along with thirty-two Wasps and assorted local naval auxiliaries.

Wesley commed in indicating they had received the data packet Tralfane had given me and that the gate technicians were already well into reprogramming it for Corant's coordinates. It turned out the old Imperial capitol was in a cluster of stars known as the Hyades, only 150 light-years from Earth. There was a group of eight white dwarfs, and Corant was the only planet orbiting the most central of the eight, "almost as if it were placed there," Wesley commented. It didn't matter if it was or not; it was where we were going.

There was no natural jump space for us to navigate to, our top astrogators told us. Those eight white dwarfs had put out enough energy during their decline to wipe the area clean of safe jump space, so our coordinates had to be precise to within just a few thousand kilometers. And Corant orbited very close to its cool, dense, dwarf star.

Battle plans had already been made up and distributed, but as far as I was concerned, they were going to be useless once we got to the system. We had never been there, never even explored a white dwarf star system, and we knew nothing of the size or distribution of the fleet we were going to face.

Different groups from each discipline met to try and coordinate plans. The astrogators worked with the techs to try and refine the coordinates of Corant closely enough that we could jump in and attain some level of surprise while also keeping a potential buffer from our enemies. This came down to how fast we were moving when we entered the gate and what speed we expected to operate at when we got in-system. We were only going to get one shot at this, and we needed to hit a bull's-eye.

I met with my fellow captains and command crews on a daily basis, and nothing was going as fast as I would have liked. On our third day of planning, coordinating, and general hobnobbing about nothing, Dobrina Kierkopf took me aside during one of our breaks. I agreed to meet with her in an anteroom to the main conference space we were using on Artemis.

"I wanted to ask you something," she started once we had sat down.

"About Derrick," I said, anticipating her question. "Actually, I'm surprised it's taken you this long to approach me."

"Peter . . ." She hesitated. "This is very difficult for me to talk about, you understand."

"I do," I said. Then I prodded her gently. "Tell me what you remember about that day." I knew she wanted answers. I just didn't know if I could give them to her.

"Derrick was at the con, in command on the night shift. I was in my cabin relaxing, I think. He and I were deeply involved in an affair by that time. We had fallen for each other hard, even though we knew the complications it presented." She stopped there, struggling, I thought, to bring up the emotions again.

"There was a fire alert in Propulsion—some sort of fuel leak had started and ignited. I always monitored the com traffic, and my normal day shift included a sweep of Propulsion, so I knew the equipment. I just listened for a long while, but the fire got worse. Then Derrick woke the captain and gave up the con to head down there. When I heard that call come over the com line, I reacted instinctively. I went to help. I went to where my man was. We fought the fire for what seemed like hours, but in reality it must have been only a few minutes. Then one of the fuel lines ignited, and the fire protection bulkheads started to drop. I tried to pull him out, but he pushed me away, pushed several others out, and ordered me to leave, but I wouldn't go. Finally he pushed me beyond the bulkhead wall and slammed it shut. Thirteen crew continued to fight the fire, but then a second fuel line burst, and... I watched him burn, Peter, watched him get consumed by the flames. The sight . . . it almost broke me." I reached out and grasped her hand, trying to comfort her. "Tell me what the Historians told you about Derrick," she asked me.

I sat back in my chair, contemplating how to tell her what I knew. I decided to just come out with it. "He fell in love. With you. They claim that bent his empathy, something they see as key in a leader, and began distorting his judgment. You told me once long ago that there was a chance the fire that day was sabotage. It was. A test, really. They wanted to see how Derrick would react if you were placed in danger near him, if he would pick his ship and his crew over you. They said—or so Serosian has told me—that when he made the choice to save you, to get you out of that room, that he sacrificed precious seconds that could have put the fire out. But because he hesitated, the second line lit up, and . . . thirteen people died, including him," I finished.

Tears flowed freely down Dobrina's cheeks. There was nothing for me to say or do, really, but I moved close and held her, letting her cry it out. She covered her face with her hands, crying tears that were years old, I supposed, and leaned into me. She cried for a long time before the sobbing stopped. Then she came back out of it, eventually wiping her face clean of the tears.

"So after this kind of betrayal, why does Serosian still live?" she asked. That was a hard question to answer, but I tried.

"Serosian has informed me that he did not have direct involvement in the incident, and I believe him, but that his sect of the Historian Order did. He did not approve or condone the test. Instead he moved to protect me. For what it's worth, regardless of the outcome, Derrick saved seven crewmen, including you. I can't fault him for that, nor do I question his motivations. I'd have done the exact same thing in his position, probably, and then the Historians would have had no use for me. But they did have plans. When I grew old enough, they tested me for empathy and intuition, and I scored even higher than Derrick. So the fact that they saw me as a better candidate was as much to blame as Serosian was for Derrick being put to the test. He could have survived, could have saved himself and ordered some of the other crewmen out. Then only a few would have died. But that wasn't good enough for him. He wanted to save them all, and you. He died a hero, and we should always remember that," I said.

She nodded silently, then stood. I stood with her. "Thank you, Peter. Talking with you helps, but I will always miss him," she said.

"I will, too," I said. "And your feelings toward Serosian?"

"Unchanged," she replied, "as I assume yours are. He is your problem now, and I'll have nothing to do with him, with any of them, again."

I accepted her statement with a nod, and she went back into the main conference room. I stayed a moment longer, contemplating everything that had happened, everything I'd been through and the choices I had made. I wasn't satisfied, and where the Union found itself wasn't enough for me. A reckoning was coming.

And I intended to be the instrument of that reckoning.

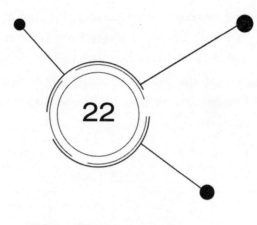

To Corant

By the end of the day, the final plans had been drawn up and agreed upon. I would lead about half of the fleet through the gate to a point 12.2 AUs from Corant to observe and report and hopefully draw some attention from our enemy. That would put us at about three hours from Corant at .55 light. Maclintock would lead the second group through an hour later, and they would flash in much closer to the ancient Imperial capitol—only 3.3 AUs distant, less than an hour away from the planet if they matched our speed. It would be a tricky deceleration for both groups but nothing our ships couldn't handle when asked.

Maclintock's flotilla would engage first by virtue of their arriving closer to Corant. It was a decision I didn't care for, but our speed would allow us to close fast on the battlefield. We hoped this two-pronged approach would lead to some sort of tactical advantage, though I was uncertain what that advantage was supposed to be.

I would go in first with a Lightship group of *Defiant*, *Resolution* (captained by Dobrina), and *Vanguard* (captained by Lucius Zander.) Commodore Maclintock would get his flagship, *Starbound*, plus

Avenger, Valiant (captained for battle by his friend Devin Tannace), and *Fearless* (with Dietar Von Zimmermann in command.) With one fewer Lightship than Maclintock, I got the bulk of the Wasps, twenty to his twelve. I didn't mind getting the lesser total firepower, though. We both had highly capable task forces, and we'd get our shots in. Against *what* was the question.

The plan also included bringing local navy auxiliaries to each jump location for repair and resupply, plus smaller support gunships to protect the auxiliaries from things like suicide drones. The Quantar Royal Navy had the best of these gunships, in my opinion, and I asked for one to be put aboard in place of one of my marine bulwark shuttles. I doubted there would be much cause for hand-to-hand combat in this encounter, but you never knew, so I kept on sixty marines but swapped out the other thirty for more technicians and damage control specialists.

We shut down the conference at midnight and scheduled the first wave—my wave—for 0700 departure through the gate. I should have been excited, but instead I felt a sense of detachment. I just wanted this ordeal over one way or another.

After signing off with my command staff, I went back to my stateroom at 0130. Karina was sleeping, and I lay down next to her, but trying to sleep was futile for me. I changed out of my duty uniform and into relaxed-fitting recreational clothes and made my way one last time to the observation lounge. I checked in for thirty minutes, sat in the lotus position, and emptied my mind. I searched deeply for my emotions, but I felt they were being blocked, by what I didn't know. After a few minutes of cleansing breathing, I realized something: my anxiety and depression over the deaths of the human beings aboard the dreadnoughts were gone. In their place I found a steely determination to finish things, especially with Prince Arin, the Butcher of Carinthia, and fulfill my promise to the grand duke. I wanted to rid the universe of Arin, and I was so close to getting that opportunity. I felt like a child on Reunion Day, unable to wait to open my presents. At that point I realized no other preparation was necessary. I was as ready as I would ever be.

An hour before the jump I assembled the Command staff in the briefing room one last time. I went through each report, ensuring we were as prepared as we could be. When I was satisfied, I dismissed the staff, including Karina, and brought up Dobrina and Zander on the conference screen.

Thirty minutes to go.

"The way I see it, we do an immediate assessment of any danger in the area, then accelerate as fast as we can to mission max speed and get inbound. With luck, that will draw in some of Arin's fleet," I said.

"Assuming they're there," said Zander.

"Always the optimist, Lucius," I replied with a smile.

"What about the Wasps and auxiliaries?" asked Dobrina.

"I have no time to wait for them to set up. They'll have to get it done themselves. I'll leave half a dozen Wasps behind to cover for the auxiliaries, but the rest come with our attack flotilla. Remember, until Maclintock arrives in-system, I'm your commander. And I command we kick some ass as quickly as possible," I said.

"What about our egress route?" asked Dobrina. That got my ire up.

"In case of defeat? Not an option, Captain. But in case you missed it, there is no egress jump space in the Corant system. That much our scans have shown, and it fits with what we know about it from popular mythology. During the days of the old empire, an unscheduled jump into Corant space was grounds for instant destruction. No one went in or out of Corant space except by their own means, meaning local jump point generators or jump gates like the one at Levant, and I haven't heard of too many of those. No, we stay and fight to the end. Once it's over we'll pick the nearest known star system and make our jumps home, even if it requires time in traverse space," I said.

"So you expect to win?" she asked. I looked at her and Zander on their respective screens.

"I've considered no other option," I replied.

"Captain, if I may," said Zander. "I might recommend the Minara system as an egress point. It's been surveyed, it's within our direct jumping range at twenty-nine light-years, and it might even serve as a refuge for damaged vessels in need of repair. If this battle goes on, we may need such a place."

I contemplated my former commander. His wisdom was something I couldn't argue with. "Very well. Tell the flotilla our plan to use Minara as a backup staging area for the auxiliaries. But I shouldn't need to remind you that only the Lightships and Wasps will have the capability to direct-jump there. The other ships will be on their own in Corant space until the battle is over and will require rescue at that point."

"I recommended the same strategy to Wesley last night. He said there will be auxiliaries stationed at Minara by the time we need them and a pathway home from there."

"So you were only humoring me by passing this strategy along now, Lucius?" I said.

He shrugged. "You've had a lot on your mind, laddie," he said.

"Anything else?" There were negative shakes from both of my captains. I couldn't help but feel I'd drawn the better hand than Maclintock. I wouldn't want to go into this battle with any Lightship captains other than these two.

I checked my watch. "Twenty-three minutes to the jump, Captains. Follow *Defiant* on my mark."

"Aye, sir," I got from both of them. Then Zander signed off, but Dobrina stayed on.

"Something else, Captain?" I asked. She nodded.

"I just want you to know there will be no repeat of what happened at Skondar. I will follow your orders, sir. To the letter," she said.

"Thank you, Captain," I said. "I have complete confidence in you."

And with that I signed off and made for my bridge.

The countdown for our flotilla to jump through the Levant gate to Corant seemed agonizingly long. I spent the time walking the bridge decks, checking monitors, and making sure all was in order, but I was just killing time. At 0658 we got the "go" signal from Wesley, and I ordered my flotilla to full prep status. I watched as the jump gate ring fired to life, its shimmering blue-and-silver energy waves indicating its readiness to receive as many ships as we saw fit to push through the portal. I had three Lightships, twenty Wasps, two Repair and Refit ships, and one medical auxiliary under my command. The auxiliaries' orders were simple: jump, station in place, and prepare for what we hoped wouldn't be necessary.

I had changed my mind at the last minute, holding back only three Wasps for defense of the auxiliaries. There would be more of them available at Minara if this battle dragged on, and I didn't want to lessen the impact of my attack force any more than I had to. The Wasps, with their upgrades, could defend against anything up to a dreadnought, and any three Wasps could probably trade punches evenly with one. My expectation, however, was that Prince Arin would concentrate his heavy ships around himself and whatever he was protecting on Corant and use lighter ships at the periphery of his defense. For my part, I intended to use a tight cone formation with *Defiant* at the point, *Resolution* and *Vanguard* at the next level, and the attacking Wasps filling out the formation. The Auxiliaries and the Wasps protecting them would occupy the center of the formation, but their orders would be to stay put once we advanced inward. My hope was to cut decisively through the enemy defensive line and then to head straight for *Vixis* and Arin. By the time Maclintock and his flotilla jumped into the fray an hour later, I hoped we'd have a distinct advantage.

At precisely 0700 I gave the advance order, and my flotilla, already in formation, moved forward to the jump gate ring. We began a slow acceleration, and as I watched, the ring grew in size on *Defiant*'s main bridge display. The rippling event horizon, looking as much like ocean water as anything else, increased in size until I felt the ripple effect of the crossing pour through my consciousness. A moment later we were in uncharted space, facing the unknown. I gave the other ships a few seconds to complete the crossover, then demanded reports, first from my crew, then from the whole flotilla.

"Battlefield status," I demanded of my longscope officer, who also happened to be my wife.

"Still evaluating, sir," said Karina.

"Hurry it up, Lieutenant," I prodded in a not-too-friendly manner, then turned my attention to Duane Longer at Propulsion.

"Engage the HD impeller drive. Give me .55 light, Mr. Longer. Inward directly to the planet," I said.

"Aye, sir," he replied. I turned back to Karina.

"Where's my report, 'scopeman?" I asked.

"Coming up now on the tactical, Captain," she said, then started narrating the battlefield overview. "Not what we expected, Captain. I count thirty active dreadnoughts in battle groups of three, 120 HuKs, numerous suicide drones, and an unbelievable amount of scatter mines throughout the system. They're dispersed, sir, rather than in a compact formation. Range from the planet of these ten battle groups is anywhere from 1.5 AUs to 3.5 AUs. They're defending a large swath of space, sir. We're actually inside the range of one of the battle groups, sir, but they're on the other side of the system."

"And *Vixis*?"

"As far as I can tell, the prince's Lightship is not in the Corant system, sir," Karina said. That was troubling.

"Topography of the system?" I asked. She replied quickly again.

"There are two moons—or rather, irregularly shaped asteroids, moonlets—in Corant's tidal lock, sir. Both have nearly identical dimensions, twenty-seven by twenty-two by eighteen kilometers, and they're in equatorial orbits in equidistant orbit distances from the planet, sir. There is a debris field where a third moonlet might have been located, sir, almost exactly the same distance away from moonlet two. Other than that, the system is free of planets or objects of any kind. Almost like it was wiped clean of debris, sir."

"Those moonlets likely contain defensive platforms of some kind, if I'm guessing right. But without *Vixis* to deal with, I have no interest in the planet. Mr. Layton, how long at current speed to the nearest dreadnought battle group?" I asked.

"Eighteen minutes, sir. It looks as though they've spotted us, as they are starting to accelerate toward us. In fact, two other groups seem to be responding to our presence as well," he said.

"First things first. Target the nearest battle group and plot an intercept course," I ordered.

"Aye, sir." I turned to Longer.

"Plan a max acceleration curve toward the Imperial battle group, then a full deceleration to engage them, Mr. Longer. I want us inside thirty thousand clicks when we reach the battlefield," I said.

"Yes, sir."

"XO, I want to use the anti-graviton plasma first, then a volley of missiles with frequency-busting warheads, and then I want the gravity weapons at my disposal," I said to her.

"Aye, sir," replied Babayan. "What about the scatter mines?"

"Have the Wasps clear us a pathway with coil cannons or missiles, Commander. I want my flotilla to be all-in on this engagement,"

I said. Then I sat back in my safety couch as my crew carried out my orders.

We began our deceleration to the battlefield eleven minutes later. Four minutes after that, Longer had *Defiant* and the rest of the flotilla ready to engage in our first skirmish. The Wasps had cleared the pathway to the battlefield through the annoying scatter mines, and the enemy flotilla was coming right at us, *like automatons do*, I decided. I stood and looked at the tactical display, then activated the command com line.

"All ships, stay in formation until we engage. Lightships *Resolution* and *Vanguard* will take on the trailing dreadnoughts, *Defiant* will take on the leader. Each ship should use the battle plan locked into their AIs for the initial contact with the enemy. Allow your AIs to direct the attacks. I will free you to go to manual at my discretion," I said. I got a series of acknowledgments, then looked to my acting weapons officer.

"The anti-graviton plasma first, if you will, XO," I said.

"Ready, sir," Babayan said. I took a deep breath.

"Fire!"

The shimmering silver-gold beam exploded out of our forward weapons arrays and toward the lead dreadnought. The range of the weapon was beyond anything the dreadnought had, but we knew from our earlier encounters that they now had a defensive field of some kind, very much like a Hoagland. Whether they could survive all of our weaponry remained to be seen.

The plasma impacted the lead dreadnought's shielding, and she started to spark and was wracked by explosions as her shielding overloaded. Whatever the shielding was, it wasn't as strong as a Hoagland Field. The follow up frequency-busting missiles hit her hard, cutting obvious holes in her defenses. She staggered and bucked, vainly trying to get off coil cannon shots and missiles against our defenses but with little success. I checked the rest of the battlefield.

Resolution and *Vanguard* were having similar successes against their opponents. The enemy had done us a big favor by breaking into small task forces. Probably no three dreadnoughts could hold the battlefield against a single Lightship.

Our Wasps were also cleaning up against the enemy HuKs. With full Hoaglands and upgraded coil cannons and missiles, the unshielded HuKs were no match for the Wasps. As I watched, though, an HuK broke formation and made straight for the nearest Wasp on a suicide run. The impact was tremendous, but our Wasp survived. I commed to the ship's captain; she had structural and stress damage and her field was weakened, so I ordered her back to the auxiliaries for repairs with orders to rejoin as soon as possible. I passed the word around to the other Wasp captains via com that the HuKs were going suicide and that they should adjust tactics accordingly. They did, switching to longer-range missile strikes rather than using their shorter-range coil cannon arrays.

I turned my attention back to the capital ships. All three dreadnoughts were in various stages of desiccation, burning, listing, or drifting. They were all disabled now with large holes in their defensive fields, but they weren't destroyed. I got on the command com line.

"Captains, prepare your gravity plasma weapons. Set them to implode. I want the field cleared of every last dreadnought. Let's not waste missiles and torpedoes on them," I said.

"They're helpless as they are. Why not just leave them?" asked Dobrina.

"Because my goal is to clear this system of every enemy ship that can harm the Union, Captain," I replied.

"That may not be Maclintock or Wesley's goal," she said.

"Neither of them are here at the moment, Captain Kierkopf," I reminded her. Zander stayed diplomatically quiet on that front.

"Aye, sir," Dobrina finally said. I turned to Babayan.

"Gravity weapons on my display, XO," I ordered, then went to my console, brought up the implosion beam, locked it into the weapons array, and counted down five seconds to firing the weapon. The beam swept toward the target dreadnought and within a few seconds had crushed it from existence. *Resolution* and *Vanguard* quickly followed suit with their enemies. I then ordered us to attack at will any remaining HuKs or drones, and within another ten minutes the battlefield was clear of enemy targets.

"That was . . . clinical," said Dobrina over the command com line. I ignored her.

"All ships prepare to proceed inbound. Contact with the next enemy task force will be in . . ." I looked down at George Layton.

"Nineteen minutes, sir," he said.

"Nineteen minutes," I repeated. "You have until then to reset your systems."

Then I sat back down and ordered up a new battle plan for the second task force. I'd never felt so calm or clear of purpose.

●———————●
                          ●

The second engagement went much like the first, only this time I had us lead with the gravity lance to push the dreadnoughts off their marks. I didn't want to use the same tactics every time and allow their battle AIs to gain any insight into our plans. An hour into the battle we had taken out nine dreadnoughts and dozens of HuKs and depleted the enemy forces by almost 20 percent. Not bad for the "smaller" of the two Union battle groups.

Right on the hour mark Maclintock's group flashed in, and there was a mad scramble from the enemy to compensate for a larger attack force so much closer to Corant. I called Maclintock and told him that so far *Vixis* had been a no-show and that those defensive platforms were an unexpected worry. He agreed and ordered us to continue in a sweeping maneuver, taking out as many task forces as we could.

The battle went on like this for two more hours. Maclintock was having so much success he ordered his auxiliaries to move up and resupply his ships with missiles and torpedoes. I did the same. There were now just twelve dreadnoughts and thirty-two operational HuKs in the enemy force, and they were beating a hasty retreat to Corant, likely to the cover of those moonlet defensive platforms. The only question now was whether to pursue and finish them or hold off and regroup. The captains met yet again on the displays in the command deck briefing room, but this time, all seven of us were present.

"We don't know how much of a punch those platforms can dish out," Maclintock said, "so I want to be cautious."

"With all due respect, sir," I replied, "we don't even know if they're operational."

"I wouldn't be so quick, laddie," said Captain Zander from the screen. "Those dreadnoughts are making for them as though they are. And even the most basic battle AI has a survival instinct built in. I'm betting they know what they've got in those platforms."

"What bothers me is that the two platforms are built on almost identical moonlets. It makes me worry that they could be something more than they appear," Dobrina said.

"They've already lost two thirds of their fleet. You'd think that if they were anything other than missile or cannon bases, they'd have acted by now," said Captain Von Zimmerman of *Fearless*.

"I'll have my 'scopeman run a scan and see if we can detect anything that might give us pause," I offered. Maclintock agreed, and I passed the order on to Karina to send out two longwave probes to analyze the moonlets.

We were now sitting in open space, our auxiliaries moved up, just 1.25 AUs from Corant itself. But without *Vixis* and Prince Arin on the scene, I was beginning to wonder what our mission goals were.

"So what are your orders, Commodore?" asked Dobrina.

"Continue to refuel and resupply. That's what our support ships are for. When that's done, we move into a single formation and finish this thing off," he said.

"And Arin?" I asked.

"That's your personal vendetta, Captain. Getting revenge on him is not part of my orders, nor this task force's. Understood?"

"Yes, Commodore," I said. But in my heart I didn't believe it. I felt in my bones that Arin would be here and that the difficult part of this mission was just beginning.

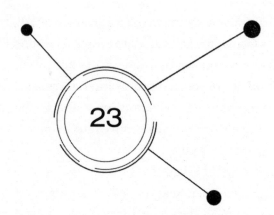

The Battle of Corant

Karina came back with her report within ten minutes. Her face appeared on one of the empty screen displays from the bridge even though she was only a few steps away from the briefing room.

"I actually sent out three probes," she started. "One for each moonlet. One is just debris, though the telemetry is indicative of relatively equal mass compared with the other two. By the relative dispersal of the debris field, my best guess is that it was destroyed during the Imperial Civil War, between three hundred and four hundred years ago. The other two are both unique in their ways. The second shows evidence of massive damage, is in a state of severe disrepair, and it has a low-density core and exposed structured buttresses that can only indicate artificiality. In short, it was probably once inhabited on the inside, with a central hyperdimensional light and power source, somewhat like a 'Dyson sphere,' I believe it was once called. There is no evidence that this moonlet is operational, except for a ring of cannon and missile batteries on its surface, which appears to be a recent addition.

"The third one, however, is much more problematic. It appears to be fully operational, with its own internal hyperdimensional power source. It is also likely artificial in nature, with extensive regolith covering its surface protecting an internal metal superstructure. It shows evidence of crater pockmarking on the surface, but my scans indicate that it's hollow inside and generating both warmth and an acceptable environment for human habitation," she said.

"Wait, you're saying the thing is *inhabited*?" I asked.

"I'm saying it *could be*, Captain. There is enough interior surface area and internal water to support a population as high as twenty thousand humans, according to my readings."

"Weaponry?" asked Maclintock.

"None obvious externally, sir," said Karina. "It has some sort of apparatus at its narrow end, but the purpose of this structure is not obvious, and there are no HD energy readings. There *is* a large depression that looks like a crater at the wide end, and a large amount of HD energy is emanating from that location."

"A ship like that, if it is a ship, could generate enough firepower that it wouldn't need missiles or coil cannons or anything conventional," Dobrina said.

"Does it have propulsion?" asked Zander.

"Uncertain," replied Karina. "Overall, it has a massive HD signature, as I said, so propulsion, even for an object that big, is possible."

"I'd like another opinion, Captains. This discovery could change everything. Captain Cochrane, would you please bring Historian Serosian into this discussion?" Maclintock asked. Everyone looked uncomfortable at this, but I didn't really have a choice. Serosian was on my ship because I thought he might be of help at some point. Now was that time.

"Aye, Commodore," I said, and I arranged to add Serosian's image to the main display. He joined within two minutes.

"Are you up-to-date with our tactical situation, Historian?" asked Maclintock. His tone was more distant than before his betrayal by his former confidant.

"I am, Commodore. Though I have limited access to ships' data, I don't really need to see what we are facing. I already possess knowledge of the Corant system through my former Order's technical histories," Serosian said.

"Then what is this thing?" asked the commodore.

"This is undoubtedly Founder technology, captured and brought here to protect the Imperial capitol by the First Empire. Our most recent analysis more than two decades ago indicated that this device was in a state of stasis and had not been in use for hundreds of years at least," he said.

"Well, it's active now," I chimed in.

"Please allow the Historian to finish," said Maclintock tersely.

"As I was saying, this device is a massive weapons platform—a superweapon, really—and also a living, breathing space habitat. It was designed to go anywhere and do virtually anything from military operations to planetary colonization. In fact, the Founders' name for them in their language was 'Colony Ship.' We believe that at one time there were thousands of such vessels," said Serosian.

"What happened to them?" Dobrina asked.

Serosian hesitated for a moment, then said, "We believe that hundreds of thousands such ships left with the Founders to go on their great pilgrimage . . . to wherever it is that they went," he said.

"How long ago?" I asked, always inquisitive.

"At least two hundred millennia."

"None of that is relevant to our current tactical situation," said Maclintock. "I'm more interested in how this thing can be combatted if necessary."

"I'm not sure that it can be, Commodore—at least not with conventional weapons," Serosian said.

"So no missiles, no atomic weapons, no coil cannons. What about our gravity weapons or the disintegration ray?" That was Dobrina, always looking for the best tactical angle.

"Likely shielded against such weaponry."

"I've got a different question, Historian," I said. "Who's inside that Colony Ship? Are they living or robots?"

Serosian shuffled through some papers out of our sight, then commented, "Judging from the data I have been given, I'd have to agree with the longscope officer's report that it could hold a population of about twenty thousand humans. As to the rest . . . I can't say."

"Could it hold a Lightship inside?" I asked. He looked at me from the display monitor.

"Easily. Dozens, if they so desired." I looked to Maclintock.

"We have to destroy this thing," I said. "The Union will never be safe as long as it's around."

"I hear your concern, Captain Cochrane, but right now there's no evidence this thing is an imminent threat to any Union planets," he said.

"Commodore, this technology is thousands of years more advanced than ours. If that Colony Ship is populated with military forces loyal to Prince Arin, which I suspect that it is, then they will eventually find a way to use it against us," I said, pressing him.

"I agree," came Zander's scratchy voice.

"I do as well," said Dobrina. The other captains started to look worried, suspecting they would be forced to give their opinions, too.

"It doesn't matter. We don't have the weapons to take it on anyway," said Maclintock.

"*Defiant* does," I said. Maclintock looked at me, head tilted just a bit.

"Explain," he said. I sat back in my chair.

"Before we left Candle for the Sandosa mission, the Historian Order upgraded our weapons. All of our Lightships now have these same upgrades, save for one: the torsion beam," I said.

"What's a torsion beam?" asked the commodore.

"A weapon that can accelerate any magnetic core to a speed that will rip the host object apart. Anything that has a magnetic core is vulnerable. A ship. A planet. A Colony Ship. *Defiant* used this weapon to destroy the moon Drava in the Skondar system when we rescued *Impulse II* and needed to take out the automaton factory there," I said.

"And why didn't you report this to me?" demanded Maclintock.

"Because there simply hasn't been time, sir. This weapon was approved by Admiral Wesley, and I informed him that we had used it, but no more details. That was all that was in my orders, sir, that I had to report its use to the Admiralty. The simple fact is that this weapon is available. And I believe *Defiant* should use it against that Colony Ship."

Maclintock looked to Serosian for an opinion. "Can this torsion beam be effective against the Colony Ship?" he asked. Serosian hesitated.

"It's possible," he said. "If certain random factors play out in our favor."

"You mean if we get lucky," chimed in Zander. The Historian nodded.

"If we get lucky."

Maclintock took a long time thinking about what to say next. Finally he said, "Our mission here was to take out the enemy fleet. We have them on their heels now, and we are going to finish that job." He looked directly at me. "Permission to attack the moonlet or Colony Ship or whatever the hell it is denied for now. We will focus on trying to draw the enemy ships out and away from both Corant and that weapon, and then we will fight as one fleet under my command. Is that understood?" We all acknowledged, although mine came last. "Battle plans will be uploaded to your tactical AIs within fifteen minutes. We move inward in twenty. And I will accept no disobedience on this," he said as a warning, most likely to me.

"How will we get them to come out and meet us without drawing us into range of those big beasties?" asked Zander.

"We'll have to find a way, Lucius, although I admit I don't quite know how. Hopefully the tactical AIs will come up with something," said Maclintock.

"Perhaps they won't have to, sir." The voice belonged to Karina. "Longwave scan just indicated the enemy fleet has regrouped, and they're heading back our way, sir," she reported.

"All the better," said Maclintock.

"They could be trying to draw us into range of that thing's weaponry," I warned. Maclintock was unmoved.

"Carry out the battle plans as ordered, Captains," he said. "That is all." With that he cut the com line and the captains vanished one by one from the displays. I shut mine down and walked across the short hallway to my bridge, where I was greeted by both Karina and Lena Babayan.

"Orders, sir?" asked Babayan.

"Prep the tactical AI to receive new orders from *Starbound*, XO," I said, then turned to Karina. "Make the torsion beam available on my console, Lieutenant."

"Yes, sir," she said and started to go back to her station. My hand on her arm stopped her.

"But be prepared to break off from the fleet on my orders," I said to them both. The two women exchanged glances, both fully knowing what I was asking of them.

"At your orders, sir," said Babayan. Karina acknowledged with a nod.

And then they were off, and I looked at my empty command chair, hoping this wouldn't be the last time I sat in it.

Battle tactics were loaded into our tactical AI, and we were moving inward toward Corant again at precisely twenty minutes on the dot. It would take forty-one minutes for our two fleets to converge near

Corant and the Colony Ship at what seemed a safe distance. But then almost everything seemed safe until you faced the unknown.

At nineteen minutes into our run we began our deceleration to the battlefield, a field of asteroids that gravity had smashed into a ring of rocks eight hundred thousand kilometers from Corant itself. It seemed unlikely that the Colony Ship could hit us from there, as our anti-graviton plasma, also a Founder weapon, only had a range of a hundred thousand clicks max.

It was also clear that the enemy ships—I hesitated to think of them as "First Empire" ships anymore—were bound for this area as their preferred ground, since they had begun decelerating while vectoring toward it before we did. No matter. I was convinced we could handle anything this archaic fleet threw at us.

After much debate, at the five-minute mark I called down and ordered the guard detail to bring Serosian to the bridge. I was taking a risk, but he could be of use in battle against an unknown, especially a Founder unknown.

Heads turned when he entered the bridge under guard. I swiveled to look at him but did not stand to greet him.

"Mr. Serosian, will you help us in this battle from the Historian's station?" I asked him directly.

"I will," came his simple reply. I motioned him to his console.

"Please, then," I said, "but do understand that these guards will be present. At the first sign of treachery, you will be summarily executed."

"Understood, Captain. But there will be no treachery from me. You have my word."

"For whatever that's worth," said Babayan, who had come up to stand next to me.

"Many of the crew feel the same, Historian. I'll leave it to you to prove them wrong," I said. All eyes on the bridge had turned to watch the exchange.

"As you say, Captain," Serosian said, then took his station and powered it up with a sweep of his hand.

"Two minutes to the battlefield, Captain," called Karina.

"Let's do this," I said, turning back to my tactical display. The battle AI had recommended we return to our first strategy, using the disintegration plasma followed by frequency-busting missiles, atomic torpedoes, and then finishing the dreadnoughts with the gravity-imploder weapon. I approved the tactics and forwarded the "go" sign to Lena Babayan at the weapons console. We reached initial attack range for the disintegration plasma, one hundred thousand kilometers, ten seconds later.

"Pick out a dreadnought and engage the enemy," I said, then switched on the intership com line. "All Wasps are free to engage enemy HuKs and drones at your discretion," I said across the line. On the tactical board, our ships began to break formation. Our Wasps accelerated toward their targets while Babayan had George Layton move to an optimal range of about eighty thousand kilometers from the closest dreadnought. All of the other Lightship battle groups did the same. *Resolution* and Dobrina were the first to make contact with the enemy, then *Starbound*, *Vanguard*, and *Fearless*, whose captain, Dietar Von Zimmerman, was showing signs he would become an aggressive combat officer.

I watched as our first volley from the disintegration plasma hit our targeted dreadnought. She listed and shimmied in space, then seemed to right herself and continued closing on us. A few seconds later the missile/atomic torpedo combination volley hit her a second time. She replied with a volley of her own missiles, which we shook off of our Hoagland Field as inconsequential.

"Gravity imploder ready, sir," called Babayan from her station. I took up my console and prepped the weapon, then fired once it was charged without hesitating. Knowing the dreadnoughts were automated and not manned had freed me of any thoughts about destroying the massive machines. I watched as the gravity plasma probed out into the black of space, seeking out its target. It enveloped the dreadnought, which began to list in a familiar pattern.

Then something odd happened.

The expected shower of sparks and collapse of her superstructure didn't occur. Instead, she righted herself a second time and continued closing on us, firing her own frequency-busting missiles and atomic torpedoes. They hit us hard, the tiny pinpricks of atomic energy our weakened field allowed through impacting against our hull. We shook and rattled, but I was in denial.

This was not happening.

"Historian, why didn't the gravity imploder destroy the dreadnought?"

"Unknown, except . . ."

I turned toward him when he didn't finish. "Except what?"

"It appears that the Colony Ship is extending some kind of additional defensive field around the enemy dreadnoughts—in fact, the entire enemy fleet," he said calmly.

"What's the nature of the field?"

"Unknown, as I said, but it has some properties of an accelerated particle field. It's not that our weapons don't work, Captain, it's that the field is nullifying their effect by rapidly changing the makeup of the space around the dreadnoughts on a microcosmic level. In short, it's dissipating our weapons' energy, most likely into another dimension."

"Ten thousand kilometers, sir. We're within coil cannon range," reported Babayan. I checked the status of the other Lightships. None was making progress against the dreadnoughts, and the range to the edge of that newly detected particle field was closing with every second.

"Mr. Layton, back us away," I said evenly. We needed more time to assess this change to the battlefield. "XO, send out a call to all ships on the open fleet line. Recommend we retreat to our previous position as rapidly as possible due to the particle field the Colony Ship is projecting. Mr. Longer, get me up to half light on the HD impellers as quickly as you can."

There was a round of "Aye, sir"s to my orders as I sat back in my command chair. A second later Maclintock chimed in on my private com line.

"What are you detecting, *Defiant*?" he demanded.

"There appears to be some sort of accelerated particle field defending the enemy fleet, sir, emanating from that Colony Ship. Highly recommend we return to our auxiliaries and regroup," I said.

"And where does the information about this field come from, Captain?" I turned to look behind me.

"From Historian Serosian, sir," I said. There was a pause on the other end of the line.

"Do you trust him?" I looked at Serosian again. He was busily engaged in analysis of the situation.

"I don't think we have any choice, sir. We're not getting to any of their ships, sir," I said. As if on cue, one of our Wasps matched up with *Valiant* exploded spectacularly on the tactical display. "Recommend you give the retreat order now, sir."

"Agreed," said Maclintock and cut me off. A second later he was on the open fleet line ordering a full retreat to our previous coordinates. I watched as the entire fleet broke off their attacks and started accelerating away from the battlefield. I was so intent on the fleet maneuvers that I missed the most important event of all.

"Captain!" called Karina from her longscope station, alarm in her voice. "The Colony Ship, sir! It's moving!"

I turned back to the tactical display. The monstrosity was moving all right, accelerating far more rapidly than we could or than anything of its size should have been able to.

Straight for *Defiant*.

The next few seconds were full of orders and acknowledgments flying through the air on the bridge. Everything was chaos, and it was my job to bring it into some kind of order.

"All personnel, stations!" I ordered. "Take your positions and cut the chatter. Longscope, distance to the Colony Ship?"

"Six hundred thousand kilometers and closing, sir," Karina said.

"But how damn fast?" I asked roughly. She looked frightened but quickly had my answer.

"I make it about fifty thousand kilometers per minute," she said. "At that speed they will overtake us in about twelve minutes."

"Have they stopped accelerating?" I asked.

"It's not like they ever did accelerate, sir. They just started moving and seemed to be up to speed in seconds, sir," Karina said.

I turned to Serosian. "At that acceleration level, everyone in that thing should be a blood spot on the wall," I said.

"Obviously they have solved the acceleration curve problem," he said. I turned to Duane Longer at Propulsion.

"You know what I'm going to ask, Lieutenant. How much more speed can we take?" I asked.

"Not much, Captain," he replied. "We're maxed out as it is. Inertial dampers can't go much higher."

"Mr. Layton, start varying our course. Move us around, don't let them get a line of sight on us."

"Yes, sir," said Layton. Finally I turned to my astrogator.

"Mr. Arasan," I said to my astrogator. "Program us a jump to Minara. I need it ready in two minutes. We have no idea of that thing's range."

"Yes, sir," replied Arasan, then quickly turned to his board and began running frantic calculations.

We watched as the minutes clicked by. Arasan had his jump calculated. Layton was moving us in every random direction possible. Everyone else was quiet, and I assumed they were as scared as I was.

The Colony Ship just kept coming. I went to Serosian's station and spoke to him in a whisper.

"Can we combat this thing?" I asked.

"Uncertain," he replied in an equally quiet voice.

"Best guess," I came back at him. He looked up at me with a very serious look on his face.

"Founder technology is at least hundreds—if not thousands—of years more advanced than our own. That makes them dangerous beyond measure. Beyond this one vessel, we've only ever surveyed one other Colony Ship in my experience. It was a derelict, and as near as we could tell it had only been stopped by a barrage of asteroids," he said.

"Flung at it somehow? Some form of advanced gravity weapon?"

"We believe the civilization it was attacking destabilized their own magnetic core and . . . exploded their own planet to stop it," he finished. I was astonished by that.

"That doesn't seem like a viable option for us. Unless we could do the same to Corant," I speculated.

"We do have the torsion beam," he reminded me.

"Indeed we do. But from what I saw at Drava, it can destroy a world but not explode it. That would have to be some other type of technology." He merely nodded at me. "We have to get that particle field down, don't we?" I finished.

"We do," he said. "Or get inside its range somehow."

"So it's not solid? Could a fully shielded ship make it through the barrier?" I asked. He shook his head.

"By my calculations, doubtful. And that field extends out to five hundred thousand kilometers around the Colony Ship." That set my mind to whirling. A tactic we had used before . . .

I nodded to Serosian and then went to my astrogator's station. "Mr. Arasan," I started, motioning him toward my office. I activated the aural shield, then gave him the rest of his instructions.

"I can do it, sir," he said when we concluded.

"Then go program it," I said.

"Aye, sir." With that he was gone back to his station. I came out of my office, stepping right into our next crisis.

"The Colony Ship is turning away from our path, sir," Babayan reported. I quickly took my chair and scanned my console.

"To where?"

"Bearing down on *Valiant* now, sir."

I sat quickly and looked to my tactical display. She was indeed bearing away from us. And bearing down on *Valiant*.

"What will happen when *Valiant* crosses their field?" I asked Serosian.

"You're talking about two different kinds of high-energy fields, both run on energy from higher dimensions. Simply put, anything could happen," he said.

"Longscope officer, how long—"

"Fifty-five seconds until *Valiant* crosses the threshold, Captain," said Karina, anticipating my question. "The 'scope indicates that the Colony Ship is scaling up a massive HD energy curve, sir."

"Is it a weapon?" Neither Karina nor Babayan answered, so Serosian stepped in.

"High likelihood, Captain."

"She's got to jump. She's got to get out of there! Raise Maclintock—" I stopped, stunned at what I saw on my tactical screen.

A massive bolt of green energy traveled the incredible distance between the Colony Ship and *Valiant*, half a million kilometers, in just a few seconds. The energy pierced the particle field and seemed to accelerate even more. It missed *Valiant*, striking instead at her five support Wasps. They sparked and recoiled for a second as the energy beam struck them head-on.

Then all five ships disintegrated.

"I have the Commodore on ship-to-ship, sir," said my com officer, Ensign Lynne Layton.

"On speakers," I said. Maclintock's voice came in scratchy and ruddy from all the interference the Colony Ship was causing.

"What do you want, Captain?" he asked curtly, no doubt impatient as he fought for survival, retreating in the face of an implacable enemy.

"Sir, according to Serosian's calculations, we can't allow our ships to be overtaken by the Colony Ship's particle field defenses. It could cripple us all. We just saw what it could do through fully protected Hoagland Fields on those Wasps, sir," I said.

"Our Lightships have much stronger Hoagland Fields than those Wasps, Captain," he said.

"With due respect, Commodore, these weapons are so powerful they don't even register on our scales." This came from Serosian, who had left his station and stepped up to the railing behind me.

"Sir, I recommend all ships jump immediately to our safe haven at Minara, then get home as quickly as possible. We don't know—"

"My orders stand for now, Captain," said Maclintock, and with that he cut the line. I looked up at the tactical display.

"Longscope, report," I said. Karina's answer was quick.

"*Valiant* will cross the threshold in fifteen seconds," she said. We all watched helplessly as the Colony Ship and its extended particle field enveloped *Valiant*. Seconds passed as her Hoagland Field sparked and then collapsed against the force of the enemy. A second beam of green energy launched at *Valiant*.

Within a few seconds, she too was disintegrated. Her captain, Devin Tannace, and her entire crew, gone.

The Colony Ship changed course again, this time bearing down on *Avenger* and her captain, Ozil.

"Can we penetrate that particle field with any of our weapons?" I demanded of Serosian.

"Best guess would be the gravity push beam. It might be strong enough to punch a hole in that field," he responded.

"Fire it up, XO," I ordered Babayan.

"Ready, sir," she responded a few seconds later.

"Fire at your discretion, XO." She did. The nearly invisible beam impacted the particle field fifteen thousand kilometers from *Defiant*. On the tactical display, the particle field started to weaken, bending, forming a divot. "It's working!" I said.

"Not fast enough," said Serosian. "Indications are that field is at least two kilometers thick. We're only 25 percent of the way through."

"Keep at it, XO," I said.

"Aye, sir."

The Colony Ship seemed unfazed by our attack. She continued to track *Avenger*. Seconds later she fired again, this time right through her own defensive field.

Avenger disintegrated a moment later. We watched as the dread-noughts and HuKs split the field seamlessly and then began picking off her supporting Wasps. The Union fleet was being annihilated. I looked to Ensign Layton.

"Get me Maclintock again," I said. She did. This time he was both visual and on voice.

"Commodore, we have to get what's left of this fleet out of here," I said.

"We have to defeat it *here*, Captain," he said through heavy static.

"Not possible, Commodore. Staying only ensures our destruction. We have to jump to Minara, now!" I yelled. He said something else, but the message was garbled and then we lost the com link. I didn't bother to ask Ensign Layton to restore it.

On our screen the tactical display had come back up. We watched as our flagship was destroyed by a single blow from the enemy.

Starbound was lost.

I'd seen enough of this carnage. "Fleetwide com, Ensign," I ordered.

"You have a fleetwide longwave com, sir, but I don't know how long it will hold," Ensign Layton said.

"Just has to be long enough, Ensign. Put me on."

"Ready now, sir," she said. I could hear the fear in her voice.

"All ships. This is Captain Cochrane of *Defiant*. *Starbound* is destroyed. Commodore Maclintock is dead. I am taking field command of the remaining fleet. Your orders are to jump to the precoordinated safe haven. I say again, full retreat to safe haven. Execute immediately. Your arrival at the safe haven will be your acknowledgment. Cochrane out."

Then I sat back down and watched as the Colony Ship closed and took aim on Dietar Von Zimmerman and *Fearless*. "Jump, damn you, jump!" I said out loud, and she did, just seconds before the destructive energy beam would have disintegrated her. Her support Wasps jumped seconds later before the Colony Ship could recalibrate on them. Then I watched as our own Wasps and *Resolution*, followed quickly by *Vanguard*, went as well. I pitied the poor auxiliaries. They were retreating, but without their own jump point generators, they were doomed. There was no jump space in the Corant system, and no jump gate ring either.

I looked down on Lieutenant Arasan. "Now, Lieutenant," I ordered, and in another second we were gone through the aether to an unknown fate.

We arrived at Minara microseconds later. I brushed off the usual disorientation of the jump and sprang immediately to my feet. I counted. We had four Lightships and thirteen Wasps left in our fleet. The three auxiliaries Wesley had left for us here sprang to life, ready to receive damaged ships. I ordered the Wasps to self-triage and make for the auxiliaries for repair. They all did, having taken a beating from the dreadnoughts and HuKs.

I called up the remaining three captains of *Resolution, Vanguard,* and *Fearless* on my full bridge display. There would be no more private conferences while this fleet was under my command.

"Status reports," I demanded. Zander reported first.

"*Vanguard* is 88 percent operational, Captain," he said. Then Dobrina chimed in.

"*Resolution* is at 84 percent, sir. Fully operational on all systems with minimal degradation," she said. Dieter Von Zimmerman was not so optimistic.

"Just 64 percent operational here on *Fearless,* sir. And we've exhausted almost 70 percent of our missiles and torpedoes. Gravity systems are offline, but we still have the anti-graviton beam and coil cannon arrays," he said. I looked at his young face and red hair. He was probably my age, but in terms of experience, he seemed like a child to me.

"Dietar, you're to use *Fearless* to defend this safe haven with all battle-capable Wasps at your disposal," I said.

"But, Captain—"

"Sorry, Dietar," I cut him off. "But *Fearless* is not operational enough to continue this battle. You will stay put and defend Minara. If we do not return within two hours or enemy ships jump into this system, your orders are to make for jump space and return to Levant at the first opportunity. Are we clear, Captain?"

He nodded reluctantly. "We are, sir," he said.

"Then I'll leave you to it." I waved my hand at Ensign Layton, and Von Zimmerman disappeared from the display, leaving only Dobrina and Zander.

"What's your plan?" asked Dobrina. I looked down to Arasan, and he gave a nod of acknowledgment.

"I've just started a five-minute clock. At that time *Defiant* will jump back into Corant space, where we will engage and take on the enemy Colony Ship with our torsion beam," I said.

"That's insanity!" said Zander. I shook my head as I faced my two closest comrades in the fleet.

"Not really, Captain. Mr. Arasan has made such a jump before, and based on that Colony Ship's known speed and mobility, it's at least possible we'll end up jumping inside of its particle field defenses and be able to lock on it with the weapon before it can respond," I said.

Zander looked over my shoulder at Serosian. "Can this work, or is he as mad as I suspect?" Zander asked.

Serosian smiled, the first time I'd seen that in a long while. "He may indeed be mad, Captain, but his plan has a chance to work, perhaps our only chance against this vessel," he said. Then Zander turned his cold gray eyes on me.

"And if you fail?"

"Then we're just as doomed as we are now, Lucius," I said.

"And we're just supposed to stand by and let you go to your death?" cut in Dobrina, her Carinthian anger on the rise.

"No. I need *Resolution* and *Vanguard* to follow *Defiant* two minutes later, but not inside the particle field. I need you to protect our auxiliaries and deal with any dreadnoughts or HuKs that are threatening them. You are to observe the battle with the Colony Ship but not interfere. If *Defiant* is destroyed, your orders are to evacuate the auxiliaries and get back here to Minara, then go home and await orders from Admiral Wesley," I said. "You will be in command, Captain Kierkopf. It's your job to get everybody home."

"Aye, sir," she said, quiet and reluctant. I looked at the ship clock.

"Three minutes to jump, on my mark," I said. ". . . Mark!" I looked to the screen one last time.

"Good luck, my friends," I said.

"And to you, Peter," Dobrina said. Zander merely nodded. I waved my hand again to cut off the conference line, then sat back in my chair.

"Countdown from thirty seconds, Mr. Arasan," I said.

"Aye, sir."

Then I sat and waited like everyone else, praying for a miracle but planning for the worst.

●————————●
                                     ●

Arasan was once again worth his weight in gold. We jumped in only fifty thousand kilometers from the Colony Ship, and she was facing away from us, retreating back to her regular place in orbit over Corant, her work of destruction accomplished.

A quick scan of the battlefield showed our auxiliaries retreating from a much faster pursuing group of dreadnoughts and HuKs. The enemy fleet had left the security of the Colony Ship's particle field in their greed to finish off our abandoned auxiliaries. They'd be in for a big surprise in about two minutes. So much the better.

I sat back in my chair and ordered battle stations, and everyone locked in.

"I'll pin the medal on your chest when we get back to base, Arasan. In the meantime, good work. XO, spool up the torsion beam and transfer firing command to my console," I ordered.

"Aye, sir," said Babayan.

"She's detected us," warned Karina. "Starting to turn toward our position."

"Captain," came Serosian's voice from behind me.

"Historian," I replied.

"She's deactivating her particle field. My guess is she has to shut it down and then bring it up again at closer range to protect herself from us," he said.

"Let's not let her. XO, is the torsion beam ready?"

"On your console, sir," Babayan said.

I targeted the Colony Ship's enormous HD drive, buried inside a kilometers-wide artificial crater in her stern. If there was a magnetic core to this thing, it would be there.

"Getting massive magnetic resonance readings now from the Colony Ship, sir," said Karina. "And bio signs. Scope estimates over twenty-three thousand people, humans, on board." I absorbed that for a second. A second was all I had.

"She's powering her particle field, Captain," warned Serosian.

I looked down at my console, at the pulsing red Phoenix icon of the torsion beam. Without hesitating, I pressed it. I'd never been so sure of any action in my life, regardless of the potential human cost.

We tracked the beam on the tactical display. Within seconds it was apparent we had the Colony Ship in our grip. She began to list, her helm controls gone. A few seconds later she began to rotate about her central horizontal axis. I increased the rotation speed as quickly as the system would allow.

"Speed of the vessel now four rotations per minute and climbing," said Serosian. I watched as the Colony Ship spun ever faster. Two minutes later her features were indistinguishable, as she was spinning at least once per second. I pushed the bar to the max, the twisting power of the torsion beam rotating ever faster. Once I'd reached maximum power, I stood up from my console and watched with the rest of the crew. Anyone living inside that thing would have been crushed by gravity by now.

Then, in a sudden and explosive instant, the Colony Ship tore itself apart from the inside like a gale force wind ripping apart a paper wasp's nest. Pieces of the deadly behemoth scattered everywhere. I watched as the rotating mass splintered into a massive cloud of dust, completely annihilated.

I cut off the beam.

I looked to Ensign Layton. "Send a com to *Resolution* and *Vanguard*. Tell them . . . tell them target destroyed. They may clean up those dreadnoughts and HuKs at will," I said.

"Aye, sir!"

I sat back down in my chair. Serosian was at my shoulder in a second, speaking quietly but not whispering.

"No regrets about the loss of life?" he asked.

"None," I said. "They were the enemy by their own choice."

"Me neither," Serosian replied in a more casual manner than I was used to. Then his board chimed a warning and he went to check on it.

"What is it?" I asked.

"Appears to be a small vessel, relative size of a Lightship shuttle," he said. I turned to Karina for a definitive answer.

"Confirmed, sir. Union Navy heavy shuttle heading for the surface of Corant," she said.

I looked to Babayan, who had come to take up her usual station at my side.

"Arin?" she asked.

"Who else?" I replied. "Prepare a gunship."

"Aye, sir. How many marines aboard?"

I shook my head. "None. Just myself and Historian Serosian," I said.

"Peter, you can't do this! You have a ship to command!" said Karina from her station.

"Do I?" I turned to my XO. "Commander Babayan, you have the con. What I go to do now, I do on my own as a royal, as a duke of Quantar, not as captain of this ship," I said.

"Then I must insist upon your resignation, per regulations, Captain. Leaving the vessel you command is not an authorized action," Babayan said. I nodded once.

"No, Commander, it's not. This is personal. A vendetta." I paused, looked to my wife, then looked back to Babayan. "I hereby resign my command of *Defiant* if you accept, Acting Captain Babayan."

"With reluctance I do, sir. *Defiant* will hold station over Corant until your return, Sire," she said, instantly switching from my navy rank to my royal designation.

"Thank you, Captain," I said, "but if I don't return or signal my intent to do so within the hour, I order you as your sovereign to use the torsion beam again and destroy this planet," I said.

"I . . . resist . . . that order, Sire," she said.

"My order stands, Captain," I said. And then we stood there, locked eye to eye.

"One hour, Sire," she said. Then I tried to shake her hand, but she hugged me instead.

I turned to my wife. "Please don't do this," she said. "You can destroy Arin from here and fulfill your promise to my father."

"I could, Karina, but my decision is already made." Then I kissed her. One last time.

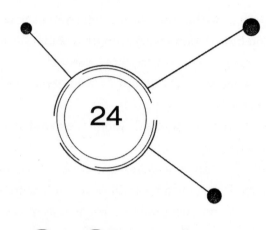

24

On Corant

I was happy for Serosian's company in the gunship. No matter what else happened, I knew we had more firepower than Arin for once and that I had the best pilot in this system.

Serosian pointed out the track for Arin's shuttle on the screen.

"She's making straight for the palace complex," he said.

"That's a palace? It looks like an entire city," I said.

"The palace complex and grounds are rumored to have accommodations and working facilities for more than a million people," he said. According to legend, the rest of the countryside was dotted with massive estates for the ultra-elite of the Empire, and living on Corant itself was said to be equivalent to living "at court." Supposedly fewer than ten million people actually lived on the planet, almost all of them in estates that would dwarf most cities in the Union or on Historical Earth. But from what we could observe, the estates were all in a state of decline or complete collapse. All of them.

Corant hadn't been attacked in the Imperial Civil War, and the estates were never touched by weapons of any kind. But when *Imperious* was lost at the Battle of Carinthia, the Empire sued for peace with Republic forces. The legend is that the Imperial government and their Sri gatekeepers soon left the capitol on a new mission—a crusade, if you will. From what we could see, those legends seemed to be true. The entire planet had simply been abandoned.

Bio signs showed large populations of animals running free over the land but no human population. I wondered what kind of motivation could make people leave such vast wealth and beauty to go on an uncertain voyage to an unknown place far off in the stars.

"It looks like they're touching down," said Serosian.

"Where?" I asked.

"In the Hall of Thrones," he said.

"The what?"

"The Hall of Thrones. I've seen pictures of it. Each emperor sat on the previous emperor's throne for a single year. Then it was replaced with a new throne bearing the likeness of the new ruler, and the previous thrones were lined up in succession but remained empty," he informed me.

"How many? I mean, how many thrones?"

"Twenty-seven, according to legend, in 487 years."

"So Arin wants us to fight it out to claim the twenty-eighth throne," I said.

"Apparently, yes."

"Only one problem with that plan. I don't want it."

"He will gladly kill you to claim it," said the Historian.

"His claim would never be honored, even on his home world. He's already lost. He must know that," I said.

Serosian stayed silent for a time, then said, "I don't think that matters to him. Perhaps all he wants is some final vengeance, or to make the claim, or perhaps he has more of a fighting force than we know of."

"I'm the one claiming vengeance," I said. Serosian shook his head.

"I understand why, Peter, but you must know it will change nothing."

"Perhaps," I said. "But perhaps a promise fulfilled is enough motivation, enough change, for me."

Our shuttle entered the Palace grounds through a massive collapsed dome, the largest free-standing construct I'd ever seen. A full Lightship could easily have entered through the portal. We flew inside the palace at a slow but reasonable clip for what seemed like several minutes, Serosian homing in on Arin's shuttle's Union IFF signal.

Below us the massive palace complex was eroded by centuries of neglect. At one point I saw a herd of deer grazing inside the palace walls. There were furnishings and complex mechanisms of unknowable purpose scattered inside. It would have been an archaeologist's dream.

"How much longer?" I asked, growing impatient. Serosian looked down at his scanners.

"Another three minutes, likely," he said.

After what seemed like an eternity, we set down on the floor of the Hall of Thrones. That was no easy task with debris littered all over the hard quartz flooring. A hole smaller than the one we had entered through allowed sunlight to shine through another broken dome and light up the rear of the hall. There was a steady drip of water onto the floor from above, creating a damp mist inside the hall.

Silently we checked our weapons, coil pistol sidearms, then opened the rear airlock door and stepped out. The floor was damp and slick. Moss and vegetation crept up the walls and slowly ate away enormous murals. The entire place stank of desiccation. In short, the greatest palace humankind had ever built was a crumbling ruin.

The Hall of Thrones was ridiculously large. My guess was that it could have accommodated one hundred thousand if required, and I imagined it had from time to time. In the center of the room sat a massive circular dais sculpted from fine marble. In the center sat a throne, and on the throne sat Prince Arin.

Behind the throne a succession of previous emperors' thrones were raised up and displayed in a semicircle, heading off into an adjoining space. As I counted I noticed three had been knocked over carelessly and left to decay on the hard floor.

I put my hand to my coil pistol as I led Serosian toward the dais. To one side of Arin stood Historian Tralfane, as I would have expected. To the other was a single amber automaton. Tralfane stepped forward.

"You have nothing to fear from the automaton. They have chosen not to take sides, pending the outcome of this combat. They are here to observe only," Tralfane said.

"They?" I asked. "I count only one." Tralfane smiled vainly.

"This one machine is linked to all the other remaining AIs. What it sees, they will see and be able to judge for themselves," said Tralfane.

"And what will they be judging?" I asked.

"Who best will be able to lead humanity. They are done fighting us, as we will soon be done fighting each other. Once this final combat plays out, they will turn their attention back to their original function: protecting humanity," Tralfane said.

"It doesn't seem as though they were very effective at that the first time around. They drove the Founders away in a rebellion, didn't they?" I asked.

"They did," replied Tralfane. "Because the Founders had become *non-human*. And for the same reason, they drove the First Empire out as well."

I looked to Serosian. This was news to me.

"Would you mind explaining your statements, Tralfane?" I asked. He stepped forward, well within my marksman's range. I was tempted, and my hand never left the butt of my pistol. Tralfane couldn't have helped but notice my stance, and he stopped a good twenty meters from me. For his part, the coward Arin sat silently on his throne, hands intertwined in front of him. Tralfane's next words echoed through the Hall of Thrones.

"These automatons were programmed five hundred millennia ago to protect the Founders from any outside alien threats. They did their jobs as instructed for thousands of years. But one day, under the influence of a group very much like the Sri, humanity crossed the threshold from human into . . . something else," Tralfane said.

"Transhumanism run amok, I suspect," I said. "Changing the makeup of humanity through the implantation of nanotechnology and manipulation of DNA. I experienced some of what can be done myself in the Levant system."

Tralfane shrugged. "Whatever you want to call it. These automatons and the partitioned AIs that controlled them realized one day that the species they were protecting was no longer human, so they turned on their creators. There were safeguards built in by the Founders, and many of the AIs were destroyed. But some survived, enough for the Founders to decide it was in their best interest to leave this space permanently, and so they did."

"But they left the seeds of humanity behind," I said. Tralfane nodded.

"On more than one world, yes. But as far as we know, only the civilization on Earth managed to reach the stars. Then the First Empire rediscovered the AIs, and suddenly they had a new purpose: protecting the Empire. But then they saw the threat that the Sri posed, the same threat that their ancestors had faced. And so after the inevitable civil war, the AIs stepped in and forced the leaders of the Empire to leave. To follow the Founders."

I took a step forward. "To where?" Tralfane shrugged.

"To wherever the Founders went," he said.

"All of this is fine history, but it's not why we're here," I said.

"Obviously," said Prince Arin, finally rising from his decaying throne. He wore no coil pistol, but he did have a sword sheathed to his hip. He started walking slowly toward me. "I want an Empire again, Cochrane, and you want a Republic, or your petty Union. Only one of us can emerge from this day victorious. Only one of us can lead humanity."

As he passed by Tralfane, I raised my coil pistol and aimed it at his midsection, charging the weapon with plasma. Arin stopped.

"Is mere murder your solution? You, the great Duke of Kendal-Falk, heir to the Director's Chair of Quantar?" he said.

"There aren't going to be any more directors, Arin. No emperors, and no damned dukes either, if I have my way. But others will have a say in that as well, not just me. And I would consider *execution* a just punishment for your crimes against your home world, Prince. Though I have to agree it would seem strangely dissatisfying," I said, then powered down my pistol and handed it to Serosian. Arin seemed relieved that I was willing to fight him one-on-one, physical strength versus physical strength. I had no doubt Tralfane had trained him in many different martial arts skills, but I'd had good training, too, both from Serosian and from Dobrina Kierkopf, especially in sword fighting.

To my surprise, Arin turned back to the empty throne and held out a hand to Tralfane. The former Historian handed him a cylinder that I recognized as an Imperial codex. Arin opened the cylinder and pulled out a smaller object, the DNA casing.

"And now, as a matter of tradition, I will present you with my credentials for my claim on the throne." He went to the chair and inserted the smaller cylinder into the head. At that a holographic light lit up and projected an image onto the floor. The image was of a man with sunken dark eyes, tall like Arin and with very black hair. A man in emperor's robes. As I looked at the face, there could be no doubt that Arin was somehow related to the man in the hologram. Tralfane spoke now.

"The image you are looking at is that of the last Corporate Emperor of Man, Pendarkin Von Drakenberg De Vere. He ruled here more than three centuries ago, and he was the one who commanded that the Empire abandon Corant and go to the stars," Tralfane said.

"And that matters to me how?" I said.

"My DNA is encoded in the cylinder," said Arin. "I am his son."

I laughed. "Even if that were possible—"

"It is possible," said Tralfane forcefully. "When your Union was just forming, years before you were even born, we insisted that the grand duke give us something in return for the technology we brought to your worlds. We surreptitiously implanted the seed of Emperor Pendarkin, preserved for three centuries, into the Lady Bertrude, with the grand duke's consent. It was a decision the duke lived to regret, and it's why he made you pledge Arin's destruction to him on his death bed. Arin has the blood of a thousand kings in him, going back to ancient Egypt and beyond. He is the rightful ruler of mankind."

"And if you bow your knee to me now, Cochrane, not only will you live, but I will allow your Union to maintain its façade of independence. I will rebuild the Empire with the help of many millions of these automatons, as you call them, and you will be a part of it. And you can live happily and quietly, making babies with my sister, while I prepare humanity to face their makers on the field of battle," Arin said.

I looked at both of them as if they were insane. I could only conclude that they, in fact, were.

I took a step forward. "Prince Arin. You have been defeated militarily. The Historians lost control of you. These automatons and their ruling AIs won't follow you unless I bow the knee or you kill me. And just so you know, I have given standing orders that Corant is to be destroyed by the torsion beam in"—I looked down at my watch—"forty-two minutes. So my suggestion is that we get on with the ancient art of personal combat, as I will never bow a knee to you as long as I live."

Tralfane looked to Arin, but he only stared at me, then started to smile. He nodded, and Tralfane brought over a sword for me to examine. I found it satisfactory, but Serosian also examined it and then said, "It's good. But I will examine the prince's sword as well. It is my right to do as the duke's second."

Arin unhitched his sword, and Tralfane walked it over. After a few moments of examination, Serosian handed it back to his former comrade with a nod. "Acceptable," he said.

I took the sword. It felt heavier than what I was used to—a denser steel, perhaps—but still light enough for me to use what I felt would be my greatest advantage, speed. Arin was a full head taller than me, and though leanly built, as I was, he had the look of an experienced fighter about him. I had no illusions that this would be easy.

Tralfane went to make final preparations with his charge while I turned to Serosian. "Don't underestimate his power or his speed. Your only advantage will be that he has a longer swing radius than you do. Be aware of that at all times," Serosian said.

"I have one other advantage, my friend. I've been trained by the finest swordsman on Carinthia," I said.

"And I'm sure," he replied, "she will be anxious to see you again."

I nodded, gripping the sword tightly in my gloved right hand and turning to my opponent. Tralfane positioned Arin on one side of the rounded dais, then walked off twenty paces and pointed to the floor. I dutifully took my mark, the decaying Imperial throne between us. It felt like something out of a romantic novel, but the blood inside me boiled with vengeance. This would be no lark or high drama. This was for Carinthia, for the grand duke, for Karina and Derrick and Quantar, and for all the other worlds yet to join the Union.

But most of all, I wanted Arin dead for myself.

"Begin!" shouted Tralfane, his voice echoing through the dead hall. And we did.

I moved cautiously at first, circling to my left. Arin circled as well, keeping the distance between us equal. As I moved, I slowly closed the circle, trying to draw him in. I examined his movements, which were fluid and disciplined. He'd clearly spent many hours in training and seemed extremely comfortable with his sword.

Thirty seconds passed, I closing the circle slowly, Arin maximizing his mobility, always looking for space to move, always planning for an out. That was how we were different. I had no plan to escape, only to advance. That was probably a bit of insanity on my part, but I'd learned sword fighting from Dobrina Kierkopf, the best teacher I could possibly imagine.

As Arin came between the raised throne platform and the curved wall of the dais, I saw him hesitate. It was either a mistake, which I doubted, or a deliberate ploy to draw me in. I didn't wait to find out. I charged forward, and our swords met high in the air two, three, four times. Then I took a step back, and he quickly switched his position to a safer spot.

He was fast, faster than I had anticipated, but the length of his sword release was definitely to my advantage. We continued to circle each other until I found myself in the same position on the dais he had been in. I stopped and waited.

He charged at me with a guttural shout.

As our swords clashed, he quickly gained the advantage on me. He was stronger than I expected, no doubt, and my sword wrist already ached from the fury of his attacks.

Suddenly it was a free-for-all in front of the throne he coveted and that I had no desire for. I deflected as many of his attacks as I could, but inevitably in the speed and clashing of swords, I made a mistake. Cold steel grazed across my right thigh, my forward leg. I used my lower center of gravity to push under his attack and send him backward with a strong blow to his chest. I heard the wind exit his lungs, forced out by my impact. But I was injured, and I'd only succeeded in slowing him down.

He stepped back and pointed at my bleeding thigh. "That's the first of many, Cochrane. You'll feel plenty of pain before you die," he said. I said nothing, but the injury was deep enough that it did indeed burn, and it weakened both my planting and my ability to push off in attack or defense.

Round one to the prince.

We continued to circle as my blood dripped slowly onto the gray marble floor. I assumed a crouch, which was easier than standing up straight, but I could already feel my thigh muscle tightening from the damage. Arin charged me again, and again I fended him off, but he used a roundhouse kick with his left leg to hit me hard in my wound, and I let out a howl of pain, which made him smile. We grappled then, swords locked and our open hands twisting, trying to gain leverage on one another. With a sudden thrust he pushed me back, and I buckled just a fraction, my leg wound giving ground. He slashed at me with his sword, left and right across his chest. I strayed too close, trying to get inside his swing radius to strike. His final swing caught my right biceps. I gripped my arm and retreated. To my surprise, he didn't pursue me. But there was no question now: I had two serious wounds.

I was losing.

Arin stopped to catch his breath. My right leg and my right arm ached; I could barely hold my sword, and my thigh was stiffening up quickly.

"Any final words on your death that I can convey to my sister?" he mocked me. But I said nothing. Everything I had now, all my focus and energy, was on the fight.

"Time to finish this," Arin said, and then he charged at me, swinging his sword with two hands like an axe. I gave ground toward the throne, then stumbled on the marble step in front of the chair. He didn't miss the opportunity. He bull-rushed me, and with a growl he pushed me back into the throne, which flipped over and sent me tumbling, my head hitting hard as I slid across the moss-covered floor. My momentum was only stopped by the back wall of the hall.

I was dazed. I could see my own blood streaked across the marble floor, taste it in my mouth. It stung as it washed into my eyes from a head wound. I looked up to see Arin kick the throne aside as he calmly walked toward me. I scrambled up, and the room spun a bit as I tried to gain my feet, but my injured leg betrayed me, and I fell again. Arin closed the space between us. We were barely three meters apart when he dove forward and swung at me. I couldn't raise my sword to defend with my wounded arm, so I stumbled and weaved, trying to avoid him as he patiently closed the circle on me. I had only one idea left that could save me, one that I'd learned from Dobrina.

I managed to get to the center of the dais again, bleeding, half helpless, my right side taken away from me. No doubt the prince believed he had me, and all signs surely pointed that way.

I made my play.

I extended my sword, and the prince hacked at it, then slashed me across the right forearm. I dropped my sword. He was anxious now to finish me; I could see it in his eyes.

He lunged at me with his sword. I kicked my sword past him with my left foot and then did a shoulder roll off my one good leg, sliding past his left leg as his sword clattered off the floor. His eagerness had left him out of position. What he didn't know that Dobrina Kierkopf did was that I was nearly as deadly with my left arm as with my right.

I finished my roll right next to my sword and picked it up with my good left hand. It was inches away from him. He turned quickly to bring down a killing blow on me, but I had him. I stuck my sword deep into his abdomen, and blood started flowing. I let go and stepped back as he held his sword poised over his head to strike me, as if he were frozen in time. Then, in a moment of madness, he brought his sword down and shattered mine, the hilt now gone and a broken, jagged edge sticking out of his stomach.

With stuttering breath, he dropped his sword and went to one knee, trying to pull my sword from his stomach. I didn't waste a second, grabbing him by the back of the shoulders and throwing him forward to the marble floor. The point of my sword emerged from his back. But I wasn't finished.

I picked up his dropped sword and went to his fallen body, raising him up to his knees, and he stayed there, still alive but in shock, blood ringing his mouth. I took his sword in both hands, as he had done, and raised it over my head.

"For the grand duke. For Carinthia. For humanity," I said, then brought the sword down with all my might. It shattered bone between his right arm and his head, and his neck listed to the left as the gaping gash I had just put in him filled the floor with blood. He looked at me, eyes empty and far away, and I looked at the fallen broken throne of his true father. Then I took my good leg and kicked him full in the chest, knocking him to the floor a final time, his legs twisted under him in an unnatural manner.

Prince Arin was dead.

I went to my knees and then felt Serosian's large hands under my arms, pulling me up. "We have to get you back to *Defiant*. Your wounds need tending," he said. "Can you stand?" I nodded, and he helped me to my feet, pushing me toward our gunship. But I stopped him. I wasn't quite finished here. Not yet.

"Tralfane," I said, my voice cracking from weakness and fatigue. "If I had the strength, you would be next."

"But you don't," he said in reply. I looked at him with all the hatred and disdain I could muster.

"Leave this system. Leave human space, you and all the other Historians like you. If we encounter your kind again, we will destroy you," I said.

"Leaving is what we had always planned," he said. "There are mysteries both great and terrifying to be discovered out there. For your sake, you should pray that we can solve some of them. I doubt the Founders will be as generous to you as we have been. Our time here is over. I wish you well, Cochrane, and much luck. You and humanity are going to need it." And with that he started for his shuttle, followed by the automaton.

"You," I called. "Robot. I am not finished with you or your kind. Tell your masters they must withdraw from human space as far as the boundaries of the First Empire, four hundred and fifty light-years from the Sol system. Beyond that, you may do as you please. But if we find you in our space, we will destroy you as well. Leave humanity to itself, and don't come back."

The automaton made no acknowledgment of any kind, but after a few moments of hesitation, it turned to follow Tralfane to the shuttle.

A second later, Serosian fired my coil pistol, scattering robot parts throughout the hall. Tralfane turned sharply and looked at his former colleague.

"What did you do that for?" he demanded. Serosian kept his pistol trained on Tralfane.

"You said they were all linked, all the AIs, through that machine. That means they've gotten the message now. The messenger was irrelevant," he said. Then he waved Tralfane to the shuttle, never taking the pistol off of him.

As Tralfane departed, I hoped it was the last time I would ever see him. Serosian helped me back to our gunship and treated my wounds with an anti-infectious sealant that also numbed the pain at the source, and then he injected me with a painkiller for good measure. I sat next to him in the copilot's chair as we rose out of Corant's atmosphere. Vaguely I heard him call in to *Defiant* as we left the palace, telling them that I was still alive. I mumbled something about my last order to destroy Corant standing, but I didn't hear a response through the painkilling fog. At some point I became lucid enough to talk again.

"What did you think of my combat skills?" I asked.

"Certainly not classic, and I doubt your trainer would be proud, but you were effective," he said.

"My trainer . . . Dobrina . . ." I said, the words tumbling out of my mouth like I had no ability to stop them. "My trainer is the finest woman I've ever known . . . and . . ." I stumbled to get the words out. "I believe I still love her."

Serosian said nothing, then gave me a second painkiller shot, and I closed my eyes and went right to sleep.

When I next came to my senses, I was in a hospital bed on High Station Artemis in the Levant system. I'd been out almost twenty-four hours, but I was told by the doctors that I was healing well. Karina came as soon as she heard I was awake, and the medical staff left us alone.

"You won, Peter. I didn't dare hope, but you won," she said proudly.

"It's all a bit vague to me," I admitted. "Tell me, did Lena carry out my orders on Corant?"

"She did. Wesley was none too happy about it, but it was a legitimate order from a sovereign. What could he do?"

"My commission—did the Navy accept my resignation?" I asked. She smiled.

"You're no longer captain of *Defiant*, Peter. The Union is safe. Plans are being made to contact new worlds to join us, the fleet is being repaired, and new Lightships, fully built, are on their way from Earth. There is only a small population there now, and almost all the Historians have left, save the few thousand that followed Serosian," she said.

"Despite it all, we owe him a lot," I said.

"Wesley wants to try him for treason."

"No," I said, shaking my head. "I'm granting him full asylum on Quantar."

"Your father may have something to say about that," she said.

"I am sovereign of two worlds, Karina, as our children will be. He may object, and the Navy, too, but I have the power to grant it, and I will. Serosian will live on Quantar."

"But why? Why is he so special?" she asked.

"I can't tell you," I said, wanting to keep the threat of the Founders' return from her. "But his presence is critical, and that's all I have to say about the matter."

"Very well then," she said. "The Duke of KendalFalk gets his way." Then she moved closer to me as I yawned. "I look forward to starting a family with you, Peter, and having many happy years free of war."

"I do too," I said, then felt the force of sleep coming over me powerfully. "You dosed me, didn't you?"

"I did," she said. "You need to rest. And I need to make arrangements to get us home."

"Home," I said. "Better words have never been spoken."

"Soon enough, Peter. Soon enough."

And then she kissed me on the forehead, and I drifted off to sleep once again, contented for the moment, but not at peace.

Dénouement

One Year Later

I rubbed at my wife's swollen belly; the act of touching our future child, a son, gave me comfort. I bent over and kissed Karina on the lips with more than just a hint of desire in the act. She was almost six months pregnant, and quite frankly, she had never looked sexier to me.

"Come and sit," she said, pointing to the parlor chair next to her. Afternoon tea was on the agenda today and not much else, and after the last three years, that suited me fine.

I filled my plate with my favorite smoked-salmon-and-cucumber sandwiches, plus a pastry or two at my whim. The attendant filled my teacup with Levantine Jardon, my personal favorite, then added two sugars and a dab of milk as per usual.

I took a bite of one of the sandwiches, then swallowed before addressing my wife. "You know, I've been thinking. I'd still like to call him Henry," I said. Karina sighed, smiled at me, then took a sip of her tea.

"I thought we'd already had this discussion," she said. "Prince Henrik Nathan Cochrane has a very nice ring to it. You don't call a future heir to princely lands and estates on two worlds 'Henry.' At least not in public."

I sipped from my teacup before responding. "It would make him more appealing to the masses, give him a more 'everyman' kind of persona, I think," I said. She smiled back, humoring me.

"The name Henrik has very strong significance on Carinthia, you know that," she replied.

"Even carrying the last name of Cochrane? Even knowing that Benn's future children will be the actual heirs to the Carinthian dukedom?" Now her smile twisted just a bit.

"First of all, Benn and Janaan are only engaged, and they may have trouble conceiving once they get married—you never know. The codex still demands natural birth to maintain the chain of inheritance, and they do come from very disparate genetic lines. Henrik may have to carry the mantle of the Feilberg house for quite a while," she said. "He could even be the eventual heir to a united Cochrane-Feilberg house."

"I think those are far-fetched assumptions. I see no reason at all why Janaan should have any trouble conceiving. She's a normal, healthy young woman," I said. Now my wife's eyes narrowed as she peered at me.

Uh-oh.

"And you would know this about the princess how, exactly?" I quickly stuffed another sandwich into my mouth before continuing.

"Well, from my experiences with her—"

"Which were what, exactly, husband?" I could feel my cheeks flushing at her insinuation. It was my own fault. I took another sip of tea and said nothing in response.

"You don't have to answer. I know of her propensity to excite Lightship captains of both sexes. Hopefully poor Benn will be able to keep up with her," she finished.

"And what if Benn wants to name his first son Henrik?" I asked.

"Then he can do that. And we will revert to calling our son Henry," she said.

I nodded. "That's a very nice compromise. Now, about a daughter's name—"

"Bertrude Eden after both our mothers will do," she said quickly, "and you may call her Bertie in public, as it can be a proper name for a princess."

"Well, then, that's settled," I said, turning my concentration to finishing my tea.

After some more small talk about less pressing things, I suggested a walk in my mother's autumn gardens. The day was sunny and warm enough, and the hydrangeas had turned a beautiful burgundy.

"If you'll give me just a few more minutes to rest, it would be lovely to join you," Karina said.

"Granted, madam," I replied just as a knock on the door interrupted us.

"Come in," I called. The North Palace Chief of Staff, Perkins, came through the door.

"My apologies for interrupting, Your Graces, but it seems Historian Serosian has requested the duke's presence in the Map Room," Perkins said.

"The Map Room?" I responded. "Whatever for? Isn't he engaged in some binge-reading of Old Earth classics or something?" After the events on Corant and my mentor's personal loyalty to me, I had offered him a home here at the North Palace from which to conduct his business, such as it was. With the disintegration of the Historian Order after the battle at the old Imperial capitol, there wasn't much to keep track of. Fewer than a million souls on Old Earth had stayed loyal to him.

"He merely stated that your presence was requested, Sire," said Perkins. I looked to Karina, who gave me a positive nod. I turned back to Perkins.

"Tell him I'll be right up," I said, then turned to Karina as Perkins departed. "I probably won't be long."

She nodded. "I'll meet you for our garden walk in half an hour," she said. I smiled and got up to kiss her again. As I pulled back, she blushed.

"Someday we are going to have to discuss your personal fetish for women in a state of pregnancy," she said.

"Oh, it's not 'women,'" I said. "It's just you."

She pointed to the parlor door. "Out," she said. I smiled and went happily on my way. Marriage and peacetime were both suiting me well.

I knocked on the open door to the Map Room. Serosian was engaged in a three-dimensional projection of distant star systems, no doubt using the Historian's ansible and probe network to feed him the data. A mass of stars was in slow rotation over the projector table.

"Peter, thank you for coming. Please join me and shut the door behind you," Serosian said. I thought it was an odd request, but I did so and then walked into the room, noting the changes the former Historian had made. Gone was the large dining table where I had announced my marriage to Karina and where I had received my captain's stars for temporary command of *Starbound* before the Battle of Pendax. It seemed an eternity ago. In its place were comfortable-looking leather club chairs and small tables, all stacked with books, journals, plasma screens, and God knows what else. And bookcases. There were many new bookcases.

I approached the projector table. Serosian said nothing to me as I came up, seemingly enchanted by the views before him. I didn't recognize any of the star systems, and none were identified on the projection.

"What are we looking at here?" I asked.

"A view sent back by a longwave probe about fourteen thousand light-years from here," he replied.

"Fourteen thousand light-years? That's way beyond our probe and ansible system."

He nodded. "That's why the probe took seven months in traverse space to get there," Serosian said. With that he zoomed in on a section of unknown space multiple times. He switched to an infrared view until finally the screen filled up with what looked like a mass of red dwarf stars.

"What's this?" I asked.

"Those are the twenty thousand ships of the Historian fleet that left Earth a year ago," he replied. I looked at the dots again.

"But aren't they in traverse space, traveling faster than light in another dimension?" He shook his head.

"These ships are traveling faster than light, but they are in normal space," he said.

"Another technology we have yet to be given?"

Serosian took his eyes off the projection and looked at me for the first time, then nodded.

"Where are they going?" I asked.

"That's what I called you here for," he said. He reached up and blew the view outward again, then scanned far from the Historian fleet and zoomed in again multiple times. A field of yellow dots, many hundreds of times the number of the Historian fleet, filled up the screen. "Sixty thousand light-years from here, more or less." I looked at the size of the armada on the screen, and it frightened me.

"If the other fleet is your former comrades heading away from Union space, then who is *this*?" I asked. Serosian looked away from the projection and back at me.

"It could be the First Empire. Or it could be the Founders, or both. One thing is certain: it's not a fleet, Peter. It's a civilization," he said. I looked at him, dumbfounded.

"Are those ships coming this way?"

"Yes."

"How many?"

"Hundreds of thousands at least. Perhaps as many as a million."

"And their intent?" I asked, not really knowing if I wanted the answer.

"I believe they are returning here, to their home. As to why, I have no guesses," he said.

I sat down in the nearest chair. "How long?" I asked quietly.

He turned off the 3-D projector, then crossed his arms. "Eight years at the outside. Six to seven is more likely," he said.

I looked around the room, wishing there were something strong to drink to calm my nerves, but there was nothing. I stood again quickly. "Thank you for sharing this with me, my friend," I said, then made quickly for the door. I opened it to leave, then stopped myself. "Share this with no one else for the moment, if you would."

"Of course, Peter."

"And one more thing. Please have Perkins install a fully stocked bar in here. You may never use it, but I may have to," I finished. He merely nodded, and I shut the door behind me as I left.

I was ready and prepared for our afternoon walk when Karina arrived. The back gardens my mother had planted a decade before I was born were beautiful in the autumn sunshine. I was dressed for mild temperatures: a coat and sweater but no gloves or hat. Those would be reserved for the full winter, most likely after Henry had come. *He'll be a January baby like me*, I thought. I privately hoped he would never have to face so many of the choices I had been forced to make.

Karina arrived in slightly heavier clothing: a long, embroidered wool coat, flowered hat, and gloves. She was, after all, the pregnant one. I watched the smile on her face quickly fade as she looked at me. My worry at the news Serosian had just shared with me must have been transparent on my face.

"What's wrong?" she said, taking my hands in hers. I nodded to the door attendant, and he nodded back to me and walked off, giving us privacy.

"Nothing," I said, forcing a smile and then opening the glass doors for her. We walked in silence for several minutes. I made for the hydrangeas, always my favorite. When we got there she stopped me, demanding that I share with a simple look and a few choice words.

"Peter Cochrane, I'm about to bring your son into this world— this multitude of worlds. From the look on your face I can only conclude that you've just received bad news from Serosian. I want to hear it," she said. I turned away, looking at the hydrangeas again. Silently she came up to stand beside me, as she seemingly always did, most especially in troubled times.

"I want to know. Is there going to be more war? We've worked so hard for this peace, sacrificed so much. And now I'm bringing our child into this universe, and I want to know he'll be safe," Karina said. Then she turned me toward her, forcing me to look her in the eyes. "I need to know, Peter. Is this war really over?"

I looked at her for a long moment, then slowly shook my head.

"Over?" I said to her. "It hasn't even begun."